unnatural causes

In Memory of

Marge Davis

unnatural
causes

LEAH
RUTH
ROBINSON

avon books
new york

AVON BOOKS, INC.
1350 Avenue of the Americas
New York, New York 10019

Library of Congress Cataloging in Publication Data:
Robinson, Leah Ruth.
   Unnatural causes / Leah Ruth Robinson.—1st ed.
      p.   cm.
   I. Title.
PS3568.0297U56   1999   99-25043
813'.54—dc21   CIP

First Avon Books Printing: August 1999

For my wonderful stepsons,
Will and Dana Rousmaniere
With love

And in memory of three dear friends
who died while I was writing this book:
The Rev. Dr. Raymond E. Brown, S.S.
Anne Walker
and
The Rev. Dr. James M. Washington, Jr.

unnatural causes

one

Even Death can become bored.

Death is a very busy person. Just pick up the newspaper any day of the week and turn to the obituaries. Death beckons to the dying after a fall in the home, after a long illness, after a brief illness, after cancer, AIDS, Alzheimer's. There are heart attacks, asthmatic attacks, strokes, thrown emboli. The possibilities seem endless.

But every now and then, there's an obituary that makes you wonder if maybe Death got up that morning and said, I'm bored. Let's do something just a little bit different.

Which might explain how Death arrived shortly before seven A.M. one cool, wet Saturday in early October driving a car, although it would be days before we knew that.

Specifically, driving a car into the parking garage under the Storrs Pavilion of University Hospital, on Manhattan's Upper West Side. Death parked and got out. He or she—for a long time the sex of the individual wasn't clear—unlocked a fire door at the far end of the garage, using a key that only hospital personnel are issued, and descended into an underground tunnel that connected the Storrs Pavilion to the main hospital complex across Amsterdam Avenue. A little while later, this same person returned to the parking garage, now wearing a white clinical coat with a physician's ID badge clipped to the breast pocket. She—or he—opened the back of the car—it was, we later found out, a station wagon—took out a strange wig of dubious quality, donned it, and also put on very dark sunglasses.

Thus attired, and carrying a large, woven basket, Death returned to the tunnel and this time followed it to a second fire door leading into the basement of the doctors' residence. A key was required for this door as well.

The basket contained, among other things, poisonous and hallucinogenic mushrooms.

But we didn't know that then.

Six hours after Death drove into the parking garage, what we did know was this: It was very, very quiet in the hospital's emergency room.

Which always made the docs and nurses very nervous.

Oh, we had patients. I was juggling four of them, in fact. But they were all walk-ins. We hadn't seen one single ambulance since the shift began at seven A.M. No gunshot wounds. No stabbings, assaults, or motor vehicle accidents. Not one single attempted suicide. No heart attacks. No strokes.

Not yet.

But emergency room physicians are nothing if not brave. Even while we snuck anxious glances at the ambulance bay door, we carried on as usual, as if we had stabbings, assaults, and MVAs galore. There were the usual quiet conversations, the usual boisterous exchanges. And those of us who had other things bothering us went right on being bothered, quiet or no.

"Ev, thanks again for going to bat for me when I almost

killed that patient the other day," Dr. Mark Ramsey said for the fifth or sixth time that morning. "I really appreciate it."

I sighed. Ramsey was one of my new interns; as his "Three," or third-year resident, I was responsible for overseeing the care he rendered. "First, you didn't almost kill the patient," I said. "Second, what's done is done. Just be more careful next time."

"Is anything bothering you?"

"No." At least nothing I wanted to discuss with Mark Ramsey.

My boyfriend, Phil Carchiollo. Today was the anniversary of our first date. That evening, my brother Alan, a student at the Culinary Institute, was hosting a celebratory dinner for us and a small group of friends in my apartment in the doctors' residence. The only problem was, Phil and I had had yet another quarrel over breakfast and were barely speaking. Phil wanted to marry me. I wasn't ready for marriage, which wounded him grievously. And celebrating the anniversary of our first date just seemed to grind salt into the wound.

The upcoming hospital merger talks. University Hospital was wooing two potential merger partners, Mount Scopus Hospital downtown, and St. Eustace Hospital uptown. Our entire hospital staff down to the last janitor was polarized either for or against one potential partner or the other. My own personal stake was the emergency medicine residency program. Currently, as residents, we were affiliated with the University College of Physicians and Surgeons, as were the emergency medicine residents at St. Eustace. If we merged with Scopus, we'd all have to "reaffiliate"—in other words, switch to the residency program at Mount Scopus's Albert Schweitzer School of Medicine. Our program was three years; theirs was four. I didn't even want to think about the problems reaffiliation would cause.

The twenty-four-hour nurses' strike, scheduled for the following Monday. My best pal in the emergency room, Gary Seligman, R.N., was the nurses' union rep. Some docs, particularly the residents, were showing their support for the nurses by wearing buttons that said "Some Cuts Never Heal." We planned to join the picket line on our lunch breaks. But many docs were vociferously against the nurses. As if we didn't have enough polarization and acrimony already from the merger talks.

And then there was that worrisome note, *Ut quod ali cibus est aliis fuat acre venenum,* "What is food to one is to others bitter poison," or "One man's meat is another man's poison." Someone had slipped it under the door to my apartment a week ago Thursday. I still didn't know who—or why. Somehow, though, it didn't sound friendly.

All that, and an ominous quiet in the ER, too. Who could ask for anything more?

"Something's bothering you," Mark insisted. "You can't fool me."

"I can try," I said.

"Maybe. But why would you want to?"

Laughing, I took the chart he was holding out to me and opened it. "Thomas Kennaugh," I said, scanning Ramsey's notes. "Guy is a charming, well-dressed yuppie businessman, Rolex watch, Armani suit, Coach briefcase, the whole shtick. Three-day history of extreme weakness, nausea, lightheadedness. Alert and oriented, with slightly slurred speech. Reports one or two bouts of apnea in the car on his way here. *Very* anxious, and not just because he's having trouble breathing. Shoots heroin 'recreationally,' he says. So. What are you thinking?"

"He got some of the Mott Haven tainted heroin the cops are talking about."

"Good call. Most of the cases have been going to Lincoln in the Bronx, or Harlem Hospital. But we may start seeing some here. What are they saying the heroin's contaminated with?"

"Methyl fentanyl. Overwhelms opiate receptors in the brain, causing the user to stop breathing."

I snapped the chart shut and handed it back. "You seem on top of this. What do you want to do?"

"Opiate antagonist and release. You think it's quiet in here?"

"No, I think it's picking up," I said.

"Think so?"

"Oh, yeah, definitely. Usual crowd's here."

Ramsey and I stood shoulder to shoulder at the nurses' station. Swarming around us were a steady stream of doctors, patients, nurses, patients' family members, chaplains, you name it—talking, crying, whining, shouting, swearing, whispering, begging, apologizing, confessing, absolving. A fireman went by in full gear, pick ax and all. As usual, I was handling several things at once. Debriefing Ramsey. Writing a note in Patient One's chart. Waiting on hold for Patient Two's private physician to come to the phone. Trying to track down Patient Three's lab results. Squinting at Patient Four's X Rays.

It's not quiet at all, I told myself firmly, looking at my watch. Four minutes. Patient Two's physician had sixty seconds to come to the phone. Five minutes was my limit. "The cops are driving around Addict Land with loudspeakers announcing, 'Toxic heroin was sold, seek medical attention immediately!' You know what that means."

Ramsey nodded. "Next we get the ones who heard it was pure and potent, and copped a bag on purpose."

"Call the Organized Crime Control Bureau," I advised. "They're keeping stats. And let's discuss it at Morning Report."

"I don't know if I can wait that long," said Mark. "I think I'll go ahead and discuss it now."

5

I shook my head as Ramsey trundled off to check Kennaugh, reviewing methyl fentanyl under his breath. For a moment, I considered administering a little methyl fentanyl to Ramsey. During my intern year, I had yammered, too—but Mark never shut up. He often kept right on talking whether or not anyone was listening. Sometimes he supplied both halves of the conversation himself, the one in his normal pleasant tenor and the other in a kind of gravely, stentorian baritone. "You never heard of the talking cure?" he asked people who commented. "It's talk or Prozac. Me, I don't like to self-medicate."

I wondered as I often did how he ever managed to get through Yale. How did he get *into* Yale? Although he fit right in here, in the maws of Welcome-to-the-Big-Time-Medicine: Manhattan's University Hospital. IV drug abusers, tainted heroin, Organized Crime Control. Admittedly, probably not what the hospital's founding forefathers and mothers had in mind when they broke ground at the turn of the century on a bluff overlooking Harlem. There they built the original five buildings with exteriors ornately patterned after the Luxembourg Palace in Paris, while the interiors were—according to a contemporary assessment—*exceedingly plain, as is right and proper in a place where war is to be waged on germs.* Sure would like some of their old-fashioned idealism to fight the modern-day wars on drugs, AIDS, social ills. Not that I wasn't dedicated. I was. But—

Brrt! My internal Cynicism Alarm went off.

Time to renew my vows.

Closing my eyes for a moment, I set in play my old medical school fantasy, scripted long ago, when the germ of the idea of actually becoming a doctor was first sprouting into reality:

Heartbeat. Heavy breathing. The sound of running. The twilight of a green-tiled hospital corridor, not quite day, not quite night. A tall slender woman rounds the corner and enters the homestretch. Overhead, the PA crackles with tension: "Dr. Evelyn Sutcliffe to the ER, *Stat!*" That's me. Light brown hair cut short but full, hazel eyes, tortoiseshell eyeglass frames. My stethoscope bounces on my neck. My hospital badge flaps on my breast pocket. My white coat floats around me like Super-woman's cape. The theme music from *Chariots of Fire*—

"Dr. Sutcliffe?" the clerk's voice interrupted my reverie. "Call for you on one-eight-one-three."

Damn. It happened every time. Just as I was about to give mouth-to-mouth to George Clooney. . . .

Patient Two's doc still had me on hold; I hung up on him and pushed the blinking button for 1813. Evelyn F. Sutcliffe, M.D., physician to the stars. The stars just didn't happen to know it. Yet.

"This is Dr. Sutcliffe," I said.

"This true, Ramsey lost the guide wire trying to put in an arterial line?" Dr. Diana Clausson asked without preamble. "And the patient had to be taken to surgery to have it removed?"

In another life, Clausson could have been Annie Oakley: point, aim, shoot. In this life she busied herself with running the hospital's Ear, Nose and Throat Clinic, and keeping herself "informed," as she liked to say.

"Do you have spies?" I asked. "Or are you just wired for sound?"

"Both. I hear Mikey Wells wanted to put Ramsey on proba-tion, but you stood up for him."

Dr. Michael Wells was one of the ER's attending physi-cians. He considered it his job to get at least one intern a year kicked out of the program. Just to keep up standards, he said.

"Ramsey's honest," I said. "When he fucks up, he says so."

"I dunno, losing a lead wire . . . That's serious. What if push comes to shove? You going to stand up for Ramsey?"

I tried to deduce the political ramifications of standing up

7

for Ramsey; Clausson usually had political ramifications in mind when she wanted to know anything. She hated Vittorio von Laue, the trustee who chaired the hospital's Q&A—Quality Assurance Committee—before whom I would be standing up for Ramsey if it came to that. Von Laue, like Ramsey, was a Yalie, and they had even attended the same boarding school. Then again, Julian Case Hamilton, chairman of the board of trustees, also sat on that committee, was a Yalie, and also had attended that same boarding school. And Hamilton was the board's main advocate for a merger with Scopus—

"Hel-*lo*," Clausson said in my ear.

Or maybe she was just interested in Ramsey for personal reasons. We were all still fanning ourselves over the Clausson-Ramsey affair that summer. Talk about torrid.

"Of course I'm going to stand up for him," I said. "He's certified to put in a central line."

"Who certified him?" Di asked.

"I did."

"For being proficient, or for making a good effort?"

I sighed. "He missed the vein repeated times. But he attempted five under supervision, so I gave him credit. Board policy allows me to do that."

"Don't sigh," Clausson ordered. "And get that defensive tone out of your voice."

"Di, what is this? Am I going before the Supreme Court?"

"Don't get exasperated, either. You want to convey your willingness to help them."

I put the phone down. Thrusting my left leg out behind me, I did a runners' stretch. Then I stretched the right leg. Picking the phone up again, I asked, "Who's 'them'?"

"The members of the Q-and-A. Just in case the matter comes to their attention, okay? Here's the rest of your argument. You realize that losing a wire is grave, but the system is designed with fallbacks to deal with this sort of thing. That in this instance the supervision put in place by the Bell Regulations actually worked exactly as it was designed to work. Because of close supervision of the intern, the resident was immediately made aware of the problem, and an adverse outcome was avoided." There was a click as she replaced the phone in its cradle.

"Why is that woman always so goddamned cryptic?" I complained aloud as I rifled through Patient Two's chart for his private physician's number again. "And why can't she learn the simple courtesy of saying hello and goodbye?"

Wait a minute.

The Latin note.

"You're the one who sent me that note," I fumed when I got Clausson back on the line. "*Ut quod ali cibus est aliis fuat acre venenum*. What is this supposed to be, a test of my Latin?"

"You could say hello, don't you think?" Clausson said.

"Why? You never do."

"I'm a honcho. You're not."

"I'm sure that's hon*cha*. But don't change the subject. Phil had to call the priest at his church to find out what the damn thing meant. 'One man's meat is another man's poison.' "

"I'm sure that's 'One *woman's* meat is another *woman's* poison," Clausson drawled. "Other than that, though, I have no idea what you're talking about."

"C'mon. It's just like you to send a cryptic message like this."

"That's true, but it doesn't mean I sent it."

I counted to ten. "Fine. What do you think it means?"

"Well, I'm just talking off the top of my head here, but it could have to do with the hospital merger talks. The Saint Eustace faction's meat is Mount Scopus's poison. And vice versa."

"But why send that message to me? I'm not a player in the merger talks."

"No, but Vittorio von Laue is. And he's your brother Alan's boyfriend."

"Still, why send it to me?"

Clausson thought a minute. "Could the note have to do with Phil? Doesn't he have some whacked-out patient who's in love with him and sends him weird notes?"

"Former patient," I corrected. "Phil's a shrink. It happens. But how do you know about that, Di?"

"You know I never reveal my sources."

"Well, could you not reveal the goddamned substance, too?" I snapped. "I mean, just this once? Surely you've heard of patient confidentiality. Or is that a new concept for you?"

Clausson loved pushing people's buttons. I could almost hear her grinning on the phone. "Mum's the word," she assured me. "But think about it. 'One woman's meat is another woman's poison.' Phil might be meat to you, but he's poison to the former patient. Or vice versa."

She hung up before I could respond. I slammed the phone down. The most galling thing about Diana Clausson was, she was almost always right.

But Phil's patients and former patients were his own professional business, I told myself. He didn't need me to advise him on patients with "difficult transferences," as he called it.

I didn't know then how wrong I was. Any more than I knew that Death sometimes wore a frightful wig and carried a large basket.

For the next hour, I saw patients.

Then, since it was so quiet in the ER, I took twenty minutes for a very late lunch.

Tempting fate.

two

It was not so quiet in my apartment when I got there.

Pots and pans clanged. The tea kettle whistled. Garlic sizzled, wafting its pungent odor out of the kitchen. From the foyer I could see the overladen dining-room table, heaped high with the wares of a Provençal marketplace: hunks of cheeses, little piles of fresh herbs, heads of garlic, onion, shallots, several kinds of vinegar, eggs, milk, flour, a bottle of Marsala wine, another of cabernet sauvignon, cans of beef broth, cans of chicken broth—

And Gary Seligman, R.N., the ER's best charge nurse, was in the kitchen, belting out cabaret songs. "Alan? Is that you?" he hollered, launching into a deep-throated, sultry, "In the Wee Small Hours of the Morning."

"Gary?" I could feel the grin spreading across my face. "What are you doing back so soon? I thought you went to your high school reunion."

Gary came out of the kitchen in his guise of sous chef for the evening's festivities. With a paring knife in his hand, and wearing a long red apron dusted with flour, he pantomimed embarrassment that I had heard him crooning a love paean to Alan. Kissing me on the cheek, he said, "I did go to my reunion—made it all the way through the class dinner last night, in fact. But by then it was getting old. People started taking out the baby pictures. So I told them I had to leave early the next morning, before breakfast even, to get back to the city in time to cook for a dinner party."

"You sound disappointed," I said.

"Oh, you know how it is. You go to these events with expectations, which are never met. Then you start examining your whole life, comparing yourself to classmates who are more successful or seem happier or make more money or whatever. Finally you remember the dreams you had for yourself when you were eighteen, which you haven't realized. Life is passing you by." He laughed and waved a hand dismissively. "Rather help Alan cook any day. Not that he needs my help."

I looked at him closely. "That reunion really unsettled you, didn't it? You're not usually this philosophical."

But just as I had evaded Mark Ramsey's inquiries about what was bothering me, Gary neatly sidestepped my asking about what was bothering him. "Let's not dwell on unpleasantries," he said, with exaggerated good cheer. "Alan nipped down to Zabars and Fairway for some last-minute supplies. He'll be back in a jif." Bowing with a flourish toward the dining-room table, then in the direction of the kitchen counters, Gary chattered on, "For ze dining pleasure of Madame et Monsieur et ze distinguished guests, we are serving, ta-da! Grilled polenta with wild mushrooms, the mushrooms finished with a dry Marsala. Breast of duck in a sauce of cream and Port wine, served with a *confit* of sour cherries and shallots. Also, pancakes of wild rice and sautéed carrot, celery, and onion.

Haricots verts. A *tricolore* salad, dressed with a light vinaigrette and Roquefort and walnuts—"

"My god, what a menu," I murmured, still looking at him.

"And, for desert," he said with a final flourish, "a marquise of chocolate and dried fruit, with a *crème Anglaise!*"

If Gary didn't want to tell me what was on his mind, there was no point in pressing him. "This is really a fabulous spread, thank you so much," I said.

"Thank Alan. He devised the menu and did all the shopping. He's already made the *confit* and the polenta. I'm just the chief chopping boy; I get to cut up the carrots and mince the onions." His mien turned serious. "Who knows, after Monday I might be chief chopping boy permanently instead of charge nurse. There's going to be a lockout, you know."

I hit my forehead with the heel of my hand. Of course Gary was on edge. The nurses' strike. "You know the residents support the nurses one-hundred percent," I assured him.

He shook his head. "You attend grand rounds this morning?"

"Yeah."

"Dr. Herrera say anything?"

Keith Herrera, a third-year resident in Internal Medicine, was the union rep for the Committee of Interns and Residents. "About the nurses' strike? No, was he supposed to?"

"That bitch," Gary breathed vehemently. "She threatened him."

"Who?"

"Clausson, goddamn her. Herrera was supposed to make an announcement at Rounds that the interns and residents are within their legal rights to take lunch whenever they want, and if docs want to take lunch on the picket line, the Committee will back them—there's nothing the hospital can do. Clausson said to him, 'You want that otolaryngology fellowship next year, you keep your mouth shut.' "

"Why would she do that?" I asked. Although no maneuver of Diana Clausson's would ever really surprise me. Had she lived in Machiavelli's day, he would have written *The Princess.*

Gary shot me an exasperated look. "Clausson's the chief of the Ear, Nose, and Throat Service. If University merges with Saint Eustace, Eustace will close ENT—Eustace has its own prestigious ENT Service; it doesn't need ours. But if we merge with Mount Scopus, Scopus will set up a new center for cranial base surgery, combining their neurosurgery service with Clausson's ENT service—and they'll ask Clausson to run it. The only fly in the ointment is, Scopus is pressuring University to cut back its nursing staff before they'll talk turkey at the merger table. Ergo Clausson is against the nurses' strike."

I flashed back to an acrimonious exchange Gary had had with Clausson a few days earlier, in the ER. But he and she were always at odds.

Gary suddenly dashed back to the kitchen. He yanked a sauté pan off the fire. "Almost burned the garlic," he said. Tossing a handful of chopped mushrooms into the pan, he inhaled the aroma greedily. "Very high stakes, this replacing nurses with aides. We can't let the hospital get away with it— next thing you know, the laundry workers will be installing IVs. Already some hospital in Brooklyn has instituted a policy where nurses can't wear name tags with R.N. on them any- more—hospital administrators don't want the patients to know whether a nurse or an aide is caring for them. Of course, Vit- torio's going to come in here this evening full of bullshit about cost-cutting measures in response to the sharp decline in reve- nues, blah-blah, managed care, and the deregulation of hospi- tal pricing, yadda-yadda—God, I get sick of arguing about it."

"I'm sure you can disarm Vittorio with your scintillating wit," I said. "In fact, I'm counting on you."

I counted on Gary for a lot of things, both in and out of the hospital. His humor. His light touch. The way he made fun of everything and laughed it off, but still managed to keep his compassion for others. I particularly appreciated his gift for the most astute analysis this side of psychobabble, and his patience. As did everyone else, especially the interns and med students who were his special charges. On Gary's last birthday, the ER docs had serenaded him with a revised version of the old Beatles tune "Let It Be"—but in our version it was Mother Gary who spoke the words of wisdom.

More than any doc in the hospital, Gary Seligman was my own mentor. We were the same age, now in our mid-thirties. But I considered him many years older and wiser.

So what does this guy look like? friends would ask when I raved about Gary. Red-blond hair that seems sun-streaked even in the winter, I'd say. Freckles, a near-permanent tan augmented by frequent trips to visit Bubbie in Florida, nice-Jewish-boy face, and a hardened, muscular body kept fit through jogging, sit-ups and push-ups.

And guess what, I'd add with wry admiration. *He cooks!*

Is he single? my women friends yelped in unison. Can you introduce me?

Yes and no, I always answered.

Oh. Sigh. *The best ones always are.*

Yeah, but they make great friends.

A large vellum envelope on the dining room table caught my eye. "What's this?"

He glanced up from his sauté pan. "Card with the basket."

"What basket?"

"In the fridge. I took a couple of the mushrooms. Didn't think you'd mind."

I picked up the card and a peculiar sensation came over me. The envelope was lined with silver paper. I slid out a correspondence card. It read: HAPPY ANNIVERSARY, XXX.

On the top shelf of the refrigerator, jammed in under the freezer compartment, was a huge gift basket of vegetables from

McNeely & Wang, the new très-très-chic SoHo grocery. And what gorgeous vegetables! Round, juicy-looking tomatoes that actually smelled like tomatoes. Slender haricots verts. Scallions. Yellow and red peppers. Several kinds of exotic mushrooms. Baby carrots. Radishes.

"Wow," I said, laughing with sheer delight. Phil had got over his fit of temper that morning and was wishing me happy anniversary after all. "I resolved on Rosh Hashanah to eat more healthy foods," I explained to Gary as I grabbed a little bag of carrot sticks, a piece of Swiss cheese, and a few crackers. "I have to get back to work." Scooping up an apple from a bowl on the table, I moved toward the door.

But something stayed me. I turned back.

A loud sizzle filled the room as Gary poured white wine on the mushrooms. As I watched, however, he put the wine bottle down and leaned back against the kitchen counter, his hands behind him on the counter edge, shoulders hunched. He sighed loudly and stared at the floor.

"You look so resigned and defeated," I said. "Are you sure you don't want to tell me what's wrong? I mean besides the reunion and your fight with Clausson and the nurses' strike."

The barest flicker of a second before he averted his eyes. He shook his head, then cracked an unconvincing smile. "What, those three things aren't enough to worry me?"

"Gary, you're sighing like you want to tell me something."

"I do," he said. "And I will. But right now, I can't."

A long look passed between us.

"Okay," I said. "I'll take a rain check. You'll tell me later."

And then, without a second thought, I went back to work.

"Something happened in the subway," Dr. Jasmine Washington announced when I arrived back in the ER. She shrugged into a lead X-ray apron and pulled on a yellow trauma gown over it. "We don't know what. Might be a shot cop."

"You call Trauma?"

"Coming down."

Quickly, I suited up, too. Medieval-like gown, armorlike apron, visorlike splash shield, gloves. As always, I briefly entertained the idea that all I needed now was a lance and a charger. My heart began to pound. Joining my colleagues at the door to the ambulance bay, I looked at my watch. Three-fifteen P.M.

We waited.

Nothing happened.

A cool breeze blew in from the open door. The remnants of Tropical Storm Judy or Josey or whatever her name was were still passing through; it had stopped raining for the moment, but the sidewalks were wet and littered with fallen leaves and branches. I lifted my visor and greedily sucked in the cool, humid air.

Mark Ramsey joined the queue. "Fall's my favorite time of the year," he announced.

"Me too," murmured a couple of voices.

"I hate summer in the city," he went on. "Fall always seems like the new year. In fact, I'm thinking of becoming Jewish like Ev here so I can make New Year's resolutions in the fall instead of in January."

"Ramsey, you talk this much nonsense before you got head-bonked in that accident?" a surgeon from the trauma service asked.

"Absolutely," said Mark. "Except when I did my clinical clerkship here."

"How'd you keep your mouth shut then?"

"Hypnotized myself."

"Yeah? You think you could hypnotize yourself now, too?"

Ramsey laughed easily. As usual, teasing rolled off his back like water off a duck. Ramsey got as good as he gave.

He was a nice-looking guy. Twenty-seven years old, about

my height, chestnut-haired, slightly built, with beautiful, pianist's hands. His face had been smashed in the car accident a little more than a year ago and the plastic surgeons were still tinkering with it, but if you didn't know that, you'd probably think he'd had a couple of beer bottles broken over his head in a bad barroom brawl. He really was very appealing—especially to a crowd of war-weary ER cynics.

Now if he could just convince patients that he knew what he was doing . . . Although, to be fair, he had at least stopped saying to the nurse—in front of the patient—"So, what are we doing here?" Thank Gary Seligman for that.

Two weeks after Transition Day—July first every year, when all the freshly minted medical school graduates arrive in hospitals across the country to take up their duties as new interns—Gary had pulled Ramsey into the nurses' supply closet for a little chat.

"The patient does not know you from Adam," Gary reportedly told Mark. "The patient does not know, as I do, that most of the time you actually know precisely what you're doing, and that this *I-know-nussing* shtick is exactly that—shtick. The patient sees a doctor with facial scars, who may or may not have had a few marbles knocked loose while he was getting those scars."

"I did have a few marbles knocked loose," Ramsey said. "My best friend died in that accident, and I was driving. You know that."

"Yes, I know, but no, you have not lost your marbles," Gary countered. "Well, your emotional marbles, maybe. I'm sure you're still grieving for your friend. You may grieve for the rest of your life. But there's nothing wrong with your mental marbles, and I don't understand why you insist on pretending there is."

"Survivor's guilt," Ramsey explained.

"If you know that, you can compensate," said Gary. "Unless you're just pigheaded."

"That, too," said Mark.

"I don't think he's going to kill any patients," Gary told me afterward, when he reported his conversation with Mark to me. "He did a clinical clerkship in the ICU when I was charge nurse up there, and he's got a good medical acumen. He's weird, but not weirder than some of the interns who've come through here. And he still panics and freezes up, but that's par for the course, they all do the first couple of months. He does need therapy for his grief. But I'm hitting the ball into your court on that one, Ev, you're the one with the psychiatrist boyfriend. See if you can get him to talk to one."

"I'll do my best," I'd said.

Three-eighteen. By now we could hear all kinds of sirens a couple of blocks away. They throbbed tantalizingly closer, but then faded. No ambulances arrived.

"Julio, can you find out what's going on, please?" I asked finally at three-twenty.

"They're saying multiple casualty, civil disturbance," the ward clerk informed us breathlessly a moment later. "So far two cops shot, a pregnant woman shot, and a suspect firing indiscriminately in the train tunnel."

"*Where?*" I demanded.

"Broadway and a Hundred-and-Tenth." Two blocks away.

"You inform Cabot?" Our fearless leader, Dr. Christopher Randolph Cabot III, director of the Emergency Department.

"Beeping him."

"Get him now. How many coming here?"

"I don't know, doctor. I'm trying to find out."

A moment later, the first ambulances arrived, discharging the wounded: a police officer shot in the thigh, and a man bleeding from a laceration of the forehead. Behind them came the dozen or so officers who always accompany a shot cop, and behind them the police brass. The ER buzzed with adrenaline as we inhaled one another's sweat and excitement. By the time it sank in that initial reports of a multiple-casualty civil disturbance were unfounded—there was no second shot cop, the pregnant woman had not been shot, but had only fainted, there had been no suspects firing indiscriminately in the train tunnel—we were high and it didn't matter. If anything, we could now enjoy the sweet aftermath of the rush without feeling guilty.

"Who knows?" said one cop as we assessed the shooting victim. (His wound was little more than a graze, and by now he was chortling with embarrassment.) "We get a report of 'man with a gun' on the platform. We respond. People running out of the subway, hollering and pointing this way and that way, all kinds of contradictory stuff, and we're going, 'What happened? Who's got the gun? Where are they?' Then there's shots fired. Next thing we know, it's a ten-thirteen, assist an officer. Meanwhile we hear that the suspect is hiding on the train, or in the tunnel, or he ran out of the subway. It's Columbus Day weekend, the subway's packed with shoppers carrying all kinds of stuff from the sales, but we gotta close the doors of the train and search. People keeling over from the heat in there. Shit, it was hotter than hell. They'd turned on the heat in the damn cars."

"You get the guy?"

"Yeah, petty pickpocket. Lost his gun somewhere, now we're looking for that."

By the time I finished cleaning the wound, it was after five P.M. I peeled off my gloves, and, slipping back into my white coat, headed for the phone to call Phil.

"What vegetables?" Phil said. "What are you talking about?"

Phil hadn't put the basket of vegetables into the fridge.

Nor had he written the card.

"Oh, god." I suddenly remembered. *"One man's meat is another man's poison."*

Gary and Alan did not answer the phone.

I ran the half block to my place as fast as I could. It was raining again, and the smell of wet New York City sidewalk filled my nostrils. I jammed my hands into the pockets of my white coat to keep all the stuff from falling out: penlight, otoscope, ophthalmoscope, my laminated *Normal Values Guide*. Hunkered down, running all out, my patient-in-cardiac-arrest-code run.

I didn't run fast enough. I found Gary in the bathroom of my apartment, standing in front of the sink.

"Don't kiss me, Ev," he said, as I panted on the threshold of the bathroom. "I've just been sick . . . Really sorry. I was looking forward . . . nice meal . . . afraid I'm going to have to pass." He opened the medicine cabinet and took down a bottle of Listerine. "Just lemme rinse out my mouth."

"Where's Alan?"

"Not back yet."

His speech was slurred.

He was sweating profusely.

His arm twitched convulsively as he lifted the glass of Listerine to his lips. He got half in his mouth and the other half down the front of his shirt. But he seemed not to notice.

And he swallowed the Listerine instead of spitting it out.

"Gary," I said.

I had to say it twice. He was gazing fixedly at the floor. When he raised his eyes to mine, his pupils remained undilated in the dim light of the bathroom.

"What's happening to me?" he asked. "I can't see my feet."

"Gary—did you eat those mushrooms?"

For a moment he didn't answer. Then, "You're not you," he said. "You're you two minutes ago."

I went to the phone to alert the ER.

three

Somehow Gary decided we were going to the Rainbow Room and the desert captain there was going to teach us how to flame Baked Alaska, or maybe it was the fish expert who was going to demonstrate the correct technique of slicing Nova—did I know those fish guys made $75,000 a year to slice fish? Maybe he needed Alan's toque. If we were going to the Rainbow Room—

My heart was in my throat and ears, every beat as loud as a klaxon wail. With one hand gripped firmly around Gary's biceps and the other clutching the handle of the vegetable basket, I steered my wildly delirious colleague into the elevator. The hospital was just across the street. All we had to navigate was the elevator, the lobby of the doctors' residence, the sidewalk in front of the doctors' residence, Amsterdam Avenue, and the ambulance bay entrance to the emergency room. How hard could that be?

The elevator doors closed. With a jolt, we began to descend. The waters of adrenaline closed over my head. Like a woman morphing into a mermaid, I plunged from the terra firma of reality to a world where all was suspended. No emotion here. Just heartbeat, breathing, heightened senses, and forward movement.

My mind swam through what I knew so far, what I needed to find out, and what I needed to do first.

During Gary's few moments of pseudo-lucidity after my arrival, I'd managed to establish a few details: Gary ate the mushrooms he'd been cooking while I was there—mushrooms from the basket of vegetables. An hour and forty-five minutes later, he vomited. He was now delirious and hyperactive; he was sweating; his pupils were constricted; and his speech was slurred. I knew that "poisonous mushroom" meant any mushroom that caused an adverse reaction—including hallucinogenic—and that "mushroom poisoning" covered everything from simple gastric upset to fatal liver failure and kidney shutdown.

I had no idea who had put the vegetable basket into my refrigerator. Briefly I tested theories. Was it possible that Alan himself bought the basket at McNeely & Wang? That it came packed with hallucinogenic mushrooms? Could it be somebody's idea of a joke? Alan had stopped by Phil's apartment to pick up keys, and had let himself into my apartment. Then Gary arrived. Alan immediately went out to Zabars and Fairway for some last-minute supplies. Gary opened the fridge and saw the basket.

But Alan would hardly have signed an anniversary card to me and Phil *XXX*.

Which brought us back to the note under the door, *ut quod ali cibus est aliis fuat acre venenum.* Obviously not from Diana Clausson after all, that much was clear. Whoever slipped the note under the door must have put the vegetables in the fridge—but who had let him in to do it? The super? Yeah, sure, if that person only wanted him to open the door to leave me a present that needed to go into the fridge—it was conceivable. Everyone trusted and liked the super, and we all tipped him lavishly for favors.

"Ohmygod he's coming right at us!" Gary yelled suddenly. "We're going to hit!" He grabbed at air as if turning a steering wheel, then threw himself against me, knocking me off balance. *"We're going over!"*

"We're not going over anything," I said firmly. He had me pinned to the door, which was going to open any minute and dump us out on the lobby floor. "We're in an elevator. *We're not going over.* Now let me up, please."

I had no idea what kind of mushrooms Gary had eaten; I couldn't get him to focus on the question. Something hallucinogenic. But there were four or five kinds in the basket, and he could have eaten all of one kind (leaving us no specimen to identify) or some of one kind and some of another but none of a third. He could have eaten only "magic" mushrooms— the effects of which wore off after a while without sequelae— or something lethal as well. I had never treated a case of mushroom poisoning, and off the top of my head I could not think of any doc I knew who had. Case Hamilton—the chairman of the hospital's board of trustees—was very knowledgeable about wild mushrooms, including hallucinogenics. I had gone out foraging with him a couple of times, but what little I'd learned from him was not what I needed to know to treat Gary. Besides, Case wasn't exactly infallible himself—he and his wife Jackie had misidentified some kind of mushroom once and accidentally poisoned themselves, luckily not fatally. At least Case would know whom to call. He and Jackie had that mycologist friend who taught at the university—

Better to call Poison Control first. Then McNeely & Wang. And I'd have to find the super.

And I probably should call the police.

But first things first: I would have to pump Gary's stomach.

The first pulse to take is your own.
Distance, distance.
Treat the patient, not the poison.
Lavage, adsorption, catharsis.

The elevator doors opened and Gary and I stumbled out. I kicked at the elevator to prevent the doors shutting again long enough to grab the basket. By now Gary was up and running.

Luckily, Lauren Sabot was just coming into the foyer. Juggling her briefcase, a canvas tote, and an umbrella, she headed for the buzzers.

I dropped the basket on the floor and lunged for Gary. Keeping a firm grip on him with one hand, I opened the door with the other, held it with my foot, and grabbed the basket again. With three feet and three hands, I might be able to get Gary across the street to the ER.

"Craig had to tape a confession," Lauren said, as we came out. Craig was my other brother. Lauren was Craig's girlfriend. "He'll be here for dinner, but—" Suddenly aware of Gary's demeanor, she stopped in midphrase.

"We're going to the Rainbow Room, but you need your toque," Gary announced.

"He ate something," I said.

Lauren quickly sized up Gary, taking note of his pressured speech and overfocused, wondrous expression. Lauren didn't miss much. A litigation associate at a prestigious, white-shoe law firm, she was a quick study. She sized up me; I guessed I looked grave and anxious. She sized up the basket of vegetables. Her eyes moved to mine.

"Ate what?" she asked, as Gary continued his rapid-fire monologue about the Rainbow Room.

"Mushrooms," I said. "Hallucinogenic."

Her eyes widened. "From this basket?"

"Right."

"Where'd it come from?"

"McNeely and Wang. There's a card in it."

"Who sent it?"

"I have no idea. What's the name of that mycologist friend of yours?"

"Robert Held."

"Can you get a hold of him?"

"Absolutely."

Lauren and I always talked like that. Zip-zap shorthand. To the point. No frills, no thrills. It was the way I talked to other docs at rounds or bedside, and I imagined it was the way she talked to her legal-eagle colleagues in conference or preparing for court. Nonetheless, I liked her—most days, anyway. Willowy, agile, russet haired, she dressed in a business-like manner and wore no makeup or jewelry (other than a gold Cartier watch). I envied her her poise and admired her for her brains. Most days, I sincerely hoped Craig would marry her, although that was not likely to happen any time soon. Craig was smack in the middle of a very acrimonious divorce.

And most days I worried—just a little—about Lauren's growing camaraderie with my boyfriend Phil. If I married Phil as he hoped, and Lauren married Craig as I hoped, Phil and Lauren would become brother- and sister-in-law. But was that really only budding family affection between them—or something stronger?

Lauren hefted the canvas tote of bottles—I saw it was wine for the dinner we were now unlikely to eat—in the crook of one arm, and tucked her briefcase under the other. Falling into step with me and Gary, she somehow managed to hoist her umbrella over our heads—it was raining again—as we lurched out of the doctors' residence onto the sidewalk and hurried toward Amsterdam Avenue.

"When we get to the ER, I want you to have a look at the mushrooms left and see if you can ID any of them," I said.

Lauren Sabot was Case Hamilton's niece and was herself an accomplished mushroom forager.

"Absolutely. What's McNeely and Wang?" she asked.

"SoHo gourmet. It's like Balducci's or Dean and DeLuca."

"Ah." She peered out from under the umbrella at the looming facade of University Hospital, on the other side of Amsterdam. "We going to the emergency room?"

"Yes."

"But doesn't this kind of hallucinating run its course?"

I didn't have time to explain. Gary—who suddenly seemed to notice Lauren for the first time even though he'd been talking to her excitedly nonstop since she appeared—let out a small shriek. Shaking loose from my grasp, he took off like a bat out of hell. Straight into traffic on Amsterdam Avenue.

My heart lurched. "Aw, *shit!*" Clutching the basket and trying not to spill the vegetables all over the street, I took off after him. Cars screeched to a halt. Horns blared. Miraculously, no one hit us. And luckily, Gary made a beeline for the emergency room on his own, straight across Amsterdam and east on West 113 Street.

"Code P! Code P!" I yelled at two medics standing under the ambulance bay overhang.

The medics looked at me in my white coat. They looked at the basket, which was the size of a small baby bassinet. They looked at Gary, running all out for Olympic gold. They dropped their cigarettes in the driveway and tackled Gary as he streaked by.

"Lose something?" one of them drawled when I caught up.

"He sure is flying," the other one laughed. They held Gary between them easily. Gary ran in place, still yammering. "—you know every single uniform is different, the drinks girl in the bar, the waiter in the dining room—"

"Thank you, this is Gary Seligman, one of the ER charge

nurses," I said. "He has eaten an unknown substance and requires medical assistance."

"Whoops, sorry, Doc."

"You need your toque!" Gary cried urgently.

"Ate or smoked?" the medic asked as Lauren caught up. Remarkably, she had nearly kept pace in her tight-skirted, pin-striped suit and Manolo Blahnik heels.

"Not toke as in smoke—*toque*, the chef's hat," I said. "Mushrooms. We got this gift basket."

"Oh, man," said the medic. "Someone slipped him magic mushrooms, and he didn't *know?*"

We went through the door of the ambulance bay into the ER, Gary, the two medics, me, and Lauren Sabot. The place was still swarming with cops, the walking wounded, and the not-so-walking wounded. Gurneys and stretchers were parked everywhere. Julio, the ER clerk, usually implacable, was shouting into the phone. Not a good sign.

"Is this the pool?" Gary wanted to know.

"Give me that basket," Lauren said. She took it. Looking around, she spied the nurses' station, and shouldered her way through the crowd into it.

"Excuse me," said the charge nurse for the shift, Kathy Haughey. Nothing escaped her eagle eye. Then she saw Gary. "Jesus. *Gary?*"

"She's with me," I told Kathy, nodding at Lauren. "She needs the phone. Gary's eaten something—God only knows what. Probably some kind of hallucinogenic mushroom. But it could be worse and I don't want to take any chances."

Kathy stared at Gary in horror. He was pressing his face up against the green tile wall, excitedly reminiscing about the Flying Fish, apparently his high-school swim team.

I eyed a police officer holding an ice pack over one eye. The blouse of his uniform was stained with blood. "What's going on here now?" I asked Kathy. "I thought we were winding down from the subway thing."

She shook her head. "A police van responding to the scene hit a bus and rolled. Eleven officers, only one of them restrained. Just sorting them out now. Plus the people from the bus." She shot her arm out sideways and grabbed the sleeve of a passing medical student, then shot out the other and nailed a premed. "I'll help you myself. Christ, look at him—he doesn't even know where he is. Set up for lavage?"

I nodded. "Lavage and charcoal slurry. Let's get routine labs, urine drug tox, EKG . . . we'll want to monitor oxygen levels . . . start an IV, normal saline . . ."

"He's taking his clothes off," Kathy Haughey observed. "Gary—"

Stripped down to his jockey shorts, Gary disappeared around the corner toward Holding, making breaststrokes with his arms and bubbling fish sounds with his mouth. I let Haughey go after him.

"Ev." Lauren Sabot was at my elbow.

Suddenly unguarded, I said, "I don't know whether to laugh or cry."

"Don't laugh."

I heard the chill and tremor in her voice before I saw her face. She was pale. In all the time I had known her, I had never seen her grope for words like this. She drew a halting breath and held out her hands. Resting on her upturned palms were two large white mushrooms. *"Amanita phalloides."*

"Oh, god," I breathed. "Death caps?"

She nodded.

My heart stopped, then restarted.

I went after Gary and the nurse.

four

Gastric lavage—pumping someone's stomach—is not a pleasant procedure under any circumstances and it's even worse when you have to torture your own dearly beloved colleague.

"I know this is a horrible ordeal, Gary," I said. "But you have to help us."

Positioning myself on the left side of the stretcher, I nodded to Mark Ramsey and he went around to the right. Holding up the Ewald tube, a big-bore rubber hose, I said, "You know what this is, Gary. I need you to swallow it."

"Snake! Snake!" Gary shrieked, thrashing around on his stretcher. "Get a shovel! Kill it!"

"We're going to need jaws," I sighed. I pushed my glasses up on my nose with my wrist and used my forearm to sweep my hair back from my forehead.

Not only was I torturing Gary, I had four people helping me do it: Mark Ramsey; Kathy Haughey; the medical student, and the premedical student. All knew Gary personally. Their emotions showed on their faces as they worked to control Gary with four-point restraints, those heavy-duty, leather wrist-and-ankle straps with bicycle locks, like the ones they put on Hannibal Lechter in *Silence of the Lambs.* Mark was so upset he had stopped talking altogether. Kathy was barking at everyone. The medical student looked more arrogant and aloof than ever, and the premed was awed by the charged atmosphere in the room. So far they'd managed to get the wristbands on and were now struggling to anchor the wristbands to the belt. The medical student, a sharp-eyed Eurasian from Hong Kong named Nicholson, held Gary's feet.

Gary got an arm free, swung wide. An IV pole went over; saved in the nick of time from crashing to the floor by the premed.

"Tie him low to the stretcher," I said.

"Haldol?" suggested Nicholson. Even he winced as Gary screamed. "Might suppress the agitation."

"No." I raised my voice over Gary's.

"It's too long-acting," said Ramsey, speaking for the first time since he'd come in the room. "Second, it's a neuroleptic. We need to be able to assess his mental status. Third, we don't know what he ingested." He wrestled Gary's arm to the stretcher. "But you might consider something shorter acting, Ev. The anesthesiologists like Tropofil—"

I cut him off. "I don't want to give another drug. Let's try this first, and if necessary we'll regroup."

"You're not going to get him to swallow that Ewald voluntarily," Haughey said. "You'll need jaws."

"No sharks! No sharks!" shrieked Gary.

We had an audience, too. In addition to the subway fiasco and the police van rollover, it was a normal Saturday night in the ER; by six P.M. there was no room at the inn. We had patients stacked two and three to a room. Tonight we shared the emergency room's OR Three with a state trooper in a

Smokey-the-Bear uniform—including the hat—and the trooper's "aided" case, a shady character in a flashy business suit who had lacerated his hand I forget how. Lacerated Hand was seated on a stool with his injured limb stretched out before him on a stainless-steel tray; hemostats protruded from a deep cut in his palm, stanching the blood flow, while he waited for a surgeon. Smokey the Bear stood next to him, his arms crossed over his chest. Both watched the action around Gary as if we were all on TV.

"Maybe get it in, when he open his mouth to scream," suggested Lacerated Hand. "He drop a tab of acid, you ain't gonna get him to calm down none."

"Nah," said Smokey. "He'd just shut his mouth again, right on the tube."

Two passing surgeons, who'd been called down to help with the cops, also had their two cents to put in. Old enough to have gone to college during the sixties, they hovered in the doorway and reminisced about their experiences with LSD.

"Middle of June, and I was convinced the lampposts were coated with ice and the earth was dying," said one.

"Yeah," said the other, laughing. "I had flashbacks for ten years. Still do. The new theory is, the brain stores LSD in the fatty tissues and releases it during periods of stress. I had this patient once, she was in four-points crying that the bed was rising—she was having DTs—and goddamn if I didn't see the bed rise myself! Guess I triggered this release of LSD. I decided it was time for me to leave the room."

"Yeah," I said over my shoulder, "do me a favor—it's time for you to leave the room now, too."

"Have fun," the surgeons called, and left.

I clenched my teeth. Kathy Haughey handed me the jaws. A kind of dental speculum, jaws was a stainless-steel gadget with rubber padding and scissor handles; you jammed the rubber part between the patient's back molars, squeezed the handles, and the patient's mouth was forced open. It locked in place. Theoretically, at least; I had never used it.

I took Lacerated Hand's advice and waited for Gary to scream again; when he did, I moved. "Got it! How's it lock?"

Haughey helped me. When we finished, Gary looked like the man in Edvard Munch's *The Scream*. Because he had to sit up for the procedure, the head of his stretcher was angled as high as possible, the railings slanting toward the floor; between them, Gary perched—trussed and strapped down and locked up—his mouth an open O with the gruesome handles of the jaws protruding.

"You okay?" Kathy asked me softly.

I could feel myself near tears. "Let's get this done," I said. "Gary, you are going to have to swallow this tube. I'm sorry. . . . God, I'm sorry."

Lubricating the end of the Ewald with K-Y Jelly, I checked to make sure the other end was in the bucket. Quickly estimating how much of the tube I'd have to get down, I inhaled deeply, and slid a gloved hand into the back of Gary's mouth to guide my way. Gary did not stop screaming. There were no words now, just long, pitched wails, which bounced off the green tile walls of OR Three and reverberated throughout the ER. I spoke to him all the while, soothing nonsense that caught in my throat. "Okay, ready?" I asked, as if he were cooperating. "Here we go, swallow, swallow—this will just take a second—*swallow*."

Gary began coughing violently and I withdrew the tube.

"Wouldn't it be easier to induce vomiting?" the premed asked.

"Nowadays the trend is against induced vomiting," I explained, while I paused for Gary to stop coughing. "In the time it takes to work, the patient may become lethargic, and then if he vomits he can aspirate." Inhale the stomach contents into the lungs.

"What do you do when that happens—when the patient aspirates?"

Normally I encouraged questions, but not tonight. I didn't answer. "Gary, can you lean your head further forward? We have to try this again. Please try to help me."

Gary wailed weakly. At least he seemed to be wearing himself out—which might make things easier. Kathy Haughey slid her arms under Gary's shoulders and braced him a little higher and more forward. I braced myself for the second try.

"Aspiration can cause acute inflammatory response," Nicholson explained to the premed, taking the opportunity to impress the one person in the room who was lower in the pecking order than he was. "Then you can get acute respiratory distress syndrome. The stomach acid attacks the lungs quickly and can be fatal. Usually you get chemical burn and a massive bacterial infection. And even when treated early, ARDS still has a fifty-percent mortality rate—"

"Nicholson," I snapped.

Flushing, he caught himself. "Sorry."

"Okay, Gary, here we go. . . ." I put my left hand into the back of Gary's mouth, guided the tube in with my right, and quickly snaked it down the esophagus. "Swallow, swallow—"

I held my breath.

"Damn," said Lacerated Hand. "This some Roto-Rooter."

I watched the Ewald disappear into Gary's gaping mouth. Just as it seemed that I had got the tube down—finally!—Gary gagged and his abdomen pitched.

Immediately Ramsey pushed him forward; I pulled out the tube. But we were too late. Gary seemed to empty his entire stomach contents into his lap with one long toss—and with a great whooping wheeze, he aspirated.

Jesus Christ. "Stridor!" I yelled, as the harsh, high-pitched wheezing began. "He's got stridor!"

Gary had aspirated and his larynx was obstructed—blocking his breathing.

My perception of reality altered. Heart slamming against my sternum, every cell in my body suddenly, cleanly, electrically charged as if struck by lightning, I jolted into the hyperdrive of adrenaline. Time slowed. Focus narrowed. Abruptly there seemed nothing in the room except my fear and my adrenaline and my five senses and my body—and Gary. Gary coughed and wheezed like a strangled whooping crane, his mouth still wide around the stainless-steel O of the medical device. His eyes pleaded with me wildly.

"Suction," I said.

Haughey slapped the suction catheter into my hand. I jammed it up Gary's nose and through the nasopharynx and down, this time aiming for the trachea. Gary gasped for air. I gasped along with him. The stridor of his breathing sliced through my heart like a razor. Precious seconds passed as Gary turned blue and struggled against his restraints. I probed frantically for the windpipe, listening for the wind to pass through the tube so I would know I had it in the lungs.

"Heart rate bradying down," warned Haughey, looking at the monitor. Gary's heart was slowing dangerously. "Pulse ox eighty-four . . ."

"I'm in," I cried just as Gary's eyes rolled up in his head.

I withdrew the suction wand, undid the jaws, and whipped them out of Gary's mouth. Grabbing the ambubag from Ramsey, I swiftly snapped the face mask on Gary and hooked it up to the wall oxygen. Dissociation kicked in and I began to feel farther and farther away, as if I were looking over my own shoulder, and at the same time I seemed to zoom closer and closer. I watched my fingers set the oxygen mask over Gary's purple lips and blue nose. I watched my hands squeeze the bag. I watched Gary's color miraculously improve just a little. Hope and dread surged in my chest in equal amounts.

35

Dimly I heard myself hollering for Respiratory. Haughey called out the numbers. Nicholson drew blood for the gases, while the premed ran for ice. Behind me, Smokey the Bear vomited noisily into the sink.

"Goddamn, goddamn," Lacerated Hand said, his voice filled with awe.

"WHERE THE FUCK IS RESPIRATORY?" I bellowed, lifting the oxygen mask so Ramsey could suction Gary's mouth. "Give me the goddamn ET tube." Moving quickly, I pulled Gary's jaw up and out; Nicholson handed me the endotrach tube from the kit. I slid the tube down Gary's throat and into his windpipe. "Tidal volume of seven hundred, rate twelve," I ordered.

Hooking up the ventilator, Haughey punched the settings in. "F-I-oh-two, hundred percent?"

I nodded. The ventilator began to thump and hiss. Haughey unsnapped Gary's vomit-soaked gown and peeled it down. Ramsey and I whipped on our stethoscopes to check Gary's breath sounds.

"Rhonchi," I said after a moment. Gurgling in the lungs. Gary was in bronchospasm. Herald of the dreaded acute respiratory distress syndrome. Not good. In fact, very bad. Nicholson's words rang in my head: *can be fatal . . . And even when treated early, ARDS still has a fifty-percent mortality rate.* I took my stethoscope off, cleaned it with an alcohol wipe. "Damn," I groaned, anguished. "Oh, Gary, I'm so sorry."

I turned my head away from Gary's nakedness as Haughey cleaned him up, and from the vomit smell, which was overwhelming. I was in the throes of if-only, if only I had gone along with Ramsey and Haughey, who wanted to sedate. If only Gary hadn't aspirated. If only I had suctioned him more quickly and efficiently. If only he weren't in bronchospasm. The if-onlys mixed in my gorge with the adrenaline and the vomit smell already clogging my head and I lurched to the sink. Shouldering Smokey the Bear aside, I spilled my own cookies almost before I knew what was coming.

"Goddamn, goddamn," said Lacerated Hand.

five

"He's been admitted to the Intensive Care Unit," I told Vittorio. "He's conscious but sedated. Alan's at bedside."

Vittorio von Laue sat upright in his hospital bed and stared at me incredulously over his reading glasses.

I swallowed. Vittorio never made things easy. "He can't talk, of course, because of the intubation—"

"I don't understand. You're telling me Gary Seligman ate *hallucinogenic mushrooms?*"

"Yes, from the gift basket."

"Which is hard enough to believe in itself—"

"I'm sure he had no idea what he was eating, Vic."

"—but in addition to that you fucked up pumping his stomach—"

"Vic, please."

"—and almost killed him? Is that what you're telling me? Because of this incredible, unbelievable fuckup, *Seligman could die?*"

"He's stabilized. They're treating him very aggressively—

steroids, bronchodilators, the new surfactant treatment. The bronchoscopy showed no particulate matter—"

"Jesus Christ." Vittorio swept aside his bedclothes and swung his legs over the side of the bed. "Gary is the hospital's most highly respected nurses' union rep—what in God's name were you thinking, waiting an hour and a half to tell me? And I'm going to break Lauren Sabot's neck, for only saying there was a 'problem with dinner' when she rang. Goddamn her. And goddamn you, too!"

"I'm sorry."

"Hand me my robe," he ordered, pointing at the closet. "Slippers on the floor."

Vittorio and my brother Alan had been together for nearly two years. A stunningly handsome man with steel-blue eyes and brown salt-and-pepper hair, in his late forties, Vic was elegant, dignified, wealthy, and successful—or dandyish, pompous, stinking rich, and opportunistic, depending on whom you talked to. I had never really liked him. But he was a respected member of the hospital's board of trustees and a big-bucks donor. We had good friends in common. And Alan seemed very much in love with him, despite their recent problems and explosive quarreling. So I tried to be polite.

I handed Vittorio his robe. Reaching up, he grabbed his IV bag off the pole and dragged it through the right sleeve of his robe. He pulled the other sleeve over his left arm more gingerly, taking care not to snag it.

Early that week, Vittorio had fallen off his horse while riding to hounds in Westchester. He was coming down a hill, took a panel fence, and the horse didn't quite get the full take-off, hitting the top bar and flipping. Horse and rider went down in a heap together; Vittorio was lucky the horse didn't land on him. Vic sustained an open fracture of the left wrist—the bones came through the skin—and the wound was contaminated with soil. Luckily, a doc from University Hospital who rode with the hunt was on the scene. He splinted Vittorio's wrist with his riding crop and neck stock, bundled him into his car, and drove him back into the city. But the wound was such a mess that the surgeons cleaning the dirt and debris out had to cut away some hopelessly contaminated tissue.

On his left arm Vittorio wore an external fixator or "ex-fix," a contraption that looked like an erector set and immobilized the fracture with pins that went through the skin into the bones. He remained in the hospital to receive big-guns antibiotics intravenously, while the docs decided whether he needed a second operation.

Vittorio was not what you would call a compliant patient. Cavalier and a bon vivant, he had a tendency to eat too much, drink too much, work too hard, play too hard, and sleep too little. Add to that his unfortunate tendency to seek new and innovative methods of killing himself accidentally. Not only did he ride to hounds, he skied, sailed, and windsurfed. He skied the most expert, black-double-diamond slopes. Twice he'd sustained tib-fib fractures (both bones in the lower leg). Sailing to him meant offshore in vessels that had no business leaving sheltered bays. So far he'd been hospitalized on one occasion for hypothermia (freezing your ass), and on another for concussion (the boom on the boat swung around and hit him in the head, knocking him overboard). Then there was the windsurfing—one time in San Francisco shipping lanes in thirty-knot winds. No injuries there, but if he'd been run down by a supertanker there wouldn't have been anything left of him to sustain injuries.

During the two years I'd known Vittorio, he'd broken his collarbone and four ribs (horse went out from under him); dislocated his shoulder, chipping the acromium (horse refused a jump and Vittorio kept on going); and sustained this open fracture of the wrist. The joke around the hospital was that Vittorio sat on the board of trustees and gave the hospital huge amounts of money because he wanted to assure that he would receive the best care possible when he needed it—and he needed it a lot.

He shook his shoulders to straighten the robe over his crisp cotton pajamas, and tied the tasseled-rope belt. I didn't help him. He was so often incapacitated, he could accomplish almost any task one-handed. Besides, he hated help of any kind—one of Alan's biggest complaints about him. Vic was infuriatingly self-sufficient. As I watched him shuffle his bare feet into his velvet slippers, I remembered Alan's blow-by-blow description of an argument they'd had recently. It had escalated beyond all reason, until Vittorio was shouting and throwing things, and demanding that Alan leave and come back when he—*Alan*—"learned how to converse in a civil manner."

Alan's explanation: "Vittorio doesn't know how to ask for help when he needs it." My parry: "The two of you need marriage counseling. He's throwing things, for chrissake. And you're letting him throw them!" Alan's return: "At least we air our differences. Confrontation is always better than conflict-avoidance. You and Phil need to learn how to fight better and vent when you need to. He broods like the Sphinx and you let him!"

Game, match, and set, Alan's favor.

Vittorio grasped his IV pole in his right hand. "Ev," he barked, "snap to. This is no time to go into a trance for pity's sake. Alan must be *frantic*." Guarding his broken left arm against his belly, he moved out of the room and set off down the corridor. I followed.

At the nurses' station, he refused a wheelchair and rebuffed a nurse's pleas not to try to walk all the way to the ICU.

"The ICU is three buildings away, Mr. von Laue," she said.

"Thank you, I know that."

"You have to take the elevator to the fourth floor, cross

the skywalk, take two more elevators, and walk about a quarter mile."

"I am grateful for your assistance," said Vittorio. "But it is hardly a quarter mile. Good evening."

The nurse scowled at me. I shrugged.

Vittorio and I got into the first of the three elevators.

"Explain to me again," he said, "how you opened the fridge, saw this basket of hallucinogenic mushrooms just sitting there like in Alice in Wonderland with a sign saying EAT ME—and then you went la-dee-da back to the hospital, without a suspicious thought in your head!"

"I told you, I thought the basket was from Phil."

"Is Phil in the habit of presenting you with baskets of hallucinogenic mushrooms?"

"I didn't *know* they were hallucinogenic, Vic!" I snapped. "Gary is my friend, too, you know—and I love him dearly. I'm worried sick."

That shut him up for two seconds, at least until the elevator doors opened on the fourth floor. But then Vic began berating me again. "I can't believe you almost killed the nurse who singlehandedly organized Monday's strike, to say nothing of the fact that he's Alan's closest friend in the world and—"

"Vic! Could you please—I am absolutely terrified here."

"She wants pity, too," Vittorio sputtered. "Good god."

I stomped down the hall and pushed through the door to the skywalk, my face burning. How did I ever get a brother-in-law like this? He could be gracious and charming—

"This is no time for false sentiment," he said.

—or utterly mean-spirited and downright surly.

I was sorry I had ever taken Alan to that blasted hospital ball, where he met Vittorio.

Two years ago, just this time of year. A glorious, warm October evening. The University Hospital and the College of

Physicians and Surgeons were having a soirée to kick off the final fundraising drive to finish construction of the new Storrs Pavilion.

I was psyched. I felt like Cinderella, about to be transformed by the fairy godmother's wand from the abject scutgirl intern, spattered with blood, vomit, and piss, into the princess doctor of the ball. I had been chosen by Case Hamilton, then vice-chairman of the hospital's board of trustees, to sit at his and Mrs. Hamilton's table, along with Dr. and Mrs. Christopher Randolph Cabot III, Mr. and Mrs. Vittorio von Laue, and the legendary hospital patroness Mrs. Storrs. Very exalted company indeed. Chris Cabot was my boss, the director of the emergency department. Phil Carchiollo, an attending on the psychiatric service, I knew from a psych clerkship I'd done my last year in med school. And Vittorio von Laue sat on the hospital's board with Hamilton. The Hamiltons had also invited some prospective donors, a real-estate mogul and his wife, whom they hoped to woo and get on the board if possible. We doctors were to serve as the "talent" to talk up the hospital to the prospective donors.

I had all the windows open in my doctors' residence apartment, enjoying the fresh, balmy breeze after several days of lashing downpour, unusually heavy for the season. It had to be at least sixty-five degrees out, if not seventy. New York City sparkled in the twilight, lights winking on everywhere as people came home from work. I'd had my shower, washed and dried my hair, put on my makeup, and was relaxing for a few minutes in my slip and bathrobe with a cup of herbal tea. My lovely new cocktail dress—pale, sea-green silk with lace trim—hung from a hanger on the door of the closet, and I admired it while I lounged on the bed with my tea. My mom, in a grand gesture, had whisked me off to Bloomingdale's the previous week and bought it for me. "To bring out the green glints in your eyes," she'd said. I'd stopped at the makeup counter for new eye shadow and had splurged on lipstick and blusher as well.

Setting down my tea, I slipped out of my bathrobe and carefully slipped on the dress. I looked at the gorgeous woman in the mirror, and she looked back at me, slightly startled.

Normally, I considered myself modestly attractive, and hoped people thought I looked intelligent and like I knew what I was doing. My usual hospital garb consisted of chinos, Brooks Brothers button-down shirts, my white coat, and boating shoes. Before I went out the door each morning I applied a little eye pencil and lipstick, both of which usually wore off by noon.

So who was this creature in the mirror? Some parts I recognized: she was tall and slender, like me; had light brown hair cut short but full, like me; hazel eyes, tortoiseshell eyeglass frames, like me. But how did she get her makeup so perfect? And va-va-va-voom, *where* did she get that *dress*?

The phone rang.

"It's Phil Carchiollo. You and I had talked about sharing a cab to the ball. But I've got a suicidal patient and I'm going to have to cancel."

"Oh, that's too bad," I said. "I was looking forward to catching up with you." More than I was willing to say. I liked Phil a lot and was secretly sorry that he had a girlfriend.

"Yeah, me too," he said.

"Will you be late?" I asked. "Or are you not coming at all?"

"I'm afraid I won't make it. I have to admit the patient and then talk to her parents."

I looked at myself in the mirror in my pretty green dress and stifled a sigh.

"I can't reach the Hamiltons," Phil said. "Is there any chance you can rustle up someone to go in my place?"

I tried to think. "Everyone I know is already going."

"What about your brother Alan?"

I had taken Alan to the nurses' Christmas party the year before, and he and Phil had had a long conversation. Phil had relatives in Florence, Italy, and Alan had done his junior year abroad there.

"Good idea," I said. "Alan and Case Hamilton can talk about soufflés and omelet pans, and if I remember correctly, Mrs. von Laue has some kind of degree in art."

"Yeah, Alan can tell his Florence stories. Lighten up the conversation a little. No one's going to want to spend the whole evening listening to docs pitch the hospital to prospective donors."

Another pause.

"I'll call Alan," I said.

I hung up the phone with a wry smile. Gary Seligman was also going to the ball. Mrs. Storrs had apparently asked, "Why are there never any nurses at these affairs?" and Case had decided he'd better get one for his table.

I'd have to make sure that Alan and Gary didn't get out of hand.

six

W hen I phoned Alan to invite him to the hospital ball, he said, "Don't tell me. You need a walker."

"A what?"

"Ev. Don't be so naïve. Black tie?"

"Yes."

"Pick you up in an hour," he said.

Within forty-five minutes, Alan arrived in a cab and whisked me off to the ball. If I hadn't been with my own brother, I would have considered him Prince Charming. As always, he exhibited a true sense of occasion. Resplendent in his tuxedo with black silk vest, he opened a split of champagne in the back of the cab, toasted the fact that I was wearing a dress for the first time in two years—"You *must* give me the name of your dressmaker, darling," he drawled—and presented me with a delicate corsage of freesia, which he expertly pinned on my left shoulder. He wore a matching boutonniere. I was struck as I always am by how much Alan and I look alike. From the nose up, our faces are carbon copies of our mother's: the same nose, same cheekbones, same hazel eyes, same brow line. Our mouths and jaw lines come from our different fathers. My own father and namesake, Evan Farley Sutcliffe, died in a car accident shortly before I was born; my mother then married Dr. Sandy Berman, who had been her high school boyfriend, and with whom she had two boys, my half-brothers Alan and Craig. But nobody dwelled on the fact that I had a different biological father. I thought of Sandy Berman as my "real" Dad, and considered Alan and Craig my "whole" brothers. I was pleased Alan looked so much like me.

"I don't want to spoil the mood, but I have to tell you something," Alan said suddenly. He quaffed the rest of his champagne in one gulp, took a tea towel out of his grip, and wiped the glass clean. "Gary and I broke up, Ev."

"You broke up?" I echoed in surprise. "When?"

"Tuesday."

"Oh, Alan, I'm so sorry."

"Yeah, me too." His voice caught.

I put a hand on his knee. "Do you want to tell me what happened?"

"Yes, but not now."

"Well, are you going to be all right tonight, with Gary at our table?"

"We'll be fine," Alan said quickly. "We've agreed to stay friends. And . . . um . . . I just want to say, I know how much you like him, Ev, and how much you were probably hoping things would work out between us, and I'm sorry to disappoint you."

"You don't have to apologize to me or anyone," I told him firmly. Although he was right: I was selfishly very disappointed. I had liked some of Alan's previous boyfriends, but Gary was the only one of them that I had hoped was Mr. Right. I sipped my champagne. The bubbles seemed to have gone out of it.

"I thought you were seeing a counselor," I said.

"We were. We broke up in her office."

"Who . . . ?"

"I did. I'm afraid I didn't handle it very well, though—apparently it was a big surprise to him, out of the clear blue sky. He didn't see it coming at all."

"Was there anything—" I started to ask. But we had reached our destination. By the time I paid for the cab and we got out, and Alan wiped and stashed my champagne glass, the discussion was clearly over.

The ball was being held in several large white tents pitched for the occasion at Lincoln Center, in a small park next to the Metropolitan Opera. We crossed the plaza, making our way through the crowds of people milling around before the evening's scheduled performances. I began to feel upset. But Alan seemed determined to enjoy the evening. When we bumped into Gary during cocktails, he seemed equally determined. The two men shook hands formally, then conversed politely as if they barely knew each other. And when we were all finally seated at the dinner table, both Gary and Alan took to socializing with a vengeance—as if to prove that neither was hurting.

Gary, seated next to Mrs. Storrs, proceeded to woo her with questions about her lifelong interest in hospitals; even before the appetizer was served, the nonagenarian grande dame was giggling like a schoolgirl.

When I introduced Alan to Case and Jacqueline Hamilton, Alan immediately inquired about the potential donors, a real estate mogul and his wife, who had not yet arrived. What were their interests? How had they been introduced to the hospital? What other charities did they support? You would have thought Alan was a professional fundraiser rather than a keyboarder at a brokerage firm putting himself through the Culinary Institute at night. He charmed the wives, impressed the husbands, and dazzled everyone with his scintillating wit. Alan even managed to put Vittorio von Laue at ease. I had always thought von Laue, while breathtakingly handsome, was a bit of a pompous ass. But there he was, laughing at my brother's jokes and stories!

I had met the von Laues a number of times before at dinner parties. Case Hamilton I had met years ago, and we had seen a great deal of each other lately, because he and his wife Jackie often included med students and junior house staff from the hospital when they entertained in their spacious West End Avenue apartment. Some of us had even been favored with invitations to weekend house parties at their sprawling Long Island estate. Vittorio and Patricia von Laue, the Hamiltons' closest friends, were often there. They kept an apartment in the same West End Avenue building and had a house near the Hamiltons' in Cold Spring Harbor.

Patricia von Laue was modestly pretty and very, very thin, with large green eyes and prominent cheekbones. She had always struck me as exotic. Mimi in *La Bohème* singing her last aria before dying, or perhaps the soprano in La Traviata. The evening of the ball, she exuded her usual, extraordinary life force, and ate most of her food with reasonable relish. But I was shocked by the change in her since we had last met. She seemed ravaged and weak and slightly drunk. Moreover, she wore a high-necked red, gold, and blue silk gown with matching turban—a dead give-away. She was dying. Some kind of fulminant cancer, I guessed, involving chest or breast surgery (the high-necked gown was to hide the scars) and chemotherapy (the turban to conceal hair loss). And I guessed, too, that she was self-treating with marijuana.

"We've never had a chance to talk, Dr. Sutcliffe," Mrs. von Laue said to me over coffee as the band tuned up. She slid into the seat next to me where the real-estate mogul had been sitting; Hamilton had taken him and Mrs. Mogul on a tour of the room. "Case tells me you completed most of your requirements for a Ph.D. in English."

I tried to divine how old she was. Late forties, probably. "I was ABD," I said. "All But Dissertation."

"What made you choose medicine instead?"

"Well, it's a long story. My parents had always steered me toward a career in medicine. My mother's the director of nursing at a large hospital center in New Jersey, and my father's a pediatric neurologist there. To make them happy, I took a double major in English and biology. Then I went to graduate school to study what *I* wanted to study. I was working on my dissertation about androgyny in the plays of William Shakespeare when Dad had a heart attack and had to undergo cardiac bypass surgery. I needed to know what was going on. I got my hands on an old, beat-up copy of DeBakey's book on heart surgery for laypeople, and I read it. And, of course, I was sitting there in the hospital keeping a vigil by Dad's bed, watching all the goings-on, what the doctors and nurses were doing. For the first time, I realized how exciting medicine was. English lit was interesting, but it wasn't life and death."

Mrs. von Laue smiled. "No wonder Case feels so simpatico with you, Doctor—you know he often says you're his alter ego. He always wanted to leave law for medicine."

"Yes, I know," I said. "He already had his E.M.T. certification when I met him many years ago in organic chemistry. As you may know, we were lab partners. In college I was drawn to the deep, quiet types, and I gravitated to him immediately. He had such an air of dolorosa, back then. He was so—"

I stopped myself, suddenly realizing that I was saying far more than I should. Especially with Case's wife Jackie sitting right across from me. Embarrassed, I reached for my wineglass.

"Unhappy," Mrs. von Laue agreed quietly. She caught my eye and held my gaze. I had seen that look before in the dying: *no bullshit, there isn't time.* Leaning toward me, she went on in a low voice, "He hates the law. Always has. When we were younger, he yearned so palpably for a career in medicine. But he was the only male heir to carry on at the family law firm, as you know. Filial duty and self-sacrifice. All that 'white shoe stuff,' as he himself will tell you."

Across the table, Jackie Hamilton unobtrusively rose and excused herself with a dignified smile. She went off in the direction of the ladies' room.

"I shouldn't give offense," Mrs. von Laue murmured.

"I'm sorry, I shouldn't have brought it up."

"Don't be. Case often speaks of that year in organic chemistry with you. It irritates Jackie no end—she sided with his parents. It was the family firm, and Case the only son. Of course, his sisters would have made perfectly good lawyers had they been encouraged, but no—only the son would do."

Alan and Gary weren't the only people at the table pretending not to have—or have had—feelings for each other. For a moment I considered telling Mrs. von Laue the truth: Case Hamilton wasn't just my lab partner, way back when.

I was in love with him.

Of course, I concealed it as well as I could; he was married, after all. If he noticed, he pretended not to. What he felt for me—if anything other than brotherly affection—was a mystery then, as it was now. Meanwhile I aced both semesters of lecture and lab, an unheard-of accomplishment; competition was fierce. I'm sure it was pure sublimation.

We did have one "date." He took me to dinner after our final lab, to celebrate our good grades—and to tell me that he had decided to continue in law, as his family wanted.

And one kiss—to say goodbye.

Things like that have an impact on the young and impressionable. I never forgot him. A thorough romantic, I assumed I would never see him again. When I ran into him years later at the hospital, I was so shocked I was speechless. So was he. He embraced me in front of six or seven board members, all of whom looked on curiously. "Look at you!" he exclaimed finally, holding me at arm's length. "My long-lost muse and alter ego! And in a white coat after all!"

We fell comfortably back into our former lab-partner routine. He consulted me frequently about hospital matters, when he needed what he called "a grass-roots opinion." We were easy together. Old comrades. He was as I remembered him: polite, formal, slightly stiff. Kind and attentive. The air of dolorosa had softened at the edges, perhaps with resignation. He claimed to be satisfied in his role of hospital board member.

But I didn't believe him.

"Well, *ecce iterum Crispinus,*" Mrs. Von Laue said. I felt hands on my shoulders, and jumped. Case Hamilton had risen and was standing behind my chair. He leaned down, his cheek next to mine. "Having a good time?"

"Yes, thank you," I said, inhaling the faint whiff of Penhaligon's cologne. His face was close enough to kiss. I didn't. "I've been talking to Mrs. von Laue."

"Excellent." He straightened. "Ah, there you are, my dear," he said to his wife, who had returned to the table. "Let's dance." He swept her away onto the dance floor.

"I so wished I could swap with him, when we were in college," Mrs. von Laue said. "I was premed all the way through Smith," she continued. "To please *my* parents. Who are doctors. I even worked as a volunteer at my mother's hospital in New Haven, two summers in a row, and Christmas vacations. I hated it. I wanted to study art history, but Dad said he wouldn't pay for a degree in art. Art was for empty-headed dilettantes, he said."

"What happened?" I asked. My mouth was dry. I reached for my water glass.

"Well, for one thing, I married Vittorio. That pleased my parents. They'd always been fond of him. And I wasn't entirely dependent on my father for support, like Case has always been. I had a small inheritance from my grandmother, just enough to pay my graduate school tuition. So I did get my Ph.D. in art history, as I wanted. And I've been very happy working as a curator at the museum . . ." she trailed off.

Out of the corner of my eye, I caught Gary across the table exchanging a meaningful look with Alan. Although he tried to cover it, I could see that Gary was upset. Meanwhile, Mrs. von Laue gazed soulfully into her demitasse cup.

"You've had to curtail your activities?" I asked delicately.

"Yes. Sadly."

"I'm sorry," I said.

She picked up her spoon and stirred her coffee. "Well, it's come back to haunt me. . . . You know the real reason I didn't become a doctor?" She laughed bitterly.

My attention was diverted to Alan. Just for a split second. Over Pat von Laue's shoulder, I could see Alan was engaged in rapt conversation with Vittorio. My eyes moved to Alan's face, back to Mrs. Von Laue's—

Then back to Alan's.

"I thought sick people were disgusting," Mrs. von Laue said. She continued to stir her coffee, her eyes down. "And, now, of course, I am one."

I glanced around for Gary; luckily, he seemed to have left the table with Mrs. Storrs. Vittorio's back was to me. I couldn't see Vittorio's face. But I could see Alan, and Alan's half of the look that passed between them.

"I'm very sorry, Mrs. von Laue," I said.

"Call me Pat," she said.

Three months later Patricia Langhorne von Laue died in her sleep, at home, of fulminantly metastatic breast cancer. By then she and I had become friends.

Vittorio and Alan had become more than friends.

And Vic and I—although we denied it up and down—had become enemies.

*   *   *

As we went around the corner to the Intensive Care Unit, Vittorio let go of his IV pole for a moment and plucked my sleeve. "Ev."

I stopped.

"Let's be friends. For Alan's sake."

My heart softened. I smiled a little. "You mean you're sorry."

He put out his hand.

I shook. Vittorio and I routinely shook, for Alan's sake, once or twice a month. I suppose we wanted to like each other, but couldn't. "I'm sorry," I said, apologizing even if he wouldn't. He never did.

But he surprised me now. "I absolve you," he said, with unusual intensity.

I caught my breath. I knew Vic was talking about the botched lavage, but for a moment I thought he was absolving me across the board—for everything. For all the animosity I'd ever borne him. All the times I'd thought, *You betrayed your dying wife and left her for my brother.* Or, *I've never gotten over my disappointment that Alan's with you and not with Gary.*

Through a haze of complicated emotion, I suddenly realized how guilty I felt that I'd never accepted Vittorio, that I'd borne him so much malice all this time. Even though Gary and Alan themselves had long since settled into a warm friendship, all forgiven—and Vittorio had long since accepted Gary as his own friend. In fact, Vittorio graciously treated Gary like a blood relative.

"Thank you," I said. "I haven't always thought kind thoughts about you, you know, and I'd like—"

But he cut me off. "Time for sentiment later," he said gruffly. "Right now I need your help—to find out who sent that goddamned basket."

seven

"Any chance he'll die?" Detective First Grade Richard Ost, NYPD, leaned toward me with concern.

"He could," I said, my eyes welling with tears.

I'd been stoic and professional while we stabilized Gary after his *therapeutic misadventure*—as such events were called in the medical literature—and transported him to the ICU. And relatively calm throughout the bronchoscopy and the conference with the pulmonologist and the assistant director of the ICU. But I had a feeling stoic and calm were about to go out the window.

Alan had finally turned up, waving the note I'd left on my apartment front door for him: *Gary possibly poisoned—DO NOT EAT ANYTHING—took Gary to ER—Beep me immediately, Ev.* The triage nurse let Alan into the ER unescorted, and he came around the corner just as we were moving Gary out. Not a pretty scene, and a horrifying shock to Alan—who already had had shock enough for one day. Turned out he had been caught in the subway when the shooting went down. For an hour and a half, Alan crouched in a hot, darkened, and crowded train held between stations while the police searched for alleged cop shooters in the tunnel.

I'd commandeered Nicholson the med student, whom I'd delegated to call Poison Control. I debriefed him—Poison Control recommended that I consult Professor Robert Held, the local mushroom expert—then sent Nicholson uptown to the twenty-four-hour library at the University College of Physicians and Surgeons, to research the literature on toxic and hallucinogenic mushrooms. Since Lauren Sabot knew Prof. Held personally, I'd dispatched her in a cab with one of each kind of the mushrooms to show him.

I'd spoken to Phil, twice.

I'd left a message for my boss, Chris Cabot, with his answering service.

I'd called Shirley Seligman, Gary's mother, and listened with a groan to the message on her machine: *I will be away on my dream tour of China and Hong Kong from October first through the twentieth. In case of emergency, please call Gary in New York.*

I'd called Judy Seligman, Gary's sister. Same message. Great.

And I'd spoken to one of the surgeons who'd been reminiscing about his experiences with LSD, to see if he'd done hallucinogenic mushrooms, too. Yeah, he'd said. Psilocybin, in college. The effects lasted twelve to twenty-four hours. Terrific.

Ost handed me a Kleenex. "Take your time, Doc. We're not in any rush here."

We sat in the ICU kitchen, a small, multipurpose room where the nurses held rounds, the doctors caught up on chartwork, and the police, when they were required, interviewed patients' family members. Ost and I had discussed so many patients during my two-and-a-half years on the University Hospital house staff that we had given up counting.

A kind man in his early forties with graying brown hair,

Ost had what I used to think were Everyman features, until my brother Craig the movie buff pointed out to me how much Ost resembled Harrison Ford—right down to the crooked, ironic smile, bemused and twinkly eyes, and air of quiet intelligence. All of which Ost sternly repressed while working, pulling on the *de rigueur* police poker face the way other guys shrugged into suit jackets and tied ties for the office. Or the way Superman cloaked himself in his guise of Clark Kent.

I considered him a friend. I called him by his nickname, "Ozzie," and he called me "Doc." We worked well together, I thought. Joked easily. Occasionally even flirted. Once in a while, traded personal info. He knew a little about my boyfriend Phil. And I knew a little about his estranged wife, whom Ost had never quite managed to divorce, despite their having lived separately for years—and despite her ongoing relationship with another man. And Ost's two teenaged kids, Tiger Lily and Gung Ho, although I kept forgetting their real names.

"Why don't we start with the medical details?" Ost suggested quietly. "When you're ready."

I blew my nose, and recounted how I had come home to find Gary, sick to his stomach. Quickly, I reconstructed the progression of events that led to his present condition. "He inhaled some of his stomach contents—very acid, very damaging to the lungs," I explained. My voice shook but held. "Right now we're assessing and treating the lung injury. On the positive side, he was conscious when he aspirated. Which is good—he was able to cough. Since we saw the aspiration, we were able to suction immediately. That's good too."

Ost looked quizzical. "So, cautiously speaking, he's all right?"

"No. The lungs are very complicated." I drew a deep breath. "In this kind of injury, the delicate mechanisms can break down, and you wind up with a profound imbalance of the normal ventilation-perfusion relationships—"

57

"Which means?"

"The water in the blood can leak into the lungs. So your lungs fill up with fluid, and you drown. Conversely, the oxygen can't cross from the lungs to the blood. Which means it can't circulate to the brain and other vital organs. So all the systems begin to go haywire. Your brain shuts down and your kidneys fail. And you die."

"But this isn't happening . . . ?"

"Not yet. It usually takes about twenty-four hours."

"And you don't know whether this . . . imbalance will happen or not."

I shook my head. "We wait and keep our fingers crossed. The pulmonologist did see a lot of secretions and edema—swelling in the lungs—" I broke off, working my jaws to keep from sobbing. "Aspiration has a high mortality rate, but most of the people who aspirate are trainwrecks—they're very old and have ten other things wrong with them that will kill them even if the aspiration doesn't. So the statistics aren't really valid for someone young and healthy like Gary."

Ost waited while I collected myself. He watched me with enormous attention and focus, seeming at the same time to be completely neutral and without opinion. I wondered as I often did whether cops learned how to watch people like that at the academy, or if the academy accepted only those applicants who instinctively knew how to do it. Ost himself knew Gary, too. The cops always know all the nurses.

"I'm okay," I insisted. In reality, I was so shaken by events and the tenuousness of Gary's condition that my thoughts and emotions seemed to be shorting out like flickering neon lights, buzzing and zapping. Only the medical details seemed real. The medical details I understood. The rest was a blur.

"Let's cover the basics first," Ost suggested. "He have any family?"

I told him about my calls to Gary's mother and sister. "Unfortunately they're in China—and not due back until the twentieth."

Ost gave me a wry look. "And what exactly did he eat?"

"I don't know. Analysis of gastric contents takes forty-eight hours. The diagnosis is made clinically—that means you guess on the basis of the patient's signs and symptoms. Our working diagnosis is, he probably ate some kind of psilocybin mushroom. We're hoping he didn't eat any of the death caps."

"Psilocybin—that's magic mushrooms? Have a similar effect as LSD?"

"Right, LSD is a synthetic drug that's related to psilocybin."

"Heard of those. Tell me about the death caps."

"Amanita phalloides." I spelled it. "Apparently kills people right and left in Europe, particularly in Germany. We don't see this kind of poisoning so much in this country, but only because we have fewer people who pick and eat wild mushrooms. If you eat them, about twelve hours later you're violently sick for a couple of hours, then you feel better. Two or three days later you drop dead. Fulminant liver and kidney failure. People who eat *Amanita phalloides* require liver transplants and lifelong kidney dialysis—if they survive." My mouth twisted grimly. Nicholson had learned all this only a short time ago, from Lauren Sabot and Poison Control. Suddenly we were experts. "So we're hoping he didn't eat those. Or if he did, that we got it all out. We'll keep an eye on his liver function tests and hope for the best."

"When can I talk to him?"

"Not until tomorrow. They'll lighten the sedation when the docs round in the morning, so he'll be awake enough for a neurological assessment. But then they'll bring him down again—restart the sedation—right after rounds. Of course, he won't be able to talk to you. He might be able to write. But we find with patients who are sedated like this that their handwriting is sometimes illegible."

Ost smiled mirthlessly and shook his head. "So. Who do you think is trying to poison you?"

"I have no idea. Disgruntled patients usually assault you right in the emergency room, or sue you for malpractice. Of course, Phil sees very crazy people."

"But the basket was addressed to *you* and delivered to *your* apartment."

"Right."

"And Dr. Carchiollo has his own apartment."

"Right, on Riverside Drive." I gave Ost Phil's address.

"This well known, or do people think he lives with you?"

"Anybody who knew it was our anniversary would know that Phil has his own apartment. That's another thing . . . What disgruntled patient would know that it was our anniversary?"

"Maybe it wasn't a disgruntled patient," Ost pointed out. "And this is what, the anniversary of your first date?"

"Right."

"How many people know that?"

"My family, his family, a few friends. The joke is, I felt sorry for him because his girlfriend at the time was in London on business, and it was the anniversary of *their* first date—so I invited him over for dinner because I knew he would be lonely. I didn't consider it a date, really. Neither did he. It's a funny story so it gets told at cocktail parties a lot. . . . People tease us, 'So how many dates you guys have before you realized you were dating?' That kind of thing. But I doubt people would remember the date. Although they might remember the story."

"Somebody knows the date," said Ost. "Who was coming to dinner this evening?"

"Gary, Alan, Lauren Sabot, my other brother Craig Berman—"

"The A.D.A.?" Assistant District Attorney.

"Right."

"I know him. Who else?"

"The six of us and Vittorio. The plan was, Alan and Gary would cook, and I would bring Vic over from the hospital for dinner, and take him back again afterward. He's totally ambulatory, just pushing an IV pole. In fact, he's due to check out tomorrow if they decide not to do a second surgery."

"Vittorio is Alan's boyfriend."

"Right."

"Fell off his horse, broke his arm."

"Right."

"So the people planning to eat this dinner are you, Gary Seligman, Dr. Carchiollo, your two brothers Craig and Alan, Lauren Sabot, and Vittorio—how do you pronounce his last name?"

"Fun low-uh." Rhymes with *loud*, without the *d*, plus *uh*.

"German?"

"Father was second-generation German American, mother's Italian-Argentinean."

"International guy. Raised here?"

I nodded. "Born in Argentina, actually. But he's an American citizen."

"What's von Laue do for a living?"

"Venture capitalist. He used to work for Morgan Stanley, but he left to handle his own clientele."

Ost nodded, switched gears. "And this basket came into your possession again how?"

The by-now nefarious basket sat on the table between us, enclosed in plain brown wrapping made out of supermarket bags, and plastered with police evidence stickers and hospital labels that said HAZARDOUS WASTE. I told him how I had found it in my fridge at lunchtime. "We think somebody bribed the super to put the basket in the fridge."

"Who's we?"

"Phil and I."

"Super's name?"

"Sava Hadzic." I spelled it. "He lives in the building. But he usually goes to his sister in Queens on Saturday nights." I looked at my watch. "Phil went down to Housing Facilities just a little while ago to see if someone there knows the sister's name—"

"Anybody else have keys to your apartment?"

"Just Phil and my parents."

"And Phil gave his to Alan, so Alan could let himself in."

"Right."

"And Alan let Gary in, then went to the store." Ost nodded. "Gary's a nurses' union rep. He have any enemies who want to see him harmed?"

"Nobody knew Gary would be there. He was away at his high school reunion. Apparently he rearranged his schedule so he could get back to the city in time to help Alan cook. Alan will know more about this—ask him."

"I will. Just covering all the bases. Where's this high school?"

I named the small town in New Jersey where Gary had grown up.

"And he went yesterday, but came back today in time to be cooking in your apartment when you arrived there at what time again?"

"A little before three. But Ozzie—no one was trying to poison Gary. They were trying to poison *me*. The basket was addressed to *me*."

Ost nodded largely to indicate that the point was taken. "He's the one who actually ate the mushrooms. I need to start with him."

We reviewed Gary's personal life. I said he had no lover right now that I knew of. His closest friends were me, Alan, and Vittorio. I saw no reason to mention the fact that Alan and Gary had once been lovers, so I didn't. We went over

Gary's schedule. Except for the reunion, I didn't know what Gary had been doing the last several days. Like all the charge nurses, Gary worked twelve-hour shifts, three or four days a week, depending on the week. He had last worked Wednesday, and was due back in the ER Sunday.

Ost returned to the topic of Gary's "enemies." By now I was exasperated. I couldn't name any enemies. Except for Di Clausson—but she wouldn't try to *poison* him, for chrissakes.

"So," said Ost, "the guy's an angel. Everybody loves him to pieces, he quarrels with no one, irritates no one. . . . There's absolutely no dark side? None at all?"

I threw up my hands. "The interns and residents like him because he's patient. But patient can be infuriating. If you're patient and the other guy blows up, you win. So people with bad tempers don't like him much. Second, he's for justice. That gets real tedious, people get tired of hearing about the exploitation of maquilladoras in Central America or in Harlem for that matter. Also, we feel guilty because we should be as concerned about social injustice as Gary, but we're not. So we get mad at him because he makes us feel guilty. Also because he's right. Let's see, he's smarter than most of the docs, so the dumb docs are pissed—real pissed. They pick fights with Gary to assert themselves. Gary wins and they're more pissed. Finally, Gary's a patient advocate and some hospital bureaucrats see that as not being a team player. Oh—one more thing—he doesn't go through the chain of command, and he's been reprimanded for that a couple of times."

I explained how Gary spoke directly to doctors if he had a problem with them. Technically he was supposed to tell the nursing supervisor, who would take it up with the director of nursing, who would put a word in the ear of the director of the emergency department, who would take the matter up with the chief resident, who would speak with the offending resident or intern.

Ost gave me a long look. "Probably the dumb docs aren't smart enough to poison anyone," he said after a moment. "Anybody Gary argue with in particular?"

"Dr. Diana Clausson," I finally admitted. "But she's probably argued with everyone in the hospital at some time or another. Her nickname is Wonder Bitch."

"What'd she argue with Gary about?"

I flashed back to the argument Di and Gary had had a few days earlier—it must have been Wednesday, since Gary was off Thursday and Friday.

I was in the ER's OR One with one of my interns, Dr. Jasmine Washington; Jazz had noticed a problem with a patient's chest tube and had come to get me. We were trying to figure out the cause of persistent bubbling in the drainage container when suddenly we heard Clausson's voice, sharp and caustic: "Let me get this straight. Are you threatening to *blackmail* me, Nurse Seligman?"

Washington and I were crouched down next to the patient's stretcher, examining the bubbling drainage container. We exchanged a look.

And then Gary's voice, equally sharp, "I think it's a fair trade, Doctor—don't you?"

They were standing just outside the door to OR One, or Washington and I would not have heard them. Even in their anger, they controlled their voices. Probably they didn't see us crouched down behind the stretcher.

"Herrera for Christmas," said Gary. "Deal?"

"Over my dead body," Clausson shot back. "Or yours."

"Would you docs stop crawling around down there and fucking do something?" the patient cried just then. "I'm in a lot of pain here!"

By the time I stood and went around the stretcher, Gary and Diana were nowhere to be seen. If Jazz Washington hadn't been there with me, I might have thought I'd imagined the whole exchange.

Keith Herrera. Union rep for the Committee of Interns and Residents, he was to have made the announcement at Rounds that the house staff were free to support the nurses' strike on Monday—in fact, encouraged to do so. But he hadn't made the announcement.

And Gary thought that Clausson had threatened Herrera. Keith badly wanted a fellowship in otolaryngology the following year. He was in line for it, but it was prestigious, and a number of residents were competing for the slot. Herrera needed Clausson to back his candidacy.

You want that otolaryngology fellowship next year, you keep your mouth shut.

But what could Gary have meant by "Herrera for Christmas"? Gary needed Herrera to back the nurses strike now, this Monday, and get the interns and residents to back the strike. It was only Columbus Day weekend. Christmas was two-and-a-half months away.

"Doc?" Ost prompted.

Better not to say anything about Di's quarrel with Gary until I'd had a chance to ask Di about it. "They argued about the hospital merger," I said.

Ost took a moment to read through his notes. "Let's go back to the Latin note," he said finally. "It said what again?"

I reached into my pocket, pulled out an envelope, and pushed it across the table.

"It came in this envelope?"

"No, I put it in there. After Gary ate the mushrooms." Working in a New York City ER, you get the gist of evidentiary procedure after a while. "When it was pushed under my door, it was just folded in half. No envelope."

"Under your apartment door, in the doctors' residence?"

"Right."

"You at home when it came?"

I nodded. "I was sitting at my desk catching up on my journals, and I heard it come under the door. I thought it was a Chinese delivery guy slipping me a menu."

"What day was this?"

"A week ago Thursday."

Ost undid the string tie on the interoffice envelope I'd put the note in, tipped it, and let the paper fall out onto the table. One sheet of lined yellow paper, torn from a legal pad, on which someone had printed in block letters, *ut quod ali cibus est allis fuat acre venenum.* Using the eraser ends of two pencils, Ost unfolded the note and examined it.

"Several people have handled it," I said. "Me, Phil, and the priest at Phil's church. Phil asked him to translate it for us."

"You didn't learn Latin in medical school?"

I shook my head. "You learn some. Mostly connecting forms, prefixes and suffixes, that sort of thing. But not to read Latin, no. I knew *cibus* meant food, as in *ad cib.*, take with food. And I was pretty sure that *venenum* meant poison. But that's as far as I got. So Phil showed it to the priest."

Ost refolded the note with the pencils, and, using a Kleenex, slid it back into the envelope.

"Of course, you wouldn't have to know Latin to find this quote," I went on. "You could just look it up in Bartlett's under 'poison.' That's what we did after Father Barrie translated it for us. You look up the English and get the Latin."

"And you thought what when you saw this note?" Ost asked. "Your initial reaction."

I shrugged. "At first I thought it was a prank, but it didn't make any sense. Dr. Clausson thought it might be some kind of comment on the hospital merger talks—for the Saint Eustace faction, Mount Scopus is poison, and vice versa. But even that doesn't really make sense."

For some reason I pushed to the back of my mind

Clausson's second hypothesis, that a former patient of Phil's had sent the note.

"Now, McNeely & Wang—"

"Lauren Sabot called them," I said. "They do gift baskets, but none with vegetables. And as soon as they heard the word *poison*, that was the end of the conversation. Their attorney will be in touch Monday morning."

"Mm. Tell me about Lauren Sabot."

"She's a litigation associate at Bennet Archer Ayer. She and Craig are dating."

"How come she knows so much about mushrooms?"

"She learned to identify and pick them as a little girl. Her uncle—Julian Case Hamilton, the chairman of the hospital's board of trustees—is an amateur forager. Also, an old family friend is a botanist who specializes in mushrooms. In fact, this botanist is the mycologist Poison Control recommended I speak to. He's a regular consultant for them. Robert Held."

"Held's the guy Lauren took the specimens to?"

"Right."

"Who gets Vittorio's money if someone poisons him?" Ost asked suddenly.

I searched his face for some sign that he was provoking me playfully, or trying to be funny. He was serious.

"Alan does," I said finally. "Maybe not all of it. But I understand that Alan's in his will."

"Vittorio have any children?"

"No."

"Parents?"

"Both dead."

"Brothers and sisters?"

"He's an only child."

"Aunts, uncles?"

"Well, you'd have to ask him. There are some great aunts. I do remember Vic's saying that his parents were both only children. But some great aunt of Vittorio's married some great uncle of Case's—Case Hamilton again, Vic's childhood friend. Vic's still very close to Hamilton and his wife, Jacqueline. Also, Vic is Lauren Sabot's godfather, and Case and Jackie Hamilton are Lauren's aunt and uncle. The Hamiltons, Sabots, and von Laues have been close for generations. I would expect they're in his will."

Ost held up a hand. "Wait," he said, as he wrote it all down.

While he wrote, I wondered about Vittorio's will. Since Alan was in it, that meant that Vittorio had had a new will drawn up after he'd met Alan. Which meant that beneficiaries in the old will had been bumped in Alan's favor. Possibly even disinherited.

"And the von Laue–Hamilton-Sabot clan is twice connected to you now? Your brother Alan's with von Laue, and your brother Craig's with Sabot?"

"I never thought of it that way, but you're right," I murmured distractedly. Those same possibly disinherited people— Case and Jackie Hamilton, Lauren Sabot—were the ones with the mushroom know-how. But none of them needed Vittorio's money; they were all wealthy themselves.

Besides, it was just too damned obvious. Case loved to take people mushroom hunting. At certain seasons of the year, if Phil and I had an invitation from Case and Jackie to come out to the island for a day or overnight, we knew without asking to pack our hiking boots. Because rain or shine, we'd be out in the woods hunting for mushrooms.

If everyone knows your hobby is mushrooms, and you've invited everyone you know to go mushroom hunting with you at one time or another, are you going to poison someone with mushrooms? I don't think so.

Although there was that worrisome business with the Hamilton family cook.

And the fact that Case, although he professed to like Alan, clearly disliked Alan's relationship with Vittorio.

"Doc, the whole thing sounds absolutely Byzantine. More complicated than the royal houses of Europe. How do I get in touch with your super?"

"He lives in the basement of the doctors' residence."

"We'll leave him a note under his door to call us," Ost said, snapping his notebook shut and pocketing his pen. "Now, where's Dr. Carchiollo?"

"Try beeping him," I said. I gave him Phil's beeper number.

Ost rose to go, slung his raincoat over one arm. "Do me a favor, don't clean up your apartment just yet. In fact, any chance you could refrain from going in your apartment at all?"

"For how long?" I asked.

"How about until tomorrow? You're not going to want to go there tonight after what happened, anyway, right? All that stuff for the dinner party, food everywhere. Why not spend the night at Dr. Carchiollo's? I'll call you in the morning there. Give me the number."

I did. I could feel the tears coming again. On the one hand, I felt overwrought. On the other, I suspected that I was, as usual, underreacting. After years of medical training and working in an emergency room, my emotions always seemed like Mama Bear's or Papa Bear's porridge, too hot or too cold. They were never just right.

Ost was still standing there, looking down at me. "The three usual reasons for murder or attempted murder are love, revenge, and money," he said thoughtfully, almost to himself. "It's highly unlikely there's a vegetable poisoner serial killer out there. My strong suspicion is, you know the guy. Could it be a stalking situation, an admirer from afar . . . or a vengeance thing, perhaps?"

That did it. Di Clausson's voice, murmuring all evening on

the edge of my consciousness, suddenly rang out loud and clear: *Doesn't Phil have some whacked-out patient who's in love with him and sends him weird notes?*

"Jesus, what's the matter with me?" I exclaimed. "Yes! There *is* an admirer from afar—Elise Vanderlaende, a former patient of Phil's. We call her 'Alice in Wonderland.' She has a fixation on Phil, the delusion that he's in love with her. She writes him love letters." I slapped the table.

And then the anger came over me. Anger at Elise Vanderlaende. Anger at myself for not seeing sooner. For once, the emotion didn't seem too hot or too cold.

It seemed just right.

eight

The first time I saw Elise Vanderlaende, she had so much blood in her hair I couldn't tell what color it was.

"Nothing's the matter!" she screamed, her voice reverberating off the green tile walls of the emergency room. "Leave me alone! Nothing happened!"

It was the first week of July, only two or three days after the annual first-of-July transition, when all the fresh-faced young interns set foot for the first time in hospitals as *doctors*—and all the other residents are promoted en masse to the next level of competence. I was a new "Three" or third-year resident, and like every other resident in the hospital, I had new responsibilities. Naturally, I was on edge.

The day was unseasonably cool for the Big Apple, temperatures in the sixties. But the screaming young woman was dressed only in a bra and jeans. Twenty-something with a perfect, willowy body, straight out of a Calvin Klein ad except for the fact that the bra was soaked through—with blood.

"I didn't do anything! *Let go of me!*"

"Don't think she's shot," shouted one of the cops above the din. "She was standing next to the guard when he took the bullet. His head exploded right in her face like with JFK and Jackie. She tore off her blouse right on the spot and ran out of the bank so fast the gunman didn't even have time to shoot her. We tried covering her with a blanket but she wouldn't keep it on."

"The Chase bank over on Broadway," explained another cop. "Didn't you get the notification?"

"Yeah, but they don't tell us what happened," I shouted back. All I knew was, there had been a shoot-'em-up, and we had been told to get ready for an unspecified number of people with unspecified gunshot wounds.

Behind the cop, a stretcher was coming into the ER. More cops. *Big* cops, wearing SWAT gear and toting big guns. I heard the *beep-beep-beep* of an ambulance backing into the bay, then the *beep-beep-beep* of a second.

I tried to get the woman's attention. "Hey. *Hey!* You're in the hospital. I'm Dr. Sutcliffe. I'm going to help you. Look at me. *Look at me!*"

"GET AWAY FROM ME ALL OF YOU!" She swung at the cop who gripped her by the biceps. Her blows bounced off his bullet-proof vest. A lumbering, unperturbable sort, he didn't even wince. "This is the doc, she's going to help you," he said kindly. To me, "Her name's Elise Vanderlaende. Gunman comes in the bank with a sawed-off shotgun, passes the teller a note. Teller's behind bulletproof glass, she steps on the button for security. All hell breaks lose. Guy shoots security, sprays the bank with gunfire. About six people down. Off-duty cop shoots the gunman."

"How many of these people coming here?"

"Half to Roosevelt, half to here. One guy shot in the leg, another guy through-and-through." He patted his right side with his free hand, holding the flailing Elise at arm's length with the other. "Doesn't look like anything important got hit. He'll live."

"The gunman?"

"You won't be seeing him. Bought the farm."

While the officer talked, I tried to get Elise Vanderlaende's attention. I got it, all right: her fist came straight at my nose. I blocked with my forearm. Ow. Grabbing for her hand, I said, "Elise, I'm going to help you. We'll get you cleaned up, we'll see if you're hurt."

"I'M NOT HURT!"

Actually, she probably wasn't seriously hurt—nobody seriously hurt could carry on like that. But it was hard to tell with all the blood. She'd need a thorough exam to make sure.

By now nurses and docs from the trauma teams were arriving from all four corners, crashing into parked stretchers, cops, EMTs and paramedics, each other. Cops and docs were hollering. I grabbed Gary Seligman, who was delegating nurses; as he often did, he sized up whatever needed doing and jumped in himself. "Hi, I'm Gary. I'm the nurse," he said to Elise.

"GET THE FUCK AWAY!" She swung at Gary. Expertly, he leaned out of range.

"Do you have any pain anywhere?" I asked her.

"No! I said no!"

She was talking to me.

It was a start.

"We're just going to make sure you're not shot, okay? Take your blood pressure, give you something to calm down. Okay? I'm Dr. Sutcliffe."

"Maybe I can help here," said a voice behind me. It was Phil. "This is Dr. Philip Carchiollo," I told Elise and the cop. "He's a psychiatric attending in the ER on a consult." I turned to Gary. "Let's get her vitals. If the BP's okay and she's got no history, we'll go ahead with two megs of Ativan I-M."

"God, that is so horrible, what happened to you," Phil said to the young woman. "What a nightmare!"

Elise, startled, looked at him. There was a long pause while the two made eye contact. "I don't need you!" she cried. "There's nothing the matter!" But gazing at Phil as if riveted, she seemed somehow to reenter reality. Her face crumpled, and she burst into tears.

"If I had blood and brains in my hair, I'd be a mess," Phil said. "Did you meet Dr. Sutcliffe here? And the nurse, Gary Seligman?"

"Yeah," she sobbed, nodding.

"Would you let them examine you? To make sure you're not physically injured somewhere? Then you and I can talk? If you like." He held out to her a pocket pack of Kleenex.

"Okay." Still sobbing, she took the Kleenex and blew her nose.

"Gotta learn how you do that, Doc," the cop said admiringly, releasing Elise's arm from his iron grip. "You sure got the magic touch."

Seligman and I made quick work of the physical exam. As we had suspected, Elise herself was not shot. Seligman started cleaning her up the best he could, while I went to eyeball the gunshot wounds.

First, the guy shot in the leg. He was lost somewhere in a melee of docs from the trauma team who had responded to the notification. My help not needed there, I moved on to the next room and the patient who had sustained the through-and-through of the right flank, as the cop had said. More trauma team docs; I wasn't needed there either. In OR Three the third patient turned out not to be gunshot at all; he was, however, drenched in cold sweat and complaining of chest pain. But he, too, had all the help he needed: a nurse practitioner, another third-year emergency medicine resident, and a cardiac fellow doing an ER rotation. The nurse was already plunking down EKG leads on the patient's chest.

So I returned to Elise.

In the few minutes I had been gone, she had metamorphosed into a visibly different person. Gary hadn't been able to do much about her hair, which was stiff with dried blood. But he'd taken a couple of passes at it with a wide-toothed comb and a damp washcloth, and fixed it with a hairclip Elise had in her backpack, so it would be off her face at least. Someone had rustled up a purloined pair of blue OR scrubs to complete the transformation.

"Who do you have to go home to?" Phil asked her after she had dressed. "Is there someone who can sit in the next room while you shower?"

The pace of the ER wound down. Neither of the shooting victims was seriously wounded. The guy who took the bullet in the leg—fleshy part of the thigh, actually—bore his pain stoically, and seemed to be enjoying his fifteen minutes of fame. "Think I'll be on TV?" he kept asking. "Think Oprah would have me on?" The second man, shot through-and-through, turned out not to have been shot viscerally, as first reported, but only in the "love-handles"—as he told his wife on the phone, laughing with relief.

I went back to my other patients, leaving Elise in Gary's and Phil's capable hands. We had the usual ER contingency: MVAs (motor vehicle accident victims), head-bonks (people who had fallen and hit their heads, or people who had been hit over the head by someone with something), asthmatics, difficulty-breathings, chest-pains. One of my MVAs came back from X Ray; I slapped his films in the light box, and conferred with the plastic surgeon. A head-bonk was ready for release. I turfed one chest pain to the Cardiac Care Unit, and had a brief conversation with another:

"I took three nitros and nothing happened."

"You have a headache?"

"No."

"Then it's probably not working."

Every now and again I would pass by the curtain where Phil was still talking to Elise. "Do you have a job? Are you going to go to work tomorrow?" I overheard him ask her, and, "Are there people there you can talk to?" A little while later, "Do you know a good therapist?"

Finally, I saw Phil saying goodbye to her. She was crying again, but smiling at the same time and dabbing at her eyes with a Kleenex. My heart swelled with pride. Phil did indeed have a magic touch. With his patients and with me.

I never got tired of looking at him, either. He had pale freckled skin from his mother's Irish ancestry, straight, blond hair from his father's north Italian side, a sleek, slender body still carried with the grace of the high school gymnast he had been twenty years before, and all the habits and mannerisms of New York City academe and the psychotherapeutic-psychoanalytic-psychiatric circles he moved in. He dressed down with the best of them. That day he wore a comfortable pair of dark green poplin trousers and a Lacoste golf shirt in a soft, muted color, with the collar up. He wore his hospital ID on a chain around his neck. On his feet, argyle socks and moccasins. On his nose, gold wire-rimmed glasses.

Phil gave Elise his card and shook her hand. Glancing up, he saw me watching him, and smiled.

I blew him a kiss.

We didn't know then that Phil's magic touch with Elise Vanderlaende would cause so much trouble later on.

A week after Elise came into the emergency room covered with blood, the letters started.

First came a card with a Chinese character on it, translated on the back "opening new doors."

Phil handed it to me at dinner one evening. Exhausted from the whirlwind pressures of transition, we were eating out for what seemed like the first time in weeks. The Greek restaurant down the street from the doctors' residence, the one with the nice garden in the back with the brightly colored lanterns.

"What's this?" I said.

Phil smiled enigmatically. "Read it."

I opened the card and sniffed. "Ooh. Nice perfume."

He looked droll.

"Okay, okay, I'm reading."

Dear Dr. Carchiollo,

I just wanted to write to thank you for taking care of me after the bank and to say how thrilled I was by your interest. Isn't it amazing how you can meet the man of your dreams in Auschwitz! Love blossoms even in the context of death I guess, it must be Fate. That guard died, but I found you. I feel like the phoenix rising from ashes reborn and ready to fly.

I am recovered now and all the excitement has worn off. Thank god! It would seem like a dream except you are very vivid in my mind. I think about you a lot and how much you helped me. You were so kind and so calm, it had a very calming effect on me. Sorry I was so crazy!

I hope you will let me buy you lunch to thank you and we can see each other when I don't have blood and brains in my hair—won't that be nice! I do look much better normally than when you saw me in the hospital. I usually wear my hair up because I like to dance. I've studied ballet since I was a kid and dance 2-3 times a week to keep in shape. Also I always take the stairs at work. You know I work right in your neighborhood in Admissions at the University. During the school year I work in the Botany Field Office but Admissions is much better, more contact with people. I am a people person—I like to know what makes people tick so you and I have that in common!!!

So here's my phone number. Let me know when it would be convenient for us to have lunch and I'm buying! If I'm not home just leave a message, I have a machine. The message is pretty funny too you should call just to hear it.

Warm wishes always from the heart,

Elise Vanderlaende

"Huh," I said, "the young woman from the bank shoot-out. Are you going to call her?"

"Absolutely not." He laughed nervously.

I put the card back in its envelope. "Not even to hear the funny message on her answering machine?"

Phil made a face. "That's just the first one. There's more." He handed me three baby blue envelopes addressed in the same sprawling, strong hand.

The same delicate scent wafted into my nostrils. "This is very expensive perfume," I said. "She's written you three times in two weeks?"

"Four, counting the card."

"Wow, she must really be smitten." I was puzzled by Phil's anxious demeanor.

An attending physician and assistant clinical professor of psychiatry, with a private psychoanalytic practice, Phil was no novice when it came to the inner whirrings of even the most deranged patients. Patients declared undying love for him or threatened to kill him with amazing regularity. He received inappropriate letters, strange gifts, and weird phone calls from patients at all hours of the night and day. At any given time, he had patients who thought they were Richard Nixon or Madonna or God or all three, patients who failed to take their meds and flipped out, patients who took their meds and flipped out anyway, patients threatening suicide or serious self-harm—you name it, he saw it.

"This is bothering you, isn't it?" I opened the first of the baby-blue letters and read it. Its content wasn't much different from the card; in fact, it was nearly identical.

"That one was hand delivered to the hospital," Phil explained. "She must have decided when I didn't call her to take her up on lunch that I hadn't received the card."

I read the second letter. Chatty and informative, its salutation could have been *Dear Pen Pal.* An anecdote from work, more information about Elise. In September she would begin her senior year at the university. She had her own apartment right in the neighborhood, on Claremont Avenue between West 122 Street and La Salle. Her parents lived on the West Coast. She had a brother at school in Boston.

"She wants you to know she lives alone," I said. "And that her family is not nearby. What do you make of that?"

"Who knows?" Again, the nervous laugh.

"I'm surprised at how young she is. In the ER I had the impression she was in her twenties."

"She is—she's twenty-one."

"I dunno, Phil, she's still pretty young."

Clearly Phil was in no mood to be teased about this young woman. I opened the third letter. More of the same.

"Says here she's taking a course in psychology second semester," I mused, "and that she's premed and thinking about becoming a psychiatrist. Wants to know if you have any advice to offer." I refolded the letter and reached for my wine. "How are you going to respond?"

"I have no idea," he said.

Over the next several weeks, baby blue letters continued to arrive in Phil's box at the Department of Psychiatry, hand delivered, although no one ever saw a young woman fitting

Elise's description. One or two a week usually, although sometimes it was three or four a week.

"You haven't explained to me why this is *bothering* you," I said. "Usually you're so blasé, especially in the context of a single ER visit. Remember that patient who thought you implanted electrodes in his brain for the CIA to read his thoughts—you said if he got so involved with you, in a week he'd be involved with someone else and that person would be the target and you'd be off the hook."

"Yeah," Phil sighed.

"Well, you were right. The patient decided his next-door neighbor was a CIA operative, he took a few shots at her with his rusty old army sidearm, and now he's on the forensic psych ward at Bellevue raving about her, not you."

"I know."

"And just the other day I heard you tell your brother Sal that you weren't going to go out and get a gun license just because some patient said he was going to punch your lights out."

"Maybe I'll run this by Gina," Phil said. Dr. Gina Rizzuti-James, a fellow attending on the psychiatric service, and old friend.

"Nothing I didn't think of myself," he reported later. "The issue of an Axis Two is just bubbling out of these letters, somewhere on the borderline histrionic spectrum . . . Cluster B personality—"

Nothing new. Saw patients like this all the time. He and Gina concurred.

But what was the *problem?*

He didn't know.

Phil continued to dither. One night he got out of bed, poured himself a shot of bourbon, and got back into bed with it. "What are you doing?" I asked groggily. "It's three A.M."

"I get pains in my stomach just thinking about her," he said.

The next day he wrote Elise a letter.

Dear Ms. Vanderlaende,

Thank you for your recent correspondence. Let me be entirely clear in saying that we cannot meet socially. You informed me at the hospital that you have a psychotherapist with whom you're working. I suggest that you continue that work and discuss with her the letters you've sent to me. Warmest regards,

Philip Carchiollo, M.D.

Two days later, Vanderlaende's voice floated out of Phil's home answering machine, coolly and calmly: "Dr. Carchiollo, I received your letter. I am unhappy with my therapist, and I would like to make an appointment to see you professionally."

Phil asked Faith, the secretary of the Psychiatry Department, to leave a message for Elise on *her* machine: "Dr. Carchiollo has asked me to tell you that he regrets he has no free hours at this time. He would like to recommend that you call instead"—the names and phone numbers of three colleagues—"any one of whom he would be happy to refer you to."

Elise sent Phil a Mont Blanc pen. He returned it. *Thank you for your generous kindness and warm wishes in sending me this pen*, he wrote. *Unfortunately I must return it to you because it would be inappropriate for me to accept any gifts from you. I continue to recommend that you discuss this with your therapist.* "That old Mark Twain comment," he muttered as he licked the envelope. " 'I would have written a shorter letter if I had more time.' "

After that, Phil stopped talking about her.

*   *   *

Fast forward to Labor Day weekend. At twilight, the sky roiled with black clouds and the wind was picking up—we thought it would storm—as Phil and I hurried across the University campus to an end-of-summer dinner party hosted by a shrink friend of Phil's, over at the theological seminary. Phil was listing the people who'd be there, reminding me where we'd met before, who had been analyzed by whom, who was Freudian, who was Jungian, who was object relations—when suddenly a figure in a billowing cloak like the French Lieutenant's Woman seemed to appear out of nowhere.

Phil's breath caught, and I felt his sharp yank on my arm.

I glimpsed the woman's face long enough to see her freeze with shock. Then we were past her.

Phil pulled me along. "It's her," he hissed in my ear. *"Don't look back."*

I looked anyway. "Who?" By then I had forgotten her. The woman stood gazing after us, both hands over her mouth as if in horror. Her hair blew in the wind, the hood of her cloak flapping. If it hadn't been New York, New York, the tableau would have been straight out of a Gothic novel.

"Alice in Wonderland."

"The girl from the bank shoot-out? Is she still bothering you?"

"Don't look! I don't want to encourage her." He glanced nervously over his shoulder. "She's not following us, is she? And yes," he went on as we reached the far side of the campus, "she *is* still bothering me."

I looked back a second time.

Elise Vanderlaende was still standing there, as if she had been turned to stone.

nine

Ten-thirty P.M. Long past the time we would have sat down to dinner. Right about now we'd be raising our glasses to one of Vittorio's famous toasts. A little night music playing softly on the stereo. Candlelight—

Instead, I watched Gary's ventilator wheeze and thump.

Standing next to his bed in the netherworld twilight of the ICU, I held his hand as his chest rose and fell. With each mechanical inspiration, his rib cage lurched up as if he were gasping in surprise. Then came the forced exhalation, like a great heaving sigh—a sigh you might heave out of frustration, perhaps, or forbearance.

The nurses had removed Gary's four-point restraints, replacing them with a Posey vest, which strapped Gary's chest to the bed. Then they had tied his hands to the bed rails with soft cloth restraints, so he wouldn't pull out his endotrach tube or IVs in his hazy, sedated state. In addition to the ventilator, Gary was hooked up to a heart monitor and an IV administration pump; he was catheterized, his urine collecting in a bag that hung at the foot of the bed; and the phlebotomist had installed an A-line in his radial artery so the physician's aide could draw blood for Gary's hourly blood gases without having to stick him each time.

For the umpteenth time I ranged my eye over the values winking and blinking on the display monitors of the various machines. Oxygen saturation still stood at 75 percent, not good. But not as bad as might be. He was in sinus tachycardia from the oxygen deficit, his heart rate 146 beats a minute. Not good either, but it could be worse. Blood pressure was normal, the same as it had been in the ER. Thank god for small favors.

From time to time I squeezed Gary's hand. Sometimes he squeezed back, feebly. When I asked him to open his eyes, he fluttered his eyelids, straining to rise to consciousness. But like a drowning man with his feet caught in seaweed or the grip of water nymphs, he never quite managed to break the surface. After a few tries he sank back down into the depths of sedation.

I knew I should let him sleep but I needed to reassure myself that he was responsive.

And that I hadn't killed him.

My anger, which had seemed so sure a half hour earlier, had played out. Now I was wallowing in guilt. In the ICU kitchen, Phil was talking to Detective Ost about Elise Vanderlaende. I had seen Ost's partner, Detective Jude Rainey, come in, and I had no doubt that justice would be done. The cops would arrest Elise Vanderlaende. She would confess to having sent the basket. There would be a trial. She would be convicted for her part in the matter.

Her part.

Because I had a part, too. Vanderlaende might have sent the basket. But I was the one who fucked up the lavage.

And if Gary died, it wouldn't be because he ate hallucinogenic mushrooms or even the poisonous death caps.

It would be because I fucked up the lavage.

I put a hand to Gary's brow and gently brushed away his hair, running my finger along the old scar. I had no idea how he'd gotten it—nor did anyone else. But someone had asked him about it at the nurses' annual Christmas bash a few years back, and since I happened to be standing next to him at the time, I suddenly figured in Gary's imaginative—and totally fictitious—answer. "Ask Dr. Sutcliffe here," he'd said darkly. "Ah, you didn't know we went back so far, did you? The truth is, we have a secret past together—she's my evil twin." From there Gary had launched into a startling narrative, all news to me, about all the times I'd tried to "kill" him during "our" childhood. How he got the scar when I pushed him off his bike while he was learning to ride.

Before I knew it, *Ev Sutcliffe tries to kill Gary Seligman* had become the longest-running feature-presentation gag in the history of the University Hospital Emergency Room. I became one half of a stand-up comedy act. Pretending to be goaded, I would "remind" Gary of other "incidents," about which he would allege further evil intent on my part, until the assembled company—usually an entire shift of nurses in the ICU or, later, in the ER—would be doubled over laughing.

"You can't die, Gary," I whispered. "I couldn't stand the irony."

Suddenly, the floodgates opened. One moment I seemed focused on the medical details—and the next I was sobbing into a sodden, balled-up handkerchief. "Oh, Gary, I'm so sorry," I whispered over and over again, trying to stifle my sobs so I wouldn't upset him. My apologies became an ocean crashing on a beach. I was sorry that he'd eaten hallucinogenic mushrooms in my apartment. Sorry that he might be poisoned—with death caps intended for me. Sorry that I'd fucked up the lavage. Sorry that because I'd fucked up, Gary was now on a respirator in the ICU fighting for his life. Soon I was sorry for a sea of misdemeanors, both real and imagined. Gary had seemed so preoccupied when I dashed home for lunch—had I been insensitive in any way, said anything that hurt his feelings? Why hadn't I drawn him out more, when I saw that he had something on his mind? I was a bad friend. Then, when he needed my medical help, I was a bad doctor. *I'm sorry, I'm sorry.*

Washing over me, too, was the desperate realization that there but for the grace of God go I. I could have eaten the mushrooms, I could have been the one to have her stomach pumped, one of the other docs could have fucked up *my* lavage—and I could be lying there instead of Gary.

I felt as if someone had shot at me, and Gary had taken the bullet.

Squeezing my eyes shut, I gripped the rails of Gary's bed. I didn't often pray, but I did now, conjuring a long-forgotten prayer taught me when I was a little girl by my grandmother Bubbeh Hazel, may she rest in peace. Behold, the Guardian of Israel neither slumbers nor sleeps. On my right hand Michael, on my left hand Gabriel—

Anunzionata Thomasson, the ICU charge nurse, touched my elbow. I jumped.

"We've all got to leave him alone, Ev," she said. "You included. I'm sure he forgives you."

I nodded and wiped my eyes. "Just a minute."

"I forgive you, too." She slid her arm around my waist. A compact Filipina, Nuncie barely stood as tall as my shoulder. "Now come away," she said gently.

I came away. Nuncie led me to the nurses' station and sat me down on a chair. "It could have happened to anyone," she said, drawing me a cup of water from the cooler. "And you'd say the same to some other doc if it had happened to her."

I sipped the water. "I should have sedated him."

"That's hindsight. In the heat of the moment you chose not to. You don't have to justify your decision."

"Is Dr. Ulrich around?" The Critical Care Fellow. At that time of night, Ulrich was the senior physician on duty in the ICU.

"He just went over to Broadway for a sandwich; he'll be back in a few minutes."

"May I read the chart?"

She shook her head. "You know I can't allow it. It's for your protection, too—that way, no one can accuse you of altering the chart or removing anything."

Before the full implication of that sank in, Phil burst through the swinging doors to the ICU. I jumped up from my chair and ran to him and threw my arms around his neck. The argument we'd had that morning was long forgotten. So was the fact that lately we hadn't been getting along at all well. Holding him then I knew that he'd be there for me, and I'd be there for him. We'd get through this together.

Nuncie allowed Phil a few moments at Gary's bedside before firmly shooing us out of the ICU.

Outside in the corridor, a small vigil had gathered. As Phil and I came out, the quiet conversations faded to a murmur, then stopped altogether. I felt all eyes swivel to me. Some were pitying, some embarrassed, and some downright hostile. I imagined their shouted accusations: *How did this happen? He ate those mushrooms in YOUR apartment?!? How could you possibly not sedate?* Mark Ramsey came around the corner and I imagined that they all looked at him the same way.

For once, Ramsey was not self-effacing. Shouldering his way through the crowd to me and Phil, he turned and said quietly, "Let he who is without sin cast the first stone."

"Aw, gimme a break," a woman on the edge of the crowd muttered.

Ramsey waited, his head held high, until someone else

87

murmured, "He's right. Let's not cast blame." Then, turning to me, Mark grasped my hand almost ostentatiously and said, "If there's anything I can do, Ev, please let me know."

As Mark swept into the ICU I felt the doors swing closed on my shame and guilt. Several people came forward. "Could have happened to anyone, Doc, don't beat up on yourself," said an ER nurses' aide named Wendell. He squeezed my arm. "Yeah," chimed in a large woman from Housekeeping, "Don't let anyone put you on defense, Hon." Helen Yannis, one of the ER nurses, embraced me. "We're all behind you, Ev." Her eyes sparkled with tears.

The crowd dispersed. Phil put his arm around my shoulders. After a moment, I followed him down the hall to the ICU waiting room.

I could feel my anger building again, rushing in where guilt had been. The person at fault here was not me. The person at fault was Elise Vanderlaende.

Rage, I thought suddenly. Sing, Goddess, of rage.

Or however the opening line of *The Iliad* went exactly.

"What do you mean, you don't think she did it?" I cried.

"I'm not saying she didn't do it," Phil said with exaggerated calm. "I'm saying I don't know."

He began to pace the room.

A small, intimate space, the ICU waiting room was designed to soothe. It was decorated in dark, eye-resting colors like a gentleman's library. There were two banquettes that worried relatives could sleep on if necessary; a couple of side tables with lamps that cast a soft, comforting glow; and two chairs. In the closet were a tiny sink and refrigerator, a water cooler, and a coffee maker. On a shelf above the coffee maker there were dozens of paperback novels, piles of the latest magazines, and a Koran, Jewish Bible, and Christian Bible. Plus a collection of New Age inspirational readings. All contingencies covered.

All, that is, except the one now facing us: who sent that basket?

Cracking his knuckles one by one—something he did only when very anxious—Phil groaned, "I just don't know. If she did, I sure as hell missed the call. It's classic. One of Dr. Clérambeault's original patients managed to find out what kind of chocolates her object's wife liked, and poisoned them and had them delivered—" He stopped himself and a cloud passed over his face. "Ev, I feel like I'm losing it. I don't feel on top of things. I misplace stuff. My keys. Important papers. I can't concentrate in meetings. Sometimes, I even glitch out while my patients are talking to me—I tune back in, and I don't know what they're talking about. And now here's Gary lying in the Intensive Care Unit, and I can't even say whether I think this crazy woman might have tried to poison you."

Now *Phil* was going through the guilt phase. "Guilt is anger turned inward," I said.

"I thought of her right off the bat," he went on, not hearing, "but then I—aw, shit, what do I know? I'm just a shrink. Shrinks are notoriously bad at predicting any kind of violence. A history of violence is the best single predictor that the person will be violent in the future, but that's like saying that previously diagnosed heart trouble is the best predictor of heart attack—"

"Phil," I said.

"—and there's always a first time! That guy who shot John Lennon, What's-his-name—he had no history of violence!" He was pacing now.

He used to let me comfort him, I thought. But he doesn't anymore. And he hasn't for months. We've spent so little time together lately, and the times we have spent together, he's been so distant. I remembered with a pang Alan's sharp lob: *He broods like the Sphinx and you let him.*

But was this the time to pick a fight? With Gary on a respirator, struggling for his life?

I went into the little closet to put some water on for tea. "Elise hasn't done anything but write letters, right?" I asked, filling the kettle at the small sink.

"Once in a while a message on my answering machine, but not often." More knuckle cracking.

"Doesn't follow you or come to your apartment?"

He shook his head. "The only time I've seen her since I treated her in the emergency room is that one time you were with me, Labor Day weekend. I'm sure if she were stalking me, I'd see her."

"Is there anything about her you haven't told me?"

"You know the whole story," he said, averting his eyes. "She was in the bank—"

"I mean about the letters. You don't talk about them much."

"I showed you the letters—"

"Phil," I said. "The letters *now*. I mean *recently*."

He was closing down on me. I could see him going off into his own little world. "Phil, you're not thinking straight. This is a *patient*. She may have tried to poison me—us—and you're wringing your hands! Where's your professional acumen?"

He stopped pacing and shoved his hands into his pockets. "You're right."

"You've never said why this woman bothers you so much. And now because she bothers you, your thinking is clouded."

"You're absolutely right, Ev. I'm sorry."

"Don't apologize. Help me. And let me help you. Why did you grow your beard back?"

He eyed me anxiously. "You have some feelings about my beard?"

"Just a thought. That maybe you did it so Elise wouldn't recognize you."

"Say more."

"I don't know, Phil. You'll have to tell me. I haven't seen the letters. In fact, you haven't shown me any since the first ones."

He waited for me to go on.

"Maybe you grew your beard back again to disguise yourself because you resent her projecting all this crap on you," I suggested. "Or did you grow it to get a new you that's not the you she thinks she knows? Or are you disguising yourself because you think she's dangerous?"

"I wasn't aware of thinking she's dangerous," he said slowly. "At least not consciously."

"Yeah, well, you didn't think that patient in the ER was dangerous that time, the one with the gun—"

"I thought he was dangerous."

"Oh, right! We're all cowering under the stretchers and paging Security, and you walk in and say to him, 'Are you sure you want to wave that gun around like that? You're scaring the shit out of all these people—is that what you want to do?' "

Phil started to laugh. "Hey. He looked around and saw he was scaring people, and he put the gun down. So?"

"So how many patients do you have this week who've expressed a desire to kill you?" I asked, smiling.

"Only three," he chortled.

"Only three?"

"Yeah, not too many takers this week. Yorba Linda says she'd like to—well, never mind. She'd like to kill me every week. But she's way too disorganized to actually manage the deed. Then I've got two patients with psychotic transference.

One thinks I'm his mother and the other thinks I'm Captain Jack. Haven't quite determined yet who Captain Jack is."

As always, a minute or two of laugh therapy helped clear the air. It also helped us focus.

"What are you going to do about Elise?" I asked. The water was boiling. I fixed two cups of peppermint tea and handed Phil one.

"I'm not going to do anything," he said, as we sat down on the banquette. "I told Detective Ost about her, and it's in his hands now. If he wants to see the letters, I'll hand them over. She's not a patient. We don't have a therapeutic alliance. There's no reason I shouldn't give those letters to the police."

There was a long pause while we sipped our tea.

"Ev," he sighed finally. "I didn't want to burden you."

A small current of electricity buzzed through me. "You can tell me why not later," I said. "But right now you'd better burden me."

"The letters. They're worse than you think."

"And?"

"She knows a lot about us. Personal stuff. I don't know how she finds it out."

"Like what?"

"Where I live, where you live. Your brothers' names and what they do, where they live. My brothers' names and what *they* do, where they live. What books we're reading, for chrissake, what music we listen to. She knows I know Gina, and in fact she *introduced* herself to Gina at the opening of the new biology library a couple of weeks ago—the reception at the university—"

"And you think this woman's not *dangerous?*" I gasped.

ten

"Where the hell is Ulrich?" a voice yelled suddenly. "Beep him *now!*"

From where Phil and I stood in the waiting room, we could hear clearly a flurry of activity down the hall. The doors to the ICU banged open and shut, then swung to and fro.

More voices.

Running feet.

"Oh, god, no," I moaned, bolting.

In the hall, a white tornado in the form of a galloping doc crashed into me, spinning me half around. All I saw of her were her swirling blond hair and white clinical coat. Together we threw ourselves through the swinging doors. They ricocheted off the walls—*whack whack*—and it seemed like the same *whack whack* of my heart now ricocheting off the walls of my chest. Dimly I was aware of Phil right behind me; I caught snatches of his murmured Hail Mary, mixing with my own "Please dear God let it not be Gary."

But it was Gary.

The telltale frenzied activity around his bed, the intern and two nurses and med student shouldering in and out between each other's elbows, the monitor alarms shrilling, voices raised frantically:

"Is that A-tach or V-tach?"

"His pressure's bottoming out!"

"With the low oxygen state, he could have atrial tachycardia irritability, you want to try stimulating discharge of the—"

"No, it's V-tach."

"—parasympathetic nerve to the heart, massage the carotid—"

"No that never works and anyway it's *V-tach!*"

I shouldered my own way into the throng. Gary lay motionless on the bed, his head thrown back. His face was as gray as a sky threatening rain on a stormy sea. The ventilator was still going great guns, but the oxygen was not crossing from the lungs into the blood. Quickly I scanned the values displayed on the monitor screens. Heart rate nearly two hundred. Blood pressure forty. Oxygen saturation, seventy and dropping.

"That's V-tach," I said. Ventricular tachycardia—Gary's heart was beating so fast, it was not effectively pumping blood and oxygen to the brain and the rest of the body. As I spoke I could feel the adrenaline jolt my own heart so that it leaped nearly out of my rib cage, as if scrambling to catch up with Gary's—*Wait, wait for me!* My voice when it came again was a runner's voice, winded and rattled. "One hundred megs of lidocaine, IV push."

The race had begun.

Everything began to flash past as time expanded. In the wink of an eye I took in the names and ranks of my fellow runners, printed in block letters on their ID badges. L. Brett, M.D., PGY-1, postgraduate year one—the intern. T. Lanahan, M.D., PGY-2, second-year resident or "Two." Nuncie Thomasson, charge nurse. A second nurse. The med student. At the same time my mind scrolled down everything I knew and didn't know about caustic lung injury, arterial blood gases, ventilation-perfusion relationships, steroids, bronchodilators, the new surfactant treatment and a thousand other related and unrelated topics.

Not one to quibble over who was in charge here, Lanahan shot the lidocaine into Gary's IV. She began barking orders: "Get Dr. Sachs on the phone, *right away.* Get Cardiology. Get Dr. Whitney. Where the hell is Ulrich?"

"Paging him."

"Get him here *now!*"

Whipping my stethoscope from around my neck, I jammed the earpieces into my ears and put the bell down on Gary's chest.

His lungs were full of fluid.

He was drowning.

"Those mushrooms," Lanahan said, "What is that, anticholinergic effects?"

But before I could answer there was a piercing shriek from one of the monitors. The heads of all present snapped up in unison, all eyes on the overhead cardiac monitor.

"He's arrested! V-fib!" the medical student yelled.

For a moment I thought my own heart had arrested. It leaped out of my chest into my throat, then worked its way into my head and pounded behind my eyes. Overhead, the cardiac monitor showed only the unmistakable pattern of ventricular fibrillation: random electrical activity yes, heartbeat no.

I called for the crash cart, kicked a riser over from the corner, stood on it, and began cardiac compressions. My left hand on top of my right, fingers interlaced, I placed my palm on Gary's sternum and began the rhythmic down-up, down-up, counting in my head *one-one thousand, two-one thousand, don't die, Gary, please please don't die, five-one thousand.* I had never put my hands on Gary's naked chest and I had never expected to put my hands on his naked chest; I don't think I'd ever even seen him without a shirt. He was slick with sweat. And cold. I began to feel cold too and I fought the feeling because I knew it was the chill of Death, dear God, no.

The nurse was back in a flash with the crash cart; a moment later she was ready with the defibrillator console. I continued CPR, down-up, down-up, while Lanahan took the paddles from the nurse and gooped them up.

"Clear!" Lanahan cried, placing the paddles on Gary's chest. We all moved back. With a small blue spark and a snapping sound Gary's body left the bed and thudded back. All faces lifted imploringly to the cardiac monitor like penitents to the Almighty. For one or two seconds the tracing spiked and bounced and our hearts spiked and bounced with it. But the pattern was only artifact. There was still no heartbeat.

"Nuncie, start the code clock," I ordered. "Lanahan, go to three hundred and sixty joules."

She was already gooping up the paddles again. "Clear!"

Again Gary's body left the bed and thudded back. Again we implored heaven, again the tracing on the monitor spiked and bounced. But as we watched, the rhythm deteriorated into wide complexes, almost like sine waves.

"Agonal rhythm!" someone cried. Gary's heart had stopped functioning altogether.

There was a high-pitched gasp from Lanahan—or perhaps it came from me. The nurse was wiping the contact gel off Gary's chest. I placed my hands, and resumed the rhythmic compressions.

We began pumping in the drugs now, a syringe full of epinephrine—the pharmaceutical equivalent of pure adrenalin—IV push straight into the bloodstream, another bolus of lidocaine, 400 milligrams of bretylium, then a lidocaine drip. Nuncie wrote down every dose and the time given on the code sheet, one eye on us, one eye on the clock. She was crying. My hands went down and up on Gary's chest and I thought about crying, too; *no don't*, you need a clear head or you won't be able to think and Gary will die.

In the balcony of my mind voices were murmuring like a radio turned low, mine and Gary's, repeating conversations we had had when we'd first met the summer after my second year of medical school, when I was the lowly clinical clerk on the medical service and he had just been promoted to charge nurse in the Intensive Care Unit. I was scared to death then, I didn't know how to fit in, I didn't know what to do, and no one took the time to explain anything in depth—except Gary. *I'm scared to death now, Gary, I thought—what will I do without you? Who will explain things? Remember when I had a dispute with my intern and you advised me on how to resolve it? Then when I was worried about my application interview for residency, you were like Kevin Costner coaching Tim Robbins in* Bull Durham, *you coached me on politic answers to interview questions, and I went to my interview with your handy phrases on the tip of my tongue: "I feel I can make a better contribution if" and "I see a good match between my own personal skills and". Well I can make a better contribution here if you stay here with me, I see a good match between my skills and your skills, here in life, here on earth, for godsakes don't go!*

But I was flunking the interview; we were going to have to shock again.

This time we got flatline.

Again the nurse wiped the contact gel off Gary's chest, I placed my hands and resumed the rhythmic compressions. The acrid smell of burnt flesh filled my nostrils. Lanahan hadn't distributed the contact gel evenly enough on the paddles and she had fried Gary's skin. Smelling it, I disengaged completely. My emotions left the country like refugees before an invading army, taking with them my past, my future—everything except the moment at hand, the down-up, down-up, *one-one thousand, two-one thousand.*

"Give me some atropine," said Lanahan. She shot it into Gary's IV.

We were in hyperdrive now. So coordinated was the team as a single entity, it was almost as if the six-armed Shiva had swooped down from heaven to gather Gary into his fatherly, divine embrace. Lanahan pushed another epi. Dr. David Ulrich, the Critical Care fellow, arrived finally at a gallop, summoned from the delicatessen over on Broadway; he still had pastrami on his breath. He took over the show, adding his arms to the fray. Next came the Cardiology fellow, a man of serious mien and undetermined Middle Eastern origin. Dr. Whitney, the pulmonary consult, arrived; a conversation ensued about lung compliance and the gap in Gary's oxygen gradient. There was a simultaneous conversation with Dr. Sachs, deputy director of the ICU, on the telephone. All the while the great god Shiva's hands—my own hands—went down and up on Gary's chest as I seemed to watch from a grassy knoll somewhere far off, on the border of the country that my emotions were fleeing to. I was there, but I wasn't there at all. I began to think that Gary was there, but not there, too.

"Clear!" Ulrich was shocking him again. I took my hands away. The paddles came down. Snap, crackle, and pop, just like the old cereal commercial—couldn't they spread the gel better for chrissakes? My throat caught. Gary's body rose and fell.

Wild-eyed, we stared at the monitor.

Still flatline.

"Resume," said Ulrich, his voice tight. A farm boy from the Midwest somewhere, he had been raised a Mennonite, and still retained the vague air of an Old Testament prophet exorcizing demons. Maybe he can exorcize Gary's, I thought numbly as my hands went up and down. Maybe he can exorcize mine. Oh,

Gary, I'm so sorry. My breath was coming fast from the exertion of the compressions.

"Clear," said Ulrich. I lifted my hands. The paddles came down; Ulrich depressed the button; the shock went into Gary's chest. This time he hardly moved. The nurse wiped off the gel and I resumed compressions. I pictured Shirley Seligman, Gary's mother, a plump, pretty woman who resembled the actress Shelley Winters, hanging up the telephone somewhere in China, tears streaming down her face. I saw Alan again as I had seen him in the ER earlier, crying *What happened? What happened?* over and over, clutching the rails of Gary's stretcher as we propelled him to the elevator banks, cramming into the elevator with us, voice tight, face taut with worry—

"Call it," Ulrich was saying. Shoulders sagging, he snapped off his gloves. "Time?"

Everyone froze. All eyes went to the code clock. In the wink of an eye, its hands had logged one hour and twenty-five minutes. In my mind, Alan was still yelling *What happened? What happened?* We all looked at one another now and saw disbelief turn to anguish and grief, one second, two. The monitor shrieked like an air-raid wail.

"Twelve-fifty-three A.M.," Nuncie sobbed.

My gloved hands were still on Gary's chest. Dumbly, I let them fall to my sides. I fell off the riser I'd been standing on and staggered into Phil, who caught me in his arms. He'd been there all along, hovering on the periphery.

"Could somebody shut off that monitor, please?" Ulrich snapped.

By then, Gary was long gone.

No one knew precisely when he had left.

And we'd all been too busy to say goodbye.

eleven

Almost as soon as Dave Ulrich had called the code, he waved Phil away and took me aside. "Ev, I know how much you cared for Gary," Ulrich said very quietly. "What happened with the lavage could have happened to any of us. You can count on my support if you need it. But there was a therapeutic misadventure and the patient died. We need to play by the book. You understand."

Over his shoulder I could see Nuncie Thomasson, with tears running down her face, turn off the respirator and disconnect the line from the airway in Gary's mouth.

"What are you saying, Dave?"

"I shouldn't have allowed you to participate in the code. But I knew it was important for you to give your all."

I didn't point out that until Ulrich had arrived, the only other doc on board was a Two. Or that Ulrich had been the one eating pastrami over on Broadway. Instead I wondered why my emotions had fled to another country and Nuncie's hadn't. I watched her snip off the end of one of Gary's IV lines and tie it off with an overhand knot about six inches from the body. She snipped off the next line and tied that as well.

"Ev?"

I looked at Ulrich and felt like I was seeing him for the first time. A man about my age, he had soft brown hair and sad brown eyes—which he quickly averted.

"Nuncie's tying off the lines," I said, realizing with horror that she was preparing Gary's body for the Medical Examiner's, not the hospital morgue. This isn't happening, I thought. Gary's going to the M.E.'s and they're going to park his body in the hall on a metal gurney until some assistant M.E. gets around to doing the autopsy and—

It was too gruesome to contemplate. I had once seen a body parked in the hall at the M.E.'s, stark naked, in full rigor mortis, forearms straight up in the air as if the dead woman were about to do push-ups.

"It's not my decision, Ev." Ulrich held up both hands in apology. "Death within twenty-four hours—"

"Of course he has to go to the Medical Examiner's!" I snapped. "He was murdered!" I bit my tongue just before I added *You fool!* Christ. Did he think I was worried about my own skin here?

Behind Ulrich, Nuncie clipped off the leads to the cardiac monitor, leaving the sensors taped in place on Gary's chest. The other nurse handed her a death kit.

"You mustn't think that, Ev," Ulrich said. He touched my elbow. "No one will say you murdered him. Don't talk like that."

I looked at him blankly. The adrenaline was still fizzing in my chest, my heart was going about 120 beats a minute, Gary was dead, my emotions were God only knew where, and I suspected that the rest of me was orbiting Pluto, I wanted to cry again like I had earlier, like Nuncie, but I couldn't, Gary was dead Gary was dead and Nuncie was tying his wrists with Kerlix gauze and crossing his arms over his chest and swathing his face and head—

"I don't know what to say to you," I mumbled, snapping off my gloves and tossing them in the trash. Turning away, I stalked out of the ICU and down the hall, Phil hurrying after me. *I don't know what to say to you either, Gary,* I thought. *I'm sorry, I'm sorry. I miss you already. I can't believe you're gone, I was just talking to you this afternoon. I never told you how much I loved you or what a wonderful friend you were to me. . . . And I didn't draw you out when you obviously had something on your mind that you wanted to tell me. Now I'll never even know what that was.*

The doors banged behind me, then banged a second time as Phil came through. He caught up with me and wordlessly put his arms around me.

It took me a second to remember to put my arms up and hug him back. *I'm a robot,* I thought. *An automaton.*

And what was I going to say to Alan?

By the time I reached Vittorio's hospital room, I was in such a state of shock that I broke the news to Vittorio and Alan without batting an eyelid.

I listened to myself with despair. It was as if a completely anonymous patient had come into the ER and died, and I were breaking the news to his or her anonymous family afterward. "Because of the oxygen deficit, his heart began beating so fast it was no longer pumping blood effectively," I said woodenly. "He went into cardiac arrest. We tried to resuscitate him, but despite our best efforts, he died."

"Oh God no, don't tell me that!" Alan cried. "I can't—He can't—"

Vittorio got up from the chair he was sitting in, glared at me, and put his arm around Alan—while I stood there awkwardly, not even knowing how to comfort my own brother. All I could think was, *Alan's always been the emotional one, and I've always been the stoic. Even when we were small children.* Ashamed, I embraced him tightly as soon as Vittorio let go.

We sat on the edge of Vittorio's hospital bed, the three of us—Vittorio, Alan, me. Vic held Alan's hand. Phil sat on a chair near the bed.

Eventually Alan stopped weeping, blew his nose, and wiped his eyes. Vittorio, calm and still with anger, said something about calling Gary's sister and mother in China. "They're not going to want to hear it from you, Ev, after that botched lavage," he said bluntly. "Baldric Case has dealings in Shanghai and Beijing, I wonder—"

"Absolutely not!" yelled Alan, jumping up from the bed. He turned on Vittorio furiously. "What is wrong with you? You're not involving Case Hamilton's law firm in this. Case is probably the one who sent that basket!"

There was a stunned silence. Phil's mouth fell open. Even Vittorio's face went slack with astonishment; almost nothing catches Vic unawares, but that did. "Alan, what in God's name are you saying?"

Alan gaped in mock astonishment, mimicking Vittorio's surprise. "Don't give me that bewildered look, Vic. I'm not saying anything different here than what I've been saying all along. Case hates me. I'm not Patricia. I don't fit in. You can't take me to all those chummy little dinner parties you and Pat and Case and Jackie used to go to. And moreover I'm in your will now, and in Case's mind, *he* should have been your rightful heir after Pat's death."

"Alan, please, you're upset," said Vittorio. "Sit down, darling, we'll—"

"Don't patronize me," Alan snapped. "You always act like I'm making this up. I'm not."

"Case doesn't hate you, he dislikes you. That will pass with time. He and Patricia were very close."

Alan chortled. "Case hates me, and now he's tried to poison

me! Would you fucking *wake up?*" Turning to me and Phil, he went on, "Would somebody please tell me why this sounds so much like the story of the Hamilton family cook? How do you explain *that*, Vic?"

And then the transformation took place. Alan, an uncanny mimic, could impersonate anyone flawlessly and he now launched an impersonation of Case Hamilton so spectacular it was as if Hamilton himself had materialized in the room:

"Mummy having one of her spells, moody and weepy," Alan began in Case's trademark staccato. "Take to her room and emerge only to rail at the staff. Make their lives utterly impossible, the maid crying in the hall, the driver sulking in the garage."

The low light of Vittorio's hospital room conspired to transport us to the softly lit comfort of the Hamiltons' living room, where I had heard Case tell the story himself countless times before. It was a set piece. When Case was a boy, the cook would serve creamed mushrooms on toast to Case's mother for lunch, whenever he "intuited" that she was ready to be carted off to the looney bin yet again.

"Monsieur le chef would arrange her luncheon tray with the best china," Alan continued with Case's voice, Case's air of aristocratic bemusement. "Little vase with flowers. Crisp linen. Cook her favorite, creamed mushrooms on toast. Take the tray up personally. Pass me on the staircase, wherever, say, 'Your muzzer is unwell, I am so sorrrry.'

"See creamed mushrooms on toast going upstairs, that's it— couple hours later there'd be Daddy looking grim and Dr. Kingsley coming through the front door with his black bag, shaking his head. Daddy saying, 'Mummy's having one of her spells, Old Chap. Needs a bit of a rest for her nerves, I'm afraid.' And off she'd go to the local 'rest home.' Come back three months later a little confused. But very subdued. Placid, even. Staff would hardly know her, she'd be so agreeable."

"Alan," I said, trying to reason with him, "first off, that story's about the cook, not about Case. Besides which, why, if Case has told this story so many times at dinner parties and we all know it, would he reenact it so precisely?"

"Because he's had a falling out with Vittorio, Ev," Alan explained impatiently. "Case wants to make up—but he sees me as being in the way. He arranges for me to eat hallucinogenic mushrooms, I'm packed off to the funny farm, and Case gains a couple of weeks of Vic's undivided attention to work out their differences. Except I didn't eat the mushrooms, Gary ate them."

"Alan, I'm sorry," I said, "but I'm not convinced." I glanced to Vittorio for his reaction. But if Vic had a reaction other than concern for Alan's distress, he wasn't letting on. I glanced at Phil. He shook his head slightly: *Don't say anything about Elise yet.*

"Ev, would you just suspend your disbelief for two seconds, please?" Alan pleaded. "Try to see it in your mind. Case gets a nice basket from McNeely and Wang. He takes it out to the island, fills it full of whatever mushrooms he picked yesterday or whenever, pays some kid to deliver it to you, and gives him money to bribe your super. So the basket is in your fridge. And I'm due to arrive any minute and start cooking."

"Gary's the one who cooks himself mushrooms on toast," I said, "not you. And how do you explain the *Amanita* death caps? Case is certainly not going to risk poisoning all of us while he's sending you off to the funny farm. Anyway, nobody gets committed anymore the way they used to commit Mrs. Hamilton. That was the sixties—Sylvia Plath and *The Bell Jar*."

"Mrs. Hamilton was a practicing alcoholic," said Phil, speaking for the first time. "She was mentally unstable, she'd been hospitalized before, and her old-line Yankee family doctor had probably never heard of hallucinogenic mushrooms."

"I didn't say Case was rational," Alan said, looking frustrated.

"Well, then, what *are* you saying?" I asked. "That Case is having a nervous breakdown, and he's not responsible for his actions by reason of insanity? He ate the hallucinogenic mush-rooms himself?"

"What if he dissociated?" Alan shot back. "Take for example that girl who delivered a baby in the ladies room at her high school prom. She stuffed it in the garbage, she returned to the party, and without saying anything to her boyfriend about the baby, she asked him to dance. That kind of thing. The girl's not insane, she just dissociated. Pregnancy was too stressful. She's going to pretend nothing happened: 'What baby? I didn't have a baby.' "

"There's an analogy here? Case . . . ?"

"Case has a devastating falling out with Vittorio. He dissoci-ates. Just like when he was a little boy, he dissociated as he watched the cook going upstairs with the tray of mushrooms on toast. He didn't challenge the cook. He didn't tell his mother not to eat the mushrooms on toast. He didn't tell his father or the doctor what the cook did. And now as a grown-up what does Case do? He makes a funny little story out of the whole thing, so he can laugh it off, and he tells the story over and over at dinner parties. *So he can convince himself no harm was done.* He didn't have that baby and he didn't throw it in the trash. Finally he comes unglued. He dissociates completely. He watches himself go through this business with the mushrooms and the basket, like, you know, he's seeing himself in a dream. When it's all over he snaps out of it. But now it's too late. Gary's dead."

"Alan," I said as gently as possible, "I'm sorry, but I just—"

"It's not Alan's theory," Vittorio put in suddenly. "It's Lauren's, isn't it?"

"*Lauren* thinks her own uncle sent this basket?" I repeated incredulously. "That he's had some kind of psychotic break?"

"Yes," said Alan simply.

"And she told you?" This from Phil.

Alan shook his head. "Craig did. He came by earlier to see how Gary was, while Lauren was off seeing Professor Held."

"Oh, Alan," I sighed, "you know how provocative Craig is, and how full of bluster—"

"Craig had no right," Vittorio growled. "There is no possible reason for him to tell you such a thing, Al, except to further upset you when you were already upset enough. Moreover, I'm sure he's blowing Lauren's concerns out of all proportion. Lauren loves her aunt and uncle dearly, and has fretted about their well-being since she was a young girl."

"Vic, you are so see-no-evil when it comes to your friends," Alan cried. "No matter what they do, you've always got some excuse. Lauren didn't hear about the mushrooms and throw her arms up in the air and yell, 'Case must be psychotic, he dunnit!' She's been saying for weeks now how worried she is about Case. He's so stressed out lately, at work and at home. She thinks he's on the verge of a nervous breakdown." Turning to me, he went on, "Maybe Case doesn't let you see him at his worst, Ev. But Lauren lives next door to him. She does see him at his worst."

"May I say something?" Phil asked quietly. "We are all devastated. Gary's dead. That in itself is so hard to assimilate, we're talking about every other thing that pops into our heads to avoid talking about Gary. We're angry. Somebody did this to Gary and we want to point fingers. But it's two A.M. And staying up all night will not bring Gary back from the dead."

"Indeed," said Vittorio. He reached over and opened his bedside table and took out a bottle of gin. "We should all try to rest. There will be plenty of time to pursue these matters in the morning." He poured a tot of gin into a plastic cup and handed it to Alan. "Please drink that, darling. It will help you sleep. Ev? Phil?"

"Thanks," said Phil wearily, "but I think Ev and I will go get drunk at home."

Which we did.

I ate an apple and a few crackers with cheese, drank two glasses of water and three ounces of bourbon, and sank down on Phil's fabulous king-sized bed with the brass headstand and piles of down pillows.

With the aid of the bourbon, my emotions finally managed to reinfiltrate the country across the demilitarized zone. Just as I was tossing down a couple of aspirin to chase the hangover, I gasped "Oh dear God!" and found myself suddenly wracked with sobs.

Phil held me while I cried and cried. For Gary. For me. For lost friendship. Out of guilt, despair, grief and anger.

Sleep, when it came, was restless.

twelve

I awoke early the next morning having dreamed of the Roman emperor Caesar Augustus, poisoned by his wife in *I Claudius*.

Augustus knew someone was trying to poison him, so he refused to eat anything except figs he had picked with his own hands off his own tree. His wife poisoned him by going out in the middle of the night and painting the fruit with aconite. While it was still on the tree.

So much for soothsaying dreams, I thought groggily. Gary didn't have a wife.

I put my arm over to Phil's side of the bed. Empty. Sitting up, I saw that the covers were thrown back. A note was propped on the night table in front of the clock:

Couldn't sleep. Seven A.M. mass, then going running. XXX.

I looked at the three Xs, just like the three Xs on the note that came with the basket. Too much for my alcohol-addled brain. I looked at the clock. Just before seven A.M.

Day One after Gary's death, I thought, and counting.

My heart heavy, I staggered into the bathroom, which Phil's

brothers had gutted and beautifully redone in colorful Mexican tiles the previous summer. Gary had marveled over the Mexican tiles when he'd seen them for the first time; he'd said that they revealed a playful side of Phil that he'd never seen before. "What's going on in Phil's head when he walks in here?" he'd asked. "Mariachi music?"

I could use Gary's help now in asking what was going on in Phil's head, I thought, as I gave myself a fright confronting the haggard visage in the mirror. My eyes were puffy from crying and drink, and I had aged ten years overnight.

Gary was the only person I'd talked to about Phil and Elise Vanderlaende. About how much Vanderlaende was upsetting Phil, and how Phil was dithering over what to do about it. We had spoken about it as recently as last Wednesday, the last day Gary worked before he died.

We were caring for a ninety-seven-year-old little old lady from the nursing home across the street; she had been brought over after suffering what appeared to be the latest of a series of strokes that had left her neither of this world nor quite of the next. Every now and again, she stirred and mumbled, and if you pinched her she pulled away, but that was the extent of her responsiveness. She couldn't—or wouldn't—squeeze my hand or open her eyes, and she didn't respond to her name. Gary and I were taking care of all the little things that needed to be taken care of before we sent her upstairs—where she would, with any luck, finally finish dying.

As Gary checked the patient's IV to make sure it was running, he said, "I've been thinking about Phil and that former patient. You know, it's very distressing to have someone be in love with you in a way that has nothing to do with you. It's like you're not even there."

I checked the patient's pupils; they were pinpoint. "But that's just transference. Phil does that for a living. What was it Freud said? The patient falls in love with the doctor and works it through. Then you terminate."

"Well, maybe something about the way she's working it through bothers him," Gary said. "It sounds very creepy to me. I've been in situations where a guy fell in love with me and then all of a sudden was making demands like we were married, when we hadn't even been out on a date! The voraciousness of it all, all that need—and all that anger! But Ev, that's not the point."

We rolled the patient to check for bedsores. "It isn't?"

"No. The point is, why isn't Phil discussing this with you? He usually talks to you about this kind of thing, doesn't he? And why are you bringing it up with me, instead of with him?"

Touché.

Turning on the shower, I adjusted the stream until the water pounded like a downpour in the rain forest, and made the temperature as hot as I could stand it. Then I got in and waited to rejoin the land of the living.

One reason I hesitated to bring anything up with Phil these days was that he was so short-tempered and contentious. Lately he argued with almost anything I said—sometimes, it seemed to me, for the sheer sake of argument. And the last thing I wanted was an argument when we were on such shaky ground together. Alan was right: I had conflict-avoidance syndrome.

Moreover, it was getting worse.

When Di Clausson had asked me the day before if the Latin note might have been sent by Phil's "whacked-out patient," I had said no.

Because Phil had made it clear to me that he didn't want to talk about Elise Vanderlaende. And I had gotten into the habit of pushing my concerns about her—and about how upset Phil seemed by her—out of my mind.

To avoid picking a fight with him about it. To avoid forcing him, against his will, to tell me once and for all why this young woman was upsetting him so much.

I'd done such a good job of denial and avoidance, in fact, that Detective Ost had to ask me specifically if there might be a stalking situation or an admirer from afar before I woke up. And that was *after* Gary ate the hallucinogenic mushrooms.

Well, I was awake now.

And Gary was dead.

Phil had some explaining to do. My job was to get myself out of the habit of denial and conflict avoidance, and to make sure he explained.

Exactly what Gary would probably tell me to do.

If he weren't dead.

The phone was ringing in the bedroom when I stepped out of the shower. Wrapping my wet hair in a towel, I dived on it just before the answering machine picked up. "Hello?"

"Sorry to call you at Phil's," Case Hamilton said without preamble. "But wanted to get you as soon as possible. Hear from you personally exactly what happened."

He had the curious habit of dropping subjects from his sentences and leaving his meaning to the deductive abilities of his listener. That, the staccato manner with which he tossed out phrases in odd grammatical pairings, and his educated, Eastern-seaboard accent conspired to make him sound at times like a less nasal George Bush. "Dreadful, dreadful news. So sorry, Ev. Know what a friend he was to you."

"Oh, Case," I sighed. "I'm absolutely blown away."

"As am I. Know it's early—could we possibly meet? Say when."

"Twenty minutes?"

"Be there." He hung up.

He doesn't sound one bit like he's having a nervous breakdown, I thought as I dried my hair and dressed. He sounds exactly the way he always sounds.

And exactly the way I remembered his sounding way back when, during our year together as organic chemistry partners.

Despite my grief for Gary and my worries about Phil, I found myself once again drawn into the memory of our one "date." All these years later, it was still so vivid in my mind.

Our year together was coming to a close. The final grades had been posted; we had both earned *A*s. Case had been accepted to four medical schools including Harvard, but bowing to family pressure, he was continuing in law. Next year he'd make partner, he told me with some bravado. He still had his volunteer ambulance work one night a week out on the Island—he'd just have to be satisfied with that.

He shyly suggested dinner together at a nice restaurant on the East Side. His treat. To celebrate our good grades, he said. We'd toast old times and wish each other well.

I met him at a French restaurant popular with habitués of haute New York. I had never been in such a place and I was dazzled. Recognizable rich people in fancy clothes were scattered around the room. A well-known author of steamy romance novels sat in a corner booth drinking champagne and eating foie gras with her girlfriend. And there I was. Me. In such a place.

With a married man, no less. I was flushed with titillation despite—or perhaps because of—my brave pretense that I was not in love with him. That evening Case seemed unusually distinguished. So debonair. Not only was he married, he was *older*. (To a college junior, an eleven-or twelve-year age difference is *a lot*.) We sat side by side on a red leather banquette, he in his lawyerly suit, I in an equally lawyerly silk dress bought especially for the occasion. Just in case we were seen by anyone who knew him, I hoped to pass as a business acquaintance.

For the first time in my life, I felt like a woman of the world. I squirmed with pleasure when Case ordered for me, calling me "Mademoiselle" when speaking to the waiter. Exultantly, I used a fish fork. I ate sorbet, to cleanse the palate. I felt so-o elegant eating salad after the main course, not before. Then there were the three different wines in three differently shaped glasses. And, finally, a cheese course—in my mind, the height of sophistication.

Perhaps it was the three different wines. Afterward, when Hamilton and I walked over to the river, lingering companionably before saying good night, I kissed him full on the mouth, even though I'd promised myself I wouldn't.

He was surprised, but rose to the occasion. He participated fully in a breathtakingly fabulous, movie-star kiss, holding me briefly but tightly. Then he politely disentangled himself from my embrace. We took our leave. There was no talk of seeing each other, and I knew we wouldn't, even though we both made noises about keeping in touch. He put me in a cab. We waved.

I was only twenty years old at the time.

He still has some kind of hold on me, I thought, as I applied eye drops and a little makeup to lessen the effects of grief and booze. After all these years.

Although many people might wonder what I saw in him. An inconsequential-looking man in his late forties, with a mildly distracted, self-effacing manner, Case often struck those who didn't know who he was as a lightweight. He had large hazel eyes flecked with green, a dimpled chin, auburn hair that was receding but as yet untinged with gray, and, although an inch or two taller than I, was slight and slim in build—all of which combined to make him seem fifteen years younger, and even more inconsequential. But those who knew him, knew him well as a man who negotiated deals and compromises with a fair hand and lent a quiet air of reason to any enterprise. After you got to know him, you realized how handsome and charming and sexy he could be, too.

Or at least I had. Alan of course might disagree. He had taken an instant dislike to Hamilton, from the word *go.*

As had Gary, now that I thought about it.

No sooner had the thought entered my mind, than the doorbell rang.

thirteen

Without a word Case set his canvas totebag on the floor and put his arms around me. I felt his cheek on mine and inhaled the scent of him, today his usual Penhaligon's cologne mixed with the peculiar smell of his Barbour oilskin jacket. The rest of him was clad in jeans, a merino-wool turtleneck, and L.L. Bean duckboots. On his wrist he wore his trademark watch, a Timex with a frayed grosgrain band.

"Absolutely dreadful," he said several times. Then, holding me at arms' length, "You'll let me know if there's anything I can do. Have you had breakfast?"

"Not yet."

We went into Phil's living room. Case took off his jacket and slung it over the back of a chair, grouped several of Phil's little Tibetan coffee tables together between the two futon couches, and started unpacking his bag. Out came a very large Thermos, three chipped Cantonese dinner plates, an assortment of mismatched silver, frayed linen napkins, a sourdough ficelle, and a stack of Tupperware containers. "Café au lait," he announced, pouring some from the thermos into a battered mug with the Yale insignia and handing it to me. He then served me two hard-boiled eggs, a hunk of bread, and a handful of cherry tomatoes and carrot sticks. There were also Robiola fresca and Caciocavallo cheeses, and slices of Salame Toscano.

"You missed dinner last night," he reminded me when he saw my bemused smile. "Now. Business. What happened?"

I started with "One man's meat is another man's poison" and went on from there. Gary's hallucinations, the disastrous gastric lavage. Haltingly I relayed the medical details of his deterioration and our unsuccessful attempts to resuscitate him. I omitted any mention of Elise Vanderlaende. Or Alan's bizarre accusations after Gary died. Hamilton, sipping his coffee, asked a few questions here and there. But mostly he let me talk unimpeded. I used medical jargon freely. As did he; he prided himself on sounding like he knew what he was talking about.

Somewhere in the middle of all this I realized suddenly that Case might not seem on the edge of a nervous breakdown, but he was certainly distressed. Normally quiet and deliberate, he seemed even more so, despite his jumpy way of talking. He sat with one arm stretched on the back of the couch, the other slung across his lap. He did not move. He hardly blinked. When I finally finished briefing him, he asked carefully, "Any theories?"

"None so far," I answered, just as carefully. "Somebody with a grudge of some kind against me or Phil. Possibly a former patient. The police are looking into it."

"Oh?"

"I'd rather not discuss it yet, Case."

Without taking his eyes from my face, he reached over and carefully put his coffee cup down on the table. "I understand.

You will tell me anything I need to know when the time is right?"

"Of course."

"In the meantime, ah, this former patient . . . Not a theory, but a possibility?"

I nodded.

"In order to make a diagnosis, you have to rule out long shots."

"Yes."

"Odds on this long shot?"

"Case . . ."

He gleaned something from my expression. "I see. Not your patient. Phil's." He coughed against the back of his hand. "Vic didn't reveal any theories to me, either. I'd be surprised if he didn't have one, though."

I noted the sheen of sweat on his face, and his slight breathlessness.

"You think Vittorio has theories?" I asked. "Or 'possibilities'?"

"Let's say working diagnoses. If there are none to be had by deductive reasoning, Vic will cook some up by inductive reasoning. Test them all to see if any are valid. Not a watch-and-wait type of person, you know. Must be doing. And doing for Vic is fighting. Fight unto death, too."

"When did you speak to him?" I asked.

"Last night. Lauren reached me at my firm."

"On a Saturday night?"

"Very important matters concerning the firm. We're meeting around the clock. Naturally, I immediately went to the hospital. Eventually chased down Vic in the ICU waiting room. Alan was in with Gary."

Whatever falling out Case and Vittorio had had, they were still speaking, at least in emergencies.

"You need to hire a private investigator," Case said, with

some emphasis. "Some very good ones are on retainer at my firm. Very discreet."

"Vittorio wants to hire a private detective?"

"No. He won't consider it. *You* should consider it. The cops are overburdened."

My mind stalled. "I'm not following you. Either you, acting for the hospital—if you think it's a hospital matter—should hire the detective, or Gary's sister—"

Hamilton leaned forward, gripping his thighs. The veins and tendons on the backs of his hands stood out. He began to speak more formally and urgently. "The detective would be pro bono. I want you also to consider some legal action against McNeely and Wang. If—"

"Case."

"Sorry. You *do* know you're the executrix of Gary's will . . . ?"

Talk about out of left field. Vaguely I remembered agreeing to do something regarding a small trust Gary had set up for his nieces if something happened to him. "I'm the executor? Of his will? Are you sure?"

"I understood Gary spoke with you about it at the time."

"You drew up the will?" That was surprising—at the very least. It brought back the feeling I had had earlier that Gary had disliked Hamilton, and I began to cast around in my mind for why I felt that.

"Yes. He did not want his sister to manage his affairs. We'll talk about that in a minute. If we fluff our feathers and threaten to sue McNeely and Wang, they'll have to tell us who their foragers are. We want to rule out the possibility that McNeely and Wang packed the basket with the mushrooms Gary ate. If they're using reputable foragers—"

"*Case.*"

He took out a handkerchief and wiped his brow. "The people who pick wild mushrooms."

"I know who foragers are." I was also trying to remember the conversation I'd had with Gary about his will. I couldn't even come up with when it had taken place. Why was I executor and not Alan, or Vittorio? Gary was just as close to them— in fact, closer—and Vic was the one with all the financial know-how.

Why would Gary ask Case to draw up his will in the first place, if he disliked him so much?

"The handpicked, local angle is one of McNeely and Wang's selling points," Case was saying when I tuned back in. "Local produce is more flavorful, more woody than what the wholesalers ship in. Commercial wild mushroom suppliers ship their stuff from France or Italy and just can't compare with, say, chanterelles that a forager picked—"

I realized that Hamilton must have been up all night. He was yammering.

"—yesterday in Connecticut. There's only one problem. You have to trust your forager. So we'll want to check the credentials of McNeely and Wang's foragers. I think it would be a good idea to make some discreet inquiries, rule out any disgruntled-employee scenario."

I wondered if he had already assigned the private detective. With or without Vittorio's or my agreement.

I leaned forward. "Wait a minute. You think *Vittorio* was the intended victim here. You're treating Gary's murder as a hospital matter, because Vic's on the board of trustees."

Hamilton started. "I didn't say that," he cautioned nervously. "It's important to proceed with an open mind. In any case, if you or Phil were the intended victims, it would still be a hospital matter."

I realized my mouth was open and I shut it. "The private detective, McNeely and Wang's foragers and packagers," I marveled, "that's all just *smoke*. Just exactly what are you not telling me, Case? Why do you think that Vittorio was the intended victim?"

"If I've given that impression, I apologize," said Case. "Perhaps, Ev, *you* have reason to believe Vittorio was the intended victim. Do you?"

"No. Just a minute. You are not going to convince me that you *really think* that someone from the Mount Scopus faction sent over *to my apartment* a basket of poisonous mushrooms just to take a potshot at the Saint Eustace faction in the person of Vittorio von Laue!"

"Ev, I said nothing of the kind."

"Of course you didn't. But that's what you want me to think *you* think."

"I'm *loathe* to consider any of my colleagues capable of trying to poison anyone," Case insisted, his voice tight with emotion. "Indeed, I consider them *in*capable of poisoning anyone."

Briefly—very briefly—I wondered if Case Hamilton needed to persuade himself that *he* was incapable of poisoning anyone. I shook that thought off. But he might need to persuade me. "Case, let's go directly to the heart of the matter, without passing 'Go' and without collecting two hundred dollars. You're laying down smoke to deflect suspicion away from yourself, because you've broadcast to the world that story about your mother's cook and the famous mushrooms on toast. You're afraid we're all going to be rubbing our chins and going, 'Hmmm, what's the connection here?' "

"Ev, please. That's hardly fair."

"I don't think 'fair' is the problem, Case. You're an attorney; you figure it out. Some people are going to draw an analogy here and think that maybe, just *maybe*, you wanted to poison Vittorio. Or Alan."

The skin on Hamilton's face seemed to draw taut. "That is patently ridiculous," he said evenly.

"No more than all this nonsense about the private detective, and the foragers and packagers at McNeely and Wang," I shot back. "Why not practice your rebuttal on me, instead of laying down all this smoke?"

By now Case was staring, his expression a mix of indignation and horror. I barreled on:

"People are saying you sent the gift basket, Case. That you and Vittorio have had some grievous falling out. Maybe Alan engineered this falling out. So either could be your intended victim. And since you and Vic have been unable to resolve your differences, you might think you'd be able to resolve them if Alan were absent from the scene for a few weeks."

There was a long silence when I finished. A professor I'd had in medical school had once advised, "Do not fill the patient's silence." I didn't. I waited.

Case got up and wandered over to the living room windows. His hands jammed into the pockets of his jeans, he spent a few moments taking in the view: Riverside Drive, the grand expanse of the Hudson River, and, on its far side, New Jersey.

Suddenly my memory jogged.

Gary hadn't disliked Case, I realized. Gary had hardly known him. But Gary had listened sympathetically to Alan's constant complaints about Hamilton's petty jealousies and interferences. In fact, Gary had listened sympathetically long after I myself had lost patience. And he always offered the same advice: *You must get Vittorio to side with you, Alan. Vic can't continue offering excuses for Case's behavior. Put your foot down—it's you or Case.*

I remembered Gary's saying about Case on one occasion, *That's an angry man. He's never missed an opportunity to miss an opportunity.*

And on another: *Alan, you have to stop this pattern of indirect communication with him.*

Still gazing out the window, his back to me, Case spoke suddenly. "Do I seem in my right mind to you, Ev?"

"Yes," I answered.

"In full command of myself?"

I hesitated. "No. You seem passive and indecisive. Frozen up."

"Panicked?"

"Well . . ."

"At the utter end of my rope? Capable of dastardly deeds?"

"I don't know," I said. "You have to stop this pattern of indirect communication, Case. Spit it out."

Hamilton turned. "My dear Madam," he drawled, with ludicrous formality, "I beg to inform you, I am a desperate man."

Alan was right. Case had never let me see him at his worst.

At least, not until now.

fourteen

V ittorio von Laue charged along the sidewalk. "No wonder health care in this country is a devil's morass," he muttered, clutching the left shoulder of his navy blue blazer as the empty sleeve flapped in the breeze. "The bloody Egyptian bureaucracy functions more efficiently."

Following half a step behind, I tried to keep pace with his long strides. "I have no idea what you're talking about, Vic."

"Never mind; it's not worth the breath. Your man knows we're coming?"

I rolled my eyes. *My man.* "Yes, he's expecting us at nine sharp."

I'd been up for all of two hours and already the day seemed interminable. Although it was a gorgeous day. The air was clean and mild, the sun shone overhead, and the sky was a huge inverted cobalt blue bowl. My head ached from the bourbon I'd drunk the night before. That at least was in keeping with my mood.

I was still shaken by my talk with Case Hamilton.

I'd spoken briefly with Phil, too, when he returned from his run. He showered, breakfasted, and left again immediately for the hospital, where he proposed to put together information about Elise Vanderlaende for the detectives.

I'd taken a call from Detective Ost, who advised me formally that my apartment was a crime scene. He was sending over two uniformed officers to secure the premises, he'd said, but he would be unable to arrive himself until ten. I of course could go in and out of the apartment as I wished, he'd told me, but the officers would follow me around and watch my every move, so I might like to wait for him. But it was up to me.

"Are the officers going right into the apartment, or will they wait for you?" I'd asked Ost.

"They'll wait for me."

What choice did I have? I'd agreed to meet Ost at my apartment at ten.

"What's his name again?" Vittorio asked.

"Sava Hadzic."

"What kind of name is that?"

"Serb."

"Anything about his background I should know?"

"His wife was Muslim. She was raped and killed by Serbs. Her father apparently came after Sava with some thugs to avenge the killing. Sava escaped in the nick of time, almost starved in the forest, and eventually made his way to Croatia. Then he came here about a year ago."

"Very dramatic," said Vittorio. "You believe him?"

I counted to five. "I see we're in fine form this morning," I said.

Vittorio ignored me. He often did. He went on asking questions about Sava. Irrelevant ones, I thought.

"And he went where yesterday?"

"To his sister's in Queens."

"Where Phil reached him by phone."

"Right."

With a glance left and right, Vittorio charged across Amsterdam Avenue against the light, holding up his good arm against oncoming cars like a traffic cop. As usual, his authority was enough to command the situation. The cars slowed to a stop obediently.

I scurried across in Vittorio's wake like a lagging member of his entourage. Vittorio was resplendent as always, in his blazer, crisp white shirt, yellow foulard tie, gray flannel trousers, and tassel loafers. I followed in jeans, denim work shirt, moth-eaten maroon sweater, and running shoes. Weekend clothes. It was, after all, Sunday. But if Vittorio owned anything in the category of weekend clothes, I had never seen him wear it. He was always dressed *for something*.

When we reached the doctors' residence, Vittorio yanked open the door to the foyer and rang the super's apartment.

"He hasn't had any trouble with the law, has he?" Vic wanted to know as Sava buzzed us in. "His green card in order?"

"Yes, Vic," I sighed.

Sava Hadzic met us at the bottom of the basement steps. A small man in his early twenties with dark hair and hooded black eyes, dressed in jeans, a flannel shirt, and work boots, Sava was gypsylike in his manner and movements, and conveyed an air of wily intelligence that I knew Vittorio would not like. I braced myself to run interference if necessary.

Hadzic was stricken. "I am very sorry for you, Doctor," he said, taking my hand and kissing it. "My fault. Sorry."

"It's not your fault, Sava."

"No, my fault. Mr. Gary is poison from this basket."

"I'm sure the cops will arrest whoever sent the basket. You mustn't blame yourself."

"Police guard your door, yellow tape. I am sorry."

"They have to conduct their investigation. We'll let them in when the detectives arrive. Sava, this is Vittorio von Laue, my brother Alan's friend."

Sava bowed stiffly from the waist, clicking his heels. He took in the sling and external fixator on Vittorio's arm, with the evil-looking pins protruding from the skin, and his eyes widened momentarily before he politely averted them. "I am very sorry, Honorable," he murmured. "Please come in."

We entered the modest studio apartment. While sparsely furnished, it was scrupulously clean, and Sava had recently polyurethaned the floor until it shone. A daybed neatly made and covered with hand-embroidered pillows against one wall faced two hand-me-down side chairs. A crate of some kind, covered with a colorful woven shawl, served as a coffee table. A frayed Oriental rug was on the floor. Behind a shower curtain, in an alcove that served as the kitchen, a refrigerator chugged and hummed.

Whatever his faults, Vittorio when he wanted to had the manners of a courtier, and respected good manners in others. He smiled politely while Sava fussed over a gleaming Turkish tea tray, served hot, sweet tea in glasses, and set out plates of cherry preserves and cookies. Vittorio drank a little tea, spooned preserves onto a cookie, took a bite, and assured Sava that we did not fault him with Gary's death. He inquired after the health of Sava's sister in Queens. He admired a picture of Sarajevo that was taped to the wall. He thanked Sava for his hospitality, praised the preserves, and asked Sava if he had made them himself. He made a brief speech about the recent rain, and how wet the weather was lately.

Sava glanced at me, clearly awed by the honor of entertaining such an exalted personage in his humble abode, and impressed with me for knowing such an exalted personage.

"Mr. Hadzic," said Vittorio finally, setting down his glass of tea, "brass tacks. Please describe for us the sequence of events from the time you took delivery of the basket of vegetables."

"Of course," said Sava. He set down his own glass. "I have already described for police. A doctor from hospital came to me with basket yesterday morning, maybe seven o'clock. Doctor was dressed in Halloween with a peruke and sunglasses, and he told me a celebration for you, Dr. Sutcliffe and Dr. Carchiollo, on your anniversaire. I was happy because I did not know you are married."

I let my marital status slide for the moment. "How did you know he was a doctor?"

"He had white coat and hospital badge."

"A hospital ID? Really? Did you get his name?"

"Well, he said his name is Dr. Moskowicz, and Moskowicz on badge, but . . ." Sava held out his hand, flipping it from side to side to indicate something flooey. "I thought that was part of trick."

"You mean, he tricked you with the basket?"

"No. For Halloween. Trick and treat. He brings the basket, yes? For your anniversaire, for the treat." His brow furrowed as he fumbled his way through his working English vocabulary. Generally, Sava's listening comprehension was far better than his ability to express himself, and he often resorted to German or French words when he did not know the English. "I see he is strange. But hard for me to understand because I am Serb, and this is American joke. So I say trick for Halloween. Maybe a doctor, maybe not. Maybe Moskowicz, maybe not. Peruke, okay, for Halloween. Strange voice like opera, okay, for Halloween. Sunglasses in rainy day—Halloween. That is what I tell myself. He gave me fifty dollars and I put basket in your refridge. I am very sorry." He reached into his pocket, withdrew his wallet, and solemnly counted out five ten-dollar bills on the tea tray. "You take this, please."

"No, you keep the money, Sava," I said. "Can you describe him for us?"

"Not so high as you, Honorable," he said, looking at Vittorio, "but maybe so high as you, Doctor. Not heavy. As I say, peruke and sunglasses."

"Wig and sunglasses," I corrected. "What kind of wig?"

"As normal. For bald. But not premiere *Stoff.*"

"Not good quality?"

"I mean so, yes."

"Cheap goods," I said.

"Ah, yes?" Sava smiled. He collected idioms like tchotchkes. "Cheap goods, okay."

Vittorio cleared his throat.

"Anything else about the man's appearance?" I asked.

"I have thought about it," said Sava apologetically, "but I did not look so closely, and because of cheap wig—yes?—and sunglasses, I didn't see all his face, and I don't know what color is his hair."

"You said he was disguising his voice," Vittorio prompted. "Could you say more about that?"

"*Basso profundo,*" said Sava, speaking deeply and dramatically.

Vittorio nodded thoughtfully. "I see. Did you think perhaps the man was not in his right mind?" He tapped the side of his head. "Crazy? Too much vodka? Too many pills? Cocaine?"

Sava considered this. "Maybe cocaine," he decided. "Speaking fast, a little wild."

"Some mental disorders seem like cocaine," Vic said.

I put my glass of tea down on the tea tray. Where was Vic going with this?

"Would you say a mental disorder like cocaine, or cocaine?"

"Maybe mental disorder."

I lifted my eyebrows.

"And the *basso profundo*—do you think the man was disguising his voice intentionally, or his voice was affected by the mental disorder?"

I had been about to ask if the *basso profundo* voice might have been due to a woman's efforts to sound like a man. I waited to hear Sava's answer.

"I don't know," said Sava finally. He looked from Vittorio to me and back to Vittorio. "Excuse me, Honorable, but you are special police?"

Vic smiled. "Not at all." He reached for his tea. "Dr. Carchiollo has crazy patients, as you know."

"Ah, yes," Sava said. But he continued to gaze at Vittorio speculatively.

As did I.

Which was when I noticed that Vic had closed down. He had a way of shutting the doors of his face, when he didn't want others to see what he was thinking, or was afraid that he would give his emotions away. He had that look now. Not quite as blank or neutral as Detective Ost's look, but blank all the same. Blank on purpose.

You son of a bitch, I thought.

You know who sent that basket.

fifteen

"No, I want to talk *now*," I told Vittorio, taking him by his good arm.

We stood on the sidewalk outside the doctors' residence after leaving Sava Hadzic. Cars rolled by. Across the street, orderlies and secretaries dashed out of the hospital to the hotdog stand and back again. Pedestrians made their way around us. A homeless man, one of my patients, solicited donations in front of the pharmacy on the corner. "Baksheesh," he pleaded. "Give me money! It's a mitzvah! Good for your karma! Tax deductible!" Another neighborhood regular, a scarecrow of an individual who wore a baggy tunic and pants on his skinny frame and wrapped his head and face in a kafiyeh—one of those checked scarves favored by Yasser Arafat—slunk along, skulking in doorways. In the middle of the street, a cop directed tourist buses thronging the cathedral. Nearby, a sanitation truck beeped as it backed up and diverted my attention momentarily.

My gaze returned with a jolt to the man in the kafiyeh. Could that be a *woman* in a kafiyeh? Could that be *Elise*?

"Well, talk," said Vittorio. "I'm listening."

Turning to face Vittorio while keeping Kafiyeh in the corner of my vision, I concentrated on the thrust of my argument. I had waited a long time to speak bluntly to Vic. "I have several things I want to discuss with you," I told him in an unwavering, urgent tone of voice. I didn't usually stand up to him like this. But I was emboldened by Gary's death. "I'm tired of 'shaking hands for Alan's sake.' There's always some misunderstanding that arises from your bluntness, or your impatience, or your insensitivity, or some other reason you and I don't communicate in a satisfactory manner, that leads to bad feelings and our ritual of 'shaking hands for Alan's sake.' Just once I want to have a decent and frank discussion with you and now is the time."

Kafiyeh was skulking closer. As she approached, I glanced at her, as anyone might glance at an approaching passerby. I imagined that behind her large, aviator-style sunglasses, her eyes met my own with curiosity, even eagerness, before looking away. She skulked on by. Definitely a woman. I could feel her eyes on my back.

Vittorio seemed momentarily taken aback. "All right," he said, gesturing toward Sami's Café, one block south. "Coffee?"

We walked down the street. As we entered the crowded café, I looked back. No sign of Kafiyeh. My heart pounding, I spotted two empty tables in the window and sat down at one of them. I sat facing out, Vittorio facing in. So I could watch for her.

Vic ordered an espresso for himself and a caffè latte for me.

"So," he said after the waiter had gone away, "shoot."

"You know who delivered that basket," I said.

His eyes flashed defiantly. "No, I do not."

"All right. You *think* you know."

"I do not know, and I am not willing to speculate."

"Vic," I said, "yesterday you told me you needed my help to find out who sent the basket. I would like to help you. It would be nice, in fact, if we could help each other. Gary was one of my closest friends. He was one of *your* friends. You and Alan were like family to him. To say nothing of the fact that Gary was one of the few people on earth I've ever seen make you laugh. You don't exactly relax with people, you know, Vic. I should think you'd treasure the ones you do relax with!"

A master of the universe, he had stared down worse than me. He did not fidget, avert his gaze, look affronted, or seem edgy. But his emotions swirled around the edges of his mask like fingers of smoke escaping from a hidden conflagration. I imagined heat lightning searing a hot, sultry night, forests bursting into flame, the acrid smell of sulphur in the air.

"The person who delivered the basket is someone you know, a person you suspect needs psychiatric treatment for some reason," I went on. "And you are very angry."

"Of course I am *angry*," he said. "Do you suppose that if I don't care to share my anger with you, I don't feel it? You're very proprietorial about my feelings. I don't know what right you think you have to them."

"Only that I have a very strong sense that you're concealing your feelings from me for a reason that has to do with Gary's death," I shot back, my voice rising.

"Lower your voice." He inclined his head. A young woman sat down at the next table, with her back to us. Probably a student from the university; she signaled the waiter, opened a textbook and notepad, and began writing.

"I suggest to you that the feelings do have to do with Gary's death," Vic went on, leaning across the table to speak quietly to me. His face was inches from mine. "Yes, I am angry. Yes, I am upset. But you misconstrue. Now let's move on."

"So don't share your feelings. Share your thoughts."

He sat back and assessed me. "I marvel that I've never seen this side of you before, Ev. But, of course, this is your emergency room persona. Very forceful, very commanding." His mouth twisted, as if in confirmation of a two-faced truth. "Not bad. I'm impressed."

"Vic," I said through gritted teeth, "*Who delivered that basket?*"

"I am not going to speculate at the present time," he reiterated. "I don't think that would be useful. I despise reckless gossip. Reputations are at stake, especially if Detective Ost continues to allege that the poisoner is someone in our own circle. I would like to see us proceed with discretion."

I began to seriously consider poisoning Vittorio myself. Or at least getting him drunk, or slipping a little scopolamine into his coffee—scopolamine has been known to act as a truth serum—to get him to let down his guard. Who *talked* like that? Did the man cultivate arrogance and pomposity, or were they unconscious traits? As I watched him tear open a packet of sugar with his good hand and his teeth, I glimpsed in my mind a scowling Napoleon Buonoparte. No, wait—right wars, wrong autocrat—it was Lord Horatio Nelson who had lost his arm. His eye, too. Maybe I should just go out and get Vittorio an eye patch, it would go nicely with the empty sleeve of his blazer.

The waiter came with our coffees.

"I think it's strange that from the start, you haven't once asked me who I think delivered it," I said. "I'm beginning to wonder if you did."

"Don't be ridiculous!"

"Well, why don't you offer some theories?" I needled him. "Case Hamilton has theories. In fact, he has plenty of them."

"None of which you take seriously, I'm sure. Shots in the

dark." He raised his cup to his lips, blew on it, set it back down. The tone of his voice hardened. "You're a Shakespearean scholar. Doesn't Case seem a bit like Hamlet to you?"

"In what way?"

"The weight of the world on his shoulders, and never sure what to do about it. A great ditherer. And, I'm sorry to say, often ineffectual or indecisive when he does act." Vittorio sipped his coffee. "Although perhaps we're lucky in that."

"Why have the two of you fallen out?" I asked.

"We haven't fallen out," Vittorio snapped. "We're like brothers. From time to time we quarrel, as all brothers do."

We were quiet for a moment. I was still trying to puzzle out some line of reasoning that would take me from the questions Vittorio asked Sava to Elise Vanderlaende. But I was distracted by Vittorio's comparison of Case to Hamlet. I couldn't resist adding, "Hamlet was right, you know. He knew who the poisoner was all along."

"Only because his father appeared from the dead and told him. He didn't figure it out himself. What else is on your mind, Ev? You might as well have at me while I'm here."

"All right," I said. "Your theories. You disdain Hamilton's, why not tell me yours?"

"You asked that already. I have no theories."

"Yes, you do. You told Sava, 'Dr. Carchiollo has crazy patients.' "

"That was a statement of fact. Not a theory."

"What about Alice in Wonderland?" There was always the possibility that Gary had told Alan and Vittorio about Elise Vanderlaende. But I didn't think so. Gary had meticulously divided all "intelligence" as he called it into two categories: gossip, and "not-gossip." He never betrayed a confidence.

He looked blank. "What about her?"

I sat there assessing his expression for a moment.

"What about whom?" Vic asked again.

"A crazy patient of Phil's. Since you seem to know so much about his patients."

"Only in the general sense," he said, making no effort to conceal his exasperation. "May we move on? Next?"

I decided, tentatively, that Vittorio did not know about Elise. "Do you think Case needs psychiatric treatment?"

"Absolutely not."

"What about Alan's theory that Case suffered a psychotic break of some kind, and—"

"Alan is overwrought. The strain between him and Case has troubled him for some time, and Gary's death . . ." he trailed off.

"Is it possible Case sent the mushrooms intending to poison *you?*" I asked softly.

"Who is putting these ideas into your head?" Vittorio demanded. "Would you be so gullible to suggestions regarding a patient's diagnosis and treatment in the emergency room? I think not."

"Is Case angry about your will?" I persisted.

"My will is my personal business," Vittorio snapped. "I am certainly not going to discuss it with you."

I decided to change tack. "Have you received any threats?" I asked.

"In what way?" He was wary now.

"Any threatening notes under the door of your apartment? In the mail? Delivered to your box at the hospital?"

"None."

"How about, 'One man's meat is another man's poison'?"

"Are you asking me who wrote that? Isn't it an old English proverb?"

"Lucretius." Suddenly, I exploded. "I don't know why you feel I should be more forthcoming with you than you've been with me," I cried, even though he had not expressed any such thought. "Second, it's so unbelievably self-referential of you to assume that you're the intended victim of the poisoning—without asking me or Phil if anyone might be trying to poison either of *us*."

His mouth fell open. "I assume nothing of the kind!" he blustered. "Why would anyone want to poison me? What nonsense! Moreover, the intended victim is moot. Gary is the one who ate the hallucinogenic mushrooms here—"

"The intended victim is *not* moot."

"Lower your voice."

"Let me tell you what the questions are," I said. "One, who delivered that basket? Two, why? And, corollary of two, was Gary the intended victim? I don't think so. Nor do you. So who *was* the intended victim? I have my ideas, which, I point out to you, you have not asked about. Which leads me to think you don't have to ask, because you already know."

But he had recovered his steely mien. "We've been through this. Let's not waste time with repetition and circular argument."

"Vic, you are truly impossible, I swear to God. It's a wonder someone *hasn't* tried to poison you."

"How nice of you to say. Next question?"

I paused to collect myself. He sees his own anger as a strength. He sees the anger of others as their weakness, which he can exploit. And he had exploited mine.

"Are you as knowledgeable about mushrooms as Lauren Sabot and Case and Jackie Hamilton are?" I asked.

An ambulance passing on Amsterdam Avenue had caught his attention momentarily and he looked out the window, but I saw him stiffen at my question. He regrouped immediately. Relaxed. Brought his eyes back to me.

We sat there looking at each other, our eyes locked in a game of chicken. "The Hamilton family cook and the mushrooms on toast story," I said at length.

"Good God. We *don't* need to rehash that!"

"I think we do, Vic," I said. "Suppose I lay it out for you. Case Hamilton told me this morning that he is utterly, totally broke. Last year Lauren Sabot bought his house from him. She was living in the carriage house and paying the Hamiltons rent. Now Case and Jackie are paying *her* rent to continue living in the main house. Pretty soon they won't even be able to afford that. Case has about twenty credit cards charged to the max. He has two mortgages on the New York apartment. On top of all this, his law firm's going under. Thursday night the partners voted to dissolve the practice as of December thirty-first. They've been meeting around the clock since. The official word is, there will be an orderly wind-up of business affairs. The reality is, the partners expect to be in bankruptcy court by the first of the year. Didn't Case tell you?

"Everyone Case knows has heard that story about the Hamilton family cook and the mushrooms on toast," I went on. "You despise reckless gossip? Reputations are at stake? Just wait until word leaks out that up until two years ago, before you changed your will *without telling Case,* he stood to inherit your entire fortune if anything happened to you."

"This is nonsense," Vittorio sputtered. "You are completely misinformed about my will, and in any case it is none of your business!"

" 'The weight of the world on his shoulders, and never sure what to do about it. A great ditherer . . . ineffectual or indecisive when he does act.' That sounds to me like someone who might send over a basket of three or four kinds of edible mushrooms, a handful of hallucinogenics, and two death caps. Unfortunately, we weren't lucky in that at all. Gary died. Would you like to speculate on what headline writers at the *Post* will make of it?"

A strange lull ensued. Somehow I did not feel like I'd won

this argument. With my elbows planted firmly on the table and my hands tented in front of my face, I stared belligerently at Vittorio and waited.

When he spoke again, his tone of voice was conciliatory. As usual, without actually apologizing, he managed to convey the idea that he regretted having upset me and wanted to make amends. Regarding Case Hamilton, Vic agreed that people might take the ball and run with it, " 'But what the great will do, the less will prattle on.' " He confessed that he and Case had been at odds, and conceded that now might be an opportunity to settle their differences. Case was an old friend who knew Patricia so well, and perhaps he did not take kindly to her replacement at first—but with time these things smoothed out, and Alan and Case were both reasonable individuals who would undoubtedly find common ground eventually.

"But, my dear Evelyn," Vittorio concluded, "Rome was not built in a day. You mustn't expect answers to everything within twenty-four hours. People have been dealt a great blow by Gary's death. You will find them vulnerable and self-protective. Not everyone will talk openly to you."

"Including you," I said.

"Including me." He graced me with one of his rare, dazzling smiles. I was struck—as I sometimes was, although not often—with a vivid and clear understanding of why Alan was in love with Vittorio despite his many faults. "Even an emergency room physician occasionally has to watch and wait. I doubt you have all of Gary's test results back. Perhaps they will tell you something that will render this conversation moot."

Against my better judgment, I softened. My anger ebbed. I began to lay Vittorio's obfuscation down to his habitual playing his cards close to his chest. Vittorio was not one to confide.

He never had been. And there wasn't anything I was going to do to change that.

We finished our coffee companionably. Vittorio thought it might be a good idea to have a quiet dinner that evening at his and Alan's apartment, with friends. We could take comfort in one another's company, and share remembrances of Gary. Vic had suggested as much to Alan.

"Vic, that's very kind of you," I said.

Vittorio paid the tab, and we went out onto the sidewalk. He shook my hand, then impulsively kissed me goodbye. Hailed a cab and climbed into it. Waved. I waved back as the cab took off into traffic.

The student who had been sitting at the table next to us came out of the café. For a moment, she looked at me quizzically, as if she were about to speak. But then she went on.

She looked vaguely familiar. About my height, slender and small-breasted. Long blond hair, tied back in a ponytail. Black leggings, black turtleneck. Oversized shoulder bag, the kind you could carry an entire weekend wardrobe in, also black. Extremely light on her feet. Unusually straight, erect posture. Loose knees, low center of gravity. Toes turned slightly out. All the hallmarks of a ballet dancer.

I started. *Was it Elise?*

She turned and saw me watching her, and waved just before disappearing around the corner of West 113 Street.

With a sudden start, I bolted after her. But when I reached the corner, she was nowhere in sight.

I moved quickly down the street, checking the wells of brownstones on the south side, and peering into the foyers of the apartment buildings on the north side. I ran clear across to Broadway, where the weekend crowd strolled along. I scanned the ATM line.

No blond in black.

No Kafiyeh.

"Baksheesh!" a familiar voice pleaded. My homeless patient again, zeroing in on me. I gave him a dollar.

Then, cursing and breathing hard, I walked back to the doctors' residence for my appointment with Detective Ost.

sixteen

Y ou can always hear Craig a mile away.

"Using a ruse to get into someone's home no matter how it's done can still be considered a burglary and 'to commit a crime therein,'" his voice boomed as I got out of the elevator on my floor of the doctors' residence.

My brother, the assistant district attorney. Always looking crisp, even on weekends. Suit, striped shirt with white collar, Cole Haan tassel loafers.

He had the righteously - indignant - on - behalf - of - the - outrageously-wronged shtick honed to courtroom perfection. His dark eyes flashed. His lips puckered. His nostrils flared. There was a tremor in his voice, pitched at precisely the level that allowed you to hear it. He was emotionally aroused, but in total control of himself (God forbid passion should triumph over reason in a court of law). A couple of inches shorter than I but a good fifty pounds heavier—all of it muscle and grist—he tensed himself like a reincarnation of one of his beloved film heroes. Spencer Tracy. Gregory Peck.

Would Counsel approach the bench? You bet, your Honor! Justice will be served!

Down the hall, I could see Craig talking to two uniformed officers in front of my apartment door, which was criss-crossed with yellow crime scene tape. From their body language, I could tell that one officer was relaxed but the other wasn't. Typical. If there were two people in a room, Craig would always manage to piss off at least one.

"Objection! Leading the witness!" I yelled.

"Code blue!" he yelled back. "Crack that chest!"

He sprinted down the hall and we embraced. As usual, Craig squeezed all the air out of me, then whopped me on the back, dislodging a few vertebrae.

Unlike Alan and me, Craig was a very physical guy. In fact, Craig was unlike us in almost every way imaginable. While Alan and I were slender, Craig was beefy. We were tall, he was squat. We were mild and easy-going—at least most of the time—while he was sassy and brassy. Even his hair seemed to stand on end. Alan and I had straight, light brown hair. Craig had black hair that waved on good days and frizzed uncontrollably on bad. Still, he was recognizably my brother, and Alan's. Same nose, same brow. Same-shape eyes, although Craig's were almost black, and Alan's and mine were hazel.

Though Craig was five years younger than I, and a year younger than Alan, people usually thought he was the eldest—probably because he threw his weight around so much.

"How you doing, kid?" he asked, letting me go finally so I could breathe. "You holding up okay?"

I grimaced. "On hold is more like it."

"Yeah, me too. I cried like a baby last night. Now I'm waiting for the other shoe to drop. Alan's a walking zombie, have you seen him?"

"Not since last night."

"He set a dish towel on fire this morning—turned on the

burner under a pan with nothing in it, forgot about it, remembered, took it off the fire and put it down on the dish towel. The whole thing went up in flames. I said, 'Out of the kitchen, dude—you're temporarily incompetent.' I called Jackie and asked her to come down." Jackie Hamilton, Case's wife. Alan might hate Case, but he loved Jackie.

"Did she?"

"Yeah. She's good people." He took me by the arm and led me down the hall. "Unlike her witless husband. Yo! Officers, this is my sister, Dr. Evelyn Sutcliffe. Ev, Officers Seth Yakir and Bud Pedersen."

They were a striking pair; Yakir was of indeterminate race, perhaps a blend of several, with dark, almond-shaped eyes, while Pedersen looked like he had just arrived from the American hinterlands; *Christ,* I thought, *a kid with freckles.* Where does NYPD find them?

"Ma'am," Yakir said pleasantly.

Pedersen nodded to be polite, all the while giving me and Craig the cop stare. "Crime scene, Ma'am," he growled. "Can't let you in. Gotta wait for the detectives."

"I've spoken to Detective Ost," I said. "He told me I could go in if I wanted, but that you would follow me around and watch my every move."

"Rather not," said Pedersen. "Ma'am."

"Oh, why don't we let her in, Bud?" asked Yakir. He smiled invitingly and motioned for me to open the door. "Don't mind my partner here. He's a little fierce."

I wondered if I could get away with saying something like, I thought they only did good cop–bad cop on TV. I decided not to chance it.

"Watch the tape," said Craig.

The door to my apartment has two locks, an upper deadbolt, and a lock on the doorknob. I put my key into the upper lock and turned counterclockwise, expecting to hear the deadbolt. But I didn't hear it; the bolt was already open. The bottom lock, on the doorknob, locked automatically. But something made me try the doorknob without unlocking it.

"The door's open," I said. I pushed it in.

Pedersen put his hand on his gun. "You sure you locked it when you went out?"

"Yes." I might have gone out without locking the top lock, but the bottom lock would have locked itself.

The two officers looked at each other. Yakir put his hand on *his* gun. They hunched their shoulders. Yakir nudged the door open with his foot, ducked under the crime scene tape, and went into the apartment. Pedersen followed, then Craig and I.

There was a strong odor of ripe cheese and fruit, and rotting food. The hall was strewn with clothes and other items. There were towels on the floor in the bathroom. The medicine cabinet was open. In the living room, papers, books, and magazines were strewn about. The drawers of my desk had been pulled out and the contents dumped on the couch.

"Shit," said Craig.

My heart began to pound with the sick brew of adrenaline and violation as I surveyed the mess. First the basket. Then Gary's death. Now this.

What next?

Yakir reappeared from the bedroom. Pedersen came back from the kitchen, his hand still on his gun.

"Nobody here, Ma'am," Yakir said.

I didn't know what to say. My heart hammering, I made my way to the bedroom, followed closely by Craig, both of us carefully stepping over the piles of stuff in the hall as if they might be mined.

"Watch the glass, he broke your mirror, looks like," said Yakir, following us.

The mirror frame was upside-down on the top of the

dresser, where it had fallen—or more likely had been thrown down—from the wall. Clothes from the closet were on the floor and bed, underneath the up-ended bureau drawers. Everything seemed covered in some kid of talcum. I sniffed. Phil's foot powder.

"Our great-grandfather brought that mirror over from Germany," Craig sighed. "Aw, Jesus."

"You can get a new mirror for it," Yakir said kindly. "Look, the frame's only chipped in this little place down here in the corner." He pointed, without touching it. "Hardly notice it."

I said, "Let's not track the glass into the rug," and went back into the living room, where I found Officer Pedersen, hands on his hips, surveying the chaos. "Happens sometimes," he said. "Neighbors know you're occupied doing something else, they hit you while you're gone. We get a lot of burglaries when there's a funeral. You're off burying your loved one, the bad guys are ransacking your place."

Craig was uncharacteristically quiet, looking around at everything with his practiced D.A.'s eye; he often went to crime scenes. "Anything you notice missing, Ev?" he asked finally.

I pointed at the desk. "My laptop computer."

"Wonder why he didn't take the printer, too," said Yakir. "TV's still here. And the sound system. Huh."

"You back up your files, Doc?" Pedersen asked.

I didn't see the plastic box in which I kept my backup discs. Of course, it could be somewhere under the piles of stuff strewn everywhere. But somehow I didn't think so. No, the burglar had stolen my computer and my back-up discs.

"You weren't writing a novel or anything, were you?" Yakir wanted to know.

I shook my head.

"Hospital exposé or anything? Article for the *New York Times* on the nurses' strike, or the big merger coming up?"

Preoccupied with my own thoughts, I listened with only half an ear while he went on talking. His wife was a nurse practitioner at University, in Pediatric Outpatient. . . .

Let me see if I get this straight. A guy wearing a bad wig, sunglasses, and a white clinical coat with a hospital ID delivers a basket of mushrooms and vegetables to Sava and pays him fifty dollars to put it in my fridge. The card reads: HAPPY ANNI-VERSARY, XXX. Among the mushrooms are edibles, hallucino-genics, and *Amanita* death caps.

Meanwhile, Phil is receiving love letters from Elise Vander-laende. He finds these letters so upsetting he is unable to sum-mon his usual professional acumen to deal with them. In fact, his professional acumen seems to have gone right out the fuck-ing window. Could she have sent the basket? He can't say.

Alan is sure Case Hamilton has tried to poison *him*. The similarities between what might be called Gary's "Mushroom Story" and the Hamilton family cook's "Mushroom Story" are so glaring as to seem ridiculous. Yet Case Hamilton, with mo-tive to poison Alan or Vittorio or both, an *attorney*, is somehow even less able to summon his professional acumen than Phil. He can't even focus on the need to defend himself.

Vittorio pursues a line of questioning with Sava that strongly suggests a conviction that some "crazy" person sent the basket. But which "crazy" person does he have in mind— Elise Vanderlaende, or his beloved childhood friend Case Hamilton?

Both Case and Vittorio seem to think that Vittorio was the intended victim. Elise has no reason to try to poison Vittorio. That leaves Case. Some quarrel is obviously going on between Case and Vittorio that no one seems willing to discuss. But how could that quarrel, or someone's wanting to poison Vitto-rio, have anything to do with my computer or my computer discs?

And why had the poisoner—whoever that person might

be, and whoever the intended victim had been—chosen such a bizarre, hit-or-miss method of trying to poison anyone? With all the other things in the basket, there was no guarantee that any of us would eat the hallucinogenic mushrooms or the death caps.

Nothing made sense.

Officer Yakir stopped talking. I turned. Detective Ost, wearing khakis and a blue blazer, was coming in under the yellow crime scene tape. Behind him I could see his partner, Det. Jude Rainey.

The two detectives looked at the mess and surmised what had happened. "Doc," Ost said grimly, by way of greeting, and, to Craig, "Counselor."

"Hey, Ozzie, Jude," I sighed.

Rainey went to look around. A compact woman with short, graying blond hair, she was dressed today in a nondescript pantsuit. But I always imagined her the way I had seen her once, smoking and chatting with medics in the ambulance bay of the hospital, wearing a sleeveless tank and cargo shorts. On her left forearm she sported some kind of U.S. Army tattoo, and on her well-defined right biceps a second tattoo that read TOUGH COOKIE.

When she came back, I asked, "Any thoughts?"

"You first," she said.

"It looks staged to me. Why toss the towels around in the bathroom? Or throw foot powder around the bedroom?"

"Yeah," Rainey said.

"My guess is, the person wanted something specific but didn't want me to know exactly what. So he or she trashed the place."

Rainey's eyes twinkled at the *or she*. "Any idea what?"

"I haven't been in the kitchen yet."

Stepping over piles of stuff, the two detectives, Craig, and I all made our way carefully into the dining room—really only the end of the living room, up one step and set apart by black iron railings. The dining room table was exactly as I remembered it from the day before: heaped high with hunks of cheeses—now very pungent—little piles of fresh herbs, heads of garlic, onion, shallots, several kinds of vinegar, eggs, milk—now sour—flour, a bottle of Marsala wine, another of cabernet sauvignon, cans of beef broth, cans of chicken broth. . . .

I peered into the kitchen. In my mind I saw Gary in there, tossing mushrooms into the pan as he complained over his shoulder to me about replacing nurses with aides. Suddenly, my eyes filled with tears and my throat tightened. I put a hand over my mouth and nose.

"Take your time, Doc," Ost said.

Amazingly, the kitchen was tidy. Clean dishes and pots and pans were stacked on the drain board. The stove top and counters had been wiped down. Gary's long red apron with its dusting of flour hung on a hook in the corner. Even the tile floor had been mopped.

And the garbage had been taken out.

"I take it you didn't come over here any time after you left yesterday and clean up," Ost said.

I shook my head.

"There was no forced entry—you noticed that, right?" he asked gently. "Who's got keys again? Only your brother Alan?"

Fumbling for my handkerchief, I mopped my eyes. "Alan had Phil's keys. I don't know whether he's given them back yet."

"Neither of them would've come over and cleaned up, would they?"

"Alan slept at the hospital last night in Vittorio's room," Craig said, a little too loudly. "I met him at his apartment at eight this morning. What time were your men on the door?"

149

Ost pointedly did not answer. There was a brief silence. I reached for the refrigerator door.

Jude Rainey grabbed me by the wrist. "Allow me," she said. Pulling on gloves, which she fished from her pocket, she carefully opened the fridge using only the uppermost top of the handle.

The top shelf, where the basket of vegetables had been, was empty. The bottom two shelves were crammed full with a large pan covered in tin foil—probably the duck—and Tupperware containers of ingredients for the dinner, in addition to all the stuff I'd had in there to begin with. I would be hard pressed to tell if anything was odd or missing.

What was missing was Gary.

And any decent explanation of why all this was happening. I shook my head and motioned for Rainey to close the fridge.

"When we're done here, Doc," Ost said, "you need to throw out all the food in the house. Everything, including things like boxes of rice that don't even look like they've been opened, or stuff in the cupboards you had before the dinner. *Everything.* Just to be safe."

"I know," I said.

"And you have to get a locksmith in here to change the locks on the door."

"Right. I will."

"I'd do that today even though it's Sunday. You'll have to pay time-and-a-half probably, but it's worth it."

I nodded. "Thanks, Ozzie."

We all went back into the living room, again carefully picking our way.

"CSU's here, Detective," Officer Yakir called from the foyer as two men wearing Crime Scene Unit jackets came in under the yellow tape, carrying large suitcases.

Craig and I left the apartment and walked down the hall to a window that opened onto the building's courtyard. We sat on a window ledge large enough for two people. Craig lit a cigarette.

"You don't think Alan *did* sneak in to clean the kitchen, do you?" he asked in a low voice.

"Why would he do that?" I asked wearily. "Whoever sent the basket must have come in to wash up the pan the mushrooms were cooked in."

"Or someone who wanted to protect the person who sent the basket," Craig pointed out.

I saw where he was going. "Vittorio can't wash dishes. Not with that ex-fix on his arm."

"I'm not so sure. Think about it. He's right-handed, and it's the left that's broken. And he's been injured before. You and I both know how well he gets along one-handed." Craig paused delicately. "But there's another possibility."

"Gary probably cleaned the kitchen himself, Craig."

"That's not what I mean," Craig said.

I knew that by now Craig would have had time to pull every possible string in the D.A.'s office, and to call in every favor owed at the Twenty-sixth Precinct, to find out exactly what the cops did and did not know about Gary's death and the events leading up to it. He couldn't share what he knew with me, of course. Or what deductions he—and the police— might be making as they surveyed the mess in my apartment.

But he could drop hints in the questions he asked.

"Absolutely not," I said.

"You're sure?" His eyes met mine steadily.

"Yes. Very."

Down the hall, Ost stuck his head out of the apartment. "Doc, you have messages on your answering machine. Could you come in here and play them, please?"

"Yeah, in a minute," I called.

I had quit smoking a while back and hadn't had a cigarette

since. But I reached over and took Craig's and dragged in a lungful of carcinogens.

"Damn you, Craig," I said, coughing, "you sure as hell better not be right on this one."

"I hope I'm not," he said.

seventeen

Phil,

I was deeply hurt & puzzled that you returned my gift esp after I've been so patient and understanding. Frankly I am so upset I don't know what to say. It is so unlike you to be so insulting and insensitive and cowardly. This is not the Phil Carchiollo I know and love, the kind and direct-speaking and decisive Phil. Are you afraid she'll see you writing with it? Why not say you bought yourself the pen? Or keep it in your desk drawer—unless she's in the habit of sneaking in your desk when you're not there—is she?

I can only think you're returning the pen instead of confessing your true feelings. You need to face reality. I can understand that this might be painful for you—why not talk it out with me? Let me help you.

Love always XXX ELISE

"This was when?" I asked, trying to keep the edge out of my voice.

"The first week of September," said Phil. "After she sent me the Mont Blanc pen and I returned it. This letter marks a turning point. First, this is the first time she directly states that she thinks I'm in love with her, but 'concealing' my 'true feelings.' Second, her affect has changed. Up until this point she's been able to make excuses for why I don't call her—I'm saving lives, I'm an important guy with a full schedule—but here she's angry. Third, it's the first time she mentions you. Although without your name. Up until now she's only said vague things like 'I know you're committed elsewhere.' "

Dr. Gina Rizzuti-James cleared her throat. Gina, an attending physician on the Psychiatric Service, was an old friend of Phil's. They had gone through residency together, and had shared a professional suite when they first started in private practice. "Elise seems to have known from the outset that Phil's in a committed relationship," she said.

"I don't know how," I replied. "We always behave very professionally at the hospital, so when she saw us together in the ER there was no way for her to deduce that we're involved. To say nothing of the fact that she was *non compos mentis* at the time. But what are you saying? This letter marks a turning point—*of her becoming more dangerous?*"

"It's possible," Phil conceded. "And she *could* deduce we're involved. You blew me a kiss in the ER, remember?"

I looked with incredulity from Phil to Rizzuti-James and back again. Never mind the kiss; I was focused on the danger. "It's *possible?*" I cried. "Phil, she wrote this letter six weeks ago! What kind of letters is she writing *now?*"

He held his hands up in a conciliatory gesture. "This was an anomaly. She apologized for it and went back to her usual tone of I'm saving lives, I'm an important guy, she understands I can't call her. Then she tells me a couple of cute little anecdotes about her psych class or her summer job in the admissions office to show she's forgiven me."

We sat in the tiny, ten-foot-square office allotted Rizzuti-James by the Psychiatric Service. The office was furnished with a hospital-issue, gray metal, utilitarian desk, a black metal file cabinet, two metal hospital chairs of the kind recently lauded by Martha Stewart, and one ergonomically correct desk chair, which Rizzuti-James had carefully chained with a bicycle lock to a bolt in the floor. She'd had the bolt installed after the last chair was stolen. So far no one had stolen the Martha Stewart chairs. Phil and I sat on them, side by side, Elise Vanderlaende's many letters stacked in folders on the desk. Rizzuti-James sat across from us in the ergonomically correct chair.

It was lunchtime. Phil had arrived with egg-salad-and-bean-sprout sandwiches, and a flask of cold herb tea. But although he had set the sandwiches out on paper plates and poured the tea into cups, none of us had touched anything. I was still feeling sick from the burglary and my hangover, which was getting worse as the day wore on.

And I was beginning to get the feeling that the reason Phil and Gina weren't eating was that they were about to spring something on me.

Phil glanced at Gina, who nodded encouragingly.

"Gina's the official 'Keeper of the Letters,' " Phil explained. "I don't read the letters anymore. I give them to Gina. The stalking literature advises that you give the letters to a third party, that you don't read them yourself."

"The *stalking literature?*" I was about to become shrill. "Phil, you said she wasn't stalking you."

"I read up. Stalking's a related topic. You do a Medline search on erotomania, the computer gives you everything and the kitchen sink." He took a deep breath. "I owe you a big apology, Ev. I really couldn't explain how anxious I was about Elise, so I treated it as a professional matter instead of a personal matter. When I did talk to you about it, I downplayed everything because I needed to convince myself it was nothing to get worked up about. I realize now that I've been depressed as well as anxious. Doubting myself, wondering whether I had done anything to encourage her . . . becoming absentminded and distracted, misplacing things. . . . She's the one who's crazy, but as the object I got sucked into her craziness, and I began to feel crazy myself. So you got a very skewed picture."

"We shrinks all think we're so on the ball," Gina said. "It's a disease of the profession to think we know what we're doing, but sometimes we miss things."

I struggled with the persistent feeling that *I* was missing something. That was a very "Mom" look Gina was giving Phil at the moment, all at once firm, no-nonsense, fiercely loyal, and encouraging.

With a lot of dark hair swept up in a Victorian do—complete with chopsticklike ornaments holding wayward strands in place—and a well-rounded figure, draped now in a loose-fitting, vaguely tailored outfit of silk and wool, Gina had "Mom" written all over her. She was actually the same age as Phil and I but gave the impression of a reincarnation of an earlier, 1950s self. In reality she was a street-smart, brassy-mouthed, first-generation Italian-American iconoclast, very 1990s, with an uncanny ability to get to the heart of the matter. The appearance was something of a professional guise. "I look like their mother when they were two or three, and I talk like her, too," she once cheerfully told me, speaking of her patients, predominantly Irish and Italian working-class stiffs bewildered by modern-thinking wives. "Helps the transference."

Not to play favorites, she gave me the same look. Gina did a lot of couples counseling.

"Miss things like what?" I asked. "Elise's anger?"

"Well, not so much miss things, more like drop the ball," Phil said. "I dropped the ball by not confiding in you. But I did everything else I was supposed to. I spoke to the charge nurses in the ER and told them if Vanderlaende came in, they should let me know—I didn't want to be surprised if she showed up. I alerted Security. I made sure if she did come into the hospital asking for me to treat her, that a colleague would see her instead."

I turned Elise's letter over in my hand. It was written on the same expensive, baby blue stationary I remembered and dated August 31. Gina had stapled it to a matching envelope. I turned the envelope over and read the date stamped in red ink: *September 3 REC'D.* "You didn't tell me about this at the time."

"I know I didn't. I'm sorry." He touched my hand. "We'll talk more about that later."

"Thank you for the apology, and I do want to talk later, but right now I'm really pissed off," I said. "Have you consulted Legal Affairs?" The hospital's in-house attorneys.

"You have every right to be angry, Ev. Yes, I talked personally to Sheldon Tardiff, the senior VP for Legal Affairs. He thought I was an alarmist. 'Has she made any overt threat?' 'No.' 'Has she been back to the hospital?' 'I receive hand-delivered letters in my department mailbox.' 'But have you *seen* her? 'No, but she knows who my girlfriend and family are.' 'But has she made any overt threat toward them?' 'No.' Tardiff's concern is bad publicity. He doesn't want to pick up the *Daily News* and see the headline 'University Hospital Takes Legal Action Against Patients.' " Phil laughed bitterly.

"They may be more helpful when you tell them about Gary Monday morning," Gina put in grimly.

Phil went on to say that, in addition to talking to Legal Affairs, he had gone to his department head, who advised Phil to discuss his countertransference with his supervisor; he had taken the matter up with his group—once a week, Phil met with colleagues for peer supervision—and he continued to discuss matters with Gina. Until Gary's poisoning, there seemed no reason to act.

"What did Detective Ost say?" I asked.

"He asked my professional opinion, and I gave it. Classic de Clérambault's syndrome, also known as delusional disorder, erotomanic type—the delusional belief that one is loved by another. The eroto falls in love with the object, but the object doesn't positively reinforce the attachment. Nonetheless, the eroto persists in believing that the object returns her love."

"There's no agreed-upon etiology," Gina added.

Phil went on: "One theory is that erotomania's a syndrome that serves some kind of adaptive function by providing an outside source of nurturing, protection, and control following periods of loss. Another theory is that the delusions provide narcissistic gratification when reality doesn't. Or Elise could have a pattern of choosing love objects who are unwilling or unable to reciprocate—Kernberg's masochistic subjugation to the unattainable object. But I have no idea really *what* intrapsychic factors come into play here—I have very little insight into this patient, except to say that she probably has some past trauma that the shooting reignited. I wouldn't begin to know what that is."

As a get-to-the-point ER doc trained to temporarily manage acute clinical problems—or "surf and turf" as the lingo had it—I was coming to the end of my get-to-the-point rope. "And?" I demanded.

"He wanted to know did I have any reason to believe that Elise Vanderlaende had poisoned Gary. I said no, except for one thing."

I glared. "Which is?"

"She's unable to stop the maladaptive behavior. That's a worry right there. Then you add on whatever projection of rejection she has—right now that's still an unknown quantity. Which may or may not set the stage for physical violence. Less than five percent of erotos actually do physical harm—"

Here it comes, I thought.

"But when they do, they don't strike at the love object. They strike at the person they believe stands between them and the object."

I counted to ten. "So Elise's fantasy is, if it weren't for me, you would declare mad passionate love for her and rush right into her arms? That's just fucking great, Phil. How long have you known this?"

"It's in the literature," Gina said.

"It's in the literature," I repeated sarcastically. "That makes it understandable, which makes it *all right?* Do you guys even listen to yourselves when you talk? You're calm and intellectual, like, like you're delivering a paper and fielding questions at an academic conference on delusional disorder, erotomanic subtype! Why aren't you *outraged* that someone tried to poison me, and Gary's dead? Why aren't you jumping up and down, pounding your chests, and yodeling like Tarzan?"

Gina wisely didn't say anything.

After a moment, Phil stood up and struck his chest three times. "Mea culpa, mea culpa, mea maxima culpa," he said. "Of course you're right."

"Too late," I said. "She's stalking me."

"What?" Phil cried. "Since when?"

I smiled widely with mock brightness. "Sometimes we miss things. And she disguises herself. For weeks now I've been seeing this skinny guy with his head draped in a kafiyeh, skulking around the doctors' residence. Well, guess what?"

"Oh no," moaned Phil.

"And this morning she came into Sami's while I was having coffee with Vittorio and plunked herself down at the next table. Because I didn't recognize her, she was able to eavesdrop on my entire conversation with Vic. For all I know, she's been following me for months in different disguises. Moreover, the person who delivered the basket of vegetables to Sava was wearing an elaborate wig and sunglasses, and deliberately speaking *basso profundo*."

Phil and Gina stared at me in horror.

"*And* my apartment's been burgled."

"When?" Phil cried.

"I don't know. Sometime after I brought Gary over to the ER, and before I arrived home at ten A.M. this morning." I told Phil and Gina about finding the apartment trashed and my computer and computer discs stolen.

"I'm really sorry, Ev," Gina managed finally.

"Why didn't you say something?" Phil asked. "Why did you let us just go on and on?"

I pushed my hair out of my eyes and shook my head. "You've made the connection between the botany office and Professor Held, haven't you?"

Gina and Phil exchanged a puzzled look. "Professor Held?"

"The chairman of the botany department. The mushroom expert that Lauren took the mushrooms to, for identification. Didn't Elise say in one of her letters that she works in the botany field office during the school year? That the admissions job is just a summer job?"

"You're right," Phil said. "Honey, I am really, really sorry."

I tried to calm down. Any minute I was going to become irrational, and I didn't want to slam Phil with all my anger and anxiety. Especially in front of Gina. I took a deep breath and made an effort to talk coherently. "Phil, you are my one and only, and I love you. I've been incredibly upset for months now that we haven't been getting along, and I'm so on edge from Gary's death . . . These last couple of months you've been moody and secretive, and when I've tried to help you, you've pushed me away. I finally realized myself this morning that you're depressed." I paused. Now came the hard part. "If there's anything else you want to tell me, now would be the time. It's easy to get sucked into things when you're depressed, your defenses are down—"

"What are you saying?" Phil gasped. "You don't think—"

"I thought it was Lauren Sabot," I said. "I thought you were having an affair with her. But it's not Lauren, is it? It's Elise."

"No!" he cried. "I'm not having an affair with anyone! Ev, how could you even think such a thing?"

"You've been moody and secretive," I said heatedly. "You and Gina have colluded in hiding these letters from me. You didn't clue me in that a total stranger who is in love with you knows all kinds of personal things about me and my brothers. Why didn't you tell me?"

"You're right," he said. "I should have."

"That's not good enough," I blustered. "I want to know the reason. Why didn't you *tell* me?"

He considered the question, his face frozen into an unblinking stare. I counted five full seconds while he neither spoke nor blinked. "I don't know," he said finally.

"You should. You're a shrink. Did you go over to my apartment yesterday to wash the dishes?"

Phil looked to Gina to see if she was as baffled by this question as he was, but her expression was inscrutable. "No. When?"

"After Gary ate the mushrooms."

"I don't understand."

I decided that he probably didn't. My heart softened. "You missed that Elise was dangerous because you didn't listen to your own intuition, Phil," I said, "and because you were worried about how I might react. Now, let's get our act together and try to solve this problem. For starters, could you lay out all your Xeroxes from the erotomania literature and your research on the dining-room table in your apartment so I can read it? Along with all these letters?"

Phil nodded and stood. He pulled me out of my chair into a tight embrace. "I don't know what's the matter with me," he said, his voice choked with emotion.

"Yes, you do." My own voice caught. "You're not sleeping well, you're withdrawn and moody, you complain you're misplacing things, that you can't concentrate—you're glitching out when your patients are talking to you—and you're irritable and argumentative. You yourself say you've been depressed. Honey, you *are* depressed. You need help."

He nodded against my neck. His face was wet.

"Will you promise me you'll see someone?" I pleaded. Phil had been in analysis for several years in the course of his psychoanalytic training, but his analyst had died the previous spring. "You've been saying since Dr. Plantz died that you need to find a new analyst—will you pursue that now?"

"Yes," he said. "I'll do it right away. Thank you, honey."

We let go of each other. Phil took off his glasses and wiped his eyes with his handkerchief. Gina smiled empathetically and reached across the desk to grasp Phil's hand. "We'll help you, Phil," she said.

I still felt that there was something wrong, something Phil wasn't telling me about Elise. But I laid it down to the depression. Depression can play tricks—on the people who suffer from it, and on those who have to live with them.

I was right.

But not in the way I thought.

eighteen

I found Professor Robert Held at a podium on the stage of a darkened auditorium in the spanking new Ruth E. Scherer Memorial Biological Sciences Building on the main University campus, where he was conducting the monthly meeting of the Morningside Mycological Society. Meetings were free, and open to the public. I slid into a seat in the back.

On a large screen to Held's right was a slide showing mushrooms growing under a pine tree. "In Russia, you can show what you've picked to the person at the desk at your hotel," Held told his audience. "They've been known to look in your bag and say, 'I wouldn't eat that if I were you.' In Europe, you just go to your local pharmacist and he or she helps you identify your specimens. If we had a huge mushroom-eating public in this country regularly poisoning themselves, we might see this as a public health issue, too. In the meantime, I suggest you go on one of our mushroom walks, with Morningside members. They can look at what you've picked and tell you what you've got."

I realized with a start that the mushrooms on the slide were the same as the ones Lauren Sabot had held out to me in the palm of her hand the night before in the emergency room. *Amanita phalloides.* Death caps. Now that I had time to look at them again, I remembered too that Case Hamilton had shown me some on one of our mushroom walks out on the island.

"During the season, I usually have an informal ID session at my apartment on Monday nights," Held was saying. He had a jumpy, rapid-fire manner of talking, like a person who thinks faster than he can talk, or who needs his lithium regulated. His body movements were jumpy, too. In the dim glow cast from his podium, I could see him bobbing and flinging his arms around for emphasis. "You can bring your mushrooms then if you like. Of course, we have the same perennial debate here that they have in France: should the ID session be Sunday, before you eat what you've picked, or Monday, *after* you eat it?"

The audience laughed. I missed the joke. I was watching Held. And looking at the death caps.

"Well, that's about it," said Held. "Can we have the lights, please? Anybody with a question, feel free to come forward. The Morningside Mycological Society secretary, Leslie, is here with membership forms. Membership is thirty dollars for students and elders with a valid ID card. Forty for everyone else. That doesn't include the liver transplant. Liver transplant is fifteen dollars extra."

More laughter. Despite myself, I joined in.

When the lights came up I saw a pleasant-looking man in his late fifties, thin as a rail, dressed informally in jeans, hiking boots, and a plaid flannel shirt. He wore sixties wire-rimmed glasses like Phil did. As I walked down the center isle of the auditorium toward the front, Held jumped down from the stage. I caught his eye and he smiled at me, crinkling all the many laugh lines around his eyes and mouth. Nice brown eyes. Nice brown hair, graying a little, standing slightly on end from all the head tossing. Fabulous teeth.

Suddenly, about a hundred people seemed to mill around him, all talking at once, shouting out questions. "Wait, wait," he laughed. His prominent Adam's apple bobbed up and down. "Line forms to the left. This lady first." He pointed at me.

I stuck out my hand. "Dr. Evelyn Sutcliffe. Lauren Sabot—"

"Yes," he said, shaking my hand up and down with such vigor I thought my shoulder might dislocate. "Of course. Of course." His expression turned to one of concern. "How is your patient?"

"Well . . ."

"Give me ten minutes here. Then we can speak privately."

"Thanks," I said.

He was true to his word and a few minutes later took my arm and led me out of the auditorium. We exited the building through wide glass doors, and I blinked in the bright, late October sunshine. "Let's go to my office, in the old building," Held said as, still holding on to my arm, he propelled me along the brick walk. Then into the hallowed halls of Old Bio with the marble floors, wood wainscoting, and lofty architectural detailing common among late nineteenth-century educational edifices. I remembered it vividly from my own student days.

Held did not wait for elevators, it seemed. He threw himself through the doors of the stairwell, pulling me after him. As we charged up four flights to the faculty offices floor, I got into the swing of things and began to present Gary's case as I might present it to an elder statesman attending at the hospital, on the run, trotting at his heels on Rounds.

"I am very sorry," said Held, upon hearing that Gary had died after aspirating his stomach contents during the lavage.

He stopped in the stairwell to look back at me. "How horrifying for you and the other doctors and nurses."

"He was a very dear friend of mine," I said. "And an invaluable colleague."

Held touched my elbow. "I certainly hope I can be of help to you, then," he said simply as he turned to go on.

We exited the stairway, and the pace having picked up again, zoomed down a hall of faculty offices. Stopping abruptly, Held rattled a large ring of keys and put one into a lock on a red door. "Have the tests come back?"

"Yes." I had tracked down my med student, Nicholson, in the physician's library at the hospital, after leaving Phil and Gina. He had given me Gary's test results, and a four-inch-thick stack of photocopied articles on mushroom poisoning. "Negative for amatoxins and phallotoxins," I told Held. Gary had not eaten any death caps. "Negative for psilocybin as well, which was—to say the least—surprising. Radioimmunoassay and thin-layer chromatography are pretty sophisticated tests. I don't understand how they could not have turned up psilocybin."

Held glanced at me over his shoulder, intrigued, as he struggled with the door. "Your friend seemed inebriated and deranged, charging around and delirious?"

"Yes," I said.

"Tendon jerks and jerky movements?"

"Some."

"Head and neck muscles convulsing?"

"No. Well, generalized muscle fasciculations, yes."

"See visions?"

"He was clearly hallucinating. I'm not sure about visions."

"Take a nap?"

"A nap?" I repeated, puzzled.

"Did he eat the mushrooms and go to sleep, then waken?"

"I didn't ask."

"But a lot of kinetic energy? Faulty lock," he explained, yanking the doorknob as he turned the key. The door released. "I like it better that way. Defeats burglars."

As the door swung in, I expected to see the stereotypical faculty office, furnished in educational oak, jammed floor to ceiling with books, boxes, and papers, and a thick layer of dust on everything. Instead I saw a pristine mahogany Queen Anne table with four matching chairs, an Oriental rug, and bookcases more orderly than those at the Morgan Library. No piles of anything anywhere. Certainly no dust. In one corner was a worn, expensive, wine red leather armchair. On a small cabinet next to the armchair, what looked like a Tiffany lamp. I looked more closely at the bookcases. They too were mahogany. Some shelves were filled with acid-free archival boxes, the costly kind, with little brass tabs. Not exactly standard university issue.

Held surveyed his sanctum with visible pride and pleasure. "Please," he said, holding out a chair for me.

I sat. Held knelt and opened the small cabinet next to the armchair, which turned out to cleverly conceal a refrigerator. He took out several small Ziploc bags and sat at the table across from me.

"Lauren's specimens from last night," he said.

Starting with the first bag, he handed them across to me one at a time. "This vase-shaped one is *Craterellus fallax,* a kind of chanterelle, also called Black Trumpet." It looked like black tree bark to me. "Next, *Pleurotus ostreatus,* the Long Island White Oyster." Tiny little mushrooms all joined together like the tentacles of a squid. "This one, shiitake. You've probably seen this in your local Grand Union, quite common nowadays. And these are honeys, *Armillariella mellea.*"

"Ah," I said. "What Case and Jackie Hamilton thought they were eating that time they were poisoned."

"Indeed. Mistook *Galerina marginata* for them. Now, none

of these"—he waved at the bags—"could have produced the symptoms your friend had. These are all perfectly edible, although honeys occasionally disagree with people. No, I believe your friend ate something else."

Held sat back in his chair, caressing the table top briefly with his extraordinary bony fingers. "The sacred mushrooms of Mexico can seize hold of you with an irresistible power," he pronounced almost dreamily. "The *Psilocybe, Stropharia,* and *Conocybe* genera. They can even seduce you into a temporary schizophrenia. Doesn't last. But it's not uncommon. People looking for hallucinogenic effects have a tendency to experiment unwisely."

I nodded.

"However," he went on, "your tests were negative for psilocybin, and there's no kinetic agent in any of these mushrooms. They produce little or no desire to move about. Judging from his symptoms, I would say that your friend ate the 'divine mushroom of immortality.' " He smiled. "*Amanita muscaria.* Also called the fly agaric. That does cause one to charge about crying and raving, or singing and dancing, as the case may be. At least according to the many published accounts, of which your friend sounds like a textbook example. I must confess, I'm intrigued. During the late sixties, several colleagues and I tried out the fly agarics on ourselves without any effects whatsoever."

I picked up something in his tone. "You sound skeptical," I said.

"No, no. Jealous, perhaps. We eventually concluded that the fly agarics' potency falls off toward the end of the season."

"And when is that?"

"Now. October."

"I'm confused," I said. "Are you telling me that this mushroom would *not* produce these symptoms . . . ?"

"Let's put it this way: the myth and lore abounds with

cases of intoxication, euphoria, reverie, extraordinary physical achievement, wondrous visions, talking for hours and hours and hours as if on truth serum—one literally cannot stop oneself. I myself, personally, have been unable to achieve this exalted state. Much seems dependent on set and setting—one's own expectations. However, there are cases of accidental poisoning with *Amanita muscaria* where individuals have become agitated and disoriented. Not perhaps to the extent that your friend did." He tented his fingers in front of his face, elbows on the table. "But this is not your worry. It doesn't matter what mushroom caused your friend's hallucinations. The effects in any case are temporary."

He paused, then launched anew. "If someone is trying to poison you, you'll want to know what type of expertise is necessary."

"Thank you for putting it so delicately," I said. "That's exactly what I want to know."

"One needn't know much," Held said bluntly. "For instance, you, knowing nothing of poisonous mushrooms, could have come to my lecture this afternoon and learned all you need to know to go out and pick some death caps to poison your near and dear. I show those slides of *Amanita phalloides* at every single lecture I give on behalf of the Morningside Mycological Society. Not to encourage people to pick them, to *dis*courage them from picking them. But how would I know if a would-be poisoner attended? And as you saw today, the meetings are open to the public. Often with a notice in the *New York Times* in the food section the week before. Anyone may come."

"I'm afraid I came in at the tail end of your lecture today," I said.

"Ah. Well. *Amanita phalloides* used to be a rare, woodland-inhabiting species," Held said. "Now it's found virtually everywhere. Even in urban backyards. Incidents of poisoning are on the rise, especially in Northern California. Most of these are among Asian immigrants, who are used to foraging in their own countries. The Asian *Amanita princeps* is safe and edible, and they mistake our death caps for that, or for straw mushrooms."

"So anyone who comes to one of your lectures learns what a death cap looks like," I concluded. "What do you think of death caps as a murder weapon?"

"I wouldn't recommend it." Held leaned back in his chair and regarded me with a speculative air. "Very few people know how poisonous mushrooms can be. Most of us don't have to think about it; we buy our mushrooms at the supermarket. But let's say you know a *little* about *Amanita* death caps. Maybe you read the article in the *New York Times* when the California wine heir died from eating them. Or you saw something on CNN about the Laotians. Probably what you 'know' is that if you eat them, you die."

"I get it," I said. "If you know nothing, you don't know how poisonous they are. If you know a little, you think they're more poisonous than they actually—"

"Precisely."

"And if you were really knowledgeable—"

"You would know that—contrary to popular belief, and mystery novels aside—*Amanita* death caps are not an efficient way to kill someone. They account for about ninety-five percent of lethal mushroom poisonings in this country. But they're only fatal about forty percent of the time. Some people who eat them survive without medical treatment. The majority will survive with treatment, and will probably not even need a liver transplant."

"So, in your opinion, the poisoner knows what *Amanita* death caps look like, and where to pick them, but not much more. He or she is not a mushroom *expert*."

"Quite a subtle puzzle, isn't it?" He smiled, tenting his

fingers in front of his face. A man obviously in love with his work.

I liked him. He was a friend of Case and Jackie Hamilton's, and I decided to trust him. "Do you know a young woman named Elise Vanderlaende, Professor?"

The question startled him, but he covered well. "I do."

"May I ask you to treat what I am about to tell you in strictest confidence?"

"My students often confide in me. My lips are sealed."

I thought about how to phrase myself. Oh, hell; just jump in: "She's stalking my boyfriend, Dr. Philip Carchiollo. He's an attending psychiatrist at University Hospital, and—"

"Oh dear God," murmured Held. A strange expression crept over his face. He began to laugh and shake his head. "Well, that would certainly explain it."

"Professor?"

"Do call me Rob. You and I are about to become acquainted somewhat better than we might have expected, Evelyn—it is Evelyn, isn't it?"

By now I was totally mystified. "Yes."

"I wondered why she stopped, although I was of course immensely relieved—I can't *tell* you how relieved—but I'm not making much sense, am I?" Again he laughed, wonderingly.

"She used to stalk *me*," Held said.

nineteen

"Held said he would question very seriously whether our person really wanted to poison anyone," I told Phil later.

He switched places with me so I could stand under the shower while he soaped up. "Yeah, easy for him to say, now that Elise is stalking me instead of him. Run his theory by me again?"

I got my hair wet and we switched places again. Sluicing the water out of my eyes, I reached for my shampoo. "If you don't know anything about mushrooms, you don't know how poisonous they are. If you know—"

"I got that part. And death caps are fatal only about forty percent of the time. I mean his theory about Elise."

"He says that during the time Elise was 'erotically fixated' on him, as he put it, she became a mushroom expert because he's a mushroom expert. He thinks she can probably identify more than a hundred mushroom species, and he's convinced that she would not confuse a death cap with an edible mushroom. So his theory is, either Elise sent the basket, but was ambivalent about poisoning anyone, *or* the person who sent the basket knows what *Amanita* death caps look like, and where to pick them, but not much more—he or she is not a mushroom *expert*. Held's a very intellectual guy. He likes subtle puzzles."

"That's subtle bordering on ethereal," Phil said.

"Anyway, he says Gary probably ate *Amanita muscaria*, which would explain why the tests were negative for psilocybin," I went on. "*A. muscaria* contains ibotenic acid and muscimol. We didn't test for those compounds."

"Now don't *you* start beating up on yourself," Phil said. "One depressed person here is enough. Elise never tried to poison Held, did she?"

I rinsed the shampoo out of my hair. "No. But he pointed out, as you told me this morning, that erotos don't usually poison the love object, they poison the person they think stands between them and the object. Held's not in a relationship. There isn't anyone to poison. His wife died two years ago and he doesn't date."

"Held knows that erotos don't go after the object? Has he been reading up?"

"Apparently he did the same Medline search you did. He's even been to a support group for stalking victims—although he didn't seem to me like the type who would go in for support groups. He says it meets on Tuesday night in a church on West Seventy-ninth Street. Experts come to address them, and he recently went to hear a detective from a domestic abuse unit and a psychologist attached to the D.A.'s office whose specialty is stalking. Most of the people in the group are women being threatened by their exes. Held went out of curiosity at first, but he's met about a dozen people now who're being stalked by erotos."

Phil gave me a very wet kiss tasting of soap and shampoo, and got out of the shower. "And he says I can call him when?" he asked from the other side of the shower curtain.

"He's flying to Boston for some kind of conference. He'll be back Tuesday evening, he says." I turned off the water and pushed the shower curtain aside. Reaching for a towel, I started drying my hair. Phil, a towel wrapped around his waist, was shaving at the sink.

Although he was still very subdued and preoccupied, he seemed a little more himself since that morning. Gina had encouraged him to get therapy instead of returning to analysis, and had recommended a former Jesuit named James Ahearn now in private practice on the Upper West Side. Ahearn had seen Phil immediately, and would continue to see him twice a week for now. Moreover, Gina had written Phil a prescription for the antidepressant Prozac.

Wrapping my head in the towel and pulling on Phil's blue terry cloth robe, I bent and kissed him on the shoulder and went into the bedroom, where I lay down on the bed for a moment.

I was so relieved that the problem had been named and addressed. Depression. Therapy. Prozac. It seemed so simple—even though I knew it had never been simple, and that the road ahead would not be simple, either. But in a day heavy with shock and grief, Phil's admitting that he'd been depressed and starting therapy was a welcome dash of leavening.

I was only sorry that Gary wasn't around to tell.

When I had seen the Prozac bottle on Phil's kitchen counter, I had briefly imagined calling Gary to say, *Good news.* But I had turned off the fantasy the way you might turn off TV. Gary was downtown by now, lying on a slab at the M.E.'s Office. And there I was thinking selfish thoughts about how Gary had always been there for me, and now he wouldn't be there for me—when actually, I was the one who hadn't been there for Gary. I had fucked up the lavage.

I kept telling myself that if Elise—or whoever—hadn't sent the basket, there would have been no lavage. But it was hard to make myself listen. The if-onlys chimed in: if only I had listened to Nicholson and Mark Ramsey, who wanted to sedate; if only Gary hadn't aspirated; if only I had suctioned him more quickly and efficiently . . .

But now that Gary was dead, the biggest if-onlys were, if only I had told Gary just once how much I loved him and what a good friend he was to me. If only I had thanked him—just once—for all the wonderful, wise, and kind advice he had given me over the years. If only I had conveyed—*on just one occasion*—how much I looked forward to going to work when I knew he would be working the same shift. How I would make lists in my mind of things I wanted to share with him while I was walking over to the hospital. How, when he would confide to me some trouble he had on his mind, I would chew it over, sometimes for hours, and get back to him later, saying, "You know, I've been thinking about what you said earlier, and I think . . ."

Now I would never get the chance to show him how much I cared.

Suddenly, Gary's argument with Di Clausson came flying up out of my unconscious. Di, sharp and caustic: *Let me get this straight. Are you threatening to* blackmail *me, Nurse Seligman?* Gary, equally sharp: *I think it's a fair trade, Doctor—don't you?*

Herrera for Christmas. Deal?

I remembered suddenly that I had asked Gary about it afterward.

Bolting upright on the bed, I swung my feet to the floor. Think. You asked him. What did he say?

Jazz Washington and I had finished sorting out the problem with the patient's chest tube. Washington, a decent enough doc but in completely over her head when it came to hospital politics, looked like she expected to be taken out and shot at dawn for overhearing a senior doc and charge nurse quarrel-

175

ing. Not wanting to contribute to her discomfort, I had pretended that nothing untoward happened. Then, as soon as I could get free, I had gone looking for Gary.

I'd found him standing at the nurses' station counter, flipping through the nurses' order book.

He was still angry. His eyes flashed, the color was high in his cheeks, and he was breathing as if he had just run up a flight of stairs. Which he may well have done. In the normal course of things, Gary almost never lost his temper. But the one or two times I'd seen him mad, he ran up five flights in one of the hospital stairwells to calm down.

"What the hell was that all about with Di Clausson just now?" I asked in a low voice.

"She's not going to blackmail Keith Herrera," he fumed. "If Herrera goes down, I'll make sure she goes with him."

"What do you mean, blackmail Keith Herrera?"

But he had waved me off. "She won't do it," he'd said. "She'd be a fool."

I reached for my bag, fished out my organizer, and flipped through it to see if I had Keith Herrera's phone number. Yes. I picked up the phone and dialed.

I got his answering machine. Damn. "Keith, it's Ev Sutcliffe. I really, really need to talk to you. It's a matter of some urgency." I stated the date and time, said I was at Phil Carchiollo's, and gave the phone number.

Then I sat with the phone in my lap for a few minutes, thinking.

Phil came out of the bathroom and looked at the clock. "We'd better get moving. You know how irate Vittorio gets when we're late for dinner."

"Mm." I went into the bathroom, still thinking.

By the time I came out, my hair dry and my makeup on, Phil was dressed in khakis, loafers, a tie, and a blazer, and was lounging on the bed, engrossed in the sports pages of the

Daily News. I remembered that tonight was game five of the baseball pennant series. Phil was an avid fan.

"What are you going to wear?" he asked, looking up. "Were you able to salvage anything from the burglary? Or does it all have to go to the cleaners?"

"Most of it has to go to the cleaners," I said, reaching for my underwear, which I had laid out on the bed. "And even if it doesn't, I'm going to send it all anyway. I can't bear the idea of wearing anything after whoever-it-was touched it. The idea gives me the willies."

"Well, do you have a nice outfit here? What about your blue suit and red silk blouse?"

I shook my head. "The dry cleaners lost the whole outfit, along with the nice silk chemise you gave me for my birthday."

"*Lost* it?"

"They mixed up the tickets. I went to pick up my clothes, and they tried to give me someone else's linen suit and silk blouse. So now they say I have to wait for the other customer to bring back my stuff and ask for her own." I got into a pair of gray flannel trousers and pulled on a pink oxford cloth shirt. Rummaging through the end of the closet he had designated mine, I found my own blazer, and put it on. Then I took it off and looked inside at the label.

"This isn't my blazer, either," I said. "What the hell is going on?"

Phil got up from the bed. "Are you sure? It looked fine when you had it on just now."

"Oh, it's the right size. But this is double-breasted and mine is single. Also, mine is from Brooks and this is Ann Taylor."

We looked at each other.

"I think you'd better have a serious chat with your dry cleaner," Phil said. "I don't like this. I feel like a poltergeist just blew through here."

I shuddered as if from a sudden chill.

"Maybe one did," I said.

"Ev, how good of you to come. *Do* come in," Vittorio took my hand, and bent down to kiss my cheek. "Thank you for your talk this morning," he said in a low voice. "Most helpful."

"Vic, you're so gracious." I kissed him back. "I thought we were quarreling as usual."

"Now, now." But he smiled as he turned to greet Phil.

I made my way into the dining room, which was, as always, breathtaking. The walls were painted a dark, rich red. At one end of the room hung a Gainsborough painting of a young boy in a maroon suit—the highlights of which matched the dining room's walls—and his English setter. The mahogany table was a double-pedestal Duncan Phyfe, paired with unusual painted chairs upholstered in celadon brocade. A crystal chandelier floated overhead, illuminating the room with candlelight. In the center of the table stood a low arrangement of lavender hydrangeas flanked by two Georgian candlesticks. Instead of a tablecloth, there were individual Madeira lace placemats.

I mentally prepared myself to eat off the gilded porcelain manufactured by a Dresden factory in France for members of the Russian royal family during the eighteenth century, wielding a heavy sterling silver fork and knife, and to drink out of delicate antique crystal glasses. I was always sure I would break something.

Alan came through the swinging doors from the kitchen. Without a word, we embraced.

"How are you doing?" I asked after a moment or two, still holding him.

He sighed. "I don't know what I'm going to do. He was my best friend."

"I know. I loved him, too."

Alan laughed sadly and let go. "You know what he'd say if he were here. 'All right, all right, that's enough *mush*.' Would you like a glass of wine?" Without waiting for an answer, he poured me a glass of red from a bottle standing on a silver tray on the credenza, handed it to me, and poured a glass for himself.

We went into Vittorio's study, a small, unpretentious room furnished with family hand-me-downs. After the formality and grandeur of the dining room, the balding Persian rug, distressed mahogany furniture, and fraying corduroy couch were a relief.

Moving a stack of manila files—some of Vic's work for the hospital board of trustees, it seemed—Alan flopped down on one end of the couch. I sat on the other.

"To Gary," he said. We clinked glasses.

I flashed on that time on our way to the hospital ball when Alan had opened the split of champagne in the cab. Then, Alan had been playful and dazzling. Now he was a shadow of himself, with dark circles under his hazel eyes from weeping and lack of sleep. "You look like the grieving widower," I said.

"I am the grieving widower. There are floods in China, did you hear on the news? Shirley and Judy Seligman are stuck in the Hu Bei Province. They designated me next of kin so I can deal with the Medical Examiner's Office and have the funeral home pick up . . . the body." In a wooden voice, he listed the phone calls he had made that afternoon, and gave me a précis of the details. He had been to Gary's apartment to pick up the mail and water the plants. He had emptied Gary's locker at the hospital. He had even worried—briefly—about whether he should cancel all of Gary's magazine subscriptions, or just have everything forwarded to Shirley in New Jersey. But so many of the magazines were in French. He didn't think Shirley knew French.

There was a long silence when Alan finished talking. My heart heavy, I reached over and took his hand. We sipped our wine.

"Vic and I went to see my super this morning," I said after a while.

Alan was deep in thought. "Yeah, he told me." Pause. "A guy disguising himself in a bad wig and sunglasses, wearing a white clinical coat." Longer pause. "It couldn't *possibly* have been Case." He chortled, then sat shaking his head for a long time.

"You still think Case sent the basket?" I asked.

"What does it matter what I think? Case made a grand show of apology this afternoon and begged forgiveness for anything he had ever done to upset me. He wanted to make sure that I knew that he knew that I thought he'd sent the basket, and he swore up and down that he hadn't. Was that your doing?"

"I did encourage him to speak to you," I admitted.

"Thanks a lot. Now I have to be nice to him. Did you also have to talk Vic out of thinking Case delivered the basket?"

"I didn't realize I *had* talked him out of it."

"Oh, who cares?" Alan shrugged. "Nothing's going to bring Gary back."

I squeezed his hand. He returned to his thoughts.

Eventually I said, "I never really understood why you and Gary broke up."

Alan looked at his empty wineglass, leaned over, and set it on the floor. "It's hard to explain. Gary was jealous of me in odd ways, and resentful of my ambition. Two years ago, I wanted to train as a chef and someday open my own bistro. Gary said, 'You'll be working hundred-hour work weeks, I might as well date an intern.' Of course, an intern eventually becomes an attending, and starts working more normal hours. I was going to open a restaurant and put in hundred-hour work weeks the rest of my life." Alan laughed hollowly. "So I left him not because I wasn't in love with him, but because he wouldn't support my career goals. Now look at me. I don't have a bistro—but I have a fabulous kitchen and a gorgeous dining room. I can throw all the dinner parties I want—and without working a hundred hours a week!"

"Are you sorry?" I asked.

"Yeah, sometimes." Grief had rendered him exceptionally raw and honest. Still, he glanced toward the door, as if to check for someone listening at the keyhole. "When things get rough with Vic, sometimes I think about quitting."

"Quitting," I echoed.

"Vic pays me a salary, you know."

I hadn't known. Although I had always assumed that Vic supported Alan.

"I'm his personal assistant," Alan went on. "Major duomo, that's me. I run the household. It's not so different from owning and running a bistro. Dinner for twelve, for example. I plan the menu, speak to the caterers if we'll be using them, order the wine, order the invitations, address them and mail them, get the cleaning people in to make the place ready, order new slipcovers or curtains if we need *that* done . . . then if we're not using caterers, I do the shopping and cook the meal." As he talked, he nodded—and kept nodding, as if to persuade not only me, but himself. "I do all the financial paperwork for the household—that's this apartment, the house in Westchester, and the house on the Island. I supervise yard-work guys, carpenters, painters, plumbers, electricians, and whoever else we need. Last week I had a very interesting conversation with the stable manager about what Vic's horses will be eating this winter. Probably I make about the same salary Doris Duke's butler made while she was alive."

"Are you being sarcastic?" I asked.

"No." He laughed again in that strange, hollow way. "I

love my life. This is what I want to do. Now, if you'll excuse me, I suppose I'm needed in the kitchen."

He got up and went out.

After a moment, so did I.

As we walked through the fabulously appointed dining room on my way to the living room, I didn't know what to think.

twenty

As conversation does after any death, the talk at the dinner table that evening rambled.

We talked about Gary, his work, his friends, ourselves. We got off the topic, then back on, then on to another altogether. It was all very stream-of-consciousness, made even more fluid by the liberal pouring of wine throughout the meal.

Somebody mentioned Mark Ramsey. How he had lost his best friend in that accident, and the fact that he had never gotten over it.

"Gary used to say that Mark Ramsey was permanently shell-shocked, because his life had been too melodramatic for him," Alan recalled. He had recovered from his earlier bout of bitter irony, and seemed bolstered by the shared sadness of his table mates—even that of Case Hamilton, who sat on Alan's right. "Starting with the fact that Mark's mother died of cancer when he was twelve, and then two years later his father's plane went down in Alaska on a fishing trip."

"Frozen solid by the time they found him," Case Hamilton chimed in. "I remember Batty Coleman—"

"You know a guy named 'Batty'?" Craig asked. "Case, tell the truth—do you know anyone named Bob or Fred or Jim?"

"*Bartholomew* Coleman, then. Rowed with me at Yale. Executor of Mark's father's estate. He called me to—"

Suddenly there was laughter. Hysterically edged, survivor guilt laughter. Boisterous with grief, we shouted him down.

"No more Yalie connections," Lauren Sabot cried.

"Let Alan finish before you start with the alumni newsletter, dear." This from Jackie Hamilton.

Phil said, "You are worse than the So-and-So begats in the Bible, Case."

Passionate, affectionate, irreverent, bittersweet laughter.

I looked around. Vittorio sat at one end of the lavishly appointed table, Alan at the other end, near the kitchen, where he could supervise the comings and goings of the wait staff. I was on Vittorio's left. Across from me sat Jackie Hamilton, Phil, and Craig. To my left was an empty place setting; the table had been set for nine although there were only eight of us. Lauren Sabot was seated on the other side of the empty chair, with Case Hamilton between her and Alan.

Alan had made arrangements with a caterer for a meal of poached salmon with green sauce, rice pilaf, and a vegetable melange. Alan hadn't exactly said so, but I'd caught his look as he called instructions into the kitchen to the caterers before we sat down: *better a meal prepared by outsiders.* A sommelier poured freely, but discreetly controlled the wine in the butler's pantry. The food was served by a waiter from platters that returned to the kitchen. Amazing, I thought. Who is the empty place for? Gary? Or Hercule Poirot?

"I don't think I've ever heard Ramsey's story," Craig said. "At least not in its entirety." What he meant was, I can't bear to talk about Gary anymore, keep talking about Mark instead.

I explained that Mark had been orphaned at age fourteen when his father died in the plane wreck. Because he had no other living relatives, Mark was packed off to boarding school by the executor of his father's estate—Hamilton's friend Batty Coleman. There Mark made friends with another boy, also fourteen, also orphaned; the other boy, Scott Something, had lost his parents in a fire when he was nine. The two became inseparable, until college, when Ramsey went off to Yale: first to college, then med school. The other boy went to professional school of some kind. I forgot where.

"Saint John's University," Case said. "Fine pharmacy school."

In any case, the two young men kept in touch, visiting each other and spending vacations together.

Then, on the night of Ramsey's med school graduation, Mark and Scott left New Haven to drive to Greenwich, Connecticut. Ten minutes from Ramsey's house there, they exited the Merritt Parkway, only to meet an oncoming car speeding the wrong way up the ramp. Ramsey swerved and lost control. The car went off the ramp and down an incline, rolling several times before smashing into a tree.

Ramsey survived with a concussion, mangled face, and a leg fractured in two places.

Scott died at the scene.

"Horrifying accident," Case said. "I spoke to Batty Coleman at the time and he said he hardly recognized Mark in the hospital, his face was so terribly broken and swollen. Mark doesn't look completely himself even today, after all his surgeries. And he still has several to go, he says."

The company fell into a ruminative silence. The loss of Mark's friend Scott had taken us right back where we'd started: the loss of Gary. Any moment now there would be keening.

Craig said with forced brightness, "I want to hear about the torrid affair with Wonder Bitch."

So I took the story up again. After postponing his internship for a year, Ramsey arrived at University Hospital on July first, only to be swept immediately into his torrid affair with Di Clausson.

"And there was certainly a big to-do over that, let me tell you," Jackie said. "Poor Dr. Clausson was persona non grata. When a male doctor has an affair with an intern fifteen years younger, no one bats an eye. But let a woman try it—"

"But my dear, it was so-o *flagrante*." This from Case.

"And she was married," Phil pointed out. "And that martial-arts-enthusiast husband of hers challenged Ramsey to a duel—"

"—which Ramsey of course declined," I picked up again, "because he didn't want to ruin all that plastic surgery."

Case said, "Dr. Hans-Albrecht Clausson, the husband—an eminent immunologist and AIDS researcher, by the way—did get his revenge. He slapped Diana with a lawsuit naming Ramsey as co-respondent in the divorce."

"The poor boy was so unnerved he spent all of Labor Day weekend with us out on the Island," Jackie laughed. "We could barely coax him out of the house!"

The collective mood began to ascend; we were like tourists driving through the Alps. Up, then down, then up again. Still winding along our detour via Mark Ramsey Road.

Case reached for his wineglass. "Mark ended it with Diana after that, I think."

"I wonder." Lauren speaking now. "I bet that relationship just went underground. The other night I was there when Mark called his answering machine to check his messages. Let's just say, when he got off the phone he was . . . passionately engaged," she confided with an exaggerated conspiratorial air.

"This was when?" Craig asked.

"Friday night." Turning to Case and Jackie, Lauren went on, "You two were in the city, and Mark was at your place out on the Island. I guess it was about midnight, and I let myself into the house to raid your liquor cabinet. Mark was in the study, listening to his messages on the phone."

Lauren paused dramatically. All of us were practically horizontal, so eager were we to hear the juicy gossip. She waited just long enough to savor having us. Then, portentously, "He wouldn't tell me a thing about it."

Guffaws, groans, and boos. *"You,"* bellowed Craig, "are a *tease!"*

"I apologized for walking in on him," Lauren went on, when the laughter had died down. "He was clearly very upset, so I tried to cajole him a little. I said, 'I thought you said last week that Diana's fireworks were too much for you.' And he said, 'Oh, you know how hard it is to resist something that's too much for you.' End of conversation."

Craig commented drolly, "What an anticlimax. Remind me not to listen to any more of *your* stories. Ev, we interrupted you."

"I remember once Ramsey was talking to Gary about"—I raised my hand to Lauren—"his tempestuous affair with Diana, and he says, 'Gary, does this kind of thing happen to everyone else, or is it just me? Is there something wrong with my horoscope? Did someone hex me when I was born? Is it because I'm *rich?'*

"So Gary says, 'I think there's an explanation here for all your *tsuris.* It's inherited. You have melodrama in your genes. Have you ever noticed, in a certain light and at just the right angle, how much you look like John-John Kennedy? What do you know about your mother's sex life before you were born?' "

We laughed ourselves silly. But soon we reached the snow-capped peaks of our hysteria. From there the road wound down again.

"You know," Case said sadly, "it was Gary who first suggested to me that Mark Ramsey could use a family for the holidays. Poor boy didn't have a soul in the world, never did get on really with Batty, don't blame him; Batty can be a dull old stick in the mud. And since Vittorio and I had been at Yale with Dan Ramsey, Mark's father, and Geoff"—the Hamiltons' oldest son—"had been at boarding school with Mark, although several years behind—"

"It seemed like a good fit," Jackie said. "We had Mark out several times over the summer, and now he comes almost every weekend."

"Sometimes when we're not even there." Case smiled. "*Mi casa es su casa.*"

Jackie laid her hand affectionately on her husband's wrist. "And you all know, of course, that we encouraged him to buy the apartment in our building here."

Everyone seemed to sigh at the same time. We descended into the valley. Sadness about Mark led back to sadness about Gary again. Try as we might to distract ourselves with gossip, the night still belonged to Gary. Tears threatened all of us like an approaching thunder shower. I snuck a look at my watch. It was after ten.

"You might benefit by having Mark so close by," Jackie told Vittorio. "Your very own on-site emergency room physician."

Vittorio smiled. "Well, at the moment I have another on-site emergency room physician. May I ask you, Ev, to do the honors after dinner?" He gestured toward his good arm, in which his docs had installed a PICC-line. This small-gage, flexible tube would allow Vittorio to undergo home infusion therapy. All he had to do was hook himself up to an IV and infuse a bag of antibiotics; when he was finished, he was free to unhook and go about his business until the next dose the following day.

"I'd be happy to talk you through it," I said. Suddenly feeling the exhaustion of the day, I jumped at the easy exit line. "You hook yourself up, flush with saline, flush with heparin, then administer the drug." I pushed my chair back from the table.

Vittorio motioned me to remain seated. "In a moment, Ev. One final tribute." He nodded to Alan, who rang the small bell next to his plate. The help came out of the kitchen and cleared the table. Then they set out glasses for dessert wine.

While the sommelier uncorked a bottle of Sauternes and poured for everyone, Jackie said, "Ev, why not show Case how to do it? Then if you or Mark aren't available, Case can help Vic."

"It's really simple," I replied. "Vic can do it himself without help. But if Case wants to buff up, by all means."

Vittorio rose, glass in hand. "I would like to propose a toast for our dear departed friend, who is very much with us this evening in spirit if not in fact." He inclined his head slightly toward the empty place setting. "Gary, you were a gifted clinical nurse and administrator. You set standards in patient care that inspired those working under you, with you, and even above you. You took fledgling medical students and interns under your wing, easing their transition from terrified baby doctors to full-fledged physicians. You taught them to fly. Some, you taught to soar. And you did all this with dedication, patience, perseverance, and humor. You organized the nurses to raise their voices in unison when you saw patient care compromised, and to raise those voices high enough to reach even the most exalted of administrators. I promise you that your voice will not have fallen on deaf ears." Vittorio raised his glass. "Gary, to you."

The sentiment echoed up and down the table. "To Gary."

We drank. Vittorio sat. I felt tears coming. At the other end of the table, Alan strangled a sob in his throat.

"Oh, Alan," Lauren said. She reached past Case to take Alan's hand. "Remember how funny he was? How about Gary's imitation of Case and Vittorio?"

Alan smiled through his tears, but shook his head.

"Darling, bring him back for us, just for a moment," Vittorio said softly.

"Okay," Alan said. He wiped his cheeks with his napkin, folded his hands in his lap, closed his eyes, drew a deep breath, and let it out slowly. Then, opening his eyes and turning toward me, he metamorphosed into Gary with an accuracy and suddenness that caught in my throat. He set his shoulders just so. Tilted his head just so. Suppressed a smile just so. There before us was Gary in the flesh, miming Case Hamilton's most earnest, thoughtful expression, channeling through Alan. " 'When I was at Lakeville I dated a girl, Muffy Something,' " Alan as Gary intoned with Case's voice, " 'who was a Forbes. She later married a Saltonstall, and her brother-in-law, Bink— or was it Jock?—who was a Cadwallader, skippered Win Huxley Bagley's boat in the Bermuda Race in sixty-three, and after he divorced his first wife Bootsie—who was, by the way, also a Forbes—he married Katherine Dunwhistle Ingersoll, and they had a daughter Caroline. Now Caroline married into the Bloggs family, and her husband Kyle Adams Wickersham Bloggs went to medical school with you, Ev. Small world!' "

Then Alan turned to his left and addressed the wall. "Wasn't she the cousin of Buffy Bowne Livingston, who went on to become la Comptesse de Manuelos y Gonzalez?" Alan asked in Gary's perfect rendition of Vittorio's Locust-Valley Lockjaw.

Alan turned to the right; now he was Case. "No, that was Biffy Bowne Auchincloss. Buffy Bowne Livingston married the seventh Argyle of Bradford."

He turned to the left; Vittorio again. "I thought that was Muffy Auchincloss who married the Argyle."

To the right; Case. "No, Vic, *Biffy Bowne Auchincloss*. You were her date at the Infirmary Ball."

To the left. "No, Case, *you* were her date at the Infirmary Ball. I took her to one of those Junior Assemblies."

Right turn; Case again. "Oh. I thought that was Missy Auchincloss. Are you sure?"

As I watched Alan's performance, chills went up and down my spine. Alan and Gary had blended into one person before my eyes. I glanced at Vittorio. He was laughing, but I could see something else entirely was going on inside him.

Oh, my God, I thought.

Alan was raising his glass. "To Gary." I drained mine. Across the table, I saw that Craig looked shaken and that he too drained his glass.

Was it possible?

twenty-one

I made my way unsteadily to Alan's and Vittorio's bedroom and the master bath, wondering.

I wondered how much I had to drink. Hard to tell with the sommelier constantly topping off my glass.

I wondered why the elaborate arrangements with the food and wine so that no one could tamper with it, if—as Alan said—I had talked Vittorio out of thinking that Case had tried to poison them. Did Vic suspect Lauren or Jackie? Or Craig, or me, or Phil? What was Vic thinking? That he'd get us all drunk and watch us spin out of control, while he sat back and enjoyed the show? Whatever you say can and will be used against you in a court of law.

I wondered if Alan was secretly still in love with Gary.

I wondered if Vittorio had secretly suspected all along that Alan was still in love with Gary. *Darling, bring him back for us, just for a moment.* Let's see whether you're still in love with him.

No, that didn't make sense. If Alan were still in love with Gary . . .

I turned on the light in Alan's and Vittorio's bedroom. Like Vittorio's study, and unlike the formal living and dining rooms, the bedroom was comfortable and understated. The rugs on the floor were well-worn. A king-sized imitation Louis-Philippe bed, blond cherry and black lacquer, dominated the room, covered with a pale-green cotton comforter and a variety of pillows tossed helter-skelter. One, a small needle-point, said, I MAY NOT BE PERFECT BUT I'M PERFECT FOR YOU. There were two matching dressers and two night tables with black lacquered tops and lion-head brass fixtures. Alan's night table, on the left of the bed, was piled high with paperback mysteries and well-worn back issues of *Gourmet* magazine. Vittorio, I saw, was reading a biography of Disraeli, Thomas Mann's *Der Tod in Venedig, Anna Karenina,* a King James Bible and, of all things, *The Merck Manual.* Each man had a slipper chair. Alan's was piled high with discarded clothing; on Vittorio's was a folded pair of trousers and a belt.

I turned on the light in the bathroom, stepped in, and closed the door.

Vittorio, like many men in his "set" as he called it, reserved his most personal photographs for the bathroom. The bottom half of the walls were tiled, but above the tiles hung chock-a-block, frame-to-frame, dozens of family snapshots. Vittorio, aged three, in a blazer and short pants, with his father down on one knee next to him. Vittorio and Case on their first day of school, Vittorio scowling directly at the camera lens, defying the indignity of abandonment, Case bravely holding back tears. Vittorio and Case at boarding school in their hockey uniforms. Vittorio's father and Case's father at the same boarding school a generation earlier in *their* hockey uniforms. Vittorio at Harvard Business School. Case at Yale Law. Pat von Laue and Jackie Hamilton, their arms entwined, the Eiffel tower behind them. Alan and Jackie Hamilton, their arms entwined, standing on the exact same spot twenty years later—someone's idea of a joke?

I found the picture I was looking for under a sconce next to the mirror.

Gary and Alan on the steps to Montmartre.

There was a light tap on the door and Craig's voice. "Ev?"

I opened the door.

"Oh, man, is this ghoulish or what?" he groaned, sliding past me and closing the door behind him. "It's like a bad Agatha Christie and a seance rolled into one. I keep waiting for someone from my office to walk in the front door to tape the confession, or two uniforms to make the arrest. Is Vic going to ply us with liquor until someone breaks down and yells, 'Yes—I admit it—I poisoned him!'? You notice *he's* not drinking anything, except a little sip when there's a toast."

"He's on IV antibiotics," I said. "He shouldn't even be drinking that."

Craig's eye fell on the picture of Alan and Gary in Montmartre. "You ever wonder about this?" he asked. He looked around for the picture of Alan and Jackie in front of the Eiffel Tower. "Look, Alan's wearing exactly the same thing in both these pictures."

"I know."

"That was a kind of honeymoon for Alan and Vittorio. Trip to Paris to mark the end of the year-long mourning period Vittorio observed for Pat. Vic was so correct about all that—not once during the entire year did he take Alan to any kind of public event—out of respect for his dead wife. Then off they go to Paris—"

"I don't know if honeymoon is the right word, Craig. Case and Jackie went on that trip, too."

"Case and Jackie is one thing. Gary Seligman's another. What's he doing in Paris while Alan's there with Vittorio? That's like you going to Paris with Phil and taking along Richard!" Richard was the guy I'd dated before and during medical school.

Since childhood, Craig and I had had a pattern of arguing. No matter what one said, out of sheer contentiousness the other jumped right in as Devil's Advocate. I could get up in the morning and say that it was raining and he would say, "No, it's sunny," and the two of us would go at each other for the rest of the day with indignation, passion, wounded feelings, and a tenaciousness that would make even God blink—and all the while enough rain pouring down outside to render the argument moot.

After years of shouting at each other, we had finally gained the insight that more often than not, Craig picked a fight with me because he really hoped I would talk him out of whatever it was—whereas when I picked a fight with Craig, I needed or at least wanted to win.

I took a deep breath. Let me win this one, I prayed. "Craig, Gary went to France twice a year if he could manage it. That was his big hobby in life: France, the French language, French films, French cooking. But let's say he snuck over to Paris while Alan was there with Vic. And let's say Alan snuck away to meet him. Would Alan then hang the picture in his and Vittorio's bathroom where Vittorio has to look at it every morning while he shaves?"

"C'mon, Ev—if I wanted Vittorio to believe nothing was going on between me and Gary, I'd be completely blatant about seeing him—'Oh, by the way, Vic, Gary's coming for dinner.' 'Oh, I meant to tell you, Vic—Gary's going to be in Paris for a week at the International Convention of Emergency Room Nurses, right when we're going to be there with Case and Jackie!' I'd ask Vittorio to take the goddamn picture of me and Gary on the steps to Montmartre, and I damn well *would* hang it right under Vic's nose when he shaves."

I sank down on the edge of the bathtub. Craig leaned against the sink and folded his arms over his chest.

"Do you really think Alan's so duplicitous?" I asked, dreading the answer.

Craig sighed. "Listen, I'm in a messy divorce because my wife cheated on me. She's already pregnant with the other guy's kid. Or so she says—how she knows whose it is, is beyond me—I have half a mind to have the kid's DNA tested to make sure he's not mine. Mom cheated on Dad all those years. When you first started up with Phil, his girlfriend was in London. So yeah, I think people are duplicitous. Do *you* really think that Alan's in love with Vittorio?"

Craig and I had had this conversation before. I always stood up for Alan. Not tonight. *I left Gary not because I wasn't in love with him, but because he wouldn't support my career goals.* The career goals had become moot, apparently. But what happened to the love?

Silence for a while. Craig chewed his thoughts. I looked at a picture of the three of us at Craig's law school graduation. Craig was grinning ear to ear, waving his mortarboard.

Craig made a second foray: "Alan's Vittorio's fucking kept boy, Ev."

"We've had *this* conversation, too, Craig."

"It doesn't bother you? What kind of life is that? Alan used to be so ambitious. He was going to work for Bouley, or Vongerichten—instead, he's running to the dry cleaners with Romeo's pants. Talking on the phone with the decorator about drapes. Organizing dinner parties for ten with lobster bisque—"

"Alan likes running Vittorio's household," I said, but with less conviction than usual. "He likes organizing dinner parties for ten with lobster bisque."

Craig set his jaw. "Maybe Alan will like it even more, now that Gary's out of the way."

"What are you saying? That Vittorio wanted to poison Gary? Don't you think if Vittorio wanted to poison someone, he would choose a method that would guarantee success? Besides, if Vic did try to poison Gary, there would be no reason for him to take all these lugubrious precautions with dinner this evening."

"That's what he wants us to think," Craig shot back. "All Vic has to do is wait for us to incriminate ourselves for our petty little sins, and he gets all the information he needs to frame one of us. No matter if the evidence is inconclusive. Case and Jackie know all there is to know about poisonous mushrooms. Let's say they want to poison Alan because they're afraid Vic will write them out of his will, and they poison Gary by mistake. Same for Lauren. She's in Vic's will, too. So she poisons Gary by mistake while trying to poison Alan. Maybe we're meant to think that Alan poisoned Gary, because Gary was going to show Vittorio photos of himself and Alan in compromising positions if Alan didn't drop Vittorio." He paused, then grinned at me. "Let's see, maybe *you* poisoned Gary. Maybe I poisoned Gary and I'm going to poison Vittorio next because I can't stand the fact that my brother likes men, so I'll just bump off the ones he likes." Craig threw his hands up in the air. "Give me a minute and I'll come up with a motive for Phil."

"Take your time." I was getting mad, although at whom or about what I would be hard pressed to say. I got up and opened the door.

There stood Phil, about to knock. He looked at me and Craig. "A little family conclave in the bathroom?"

"Just trying to figure out which one of us Vittorio is trying to frame," I said.

"Ah," said Phil. "Probably you, Ev. But tricky devil that he is, he still wants you to flush his IV before you go."

"Oh, I think he's trying to frame *you*," said Craig. He

poked Phil in the chest. "*You* done it. You were trying to poison Ev, but you poisoned Gary by mistake."

"Oh, really," Phil said. He poked Craig back. "And what's my motive?"

"You want to run off with some babe who's a patient."

Phil blanched.

"Don't even joke about it," he said.

twenty-two

It was a typical bad Monday morning multiplied exponentially.

"Day one, hour one of the Gary J. Seligman, R.N., Memorial Nurses' Strike," Mark Ramsey pronounced, surveying the scene. Residents and attendings milled around, looking worried; Rent-a-Nurses, hired for the duration, moved to and fro, trying to look purposeful. "Oh-seven-thirty hours, as Gary himself would say if he were here. Raise your hand if you have a fucking clue what the nurses *really* do." He flipped his hand to shoulder height and launched into a not-too-bad Stan Laurel imitation. "I know, Ollie! They clean up the patients so we don't have to wade through all that blood and piss and vomit and guacamole!"

I tried to get Ramsey's attention to signal him to stop.

Too late. Dr. Michael Wells, one of the ER's attending physicians, looked up briefly from a pile of charts he was sorting through. "I'll tell you what the nurses *should* do," he muttered with a scowl, "they should tape the intern's mouth shut and lock him in the meds closet. Dr. Sutcliffe, I'm going to put you in charge of chart Q-and-A. If a med student says 'boo,' I want the intern signing off on him and the resident signing off on the intern." Turning his back to Ramsey, Wells inclined his head slightly in Mark's direction and raised his eyebrows to make sure I took his meaning.

"Aye-aye, sir," I said.

Wells watched Ramsey trundle off to see a patient who was complaining of chest pain in exam room B. "Is he deranged?"

"I think all that nonsense is how he blows off anxiety," I said.

"Well, get him to stop. How can he carry on like that after that botched lavage? Were you in the room with him at the time, Doctor?" Wells asked, lowering his chin to peer at me over his reading glasses.

My breakfast began to curdle in my stomach. "When Gary aspirated? Yes."

"I heard it was Ramsey and that med student, Nicholson. That Ramsey—"

"No, Dr. Wells. Ramsey was assisting me."

"Really?" Wells looked surprised. "I thought perhaps it was . . . Dr. Ramsey's fault, but your responsibility."

I damped down my irritation and shook my head. "Ramsey wanted to sedate, but I wouldn't listen to him. It was my fault *and* my responsibility."

"Who was the attending?"

"Dr. Hollister. He was busy. A police van responding to the fracas in the subway hit a bus and rolled."

"You actually weren't on duty."

I shook my head. No, I wanted to say, and neither were you—so why are you grilling me? "Dr. Kubota was the Three on duty by then."

"But you felt you had to treat Gary personally because he was poisoned in your apartment?"

"No, I treated him personally because, ah, the only other doc available was an intern."

I watched Wells process this. I could see by his expression that he was filing what I told him under the heading *Official Party Line Version of What Happened*—while continuing to fish for clues to what *really* happened.

"You're not covering up for Dr. Ramsey?" Wells asked. "He didn't kill Gary out of gross negligence of any kind?"

"No. What gross negligence?"

"Restraint of the patient in the supine position, failure to sedate . . ."

"Gary was sitting up, Dr. Wells. He was not supine. And I told you, the failure to sedate is on *my* head. That was *my* decision, not Ramsey's. Is there something going on here that I don't know about?"

"Yes, there's something going on, Doctor," Wells snapped. "A member of our nursing staff is dead! And just our luck, a nurses' union rep."

I steeled myself. It was not a good idea to cross Michael Wells. But he was a very direct man and if you were just as direct, sometimes you could get away with it. I took the chance. "Are Ramsey and I up for review by the Quality Assurance Committee?"

He assessed me. "Let me put it to you this way, Doctor. Is there any chance at all that you were too distraught to treat Gary, but you refused to admit that your emotions were clouding your judgment?"

"Looking back, maybe," I admitted honestly. "But at the time, no."

"Did you at all consider asking a less emotionally involved individual to take over the lavage?"

"Everyone in the ER was emotionally involved. Gary was one of our own."

"You considered yourself competent."

"Yes."

"Did you have any question about Dr. Ramsey's compe- tence to assist you? I must ask this question. After three months in the ER, Dr. Ramsey is still walking around talking to himself."

"That's true," I conceded, "But he's honest." *Honest* was the highest accolade a senior resident could give a junior. "You say to him, 'So, Dr. Ramsey, what did the urinalysis show?' and he says, 'I'm sorry, I forgot to send the urine. I'll do it right away.' He never bluffs. He doesn't say he's done a rectal when he hasn't. He doesn't make the same mistake twice, so he learns. Plus I see him in the physicians' library, spending every free moment reading up. And he has a very good medi- cal acumen. So I give him the benefit of the doubt."

"If you would like to continue doing that, Doctor," Wells said very slowly and coldly, "you go right ahead. But I would advise you to rethink your priorities."

I realized immediately that I'd taken the wrong road with Wells. But before I could think of something to say to rectify the situation, a voice said sharply behind me, "Michael, are you terrorizing the residents again?"

I turned. There stood Diana Clausson, smiling pleasantly.

"Dr. Wonder Bitch," Wells said, bowing slightly. "How nice to see you. Of course I'm terrorizing the residents."

"Why do you do that?" she asked.

Wells did not want to be bested in front of me. He took his glasses off his nose and tucked them into his shirt pocket before answering. "All physicians should consider the conse- quences of their actions, and I was just suggesting to Dr. Sut- cliffe here—"

"That she shouldn't stand up for an honest intern?" Clausson finished.

Wells fumbled in his pocket and put his glasses back on his nose. "May I ask why you're interfering, Dr. Clausson?"

"All physicians should consider the consequences of their actions, Dr. Wells. An excellent maxim. You said so yourself."

A brief staring contest ensued. For the home team, Diana Clausson, five-feet-ten, one-hundred-and-thirty pounds soaking wet (we'd gone swimming together once in the university pool, and she'd weighed herself in the locker room), blue eyes sparking with intelligence, dark hair pulled back in a jaunty ponytail. Her opponent, Dr. Michael Wells, also five-feet-ten, probably two-hundred pounds (I was guessing), brown eyes dull with malice, dark hair uncombed and in need of a wash.

Guess who looked away first, and stomped off.

"Brava," I said when Wells had gone. "What have you got on *him?*"

Clausson grinned. "I have something on everyone."

"So I noticed. Herrera for Christmas. Gary Seligman beat you at your own game?"

She was good; her grin never wavered. "No one beats me at my own game," she said silkily. Holding my gaze just long enough to let me know I hadn't won, she rifled through the chart rack, found the chart she was looking for, and sashayed off.

"I want to know more about Christmas!" I called after her.

"December twenty-fifth, celebrated by Christians worldwide," she called over her shoulder. "The birth of our Lord Jesus."

She sashayed around the corner, and was gone.

Dr. Christopher Cabot, director of the emergency department, had appointed himself unofficial charge nurse for the next twenty-four hours. "Who's this?" he asked, pointing at a kid parked on a stretcher under the nurses' blackboard.

"This weekend's frat-house party boy, in for a little electrolyte tune-up," I said, inhaling the pungent fumes of eau de vomit, alcohol, and urine as I leaned over him to write on the board.

"Came in when?"

"He's been here since about two A.M., soaking up the healing rays of the nurses' blackboard."

"Ah," said Cabot. "Let's see if he can soak up healing rays in Holding, shall we?" He went off with the snoring patient.

"Ev?"

"Just a sec." I finished making my notation on the board and put the marker back in the pocket of my white coat. "Yeah?"

Mark Ramsey stood at my elbow, peering into a patient's chart and frowning.

"What's up?" I asked.

"You know Thomas Kennaugh?"

"Remind me."

"Came in Saturday A.M., complaining of weakness, nausea, and lightheadedness? We thought he got some bad batch? Naloxone and release?"

Oh, right. Mark's yuppie heroin abuser. "Why, is he back?"

"Says he doesn't want to consult his private physician."

"Of course not—he doesn't want his private physician to know he shoots up. He's a respectable businessman. Why's he here now?"

"Complains of trouble swallowing, slurred speech, blurred vision, and extremity weakness. A lot of trouble breathing—chest excursion and air movement not quite cricket. Trouble sitting up by himself. Denies pain or other symptoms."

I sighed. "I live for the day they publish the *Physician's Desk Reference to Coke, Crack, and Heroin*. God only knows what the hell they put in that shit. Okay, I'll look in."

Thomas Kennaugh lay back against his cranked-up stretcher. A modestly handsome guy in his mid-thirties with blue eyes and dun-colored hair, he wore a hospital gown and an oxygen nasal canula. Kennaugh turned his head lethargically as I entered the examining room.

I saw his distress immediately: he looked frightened. "Mr. Kennaugh, I'm sorry to see you again. Still having problems?" Ramsey had scrawled his vitals on the bed sheet next to his head, and I scanned them: blood pressure 150 over 80 (a little high); heart rate 120 (markedly rapid for a man at rest); respirations 28 (rapid); and temperature 100° (slight fever).

"Trouble breathing," Kennaugh said. He worked to form the words, like a drunk trying to make himself understood.

"Yes, I see that."

"Can't eat. Trouble seeing."

"Well, let's have a look at you." I took my stethoscope off my neck and put the earpieces in my ears. "Sit up for me now?" I had to help lift him into a sitting position. "Deep breath. Another. Once more." His lungs were clear, and, as Ramsey had said, did not seem to be moving much air.

I checked his pupils with my penlight. "A little sluggish," I pointed out to Ramsey. I showed Kennaugh two fingers. "How many fingers am I holding up?"

He seemed to have trouble focusing. "Two?"

"Are you guessing?"

"No, see two."

"You're having trouble seeing?"

"Yeah."

"How so?"

"Blurry."

"Are you having double vision?"

"No, blurry."

I finished a rudimentary neurological exam. He had trouble following my finger with his eyes without moving his head. When I asked him to bare his teeth he could only manage a weak grin, and his gag reflex was absent.

205

"Mr. Kennaugh," I said, "when was the last time you used again?"

Speaking with difficulty, Kennaugh swore he used "only recreationally," that the last time he shot up had been almost two weeks ago, and before that more than a month.

"Two weeks ago? Are you sure? I had the impression Saturday that it was much more recently." I glanced at Ramsey. He flushed. "You and Dr. Ramsey talked about the Mott Haven bad batch."

"Two weeks ago," he insisted.

That changed the clinical picture a great deal.

I asked him to show me the injection site, and he showed me a spot on his inner thigh. The needle mark was no longer visible. He had no injection wheals, track marks, or skin abscesses anywhere on his body. He claimed to enjoy good health except for his current problems, and he did appear robust. So I believed him.

"Are you still feeling nauseous?" I asked.

"Little, yeah," Kennaugh said.

"Vomiting?"

"No."

"Any cramps, diarrhea?"

"No."

I remembered from my conversation with Ramsey on Saturday that Kennaugh and his brother owned a securities trading firm and worked together at the World Trade Center. They were both unmarried, shared an apartment, and subsisted almost entirely on fast food. During the previous week, they had eaten all their meals together.

"Your brother's not sick too, is he?"

"No."

"And you've only eaten in restaurants—nothing at home?"

"Only restaurants."

"You haven't eaten any canned goods? No tomato juice, canned peaches Aunt Millie put up, anything like that?"

"No."

"Shellfish? Baked clams, raw bar?"

"Allergic."

"Allergic to shellfish?"

"Yeah."

"Okay. Do you suffer from migraine headaches, Mr. Kennaugh?"

"No."

I went back to the heroin use. "All right. I'll be frank," I said as kindly as possible. "I don't want to alarm you, and I'm sorry to have to tell you this. But with someone who uses drugs intravenously, I always have to consider AIDS."

Fear flickered in his eyes. "Never share," he said with as much vehemence as he could muster.

"Not even the first time someone showed you how to do it?" I asked gently.

His expression told me I was right. "Have you been tested for the AIDS virus before?"

He closed his eyes and shook his head.

"I'm afraid I need to ask for your permission to test you for AIDS," I said.

Afterward, Mark and I conferred in the corridor.

"If he hasn't shot up in two weeks, it's not bad batch," Mark said heatedly. "I know I went over with him when he last shot up—it would really be nice sometimes if the patient would *help*."

"Some patients are poor historians," I said. "He's clearly having some kind of respiratory difficulty—let's get him on a mask. You send blood for gases?"

"Yes."

"Let me know as soon as the results come back. He might need intubation."

"I will," said Ramsey. He was still irritated that the patient had made him look bad in front of me. "So you think it's an HIV seroconversion illness?"

I thought a minute. Seroconversion is when a person, previously negative for HIV infection on blood tests, "converts" to positive and suffers his or her first AIDS-related illness. HIV has been known to hide in the body for months, even years, only to suddenly show up on blood tests like the Loch Ness monster surfacing. "I don't know what it is. Seroconversion can cause anything from soup to nuts, so that needs to be ruled out. He hasn't eaten anything home canned and he says he doesn't have double vision. . . . His sensorium is clear, but there's obviously some kind of cranial nerve involvement. His motor function is really weak proximally. If it's not a seroconversion illness, my guess would be a lesion at the base of the brain. But that's just a guess. He really needs to be worked up. Let's think about tapping him. Test for HIV, order an MRI, get a neuro consult, and admit. They can rule out stuff like Guillain-Barré upstairs on the floor. Meantime, try to convince him to notify his personal physician. He'll need the advocacy when he goes upstairs. And move him out where we can see him, in case he crumps."

He nodded dejectedly and went off.

I sighed. Mark really should have pressed Thomas Kennaugh about his most recent heroin use when Kennaugh first came in on Saturday. Here we had been running on all wrong assumptions because we took it for granted that the bad batch heroin was causing the patient's problems. For the umpteenth time I asked myself the same question I always asked when Ramsey dropped the ball: how did he ever get through Yale? He was not stupid. He never made the same mistake twice.

But a lot of the time he seemed to know only about as much medicine as a third-year med student might know.

And something about Kennaugh's clinical picture was nagging me, but I couldn't put my finger on what.

"Dr. Sutcliffe?"

"Yes, Julio."

"Dr. Carchiollo for you."

"Thanks." I went to the phone and picked up.

"Detective Ost is here," Phil announced. "He's questioned Elise Vanderlaende. Can you come up to my office?"

"Phil, do you know what it's like down here?" I asked. "Chris Cabot is ferrying patients."

"It won't take more than ten minutes."

So I left matters in Mark Ramsey's hands.

Kennaugh crumped a few minutes later, while I was gone. He stopped breathing altogether. Luckily, Respiratory was just arriving to intubate him. He was admitted to the Cardiac Care Unit, because the ICU was full up.

Because I was off the floor, Cabot made the decision to admit.

Because of the bedlam in the ER, Mark forgot to tell me.

And because of my own preoccupations, I forgot to ask.

When I arrived at Phil's office, Detective Ost was standing in the hall with his hands in his pockets.

"Doc," he greeted me.

"Hey, Ozzie." I touched his elbow.

He smiled stiffly. "You get your apartment back in order?"

"My brother Alan offered to take care of it, God bless him. He and his boyfriend have on call a regular army of all sorts of household help. Alan and Vic do a lot of entertaining."

"How the other half lives, huh?"

"Really. Your people turn up anything?"

"Not yet. But don't expect much. You find anything else missing?"

I shook my head. "Just the computer, and my back-up discs."

There was an awkward pause. I had the peculiar sense that Ost was angry on my behalf; he had that holy-hound-of-heaven air about him.

"Where's Phil?" I asked.

"He'll be with us in a minute. Let me ask you something: Gary Seligman told you he went to his high school reunion?"

"Yeah. Why?"

"I called the school. They don't do reunions. They do Homecoming—on Thanksgiving, not Columbus Day weekend. Why do you think Seligman would tell you he was going to his high school reunion when he wasn't?"

"I don't know," I said, frowning. "Are you sure? He said he left the reunion early because they were getting out the baby pictures. Why would he make up something like that?"

"That's what I'm asking you, Doc."

But before I could answer, Phil was at my side.

"I asked Detective Ost to go over this again with you present," Phil said. He, too, seemed angry.

What the hell is going on here? I wondered.

We all went into Phil's tiny office. He closed the door.

For a moment no one spoke. I looked at Ost. He had switched gears completely, and he gazed at Phil with obvious suspicion and a small, disdainful smile. Phil met his eyes with defiance.

"I'm getting a very bad feeling about this," I said.

Without a word Phil went behind his desk. He gestured toward the two visitor chairs in front of the desk. We all sat.

"If I didn't know the two of you, I'm damned if I'd know what's what," Ost said, managing to imply on the contrary that he knew exactly. "As I was just saying to Dr. Carchiollo here, 'If you're having an affair with this Elise Vanderlaende, now is the time to tell me. Because I have to tell you, talking to her, that's what I think. That you're sleeping with her.' "

The bad feeling I was having turned into a kick in the solar plexus.

"I'm not having an affair with her, Ev," Phil said. He struggled to control his anger. "You know I haven't laid eyes on her since you and I saw her together six weeks ago, going across campus. Labor Day weekend."

"Doc, let me lay it out for you," Ost countered, turning to me. "I go visit her. Apartment over on Claremont Avenue. Identify myself, show my shield, I need to talk to her about an ongoing investigation. She invites me in. I walk into the living room, and she's got pictures of Dr. Carchiollo. Not formal pictures, like she might be able to cut out of the hospital newsletter. Actual photographs. Candid shots.

"Now Dr. Carchiollo warned me about her, that's she's in love with him and she believes he's in love with her back, but there's nothing actually going on. So right away I'm thinking, yeah? So where did she get these pictures?

"I tell Vanderlaende there's been a poisoning at Dr. Sutcliffe's apartment, and that I'm interviewing Dr. Sutcliffe's and Dr. Carchiollo's friends and patients to see if anyone can tell me anything. Right away she says, 'Who gave you my name? Dr. Sutcliffe or Dr. Carchiollo?' " Ost lifted his eyebrows at me for emphasis. "This clues me in, I'm not dealing with a dummy here. I say, 'Dr. Carchiollo.'

"I'm expecting her to come right out and brag she's sleeping with him—that is, if she's as crazy as Carchiollo says. Or I'm expecting her to realize the jig is up, I'm calling her on it, and she'll have to admit there's no affair, it's all in her head. Meanwhile I'm looking at her. She's a very beautiful girl. Long neck like a dancer, very graceful. To be honest, if Dr. Carchiollo here hadn't told me she's nuttier than a fruitcake, I'd think of coming on to her myself even, though she's not much older than my daughter. But I try not to let myself get distracted.

"She says, 'And what did Dr. Carchiollo tell you our relationship is?'

"I say, 'I'd prefer if *you* tell me what your relationship is, Ms. Vanderlaende.'

"She says, 'I am willing to do my civic duty and help you

any way I can. But my relationship with Dr. Carchiollo is our private business, and I'm not going to discuss that with you.'

"I say, 'Forgive me, but I believe it's your civic duty to tell me. Because someone has tried to poison Dr. Sutcliffe. You know about poisonous mushrooms from your work in the Botany Field Office, so you have the means. And if you're in love with Dr. Carchiollo, you have a motive. That's enough for me to take you down to the station house and question you there. But I'd rather not do that, unless you force my hand.'

"This is one smooth operator. She doesn't even blink. She says, 'Who says I'm in love with Dr. Carchiollo?'

"I look pointedly at the photographs.

"She says, 'I admire Dr. Carchiollo a great deal. That does not mean I'm in love with him. It's true that I know a little about mushrooms—not much, but a little. I've seen Dr. Held's slide presentation a couple of times, the one that he gives for the Morningside Mycological Society. But I saw Dr. Sutcliffe on the street yesterday. So she hasn't been poisoned at all. Maybe you can tell me a little more about who did get poisoned, Detective. So I can help you.' "

Here Ost paused to laugh and shake his head in frank appreciation of Elise Vanderlaende's composure. "You know, one way you nail someone is to see if they know something you didn't tell them. Another is to get them to agree with the assumptions in the question. But she was having none of it. I couldn't get anywhere with her."

My heart was pounding. As levelly as possible, I asked, "Do you think she did it?"

"She's smart enough to have done it," Ost said. Assessing me, he backed out of his confrontational stance and shifted into neutral. "And she can't account for her whereabouts Saturday. She says she stayed home all day, paying bills and reading and relaxing. No phone calls."

"So can you arrest her?" I asked.

"We could take her in for questioning," Ost said. "But we'd have to let her go a few hours later."

"Why?"

"Right now there isn't any way to make the charges stick. It's all circumstantial. We'd have to connect her to the gift basket. She's not the type of person we're going to get to confess, I can tell you that right now. She knows enough to stick to the story she's already told us, and not elaborate." Ost leveled his gaze on Phil as if Phil could provide the missing pieces of evidence to connect Elise to the basket.

"I've told you all I know," Phil protested angrily.

Ost, without so much as rippling his impassive, neutral expression, somehow managed to let me know that he thought Phil was concealing something.

I said to Phil, "You did tell Ost that Vanderlaende used to stalk Held? And that Held says she's a mushroom expert?"

"Yes, I did," Phil said through gritted teeth.

"She's not as smart as you think," I said to Ost. "Or as consistent. Why didn't she make sure I was the one poisoned? And why would she risk poisoning Phil? Her motive is, she bumps me off, she gets him—right?"

Ost looked at me with interest.

"Get her to help you solve it," I suggested. "You say she said to you, 'Maybe you can tell me a little more about who got poisoned, so I can help you.' Well, take her up on it. Stroke her ego. Then provoke her with the inconsistancies. Say, 'Ms. Vanderlaende, you're too smart to have done it, but maybe you can help us out. You're someone who would do her homework first, get a more reliable murder weapon, deploy it in a more organized manner. Clearly this person who poisoned Gary Seligman doesn't have your talents.' Then just keep needling her until she says something incriminating."

Ost let a smile flicker briefly behind his eyes.

"Maybe sending us those mushrooms was a gesture," Phil

mused, off on a different tack altogether. "Like a suicide gesture. She must be furious with me for not returning her love. She protects me from her anger by putting it on you, Ev. But deep down she's probably not sure whom she wants to kill. Sending that basket lets us know what the stakes are. You let her have me, or else."

"So you think I should take her in," Ost said to me.

"She fucking tried to poison me and she killed one of my closest friends, Ozzie!" I exploded suddenly. "Yeah, I think you should take her in!"

Ost turned his gaze on Phil. "You, Doc?" he asked softly. "You think I should take her in?"

"Of course I think you should take her in," Phil cried. "What kind of nonsense is this? Since when do you ask civilians whether they think you should take someone down to the station house for questioning?"

"Just making sure," said Ost.

There had been something really peculiar about the way Ost was acting from the outset of this strange meeting. I finally put my finger on it.

Ost was playing Phil and me off against each other.

To see whether Phil maintained his composure while Ost summarized his interview with Vanderlaende—with me present.

To see whether I was buying Phil's denial, that he was not having an affair with Elise.

To see if I might like Ost to bring Vanderlaende in to the station house for questioning, but Phil might not.

Obviously, Ost didn't know whether or not to believe Phil. Jesus.

Ost pretended not to notice the lightbulbs going on in my head. He reached into the inside pocket of his suit jacket to pull out a photograph.

A photograph of Phil and Elise Vanderlaende. Together.

Sitting on a blanket on the beach. In bathing suits. Phil was smiling into the camera, and Elise was smiling at him.

I stared at Phil in disbelief.

"It's not what you think," Phil said.

twenty-four

"Ev, *look at the picture*," Phil sputtered. "That's *your* beach blanket, *your* beach bag, and *your* biography of Charles Dickens. That *you* were reading last month. If I were going to the beach with some hot young tootsie, would I take along your biography of Charles Dickens? Who besides you would read a biography of Charles Dickens on the beach in the first place?"

For a moment, I didn't know what to think. My heart went one way and my head went the other.

Earnestly imploring, Phil leaned across his desk toward me. "She had the photo doctored!" he cried. "She had your image taken out, and hers inserted!"

"They can do that now," Ost conceded, as if he now believed Phil, although somehow I didn't think he did. "Put you at the scene of the crime when you're nowhere near the place. Maybe not your local Fotomat. But those professional labs down on Twentieth Street—" He snapped his fingers. "Like that."

I looked at the photo. The young woman I had seen the

day before in the café had taken pains to make herself unnoticeable, even mousey—I had barely glanced at her when she sat down at the next table. But here Elise Vanderlaende shone forth in all her hot young tootsiedom. She seemed very long—long neck, long torso, long arms, her long legs tucked under her as she knelt next to Phil. Proud and defiant, she wore a vibrantly colored bikini so racy I would never dare try it on—not even in the privacy of a department store fitting room—let alone appear in public in it. Her blond hair lifted in the gentle sea-breeze and she raised a hand to brush it back from her face. And what a face. Here in profile, she showed a straight, aristocratic nose and jawline.

Sitting on my beach blanket, with my beach bag, my book, and my boyfriend.

On a blissfully sunny but not-too-hot day in mid-September, Phil and I had joined a Carchiollo family pilgrimage to Jones Beach, where Phil's brother Sal spent the morning gleefully photographing everyone. And I had spent most of August and September doggedly reading a biography of Dickens. Which I had taken with me to the beach that day.

I couldn't tell by looking at the photo itself that it had been doctored. Still, clearly my image had been removed, and Elise Vanderlaende's inserted.

What I was having trouble with was the complicated emotional picture I was getting from Phil. He was indignant and angry. But he was something else, too.

And Detective Ost's now studied neutrality seemed to underscore that something else.

"Where is the original of this photo, the one with me in it?" I asked Phil.

"I don't know. You didn't like the way you looked in any of the beach pictures, remember? I may even have thrown them out."

"Is she going through your garbage?" I asked incredulously.

"How could she? Someone would see her. Besides, the garbage cans are in the alley behind a locked gate."

"You said you've been misplacing things," I reminded him. "Did you maybe show the beach photos to Faith? Leave them with her, or on her desk? Where Elise might see them when she was cruising by to deliver you another letter?"

"I don't remember," Phil sighed. He ran a hand through his hair. "That would certainly explain how Elise might have got her hands on them. Faith is the psych department secretary," he explained to Ost. "She has two daughters the same age as my nieces, and we often admire each others' family photos."

Ost's steady gaze moved from me to Phil and back again. "Anything either of you haven't told me, now would be a good time. We're not talking Halloween prank here anymore. Gary Seligman died. Now we're talking Murder Two."

"Phil?" I prompted.

There was a long pause while Phil stood behind his desk, hands in his pockets, rocking back and forth on his heels.

"I do have something I want to get off my chest," he said finally. "My judgment has been clouded in this matter. The last several months I've been very depressed, and angry. Grappling with Elise has made me even more depressed and angry. But the main problem here is, I'm hurt and angry that you won't marry me, Ev. To me it's a matter of trust. You don't trust me enough to marry me. That's the best I can explain it, and I know it doesn't make any sense rationally, but it's because of my anger at you that I haven't confided in you about Elise. I think my unconscious motivation was, if you weren't going to trust me enough to marry me, Ev, then tit for tat, I wasn't going to trust you enough to confide in you about Elise."

For a moment, I was speechless. I knew that Phil was hurt and angry that I wasn't ready to get married. Mostly he expressed this anger with sarcastic little remarks, like the one he had made the day before: "It would be nice someday if we could celebrate our *wedding* anniversary." But I had never heard him speak about trust before, or equate my not marrying him with not trusting him.

"I'm sorry," I said, when I had found my voice. "I didn't realize you felt so betrayed and rejected."

"I needed something important to withhold from you," Phil said simply. "Meanwhile, I was just getting more and more depressed, because I was too angry to confide in you."

It made sense to me. "Oh, Honey," I said. "It's not you. It's me. I want to marry you eventually. I'm just . . . some kind of phobic. You say 'Marry me' and I panic."

I glanced at Detective Ost. In the several years I had known him, I had never once seen him lose control. But he stood there now with his mouth open. "Doc," he cried, "don't tell me you actually *believe* that!"

"Yeah," I said, looking at Phil, "I do."

Back in the emergency room, there was little time to reflect. So many of the worries I'd had about Phil over the last several months seemed to disappear and my heart sang for that. But Elise Vanderlaende was still at large. And I needed to track down Di Clausson. Keith Herrera had never returned my phone call; I wanted to talk to him as well. And I wanted to find out if there was a Dr. Moskowicz on the house staff or affiliated with the hospital. Sava Hadzic, my super, had told me and Vic that the person who delivered the basket had worn a white clinical coat with a hospital ID that said Moskowicz.

And, of course, I had patients to attend to.

"Thank *God* you're back," Ramsey cried. "Incoming. MVA—we don't know anything except she's burned and there were fatalities at the scene." He looked at his watch. "ETA two minutes."

"What are you talking about? We're closed to Level One trauma for the duration of the strike."

"Not right this minute. Saint Eustace closed a half hour ago after they took sixteen patients from a construction accident, and Mount Scopus has some kind of toxic spill situation."

I groaned and suited up—gown, X-ray apron, splash shield, gloves—and grabbed a Rent-a-Nurse, a light-skinned black woman with a Caribbean accent. "Nicholson!" I hollered.

By now the sirens were whooping down Amsterdam Avenue. We lined up by the ambulance bay door.

The beep-beep-beep now of the ambulance backing into the bay. We threw open the doors and ran out onto the dock. The paramedics were already rolling. "Unknown female, Asian, approximately mid-thirties, she was the driver of the vehicle, three fatalities," one of the medics announced as he propelled the gurney into the emergency room. "BP one-eighty over ninety—"

As he continued with the litany of vitals, I looked at the patient. Her face black with grime and smoke, she moaned and writhed despite being "collared and boarded"—strapped head-to-foot to a long wooden board to immobilize her in case she had spinal injuries. "I can't I can't I can't! Help me! I'm choking!" she cried.

With any patient you always want to know three things first: Is the airway patent? Is the patient breathing? Is the heart beating? Any patient who is talking presumably has a patent airway, is breathing, and has a heartbeat. Next you look for any possible threat to the breathing—broken ribs, that kind of thing—and any life-threatening bleed. You do all this while you try to get the patient talking to you. "Hey. Hey. I'm Dr. Sutcliffe. *Look at me!* Can you tell us your name?"

"I'm gonna die!"

"No you're not. This is the emergency room and we're going to help you. What's your name?"

"I can't! I can't!"

I turned to the medics. "We have any ID on her?"

"Purse burned up in the car. Cops trying to get some kind of identification."

"All right. Ma'am, can you lie still for me please? I need you to lie still." She was tall and slim, like me. My age, too. Hair cut short but full. Sometimes it's easier when you identify with the patient. Sometimes it's harder. Today I was feeling vulnerable and paranoid so it was harder.

Glancing at Ramsey, I could see he was completely over-identifying. The color had drained from his face. To snap him out of it, I started telling him what to do, the way I would with a medical student. "We've got to get her to lie still to protect the spine. This kind of delirium, she's probably got a head injury. Let's do X rays, ultrasound to see if she's got any bleeding in the belly, stabilize, and get her up to CT scan."

Nicholson calmly set about vitaling the patient and drawing blood.

"I'M GONNA DIE!" the patient shrieked.

"You're not going to die," I said firmly. "Look at me. Look at me." I got the patient to make eye contact finally. "You've been in a really bad accident, but you're at University Hospital now. We're going to find out what's the matter, and we'll take care of you."

"I can't, I can't," the patient whimpered.

Ramsey was finally snapping to. His stethoscope in his ears, he bent over and spoke quietly to the patient. Her eyes went to him.

"Look at my face," he said quietly. "See these scars? I was in an accident just like you were. Trust me. We'll get you through this. Deep breath for me now? Good. Again?"

A few moments later, he had calmed her.

* * *

"Mark, this is no time for you to have a personal crisis about whether or not you should be in an emergency-medicine residency," I said. "I understand that seeing that MVA could make you freeze up and flash back to your own accident. But you used that experience to connect with her. You were fabulous with her. You calmed her right down."

"I couldn't think."

"You did fine. And I'd be happy to take you out for a beer and help you talk it out—*after the nurses' strike.*"

Ramsey paced the ambulance bay dock. A dull roar of shouting from the nurses' picket line around the corner filled the air: "WHAT DO WE WANT? FAIR CONTRACT! WHEN DO WE WANT IT? NOWWWWW!"

"I just don't have the right pathology for this, Ev!" Ramsey said through clenched teeth. "I'm not an adrenaline junkie. I can't think on my feet. I can't handle bam-bam-bam one ambulance after another. I hear a siren and I start gagging like I'm going to throw up—is this the day they bring in somebody I'm going to kill because I can't chew gum and talk at the same time?"

"Ramsey!" I barked.

Tears of frustration filled his eyes. "No! You don't understand! Gary covered my ass. Kathy Haughey covers my ass. All the nurses cover my ass. *Nicholson* fucking covers my ass—and makes sure I know it, that smug little shit—you know how humiliating that is? I'm going to have a nervous breakdown in there! You think those Rent-a-Nurses are going to catch me if I fall off the trapeze? I don't think so."

"Awjesus." Now I was pacing. "Mark, we all get like this. My internship year, I used to lock myself in the bathroom and cry and throw water on my face, I was so scared. I lost ten pounds because I couldn't keep anything down except cottage cheese. But I drew on my inner reserves and toughed it out. And that's what you have to do."

He ran his fingers over a scar on his forehead, back and forth. His hands were shaking.

"I know you have inner reserves," I said. "You had to draw on something to keep going after that accident, when your friend Scott died. Now please. I'll back you up as best as I can. But get back in there. We need you."

From around the corner came singing: "A tisket, a tasket, without a nurse a casket!" Then more chanting: "HOSPITAL CUTS KILL! HOSPITAL CUTS KILL!"

"Oh, man," Ramsey said. "Gary must be pissed he's missing this strike." He wiped his eyes.

"Mark, why did you choose this residency?" I asked.

"I didn't choose it. It chose me." Realizing that strange declaration made no sense, he went on, "There was a saying at medical school, 'Everyone who goes into emergency medicine is either running toward something or running away from something.' It sounded like me. I didn't know whether I was coming or going, and I thought if I signed up for a residency in emergency medicine, I would find out."

"Have you?"

"Most days I seem to be running away."

"Well, just today, don't run away."

"Okay." He drew himself up, and marched back into the ER.

An hour later our MVA patient was stabilized, but we still didn't know her name.

"Upon arrival she was talking but not making much sense," I reported to Chris Cabot. "She then became stuporous, so we intubated her and sent her upstairs to CT scan. Ultrasound of the abdomen was negative. Second-degree burns both hands—medics say bystanders pulled her from the burning car, but she ran back to rescue her friends. Pretty heroic considering her right foot is probably fractured."

"Okay, ask Julio for a Jane Doe number." Cabot rubbed his chin thoughtfully. "See if you can get a chaplain or social worker on it to liaison with the cops. What's the story with Ramsey?"

"Nerves."

"Jane Doe has several lacerations on her on her thigh?"

I nodded.

"Let Ramsey repair them. That'll get him refocused."

I nodded. I didn't want to tell Cabot that Ramsey couldn't suture worth a damn, and that I would have to spend the whole time peering over his shoulder while he was repairing the wound.

"Who's this?" Cabot pointed at a stretcher parked in the bay opposite the nurses' station.

"Ah, university professor, the Reverend Dr. David Keller. Came in complaining he'd had an irregular heartbeat at home. We ruled out MI, but he's still scared. He's a patient of Diana Clausson's. We've called Clausson and she's coming down."

"Ah, the Goddess Diana, championess of the hunt." Cabot had had a classical education, and peppered his speech with references to Greek mythology. He clapped me on the shoulder. "Anything else I can do for you?"

"I think I'm okay," I said. "Thanks."

"I *know* you're okay, Doctor. You always are." His hand was still on my shoulder, gently steering me a few paces away from the bustle of the nurses' station. "I've read your report on Gary Seligman. Very clear and comprehensive, as always. I know what great chums the two of you were, and I don't want you second-guessing yourself. Any concerns that you might like to take up with me?" he asked quietly in my ear.

"Thank you, Dr. Cabot, that's very kind. Do you have any

concerns you'd like to take up with *me,* any questions *you* want to ask?"

"I believe everything is clear. Except, of course, the murky circumstances of how he came to eat those mushrooms."

Cabot knew about Elise Vanderlaende; that morning, Phil had filed a report of his own with the chief of Psychiatric Services, with a carbon copy to Cabot. What Cabot knew about Case Hamilton and his mushrooms I couldn't say.

"Any new thoughts there?" Cabot asked.

"We're still chasing down leads, as the cops say. Do we have a Dr. Moskowicz on the staff?"

He thought a moment. "I met a doctor of that name at a reception recently. Nice Israeli fellow, first name Ilan. Pathologist, I believe he said."

I took a stab in the dark. "How about a Dr. Christmas?"

"Luke Christmas? I know him well. But he's not affiliated here."

I felt a slight tingling.

"He's director of medicine at Mount Scopus," Cabot said.

twenty-five

I sprinted to Morning Report, replaying in my mind Gary's salvo to Di Clausson earlier in the week, the one Jazz Washington and I had overheard: *I think it's a fair trade, Doctor—don't you? Herrera for Christmas. Deal?*

And Di's answering volley: *Over my dead body. Or yours.*

It was like one of those maddening analogies on an IQ test. Gary wanted Di not to hold over Herrera's head the otolaryngology fellowship that Herrera wanted. Di wanted Gary . . .

Not to hold over Dr. Christmas's head the . . .

Directorship of the new center for cranial base surgery that Mount Scopus would set up if the merger with University went through, that Di wanted.

Close, but no cigar. Let's try this again. Herrera was supposed to announce at Rounds that the interns and residents were within their rights to support the nurses on the picket line, but he didn't because Di said to him, "You want that otolaryngology fellowship next year, you keep your mouth shut."

Di had the power to withold the otolaryngology fellowship that Herrera wanted.

But Gary didn't have the power to withold the directorship that Di wanted. Christmas had that power.

Herrera for Christmas.

If you don't pressure Herrera, I won't pressure Christmas.

Are you threatening to blackmail *me, Nurse Seligman?*

Gary had had something on Di.

But what?

"The Rent-a-Nurses are all eager, but we don't know them, and they don't know us," Dr. Abby Kubota was saying when I arrived for Morning Report. "They also don't know where anything is."

A chuckle of agreement went around the doctors' lounge. I spotted Mark Ramsey and slid into the empty seat next to him.

As on any other morning, the primary raison d'être of Report was breakfast: when else would the overworked house staff find time to wolf down their daily quota of bagels, doughnuts, and caffeinated beverages? Usually while doing this, we discussed an interesting patient and heard announcements from Kubota, our mild-mannered chief resident. Today the topic of discussion was How to Get Through the Strike Without Killing the Patients.

"I know all the med students are chomping at the bit to take on more responsibility," Kubota went on, smiling at those med students present. "Just so you know, the interns are under orders to keep you as tightly reined in as possible. I don't care how many patient kills you think you need for your logs."

Boos and whistles. The med students were required to perform certain procedures—for example, spinal taps, the insertion of arterial lines, etc.—during their clerkships; these procedures were recorded in small notebooks, called procedure logs, signed by the residents, and the logs handed in at the end of the rotation.

I waved my hand at Kubota.

"Oh, and Dr. Sutcliffe wants to remind everyone that you should go out on the picket line on your lunch hour to show support for the nurses. Apparently Keith Herrera was going to make an announcement at Rounds Saturday, but forgot. Any questions?"

All eyes in the room turned to me and Ramsey. Kubota had opened the meeting by announcing that hospital administrators had asked her not to discuss Gary's death at Morning Report. Of course everyone wanted to know why not, but Kubota wouldn't say.

As our colleagues stared at us, I glanced around. Some of the docs seemed curious, others embarrassed, a few accusatory. I fought back tears and giving in to guilt again. Instead, I shrugged elaborately, and pantomimed zippering my mouth, locking it, and throwing away the key. That at least got a laugh and broke the spell.

"Any *other* questions?" Kubota asked.

Kubota, who sported a "SOME CUTS NEVER HEAL" button, went on, "Let me remind you of the issues. Staff cutbacks, the lack of progress in contract talks, and the hospital's demand to have unlicensed employees do more of the work now done by R.N.s. Those of you who still think the nurses' strike isn't about you, apply the 'my-mother' criterion. If it was my mother, would I want an RN caring for her, or an unlicensed aide?"

"So your point is, if you love your mother, go out on the picket line at lunch," one of the med students suggested.

"You're being completely one-sided," called out an attending physician in the rear of the room. "Some of us have patients—mothers, if you prefer—whose care will be utterly compromised by today's strike. I say, let the nurses work out their differences at the negotiating table, not out on the sidewalk!"

"And we'd appreciate less false sentiment, Kubota," called another. "Don't buy into that tabloid trick of fanning emotion."

"Yeah, Kubota—and you of all people should be neutral. The chief resident has no business taking sides in politics like this!"

The room erupted in angry voices. Kubota, her face flushed, angrily unpinned her "SOME CUTS NEVER HEAL" button and handed it to me; I pinned it on my own clinical coat. A few people cheered. Things were rapidly getting out of hand.

Suddenly, someone started singing the ER version of "Let It Be," where Mother Gary came to us in times of trouble. Everyone stopped talking. Other voices chimed in. Soon, most of us were singing at the tops of our lungs.

Those docs opposed to the nurses' strike groaned and looked disgusted. One by one, they filed out of the room.

The rest of us finished singing the song.

Afterward, there wasn't a dry eye in the house.

Outside on the picket line the nurses were enjoying unseasonably warm weather and sunshine, and a mild, summery breeze. The temperature was probably in the seventies. Most of the picketers had shed their jackets onto a heap by the hospital's front door, many wore sunglasses under the brims of their red nurses' union caps, and some had even stripped down to sleeveless tee-shirts and were passing around bottles of suntan lotion. An air of cocky, jostling exuberance prevailed.

The day and the strike were still young.

A television reporter stood with his back to the picket line. As I watched, he metamorphosed into his on-camera self: aroused, indignant, deadly serious. "Question: You're sick. You go to the hospital. The hospital assigns someone to take care of you *who has only had three weeks of training.* Not a nurse.

Not even a licensed technician. Doesn't even have a college degree. An *unlicensed aide with a high school diploma*. Would you say the hospital cares about its patients? The nurses at University Hospital say no."

I waited behind the cameraman. "Lunch hour" was a figment of the imagination and a joke; I had fifteen minutes to eat lunch and join the nurses on the picket line. But I didn't really feel like being on TV. I ate some carrot sticks and cold cooked broccoli out of a Baggie, then unwrapped my Swiss-cheese sandwich and bit into it.

The television reporter intoned portentously, "This strike isn't about wages and benefits. It's about providing quality care. Nurses here say hospital management is more interested in putting profits before patients. You can teach a janitor to take blood pressure, they say—but is that safe for the patient?"

I spotted Keith Herrera on the picket line.

"Hey, Sutcliffe," he greeted me when I slid into the line beside him.

A compact man wearing a blue scrub suit under his white clinical coat, Herrera was about five-foot-eight, young but balding, with dark hair, black eyes, and stylish eyeglass frames. "I called you this morning at your boyfriend's, but you had already left," he said. "What's up?"

"I need to ask you about Di Clausson," I said. "Did she pressure you in any way not to announce at Rounds that docs were within their rights to picket with the nurses?"

Immediately he was wary. "Why are you asking?"

"Just something that Gary Seligman—"

"Not here," he snapped, cutting me off. Taking my arm, he pulled me out of the line and around the corner. "Now listen to me," he said. "I know what you're thinking, and it's crap."

I jerked my arm free. "Keith, all I want to know is—"

"Whether I'm sleeping my way to the top," he finished.

Hands on hips, he leaned toward me like a bullying drill sergeant. "I am not having sex with that woman, goddammit, and if Seligman told you otherwise, fuck him in his grave! I'm competing for that otolaryngology fellowship fair and square—just like everyone else. Nobody's going to question my ethics. Not you, not Seligman, and especially not Diana Clausson!"

Turning on his heel, he stomped back to the picket line.

So much for Gary's theory that Diana Clausson was holding the otolarygology fellowship over Keith Herrera's head, I thought as I walked back to the ER.

You couldn't intimidate Keith Herrera if you tried.

Back in the ER, Doctor-in-training Chang-Hua Charles Nicholson lay in wait for me as I came through the ambulance bay doors. Eager to prove that he, a lowly extern, could handle the workload of an intern and handle it with competence, nay, *distinction*—while a certain intern-who-shall-remain-nameless wallowed in despair, barely able to perform the duties of a med student—Nicholson launched into reports on all his patients and then some.

"Jane Doe, MVA, head CT clear, Ramsey sewing up lacs. David Keller, irregular heart rhythm, Dr. Clausson's patient, she's on her way. Marie Powers, probable hot appendix—"

I held up a hand. "What probable hot appendix?"

"Twenty-five-year-old African-American, complaining of abdominal pain, guarding but no rebound. Surgeon coming down."

"Okay, good. We any closer to an ID on Jane Doe?"

"Chaplain tracked down the owner of her car, man named Jhang. Jhang says there were four girls in the car, his two daughters and two nieces. They were all on their way to Grandma's funeral. Jhang's coming in now to ID the one who's alive."

I groaned. "Think what must be going through that poor man's head, not knowing which one she is, and the other three dead. I'll talk to him when he gets here. The professor, Clausson's patient, what does she see him for?"

"Spasmodic dysphonia." Difficulty speaking due to spasm of the vocal chords.

"Know anything about it?" I asked.

Most med students wouldn't, but Nicholson had an answer ready: "Some theories about basal ganglia, but the etiology remains unclear. Nerve impulses that flow from the brain to the vocal chords become jerky and shaky, drastically reducing the ability to speak fluidly. Treatment of choice is local injection of purified botulinum A toxin, which is well-suited for many of the dystonias, including blepharospasm, spasmodic dysphonia, and swallowing disorders. The toxin acts by weakening the strength of the involuntary contractions, without interfering with fundamental neural mechanisms."

A very impressive answer. But it came bullishly, as if I had asked the question to humiliate him.

For a moment I considered the fact that if Ramsey had come back with that same answer, I would have praised him lavishly. But praising Nicholson even where praise was due just seemed too complicated. Externs—medical students on ro tation in the hospital—for the most part were either obsequiously deferential or arrogant and show-offy. Nicholson was arrogant and show-offy but with a twist: he had some kind of hidden agenda I could never figure out, and I disliked him for it. I like to be fair to people, so I felt guilty that I disliked him so intensely. I was constantly defending myself: *But it's really his own damn fault if I don't like him.* Which made me mad. Why was he so provocative—and so maladaptive? Why couldn't he figure out his place in the ER hierarchy and make an effort to fit in?

I explained as patiently as possible, "I'm asking you because Di Clausson will bite your head off if you don't know every damn thing there is to know about her patient and his problems." *And she'll bite mine off too,* I didn't add. "Now how about if we briefly discuss his arrhythmia? You ruled out MI. So what's the differential?"

I listened with half an ear while Nicholson scornfully listed several different things arrhythmia could be a symptom of and what to do about it. As usual, he was right on the money and needed no help from me.

When he finished, I made myself praise him. But this only elicited a suspicious look, as if I were somehow trying to trick him. So I gave up. Grabbing an armload of patients' charts from the rack, I sat down at the doctors' desk in the nurses station. Michael Wells had put me in charge of chart Q&A, which meant I had to read all the charts, check protocol and doctors notes, and make sure everyone who needed to sign had signed and written his or her name legibly. Especially while the nurses were out, when something might go wrong.

After finishing reading the charts, I went to look for Ramsey. I found him in the ER's OR Three preparing a tray to suture Jane Doe Jhang, now that she was back from CT Scan.

The patient lay unconscious on her stretcher. She was breathing well on her own, but she was still intubated and we had left her neck brace on. Her burned hands had been treated with salve and bandaged, and her left lower leg was in a cast. No one had washed the soot and grime off her face—a job that normally fell to the nurses—so I decided to do that now. I got a washcloth and moistened it in the sink.

"Couple of nasty lacs," Ramsey observed as he rummaged through boxes in the floor-to-ceiling supply cabinets and selected his sutures and needle sizes. When he had what he needed, he spoke conversationally to the patient as if she were awake. "I'm Dr. Mark Ramsey, I treated you when you first came in, remember? You've got some gashes on your leg here, from the accident. I'm going to suture them for you now." He peered at her for any sign that she had heard him. There was none. But you never knew, and it was always good to show the patient every courtesy possible. "I'm Dr. Sutcliffe," I added. "I'll just wash your face for you. You're a little sooty from the fire."

Ramsey sat down on a stool next to the patient's stretcher. Setting a pair of safety glasses on his nose, he pulled on gloves and placed green surgical drapes around the first wound. Meanwhile, I scrubbed the patient's face as gently as I could; her skin was reddened from the fire, as if she had overdone it at the beach. When I finished washing her, I filled a syringe with two percent Xylocaine and handed it to Ramsey—just as he said, "Shit, I forgot the Xylocaine." He smiled up at me. "Thanks, Ev."

I watched him infiltrate the Xylocaine outside the perimeter of the wound so he wouldn't track dirt in with the needle. So far so good. When he was finished, I helped him rinse the wound. "You want to use monofilament nylon," I instructed. "And you want to take extra care to match up the dermis."

"Close with silk?"

"No. The infection rate with silk is ten to fifteen percent. With nylon it's only two to three percent." I bit my tongue before I said, *Ramsey, for godssake—you've been working here for three months, don't you know by now not to use silk to close wounds in the ER?*

As I watched him work, I said, "You know, Mark, you and I haven't had any time to talk about Gary's death. Do you personally have any theories, or have you heard any theories—"

"Why we lavaged him? The possibility that he had eaten cyclopeptide-containing mushrooms justified—"

I put up my hands. "Stop. You don't have to justify the lavage for me, this isn't a test run for the Q-and-A."

"We're being brought before Quality Assurance?" All the color drained out of his face.

"Not as far as I know."

"Christ—are we up for sanctions?"

"No. Listen to the question. I want gossip. Have you heard any gossip about how Gary came to eat these mushrooms in my apartment?"

He went back to scrubbing. "I didn't want to be the one to tell you," he said, a wild note suddenly creeping into his voice. But in a rush of words he did:

"Dr. Carchiollo's patient—the one he warned the nurses he didn't want to see if she came into the ER—she works at the university for that mushroom specialist, the one Nicholson talked to when Gary got poisoned—the guy Poison Control recommended, Professor Held—people are saying this Eliza or whatever her name is had an affair with Carchiollo, and when he tried to break it off she sent the basket with the poisonous mushrooms."

Working in a hospital was like living in a small town; everybody knew your private business and believed what they heard—but wouldn't think of asking you if the rumors were true. "Elise Vanderlaende," I said as calmly as possible. "Anything else?"

"I'm sorry, Ev. Everyone's really embarrassed that he would cheat on you like this. That's why no one's said anything to you. To say nothing of having sex with a *patient*—"

"He's not cheating on me," I said with as much confidence as I could muster. At least I hoped not. "And she's no longer his patient. She's an erotomanic stalker. Like that woman who stalked David Letterman and said she was his wife. The woman's deluded. Vanderlaende may actually believe Phil's having an affair with her—" But seeing Ramsey's expression, I stopped.

Pity. It spread across his face like a sheet of cascading rainwater.

Elise Vanderlaende was not the person deluding herself.

In Ramsey's opinion, I was.

"Jesus," I breathed.

"I'm really sorry," he said for the third time. He finished scrubbing. As I rinsed the wound for him he went on, "Nobody thought you knew. We didn't know how to tell you. And then when the detective came into the ER with that photo of what's-her-name, Elise Vanderlaende? and Kathy Haughey actually *knew* her—"

"Kathy knows Elise Vanderlaende?"

The pity grew denser. If that was possible.

"Mark, you must tell me everything you know. I don't care how damning it is. Please."

For a moment he didn't say anything. He reached for a needle holder and peered into the wound. When he began to speak he did so slowly and deliberately, as he placed the first sutures deep in the wound. "Kathy knows Vanderlaende from the university gym. They take the same aerobics class. A couple of weeks ago, Kathy comes into the locker room to change before class, and there's this girl weeping in the shower. Kathy asks her what's the matter. The girl blurts out this story about how her boyfriend's broken up with her. He was going to leave his other girlfriend for her but now he's not. And what's even worse, he's her *psychiatrist.* The girl doesn't name names. But it's clear to Kathy that it's a psychiatrist at this hospital. She was seeing him for posttraumatic stress disorder because she'd been involved in some kind of shooting and was having nightmares, and this doc apparently gave her some line that a loving sexual relationship with him would be healing. The nightmares would go away if she slept with him, basically.

"So naturally, Kathy is *incensed*," Mark went on. "Kathy tells the girl to get a lawyer and call the American Psychiatric Association and lodge a complaint. I remember Kathy coming into work that day and telling one of the other nurses about it. She was so mad she was raising her voice. I heard the whole thing. But like most things that happen around here, I forgot about it."

"Then, when Detective Ost showed Kathy the photo . . ."

Ramsey shook his head. He looked incredibly pained. "After the detective talked to Kathy, she came out of the room white as a sheet. She didn't say anything. But I got this intuitive flash *that she's the girl from her aerobics class*. The one who was crying over an affair with her shrink. And someone's just tried to poison you and Dr. Carchiollo but Gary ate the hallucinogenic mushrooms instead. I put two and two together. Unfortunately so did everyone else. Now it's the buzz."

I nodded. No wonder everyone was embarrassed to look me in the eye. Not only did I fuck up Gary's lavage, they thought my boyfriend was screwing a patient.

"Am I matching this up okay?" Ramsey asked.

I leaned over him to examine his handiwork. "Looks fine. Listen, do you know anything about what Gary was doing the last few days?"

"What he was doing?" His face blanked. Ramsey was one of the few people I knew who could go from sixty to zero.

I spelled it out: "He had Thursday, Friday, and Saturday off. Did he mention to you what his plans were at all?"

"Well what does he usually do on his days off? Read French books? Watch French videos? Cook? What are you asking?"

"He told me he was going to his high school reunion, but he didn't go."

Mark looked confused. "He didn't?"

"No. His high school wasn't having a reunion this weekend."

The blank stare again; it went on so long I thought Mark had been struck dumb. I got another idea. "Mark—you said you see Elise around the neighborhood and she speaks to you?"

He nodded.

"She knows your name?"

Ramsey lifted his shoulders into a shrug. "I was there that day in the ER when they brought her in."

"She only says 'Hi, Doc'—or you've actually had a conversation with her?"

More blank stare. Then, "I didn't know about her and Carchiollo!" Mark protested, his voice rising. "I went into Sami's one morning and she came over and introduced herself and asked could she buy me a cup of coffee. We talked about the bank shooting. Then she asked about why I decided to go into emergency medicine. Then she asked about you. I had no *idea* she was fishing for information about you, Ev, or I wouldn't have told her anything!"

"When was this?"

"I don't know. Late July, maybe early August."

"And what did you tell her about me?"

"I don't remember. She asked about me about Gary, too. And Kathy Haughey. And about Phil. What I thought of Phil. She seemed equally curious about everyone who'd cared for her in the ER that day, and all the other docs and nurses who worked there. She wanted to know what it was like seeing what we see day after day and what kind of toll that takes."

"Kathy Haughey wasn't on duty that day, Gary was," I said. "You had coffee with her only this once?"

"No, maybe three or four times. They weren't dates, Ev— we didn't arrange to meet or anything, I'd go in to Sami's and she'd be there and I'd join her, or vice versa. Then sometimes

I'd bump into her jogging. It got to be a joke that we were always bumping into each other."

"And you had no idea she was in love with Phil?"

"Not until the detective came in here with the photo. Ev, I'm really, really sorry about this whole business, I—"

I cut him off. "Do you know anything about the falling out between Case and Vittorio, what it's about?"

He looked relieved that I had changed the subject. But then his expression clouded again; I had just changed it from one uncomfortable subject to another. "It's a quarrel over money," he sighed. "I don't know the details."

"Acute, or chronic?"

"I have the impression it's chronic. Case mismanages his money, Vic bails him out. What Case should do is let Vittorio manage his money for him, pay all the bills, and give Case an allowance. Jackie's suggested that a number of times. Vittorio is willing. But Case is too proud. Besides, what Case really wants in life is to be Vittorio. Vittorio does whatever he wants. Case has *never* done what he wanted; he's always done what everyone else wanted him to do."

"They really do treat you like a member of the family, don't they?" I murmured.

Ramsey laughed ruefully. "Yeah—'You're a member of the family now, so don't mind us, we'll just go ahead and argue in front of you!' " He shook his head. "Case and Vic have a real love-hate relationship going there. Vic is constantly humiliating Case. And Case is so full of envy he can't see straight. But they're like brothers so they duke it out, just like real brothers would. Then they forgive each other and start all over again."

"Anything in particular happen recently?" I asked.

"They had a big fight a couple of weekends ago. I took the train out Sunday morning to spend the day. When I got there, Jackie said Case and Vic had gone out to pick some mushrooms for dinner, why didn't I go find them in the woods? So I walked down the path, you know, the one behind the barn. I heard their voices. I realized they were arguing, so I turned around and came back." He stopped.

"But you overheard something before you turned around."

Ramsey looked up at me and bit his lip. "I've been wondering whether to tell anyone."

I waited.

"You can't repeat this, Ev. If you tell the cops and they come to me, I'll deny saying it."

"I understand," I said.

"Case and Jackie *do* treat me like a member of the family. . . . Oh, hell, here's what I heard. Case said it was one thing if Vic wanted to shack up with Alan, but it was a disgrace to Pat's memory for Vic to change his will to leave Alan the money Pat had left Vic."

He paused so long I almost filled his silence.

Finally he finished: "And Vic said, 'And what are you going to do about it, Case—send Alan a tray of mushrooms on toast?' "

twenty-six

"Y o, Sutcliffe!" someone yelled from the ambulance bay. "Heads up, sidewalk dump!"

A sidewalk dump meant that a car had pulled up in front of the emergency room's West 113th Street entrance, rolled to a halt only long enough for the door to open and the patient to tumble out, and had sped off again.

I ran out the ambulance bay door and saw a woman crumpled on the curb. Two medics from an ambulance parked nearby were running over with their gear.

"I'll get a stretcher!" I yelled.

By the time I was kneeling next to the woman, the medics had already inserted an oropharyngeal airway. "She's breathing, but just barely," one said. He hooked up an ambubag to the oxygen tank and started ventilating her.

"BP's one-twenty, pulse eighty," said the other medic. "Pinpoint pupils. Expensive dress, jewelry, makeup. My guess is, those are four-hundred-dollar shoes. What's the world coming to?"

The patient was certainly very beautiful and well turned out; in her early thirties, maybe, she looked like a young businesswoman, perhaps, or a trophy wife, or a lady who lunched—and just happened to shoot a little heroin on the side. I made a fist and ground it into her sternum. No response. I looked around the sidewalk for a purse. Nothing. "She have any ID on her?"

"Nope. Whaddya wanna bet, her stockbroker buddies are hoping she'll get a little anonymous care without her employer finding out? You want I should start a line for the Narcan?"

"Let's get her into the ER," I said.

"Suit yourself." The medic, a zaftig woman with coal-black hair and a very downtown haircut, whose nametag read "OLI-VERI," lifted her chin at her partner, a beefy, red-haired guy named Tsach. They picked up the patient effortlessly and slung her onto the stretcher. Her limbs flopped every which way.

"There's the injection site." Oliveri pointed to a tiny red spot behind the patient's left knee. "What's wrong with these people? I could afford a dress like this, I wouldn't be shooting up, let me tell you."

We ran through the ambulance bay and into the ER. I pulled the stretcher into OR One, where Ramsey was just pulling off his gloves and dropping them onto his suture tray. He pulled Jane Doe Jhang's stretcher sideways to make way for her new roommate.

Oliveri unshouldered her bag of gear onto the floor. "Offer's still good on that IV, Doc," she said to me.

"Thanks, I'd appreciate it," I said.

"This the sidewalk dump?" Ramsey asked.

"Yeah, another yuppie heroin user, looks like." I got a bag of saline and a box of burette IV tubing out of the cabinet and started setting up while Oliveri got down to work. She was fast and good. By the time I had the Narcan ready, Oliveri had drawn blood and hooked up the IV.

I shot the bolus IV push and we all stood back. Narcan, which reverses the effects of heroin and other opiates, usually works so fast patients have been known to sit bolt upright and deliver a one-two punch to the doctor's jaw before the doc has had time to get out of the way.

The patient did not stir.

"What was that, two megs?" Ramsey asked.

"Yeah," I said. I looked at my watch and prepared another dose. Medic Tsach kept pumping the ambubag, forcing oxygen into the patient's lungs. Again I noticed how beautiful the patient was, even unconscious and blue from low oxygen. On the ring finger of her left hand, she wore a diamond ring that would probably pay the rent on my apartment for five years.

"Two megs won't do much if she took street fentanyl or that Mott Haven bad batch," Mark said to no one in particular just as I shot the second bolus into the IV.

"Yeah, you're right," I said.

We all stood back.

Nothing.

Ramsey started talking to himself under his breath. "Street fentanyl can be hundreds of times more potent than heroin or morphine. It's highly lipid-soluble and goes straight to the brain, right through the blood-brain barrier. It works so fast, it sometimes kills the patient before she even has time to withdraw the needle."

"At least her color's coming back," I said. Looking at my watch, I prepared a third dose of the Narcan.

Meanwhile Oliveri cut the patient's dress off, clucking and shaking her head. "French silk underwear," she muttered, and cut that off, too.

Ramsey revitaled the patient, called out the numbers, and handed the blood tubes off to the premed for log-in by the clerk and transport upstairs to the lab. "You know, there was a study in the mid-eighties at the University of Southern California, I think, that showed that fentanyl was one of the two most widely abused drugs among physicians, especially anesthesiologists."

Oliveri stopped muttering over the patient's shredded underwear. She gave Ramsey a perfect New York look, like, *Who is this guy?* As if she hadn't been talking to herself as much as he.

Suddenly, the patient tried to turn her head. A few seconds later she put her hand up to feel what was on her face. Her eyelids fluttered open.

"Welcome back to the world, Hon," Oliveri said.

The patient stared at us wild-eyed. Pushing away Tsach's hands with the ambubag, she bolted upright, spat the plastic airway across the room and yelled, "Who the hell are you people? What the hell do you think you're doing?" Realizing she was naked, she let out a shriek and crossed her arms over her breasts. "Where the *hell* are my clothes?"

"You're at University Hospital," I said. "You overdosed on heroin and you were brought here unconscious."

"That's ridiculous. I don't know what you're talking about. Could I at least have a goddamn sheet to cover myself? Where are my things?"

I gave her a patient gown and helped her slip it on. "I'm afraid you were brought here without your things. Your friends dumped you unconscious on the sidewalk outside the ER and left in their car."

"You're making this up. Where's my briefcase?"

"Not here."

"Not here," she repeated. A lightbulb went on behind her eyes: we didn't have ID, we didn't know who she was. "You can't keep me here against my will. I'm leaving. Give me my goddamn clothes."

"I don't advise that," I cautioned.

"Who the fuck are you to advise me?" She read my name

tag. *"Doctor* Sutcliffe. Well, give me my goddamn clothes, Doctor!"

"The word you're groping for is 'Thank you,'" Ramsey said.

The patient stared at Ramsey with incredulity. "Who the fuck asked you? You don't look like *you* exactly came in here on your own two feet of your own volition, either!"

"You're right," Ramsey said. "I was in an accident, that's why my face looks like this. Strangers cut me out of my car and stopped my bleeding, strapped me to a stretcher, dragged me up the side of a ravine, and put me in an ambulance to take me to the hospital. I was unconscious for three days. When I woke up, other kind strangers were taking care of me. You can bet the first thing I said when I was able to talk again was 'Thank you.'"

The woman sat there gaping at him.

"Let me explain something to you," Ramsey said. "The duration of action of most opioids exceeds the duration of action of Narcan, the drug we gave you. What that means is, although the Narcan woke you up and you feel fine, that feeling is going to last only about half an hour. Then the heroin or fentanyl or whatever you took is going to get the better of the drug we gave you, and you could very well wind up unconscious and not breathing again. You need to stay in the hospital and get an IV infusion of Narcan to make sure that doesn't happen. Capeesh?"

The woman stared a long moment at Ramsey's face, then at his name tag, then at his face again.

"Who are you, the hospital pharmacist?" she asked finally. "No, wait—I know you! You were the med student when I broke my arm two years ago! You're a Yalie, right?"

Ramsey blinked.

"I was so impressed with how you knew the answers to all your intern's questions. You were pointing at the X Rays and saying things like 'Colles' fracture this' and 'displaced that'—Don't remember me, huh? That's okay. Better for me. I'm in a lot of trouble, if word gets out I was here." The woman smiled. "Thank you, Dr. Ramsey, for then and now," she said. She looked at each of us in turn. "And you, and you, and you. Forgive my mouth." She turned back to Ramsey. "Now, since you're the smart one here, why don't you explain to me how I can stay here, get more of this drug you say I need, pay cash, and leave without telling anyone my real name so my boss doesn't find out about my, ah, recreational habits?"

"Well, guess we're done here," Oliveri said loudly. She picked up her gear and left. After a minute, so did Tsach.

So did I.

"I think I'm having a doctor moment," Ramsey said to me a little while later. "A fabulously gorgeous patient who calls me 'Doctor' even though I talk to myself. And who actually listens to my advice."

"Which was?" I asked.

"Well, I convinced her she had to tell me her real name."

"Good. Very important."

"But I said she could keep her boss from finding out she was hospitalized by paying cash on discharge, or by having a friend pay with a check, instead of writing a check in her own name."

"Be sure to get her old chart." That would verify the woman's identity.

"Absolutely." He sighed elaborately, miming lovesickness. "Think I should marry her?"

I laughed. "I dunno, Ramsey—how come you didn't marry her when you treated her broken arm? You can't even remember her—and she's movie-star gorgeous."

"Yeah . . . Lots of stuff I don't remember since the accident. This woman, how to read X rays." He laughed and shook his head. "It really bothers me sometimes. . . . I have whole weeks of important stuff I can't remember. I know I spent that last winter break with Scott—I've got the photographs to prove it. But I have no clue where we went. Looks like the Caribbean, but I don't remember ever having been there!"

I patted his hand. "She tell you what she took?"

"Designer heroin, she said. Street fentanyl. Claims it was the first time."

"Maybe," I said. "You tell the dealer it's your first time, he sometimes gives you extra good stuff, more potent."

"Maybe I could have another doctor moment with her before she leaves," Ramsey mused. "Get her to agree to go into some twelve-step program."

"Go for it," I agreed.

I looked at my watch. It was nearly three.

Time for Dr. Clausson, Take two.

"Are you still seeing Di Clausson?" I asked Mark as casually as possible.

He chortled. "Yeah, what can I tell you? The flesh is weak."

We were taking Jane Doe Jhang up to the ICU. With her ventilator, IVs, and portable machines, transport was a two-person job.

"She quarreled with Gary last Wednesday," I said, "and I was just wondering if you knew anything about it."

Ramsey shook his head. "She hasn't said anything to me."

The elevator doors opened and we pulled the stretcher out into the corridor, then around the corner into the ICU, found out from a Rent-a-Nurse what bed Jhang had been assigned, and with her help transferred Jhang and her various machines to the bed. Mission accomplished. Ramsey went back downstairs and I waited to give report to the Rent-a-Nurse.

The nurse, a buxom matron with her gray hair pulled tight into a french twist, was on the phone. "Mm-mm," she said a few times, and "Yes, Doctor." She rolled her eyes and smiled at me to let me know she'd get off the phone as soon as possible. "Dr. Healy, Mr. Kennaugh's brother's been asking to speak with you."

Kennaugh. I'd forgotten all about him. I rifled through the chart rack until I found his chart, and flipped it open.

"Help you, Doctor?" the nurse asked as she hung up the phone.

"Yeah, this patient, Kennaugh? How's he doing?"

"He's going to be laid up a while on the ventilator."

"What's wrong with him?"

"I'm surprised you haven't heard." She leaned closer over the counter as if to impart a particularly juicy tidbit of gossip. "Medical students, residents, fellows—*everybody's* been coming by to have a look at him. Botulism poisoning."

"Botulism?"

"Mm-mm." She had a soft Georgia accent, which made her sound even more conspiratorial.

"His brother's not sick, too, is he?"

"Oh no, Doctor. He was just here if you want to speak to him."

"Kennaugh's allergic to shellfish. He denied having eaten anything home-canned. And he and his brother ate all their meals together the last several weeks—but the brother's not sick. So how did he get botulism?"

"From the heroin."

"You can get botulism poisoning from heroin?" I asked, marveling. "I've never heard of that."

"Mm-mm. The docs here had no clue what was wrong with him, not even Dr. Sachs. Then Dr. Clausson came in while the docs were rounding on Mr. Kennaugh. She knows all about botulism because she uses the toxin in her clinic. She explained about wound botulism. Only about forty-five cases of wound botulism have been reported in the literature since World War Two, Dr. Clausson says. So it's very rare. But there have been a handful of cases where people got it from contaminated heroin, and in one or two cases from cocaine. So now Dr. Sachs is going to present the case at Grand Medical Rounds on Thursday." She looked at my name tag. "Oh, you're Dr. Sutcliffe. Dr. Sachs wants to discuss the case with you."

"I'm sure he does," I said. Damn. It would have been a hell of a coup to have diagnosed wound botulism in the ER. I was a little envious not to be presenting the case myself. "Have they given the patient antitoxin?"

"Mm-mm, yes ma'am. I forget who-all they had to call to get it, the army and the board of health and the CDC." The Centers for Disease Control in Atlanta. "It's a reportable disease, you know. But Dr. Sachs says it's likely to be three months before they can wean him off the ventilator and send him home."

"Three *months?*"

"Mm-mm. Poor Mr. Kennaugh will be climbing the walls."

As I returned to the ER, I went over the questions I'd asked Kennaugh and the answers he'd given. Without ever having seen a case of botulism personally, I didn't see how I could have made the call. I'd asked the botulism questions—Are you having double vision? Have you eaten any canned food? Shellfish? And got "no" for answers. I had a dim recollection of having heard of wound botulism. But I'd thought it was something soldiers died of in the trenches during World War I.

I put it on my list of things to ask Di Clausson.

twenty-seven

Whena I came back into the ER, the EMS batphone was ringing.

"*Notificación*," a clerk yelled out as I reached over the nurses' station counter for a sheaf of lab results. The clerks always used the Spanish word whether they were Latino or not, for reasons that escaped me. Solidarity with the clerks who were Latino, maybe. Still, it sounded comical coming from the mouth of someone named Agafea Fedorovna Petritskaya.

"I'll take it, Pete," I said. She handed me the phone. "This is Dr. Sutcliffe, go ahead."

"Thirty-five-year-old male bicyclist struck with head trauma, LOC, he's been intubated, five minutes coming in," a gruff voice barked.

"You got a premium on bicyclists today?" I asked. "I've already got one."

"For you, a deal," the voice said expansively. "Two for the price of one." He rang off.

I went to see bicyclist number one.

"This is *really strange*," he said when I entered the room. "What happened?" He lay on his stretcher still wearing his white neck collar with the lavender Velcro straps. One side of his face was abraded and crusted with dried blood.

"You fell off your bike, Mr. Telsey."

"Yeah, I know. How long was I out for?"

"About a minute."

"Where did I crash?"

"Amsterdam and One Hundred and Sixteenth, in front of the law school."

"Was I wearing my helmet?"

"Yes."

"Where am I?"

"You're in the emergency room at University Hospital."

"I'm in the emergency room? Wow." There was a slight pause. "This is *really strange*. What happened?"

Jazz Washington came into the room. "He's not laying down any new memory."

"I see that," I said. "You fell off your bike, Mr. Telsey."

"Yeah, I know. How long was I out for?"

"We'll talk again in a minute."

"Where did I crash?"

"I'm going to see another patient. I'll be back in a few minutes." Turning to Washington I asked, "Has this patient been to CT scan yet?"

"Yeah, it's clear," Jazz said.

"Was I wearing my helmet?" the patient called after us as we left the room. I grabbed Nicholson and a young woman wearing a premed's coat. "Find me a nurse," I told her. "Say we've got a notification, head-bonk, ALS on the scene."

"Head-bonk?"

"Head trauma."

"Notification, head trauma, ALS on the scene," she repeated.

"Right."

I went into the ER's utility room, and found Case Hamilton washing his hands in the sink. "I thought I'd let my law firm go under without me," he said with a grim smile. "There ought to be some way I can help out here to alleviate some of the difficulties during the strike."

I shouldered in next to him at the sink, wet my hands, and lathered. "Thanks, we need every hand we can get. Listen, do you know a young woman named Elise Vanderlaende?"

"Dear God," he said, startled. "Not that young woman who was after Rob Held?"

"The same. Unfortunately, now she's after Phil. He treated her once in the ER a couple of months ago. Did you ever meet her?"

"Indeed. She introduced herself to me at a meeting of the Morningside Mycological Society." He knocked the big-bladed faucet handle with his elbow to turn off the water, pulled down a few paper towels, and handed me some. "Held saw me talking to her and afterward told me never to speak to her again."

"How much do you think she knows about you, Case?"

"About me? Let me think. I may have told her the story of how Jackie and I ate the *Galerina marginata* that time."

"Did you tell her the story about your family cook?"

"I doubt it. I don't believe I spoke to her long enough. But many people at the Society know that story. We have a lot of dinner parties. It gets told often enough. What are you getting at?"

"I'll tell you later. There's a notification."

I went out onto the ambulance bay dock, joining Washington and Nicholson. "So what's the story with Telsey?" I asked. "Are you admitting him, or what?"

"I can't get through to anyone on the floor," Washington complained. "They keep putting me on hold."

253

"Did you call the nursing supervisor?"

"I can't get her, either."

"What about the AC?" Nicholson asked. The administrative chief was the senior medical resident in charge of coordinating admission from the emergency room to the intensive and cardiac care units.

Washington rolled her eyes. Nicholson was so irritatingly know-it-all, even when he was right, no one wanted to hear it.

"Call the AC and tell him you can't get anyone to take the report and you can't find the nursing supervisor," I sighed. "If that fails, go up there in person and find some Rent-a-Nurse to take the report."

Washington went back into the ER.

A lovely breeze was wafting into the ambulance bay bringing the delicious odor of fall leaves baking in the sun. I closed my eyes for a moment and pretended I was somewhere far away. Paris, maybe—I'd once visited there in mid-October, and I vividly remembered the Garden of the Tuileries with its orange-and-red treetops rustling—

Paris. Gary. The memory took a sudden sharp turn and I found myself remembering Detective Ost's asking why Gary told me he was going to his high school reunion, when there wasn't one. Not only that, Gary had made up that little detail that he left when people started getting out the baby pictures. And then he was talking about "you know how it is" at reunions. . . . If Gary hadn't gone to his reunion, that wasn't just a lie, it was an elaborate lie.

Moreover, it was a lie I didn't catch. I knew Gary well. Wouldn't I know if he was lying to me? Later on, just as I was leaving, I'd noticed something was wrong, and I'd asked him about it. *Nurses' strike,* he'd said. *That's all.* Just a little white lie there, but I'd caught him out—I didn't believe him. Something *was* bothering him. I just hadn't had time to press him about it.

The whoop-whoop-whoop of a siren interrupted my thoughts.

Then a loud bang. Metal crunching and glass breaking.

And screams.

I jumped down off the ambulance bay dock and ran alongside Nicholson toward the noise. People ran toward us, a blur of blue scrub suits and white coats, mixed with the white and green of paramedics coming from their rigs parked in front of the hospital's side entrance. Someone going the other way slammed into me, hard. I hit the side of the hospital. Bounced once, stumbled, recovered. Kept going.

"Cars plowed into the picket line, at least a dozen down!"

"Stretchers! We need stretchers!"

"Get a doc get a doc *I need a doctor here NOW!*"

I swept my eyes over the scene. A yellow cab and a red Jeep were crumpled in a heap against the traffic light pole on the corner of Amsterdam Avenue. The hot-dog cart was over on its side. An upended blue police line sawhorse marked where the picket line had been. Small groups knelt over the wounded like Muslims praying to Mecca. The back passenger-side door of the cab was open. A dark-complexioned man with blood streaming down his face was shrieking, "Baby come! Baby come!"

I heard another raised voice, my own: "Whaddya got? Whaddya got?" as I tried to count patients and see who was breathing, who not. Bizarrely, my nostrils filled with the smell of sauerkraut as I swept my gaze quickly over people who were talking or moaning, one, two, three, four, five, six—

The front of the cab had accordioned between the Jeep and the traffic light pole. Inside the cab the driver lay draped over the steering wheel. In the Jeep, two people in the front seat, both talking and moving. Their airbags seemed to have saved them from injury.

Somebody lay half under the cab.

It was Kathy Haughey. "I'm okay, I'm okay!" she was shouting hysterically. "Get the guy!" A motionless form lay facedown next to her, his head against her hip, the rest of him under the cab. His arm draped across her belly like a sleeping lover's.

"He's breathing, he has a pulse," said Helen Yannis, another of the ER nurses, down on her knees next to the man. "Sir! Sir! Can you open your eyes? Tell me your name!"

The man groaned and stirred.

By now we had firemen from the engine company across the street running over. Out of the corner of my eye I saw Ramsey and the medics Oliveri and Tsach dash around the corner. "Let the medics and firemen get him out from under the car, Helen," I said. "I need you to triage. Eyeball, head count."

"Gotcha." She got to her feet and began to move among the fallen.

"Kathy, you have any trouble breathing?" I asked.

"No."

"Okay, stay there until we move you."

From within the cab came screams and shouts of *"Poussez! Poussez!"* and *"Voici le bébé !* Here it comes, here it comes!" Case Hamilton of all people was delivering a baby in the back seat—in French. "I've got the kid! Suction! I need suction!" he yelled.

I positioned my right foot next to Kathy's left shoulder, and, careful not to cut myself, I put both arms and then head and shoulders through the shattered window on the driver's side. I got an arm under the driver, and, holding her head, sat her up. She groaned. Her eyes fluttered open. "Try not to move," I said. "We'll take care of you."

"Wha' happen?" she mumbled.

"You've been in an accident." I bit my tongue and refrained from adding, *And you weren't wearing your seat belt, you idiot.* "I'm Dr. Sutcliffe. Can you tell me your name?"

"Mila Peña." She put a hand to her face and felt the blood. "Ay-yi," she moaned, spitting out a couple of teeth. "*¡A la gran puta!*" She tried to look over her shoulder at the commotion in the backseat but I restrained her. "Ma'am, *please don't turn your head.* What happened here?"

"Sumbitch hit me! *¡Me cago en la puta virgen!*"

A medic standing outside the car behind Case handed in a scalpel. Case cut the baby's umbilical cord and handed the baby out to the medic. "Stimulate that baby! Get someone to resuscitate him! Go! Go!"

The medic handed the baby to Mark Ramsey who dashed off to the ER. Hamilton turned his attention to the mother, and I turned back to the cab driver.

"You having any trouble breathing?" I asked. I shifted my feet slightly to give the firemen more room to maneuver as they helped Kathy and the man under the car.

"Hurts."

"Hurts when you breathe?"

"Yeah. I don't hear no baby cry."

"I'm sure the baby will be fine," I assured her. "Try to stay very still." I gently pressed one side of her rib cage. She gasped in pain. I apologized and gently pressed the other side. "What you do to me?" she moaned.

"You've got broken ribs," I said. "I need to listen to your lungs." I put my stethoscope in my ears and auscultated her; she had breath sounds both sides, but was breathing shallowly. Her pulse was strong. "We'll get you out of here as soon as we can, Ms. Peña." I angled myself out the window. A fireman stood behind me with a crowbar. "She's got broken ribs both sides," I told him. "Let's get some oxygen on her."

"Okay, Doc."

"Move her out as fast as you can. Keep your eyes open, she could crump. You need a doc, holler."

The fireman nodded and tried the car door. Amazingly, it creaked open. He leaned over the patient, said, "Excuse me, Ma'am," and made sure the ignition was off.

All the while Oliveri and Tsach had been working to get the unconscious man out from under the cab. They carefully rolled him onto a backboard and slid him out. He groaned and fluttered his eyes.

"Sir, can you tell us your name?" Tsach asked.

The patient mumbled inaudibly.

"Got both feet on backward," Oliveri said. "Legs like jelly." The man's trousers were soaked with blood. His arms and face were abraded and oozing blood.

"That's Ryan Rivera," Tsach said. "The TV reporter. He had a cameraman and producer with him—they should be around."

"See if you can find them."

Looking around, I saw there were enough docs, nurses, medics, EMTs, firemen and cops to deal with a jumbo-jet crash—who was back in the ER to receive the patients as they were brought in? I started yelling for Helen Yannis.

"I'll need nurses for this guy," I told her when she appeared at my elbow. "And we're going to need blood." By now I was down on my knees on the sidewalk next to the two medics. I checked Rivera's airway, listened to his lungs to make sure he was moving air, and palpated for broken ribs. "He's got decent chest expansion but it's not great," I said. "Give me some numbers."

Oliveri reeled off the blood pressure, heart rate, and respiration rate. She slapped an oxygen mask on Rivera and fiddled with the canister. Tsach finished shearing off Rivera's trousers. "Oh, man, Doc," he said. I looked. Rivera's legs from the knees down were a gruesome carnage of torn muscles and bone shards.

"His blood pressure's dropping," said Oliveri.

"Let's rock and roll," I agreed. In a flash, we slapped a C-collar on the patient, hefted Rivera's board onto a stretcher and took off for the ER. As we ran down the sidewalk I asked, "Anybody know what happened?"

"Cab coming south on Amsterdam ran the light and made this big swooping turn," said Tsach. "Cabbie's got a woman in labor, she doesn't want to birth in the car, they're trying to make it to the ER. They turn right in front of the Jeep and BAM! Bounce off the light pole, knock over the hot-dog cart and plow into the nurses. Lucky they hit the pole first, gave the nurses a second or two to get out of the way."

"I was going to get a hot dog," said Oliveri. "Three seconds later it woulda been me."

"Hot dogs are bad for your health," said Tsach. "Like I been tellin' you."

Back in the ER we almost mowed down Mark Ramsey, who was running around with the now squalling baby still in his arms. "The baby is crying, just relax!" someone was telling him. We pulled the stretcher into OR One. One of the Rent-a-Nurses was stocking the crash cart. "I want lines, both arms," I ordered. "But let's turn him first and get him off the board. Check his back."

Outside the OR Ramsey said, "I don't know where the mother is, where's the fucking pediatrician?"

There was a horrified gasp and then a dull thud from the Rent-a-Nurse, who had just taken her first look at Rivera.

"Going, going, gone," said Oliveri. She stepped over the passed-out nurse. "Good help is *so* hard to find."

"On my count," I said. "One, two—"

We rolled Rivera and got the board out from under him. Oliveri started putting in the IV lines herself, hanging bags, drawing blood. She worked from her own kit, which she had unshouldered onto the floor at her feet. The Rent-a-Nurse seemed down for the count. "Make sure she didn't strike her head, will you?" I asked Tsach.

"Out cold," Tsach pronounced cheerfully. He grabbed the Rent-a-Nurse by her feet and dragged her into the corner of the room. She woke up and groaned.

I took a closer look at Rivera's mangled legs and said to Tsach, "Could you go out there please and find me a nurse? One that you recognize? And tell the clerk to call Intervention, we'll need bilateral large-extremity angio. In the meantime I need X Ray and a trauma surgeon. Really stat."

Tsach went out. Helen Yannis came in with several units of blood.

"Thank God," I said. "Put that O-neg on a rapid infuser. I ever tell you how much I love you?"

"No, but you can start now," said Helen. She got the blood set up, then looked at Rivera's legs for a long moment. The X-ray technician came in wheeling his lumbering Brontosaurus machine and we got Rivera ready. Out of the corner of my eye I saw the Rent-a-Nurse pick herself up with as much dignity as she could muster and slink out. Helen, Oliveri, and I went out too when the X-Ray machine began to whir and click. I handed Rivera's wallet to Pete, the clerk, so she could start making out a chart. "What happened to the bicyclist struck with head trauma, the one we were waiting for before the crash?" I asked Pete.

"Diverted," she said without looking up from her computer screen. Taken to an emergency room elsewhere.

"Oh, good. I was worried about him. Where's Kathy Haughey?"

"X Ray."

"Mila Peña, the cabbie, fractured ribs?"

"OR One."

"What about the woman who just gave birth?"

Pete looked up. "I look to you like train master?" she asked in her almost impenetrable Russian accent, smiling. " 'What track your train?' " She printed out a sheaf of lab results and handed them to me. "Mother upstairs, Maternity. Pediatrics have baby, thanks God—Dr. Ramsey almost pass out. Father OR Three, he need sutures."

Stretchers were parked everywhere, making it almost impossible to walk. I stuck my head into OR Two, where a couple of docs and nurses were working on the cabbie with the broken ribs. Everything under control there. It appeared that no one had been seriously injured, with the exception of Ryan Rivera. Among the throng I spotted Case Hamilton. He had his stethoscope in his ears and was taking someone's blood pressure. His suit vest and trousers were ruined with afterbirth, but he looked absolutely radiant.

The trauma surgeon came barreling into the ER, a lean, aging-cowboy type with steel gray hair. His name was Potter and he'd done two tours in a M.A.S.H. unit in Vietnam, and he never heard the end of it—natch, we all called him "Colonel." Colonel Potter listened politely while I briefed him. He looked at Rivera's legs, slapped his X Rays in the light box, and got on the phone.

"All right, let's get this show on the road," he said finally. "Move'em out."

Potter, Yannis, and I rode up in the elevator with Rivera. A seasoned trauma surgical nurse who regularly worked with Potter had joined us. She had volunteered to come in off the picket line to assist him with Rivera's surgery. The nurses seemed to have conveyed upon Rivera the status of honorary nurse. And as one of their own, he would get the best care available; the nurses would see to it.

"What do you think?" I asked Potter.

He pursed his lips. He had a reputation for being laconic,

and he liked to play up to it. "He's got pieces of free-hanging bone and comminuted fractures"—bone that has practically been ground to powder—"but no actual severance. Good pulses both sides in the lower leg. Appears to be reasonable tissue, maybe some areas that need grafting. I don't think we'll have to amputate, Doctor."

When we arrived at the surgical suites, I lingered a moment, watching through a glass window as the docs took Rivera into an OR and began to prepare him for surgery. Yannis put her arm around my shoulder and gave me a squeeze. "Don't stay too long. We need you back downstairs," she said, then left.

I stayed a minute longer.

As I was leaving, a nurse or resident in full OR battle dress—scrubs, gown, booties, shower cap, visor—was just coming in. I brushed past her.

Something about her stayed with me, an odd feeling I didn't even think about until later. Remembering the famous advice of King George V of England when asked by his son for pointers on how to be King—"relieve yourself whenever you can"—I ducked into the ladies room; who knew when I'd get my next chance? As I washed my hands, the odd feeling surfaced. I thought, That person who brushed so close to me just now in the surgical suites—who was that? Why did she seem so out of place?

I left the ladies room and pushed open the door for the stairwell. The door had barely closed behind me when I heard it open again; I was still on the landing, in fact. Before I knew what was happening, there was a blur of blue scrub suit that gave me a hard shove.

Hard enough to knock me off my feet.

twenty-eight

I crashed into the metal post in the center of the stairwell and went down on all fours. There was a pop and splintering; the light on the landing went out. As I struggled to stand, I was met with a knee to the abdomen and then a sharp jerk. My assailant grabbed me by the back of my belt and yanked me off my feet. The wood banister came up hard against my belly and ribs as I bent double over the landing rail. My glasses sailed off my face. Everything happened so fast I barely had time to react. But some part of me was swifter than my brain— my hands gripped the rails so I didn't go over completely, and I kicked out and connected with my attacker. There was a muffed *Oof.* Once I got my feet back under me, I managed to stand long enough to get a quick glimpse of a figure in OR battle dress. Then a fist connected with my cheekbone and another with my nose and a third against the side of my head. A few more blows fell on my forearms now up to shield my head. Then I was airborne again.

There seemed to be a space in time. I put my left arm out

to break my fall, and came down on it hard. Then I rolled several times over.

Along the way I hit my mouth and when I finally came to a stop flat on my back on the next landing I tasted blood. For a moment I wasn't there. I was drifting through a haze where I imagined a patient bending over me and asking if I was all right. No, wait—the patient was wearing scrubs, he was the doc and *I* was the patient. . . . No, that's not right either. The woman I saw in surgery—

I opened my eyes. Case Hamilton was on his knees next to me. He was holding my face still with one hand and smacking my cheek with the other. "Ev. *Ev!*"

"Why'd you push me down the stairs?" I asked groggily, trying to focus. I sounded like I was talking around a wad of cotton.

"Someone pushed you? Are you *sure?*"

I tried to put a hand to my mouth, which seemed from the inside at least to have swollen to the size of a grapefruit. Pain shot up my arm and my vision blackened. The light seemed very, very bright and seemed to get brighter. I was staring up into the bare bulb of the wall fixture on the stairwell landing. But my assailant had broken a bulb and the light had gone out. . . . I deduced I was one landing down from where the scuffle had taken place. I'd managed not to get thrown over the railing into the stairwell. But I hadn't managed not to get pushed down the stairs.

Case had my head in his hands. He was palpating for skull fractures.

My mind cleared suddenly. "I wasn't knocked unconscious," I said.

"Uh-huh." He felt my ribs, arms, and legs for fractures, quickly and professionally. Then he whipped out a pocket penlight and checked my pupils.

"You know, you're very good at this," I said.

"Glad to hear I'm good at *something*." He gently looked in my mouth. "Say ah."

"Ah."

"Bite down."

I did, gingerly.

He held up two fingers. "How many fingers am I holding up?"

"Two."

"Show me your teeth like this." He bared his teeth and I bared mine. "Look at my finger. Follow my finger without moving your head." He sketched a large *H* in the air.

"Where'd you learn to do a neuro exam?" I asked.

"Not hard to learn. Move your feet."

I moved.

"Hands?"

The right one moved okay. When I tried to twirl the left, pain shot up my arm again.

"You've got a split lip and you did something to your left wrist," Case said. "Want to sit up?"

"Yeah."

He put his arms around me and helped. Some of my old feelings for him from our premed days as lab partners resurfaced. Apparently something stirred in him, too—I felt his nose against my ear for just a split second.

Or perhaps I imagined it.

He pulled me to my feet and held me at arms' length, peering at me. "How're you doing?"

"Mouth hurts." I ran my tongue over my lips; both the top and bottom were as Case said, split. There was blood on his scrub shirt where I had rested my face briefly. I looked down at my own shirt, also bloodied. I felt my face with my right hand. Sticky. Blood on my hand. "Aw shit, I must look like Dracula after a feeding frenzy," I said.

"Yeah, you do."

"How bad is it?"

He smiled. "Well, try to be upbeat. Some women pay to get that bee-stung, pouty look. Although without the blood. Someone really pushed you down the stairs?"

"Yes."

"Who?"

"I didn't really see him. He was wearing scrubs. That's all I can tell you." I remembered the nurse or resident up in the OR suites. Someone about my height, slightly built. "Or maybe it was a woman."

Fuck. *Elise Vanderlaende.* The woman of a thousand-and-one disguises. No wonder no one on the Psychiatric Service ever saw her putting letters in Phil's mailbox. When she came into the hospital, she dressed as a doc. Someone had given Elise a pair of scrubs the day of the bank shooting, and with those on she could go where she wanted and collect an entire wardrobe: white clinic coats, trauma gowns, OR booties, masks, caps. People would just think she was a med student.

People like me. Whom she could just push down the stairs, with impunity.

"Let's go back to the ER," I sighed. "I need to get my wrist looked at."

It didn't occur to me to ask Case where he'd been a few minutes earlier, or what brought him into the stairwell to find me.

Or why he'd changed out of his street clothes and volunteers' coat into a pair of blue OR scrubs.

Back downstairs, an air of triumphant-army-after-the-battle prevailed—the battle being the accident that plowed into the nurses' picket line. Nobody had died, only one person had been seriously injured, and a baby had been born. There wasn't exactly champagne, but there was adrenaline, and people were giddy with it. It made for an odd sight: half the patients in the ER seemed to be wearing blue or green or maroon scrub suits, guarding their sprained or broken arms across their bellies, blood dribbling down their chins and soaking their shirts—yet all talked excitedly as they recounted for each other what had happened, each person contributing his or her slightly different vantage. I fit right in with the walking wounded. Only three people asked me what I'd done to myself. I told them I'd fallen down the stairs.

Hamilton went to get me some ice.

By now I was sure that Elise had pushed me. Some small voice in a dark corner of my mind argued against it, but I was tired of listening to that voice, and I let my anger shout it down. That woman was out to get me and Phil, and I wasn't going to make any more excuses for her. So what if she was only twenty-one years old and had the neck of a swan—she'd dined out on her namby-pamby good looks once too often, suckering everyone into believing she was some harmless, neurotic, disempowered beautiful *girl*—how could a lovely girl like that do anything to hurt anyone? Well I had news for everyone: she can and she has.

My anger came over me like a sudden conflagration, and a delayed-action spurt of adrenaline goosed the fire as if I had doused it with charcoal starter. My chest burned. I felt emboldened and reckless. In my mind I saw myself back upstairs in the surgical suite, grabbing Elise by the arm, throwing her against the glass wall, hard, pulling down her surgical mask and ripping her shower cap off her head. *Page Security!* I yelled in my fantasy. I pictured her snarling and malicious, kicking at me, scratching me, struggling to get away. I hauled back and slugged her in her luscious mouth and watched the blood flow. *That's for stalking my boyfriend!*

"This is Dr. Carchiollo," Phil's voice said in my ear. I had the phone in my hand. I had dialed him without even knowing what I was doing.

"Elise Vanderlaende just pushed me down the stairs," I said. "I want you to go down to Security right now and get them to find her and remove her from the premises. She's fully gowned for surgery—gown, mask, cap, the whole fucking outfit." I hung up before he could respond.

Case came back with several cups of ice. I dumped the ice into three rubber gloves, knotted them closed, and wrapped two around my wrist with gauze. The third I held to my mouth. Shaking off Hamilton's offers to help, I stomped off to X Ray.

I had to wait a while; ahead of me were the nurses who had been injured when the yellow cab plowed into the picket line. I sat down on one of those hard, uncomfortable plastic chairs so ubiquitous throughout the hospital, leaned my head back against the wall, and closed my eyes and stewed. That stupid bitch. My arm better not be broken, or . . . or . . . or . . .

But like a blowhard ten-year-old, I ran out of threats. My anger began to abate. *Don't get mad*, I thought—*get even.* What I needed was a plan. For whatever reason, Detective Ost couldn't, or wouldn't, arrest Elise. Of course, Ost had to do everything by the book. But I didn't. Ost's hands were tied in ways mine weren't.

What could I do to help put this woman behind bars?

I sat up and looked around. Kathy Haughey was coming out of X Ray, peeling open the Velcro straps on her C-collar. "I don't care," she was saying. "I'm not going to sit around all night waiting for some chief or chairman to look at my films and tell me what I can see with my own two eyes." She caught sight of me. "Jesus, Ev, what happened to you?"

"Fell down the stairs. May I?" I got up and took her X rays and slapped them into the light box.

"Yeah, and I'm the angel Gabriel," Kathy snorted. "You look like my sister Mary after her husband's had at her. He's not beating you too, is he?"

"Who?" I asked, confused.

"Phil Carchiollo. What happened, you found out he was shtuping Little Miss Moffet, and you confronted him?" But immediately she heard herself, and apologized. "I'm sorry, I'm out of line. That was really insensitive of me."

I looked at Kathy's head and neck films, which were clear. "There's a strong possibility Little Miss Moffet did this number on my face all by her little lonesome," I said as I scrutinized the films of Kathy's fractured wrist. "Who's on for ortho?"

"Manny Hernandez." Pause. "What's going on?"

I told her about my assailant in the staircase. Then I briefly outlined what Ramsey had told me earlier, that Elise Vanderlaende had "confided" in Kathy that her psychiatrist had "seduced" her. I told her that I was standing by Phil: that the girl was an erotomanic stalker out to ruin him, and that he had never been in a therapeutic relationship with her. "He saw her *once* in the ER."

I watched Kathy's face carefully to gauge her reaction. I respected her opinions almost as much as I had respected Gary's.

Kathy looked confused, then incredulous. "She made the whole thing up? Are you kidding me? And she did *that* to your face?"

"Crazy people can be very strong," I said.

But Kathy was shaking her head. "Elise is not making this up, Ev. Maybe she's embellishing a little. But my guess would be not much. No, Phil's in this one up to his neck." Her voice softened. "I'm sorry."

I replaced her X rays in their envelope and handed them back to her, saying, "They're clear." It was one thing to have Mark Ramsey think Phil was involved with Elise Vanderlaende. Mark was young and naïve. It was quite another to have Kathy Haughey believe it. A seasoned ER charge nurse, Kathy was one of the most astute women I knew. She would not be easy to snooker.

"Please hear me out," I said. I told Kathy, briefly, how Elise had been stalking me. I said how smart Elise was. By figuring out Mark Ramsey's schedule, she was able to "accidentally" bump into him enough times to strike up a friendship with him—and pump him for information about Phil and me and other people who worked in the ER. I had no doubt that she had stalked Kathy, too, in order to strike up a friendship with her—which she had accomplished by joining Kathy's aerobics class. And once she had Kathy's ear, she could fill it with nonsense. Elise was clearly out to make friends with all Phil's and my friends, I said, and systematically turn them all against Phil—and me.

"You've known Phil for years, Kathy," I said. "Why would you believe a college girl's word against his? Phil did everything he was supposed to, exactly by the book. He warned you and the other ER charge nurses about her. If Vanderlaende came in, you were to let him know—he didn't want to be surprised if she showed up. He alerted Security. He made sure if she did come into the hospital asking for him to treat her, that a colleague would see her instead. Would he do that if they were lovers?"

"He might if he just dumped her," Kathy pointed out.

I sighed and sat back down.

Kathy sat down next to me. "It's one thing if you want to forgive him, but . . ."

"That sounds like an awfully big 'but,' Kathy."

"But don't delude yourself," she said.

"Christ, Ev!"

I opened my eyes. Kathy was gone. I was still waiting my turn in X Ray.

Phil knelt in front of me. I let him take the ice away and look at my bruised and bloodied mouth. He checked my teeth to make sure none were loose, palpated my jaw. "When did this happen?" he asked.

I told him. We had a brief, fact-filled conversation like two docs. No breast-beating or mea culpas, or touchy-feely I'm-a-shrink-am-I-doing-the-right-thing? agonies. Not to say Phil wasn't angry. He was. But it was the kind of angry I recognized: cold as steel, calm. I felt immensely close to him.

"You okay?" he asked.

"Yeah."

"Got any alcohol wipes?"

I produced a couple from the pocket of my white coat. Phil gentled swabbed the blood off my face. The alcohol stung mightily. He clucked like a mother hen.

"We're going to solve this problem," he said.

"Good. The entire hospital is convinced you're having an affair with Elise Vanderlaende, Phil." I told him about my conversations with Mark Ramsey and Kathy Haughey.

As I spoke, Phil's face became suffused with rage. "I'm going to kill that woman," he said quietly through gritted teeth. "How dare she co-opt my life like this?" He put his arms around me and hugged me tightly to him. "Oh God, Ev, I'm so sorry for what she's done to you. Can you ever forgive me?"

For one fleeting moment I flashed on my jealousy of Lauren Sabot, my worry that Phil was having an affair with her. What if I'd sensed all along—correctly—that Phil was having an affair—but just pinned it on the wrong woman?

Maybe there *was* something to forgive . . .

No. Elise might be able to gaslight all my friends, make them believe her pack of lies . . .

But I wasn't going to let her gaslight *me*.

"There's nothing to forgive," I said in Phil's ear.

There wasn't much we could do to solve any of the problems right that minute, except the one that Elise was in the hospital. Phil called Security and told the sergeant that Elise was impersonating a doctor, and that she had pushed me down the stairs. That got the guard's attention. When Phil described her, however—"She looks like the long-necked young woman on *Friends*, What's-her-name, Kudrow"—the sergeant started laughing. "Hey, Doc, Lisa Kudrow can push *me* down the stairs any time she wants!" But he promised to look for her.

X rays of my arm came back negative; nothing broken. Just a sprain. Chris Cabot personally fixed me up with a plastic splint and Ace bandage. There wasn't anything that needed to be done for the split lip and contusions on my face. I'd just look like I'd been in a fistfight for a week or so—which I had been. I felt my right cheek where the hardest of the blows had landed. Luckily whoever it was hit like a girl. But I had just enough anger and adrenaline left to swagger a bit with machismo. I swallowed four aspirin with a can of tomato juice and went back to work.

Working one-handed was not easy. I had limited use of the fingers of my left hand, and I couldn't grab or hold anything. Suturing was definitely out, which put me out of the competition to care for the injured nurses, most of whom had sustained lacs, abrasions, and bruises. So I assigned myself to see the patients who would otherwise get lost in the accident shuffle.

While I was examining my third drunk college kid of the day, Nicholson came into the examining room and posted himself next to me. Undoubtedly he had some complaint he wanted to air.

"Mr. Jhang come in yet?" I asked.

"Cabot talked to him and took him upstairs personally. Jane Doe is one of his daughters, but he can't tell which one—fraternal twins, about the same height and weight, and her face is just swollen enough he doesn't know."

"Oh my god. Poor man."

"Yeah. What a bitch." Even the cold-hearted Nicholson seemed moved.

We went to look in on Telsey, the bicyclist who hadn't been laying down new memory. He still hadn't been admitted. "Was I wearing my helmet?" he asked as if I'd never left the room. I figured he wouldn't notice if I left again. I wrote the time in his chart, scribbled a note. Nicholson and I charged on to the next patient. "The heart arrhythmia, Dr. Clausson's patient?"

Nicholson flushed. "Clausson wanted him admitted and she took him up herself."

"She give you a hard time?"

If she did, Nicholson wasn't about to admit it. I let it slide. "Your probable hot appendix?"

Nicholson flushed more, if that was possible. "Surgeon turfed to GYN."

"Don't take it personally, Chip. You can't get red in the face every time someone questions your judgment."

His mouth twisted.

"It's not about you," I reminded him. "It's about the patient. Now listen, do me a favor. I know it's busy here. But I need someone to round up everything we have on Gary Seligman. His chart should be in Admitting if it hasn't gone to the Records Room already. Find it and photocopy it, will you? If anyone challenges you, say it's for me. Be authoritative but not defensive, okay?"

"Why?" he asked.

"Just do it. And glance through the labs. I want your input."

A small smile touched his lips, then widened into a grin.

I grinned back. "Try to do it without gloating," I said.

twenty-nine

I did my best to give my patients my full attention, but it wasn't easy. Despite the aspirin and tomato juice (which I secretly believe has magical curative powers), my wrist began to throb, and if I jarred it I got a stabbing pain all the way up my arm. Also, my bruised and bloodied mouth and splinted wrist distracted the patients; instead of listening to my questions about their chief complaints, they suddenly wanted to hear about mine. *"¿Como anda la batalla, doctora?"* asked one patient, an elderly Cuban, as I took cultures of his cellulitis—"How goes the battle, Doctor?"

Chris Cabot made sure he looked in on each injured University Hospital staff member, and every person involved in the picket-line accident. Despite the strike, Helen Yannis agreed to remain in the ER and serve as charge nurse until the last injured nurse was either admitted or released. The chief resident on the plastic surgery service came down to see if anyone needed suturing on his or her face. Two general surgeons also appeared in the ER to volunteer their services.

That took care of most of the nurses wounded on the picket line, and gave the ER docs the opportunity to turn our attention to the huge backlog of patients that had developed during the hours following the accident.

By five P.M. the number of patients in the ER including the injured nurses had dropped to a manageable seventeen. Which didn't mean that we could take a break. We were still working shorthanded, with the docs and med students providing most of the nursing care.

Around six P.M. word came down from upstairs that the University Hospital Board of Directors had just voted on the prospective merger partners. By an overwhelming majority, they had elected to begin stage-two merger talks with St. Eustace Hospital.

Boos and cheers resounded across the emergency room, echoing off the green tile walls. Members of the St. Eustace faction congratulated themselves. Members of the Mount Scopus faction consoled themselves. The house staff—whose residency programs and fellowships would now not be disrupted by a merger with Scopus, jumped up and down and exchanged high fives. I knew that the nurses, outside on the picket line, would be ecstatic, too—St. Eustace nurses belonged to NYSNA, the powerful New York State Nurses Association, which two months earlier had successfully pressured management at Eustace to drop its efforts to eliminate job security. At the same time, NYSNA (pronounced "Nize-nah") had also successfully negotiated a "no-bump" clause that barred the hospital from moving nurses from one department to another.

"Oh, Gary, I wish you were here to see this," I murmured. I observed a moment of silence while I imagined him seeing it.

I looked around for Case Hamilton to offer my condolences, but didn't see him. I wondered if he had gone to the board vote in his scrub suit.

Finally, I remembered with a delicious *Schadenfreude* that

Di Clausson would not be happy to hear this news. Gary had said Saturday afternoon that St. Eustace, which had its own prestigious Ear, Nose and Throat Service, would probably close ENT at University—putting Clausson out of a job.

Around nine P.M. I got out my second cheese sandwich and wolfed it down while writing chart notes. Around ten P.M. I was able to drink a cup of tea after letting it cool to a temperature that could be gulped. Triumphantly, I managed time to go to the bathroom for the second time since I'd come on that morning at seven. I took the opportunity to wash my face, brush my teeth, and reapply eye pencil. I skipped the lipstick. I looked like an extra for *Rocky VI: Comeback*.

At a quarter after ten, my brother Alan called to see if I needed food.

"Thanks," I said, "but I've eaten. Things are so crazy here, I probably wouldn't have much time to talk to you if you came by, anyway. But if you could bring a couple of sandwiches tomorrow, I'd be grateful. How are you?"

"Better when I have something to do. Anything you need, just let me know," Alan said. "By the way, your apartment is ready for rehabitation. Berta cleaned the place from top to bottom. We laundered what clothes could be laundered and took the rest to your dry cleaners. Picked up your yellow silk dress, too."

"My yellow silk dress?"

"You had a couple of dry cleaners' tickets on your fridge, so I thought I would pick up your clothes, since I was going there. A yellow silk dress and a couple of suits. All hanging neatly in your closet."

I didn't have a yellow silk dress; another fuck-up at the dry cleaners. But I wasn't about to take it out on Alan. "Thanks, Alan. I really, really, appreciate it."

"Thank Berta, she did all the work." Berta was Alan's and Vittorio's housekeeper.

"I'll give her an envelope the next time I see her," I promised.

"I cried when I threw out all that food," he said suddenly, his voice cracking. "I wish I knew what it was Gary had on his mind Saturday. He was so preoccupied. Not himself at all."

"He didn't go to his reunion, you know," I said.

There was a long pause. On the other end I heard a door click shut.

"This is going to sound completely off the wall," Alan said in a low voice. "But I'm pretty sure that Gary did go to a reunion—just not to his own reunion."

"Whose reunion did he go to?" I asked.

"I think he went to Case and Vic's. Vic was going to go with Case and Jackie and Geoff Hamilton. Then Vic broke his arm and Case's law firm went belly up, so they canceled. I think maybe Geoff went. But last Tuesday when Gary was here for dinner, Vic was still planning to go. So Gary was asking Vic all kinds of questions about the school, where it was, how you got there, what kinds of events the school had planned, does everybody go. . . . I said, 'Why? Are you planning to go yourself?' Gary laughed and said that his own reunion was so boring, he thought just once he'd go to someone else's. There was a very strange edge to his voice. Even Vic noticed something was up. But we have no idea what." He lowered his voice even further so I could barely make out what he said next: "Vic's been on the phone all afternoon calling people. I think he's calling his old school chums."

"Can you tell me what Case and Vic have been quarreling over lately?" I asked.

Long pause. "All right, but you can't say I told you. Case became guardian and conservator of Lauren's estate when her parents died. He embezzled—he says he 'borrowed'—money from her."

"*What?*" I gasped.

"You know, you and Vic are so down on me because I've never liked Case, it's really hard not to say 'I told you so.' But I know you like him. So I'm sorry."

Standing in the nurses' station, I groped for a chair and sank into it. "God. How long have you known?"

"Only a couple of months. Lauren found out, and she went to Vic in May or June, I forget when exactly. Vic made Case sell Lauren his house for five hundred dollars. The real worth of the house is about the same as what Case embezzled from her trust funds. Then Vic forced Case to sign trusteeship over to him. Lauren forgave Case, but Vic's still mad because Case won't get his finances in order. Also, now that Case's law firm is breaking up, Vic is worried that we'll find out Case has embezzled other clients, too. Vic's beside himself with worry. Jackie also."

"This is really awful," I said. "Can anyone get Case to go to Debtors Anonymous?"

"Lauren's after him to do exactly that. But she hasn't had much success."

I heard the door opening and Vittorio's voice.

There was a soft click as Alan replaced the receiver in its cradle without saying goodbye.

I sat in my chair a full two minutes after Alan hung up, trying to absorb this news.

It certainly explained one thing: the meaningful looks that I'd seen Lauren Sabot giving Phil. She's probably been trying to get Case into therapy, and asking Phil for advice how to persuade him to go. And of course Phil wouldn't confide in me about it.

But it didn't explain why Gary would go to Vic and Case's reunion.

I went back to work. I had just finished writing a prescription for a patient who was being released when I turned around and bumped into Geoff Hamilton, Case and Jackie's oldest boy—actually, I shouldn't say "boy," he was slightly older than Mark Ramsey. A marketing director who worked for a large publishing firm, he was normally lively and funny and went everywhere with a kind of "isn't-life-interesting!" look on his face. Not tonight. Tonight he looked grim and tired.

"Geoff, what are you doing here?" I asked.

"I just brought my mother in," he said. Fear flickered in his eyes. "I'm worried she's had a stroke."

"Oh, no. Where is she?"

Geoff pointed toward an examination area across from the nurses' station. The EMTs were just wheeling Jackie in. From where I was standing, perhaps thirty feet away, I could see that she looked pale and lethargic.

"I haven't been able to reach my dad," Geoff said. "Do you have any idea where he is?"

"He's here somewhere. I'll have someone find him for you." I put my hand on his shoulder. "Geoff, I'll go see your mother personally. Why don't you go get yourself a soda or something?"

He shook his head; he had more he wanted to tell me. "Her sugar's out of whack, too—she's got that apple smell. And her blood pressure's probably through the ceiling, what with all the stress." He passed a hand through his light brown hair. A strapping guy just over six feet, he had his father's large hazel eyes flecked with green, Case's dimpled chin, and Jackie's solid, stocky build. But tonight his shoulders drooped.

"I'll look in right now," I said.

"I never should have left her alone this afternoon. She said she wasn't feeling well. I just had to go out to the Island and get the dogs, and I thought I'd be right back."

"She inject insulin, or take pills?" I asked.

"Injects. I put all her insulin in her purse along with all the kits she uses to test herself. She keeps a notebook, too. I made sure she brought it." He took a deep breath. "I should tell you that we've had no success getting her to quit drinking. She likes a glass of wine or two with dinner, and a snifter of brandy for a nightcap. She figures she can drink it if she writes down exactly how much she drinks. I keep telling her, No, Mom, you're only allowed to drink *occasionally*, like one glass of champagne *a year* at somebody's wedding. Maybe you can talk to her. Maybe she'll listen to you." Geoff got out a handkerchief and blew his nose and wiped his eyes.

I grabbed a premed student. "This is Geoff Hamilton," I told her. "His dad is Case Hamilton, chairman of the hospital's board of trustees."

"I know Mr. Hamilton," said the premed. She looked at Geoff with interest.

"Could you find him please? Tell him his wife's been brought in. Her diabetes is a little out of control."

The premed nodded and went off.

Geoff handed me his mother's notebook and purse. "She was pretty much doing all right until the shit hit the fan at the law firm—you know the partners voted Thursday night to dissolve the practice, right? There are only eighty partners, and sixty of them have already defected to Bennet Archer. Then Saturday, Gary Seligman was poisoned." He wiped his eyes again. "Dad was so upset. He went to the hospital as soon as he heard."

Something moved on the edge of my memory. But when I looked, it was gone.

"I was at our boarding school reunion," Geoff went on. "Dad and Mom didn't go this year because Vic broke his arm, and because of the problems at the law firm. Dad was at the firm almost all night Thursday and Friday, and most of Saturday and Sunday, up until dinner with you guys last night. Anyway, when I got back to the city yesterday Mom wasn't well, but she insisted on going to Vic's for dinner. I said,

'Mom, you better not be drinking,' and she said she wasn't. So I went on out to the Island. Then today the cops—" he stopped himself. "I have to see my dad. His secretary said he's here, but he hasn't called for his messages all day."

"The police came to your house." I made it sound like a statement, as if I'd known all along. "Your mother was already unwell, and then this business with the cops happened. The stress threw her sugar out of whack."

I saw him decide to confide in me. Geoff had always struck me as the caretaker child of the Hamilton brood, bearing the heavy weight of his parents' troubles all his life. He looked like he might welcome some help for a change.

"They searched the house this afternoon," he admitted. "You know the potting room, where Dad dries his mushroom specimens? They took every single specimen he had there, plus his notebooks. He's going to be sick when he hears. They searched the West End Avenue apartment, too. In fact, they timed both searches to coincide—when Mom called me to say they were searching the apartment, I was standing there watching them search the house. They wouldn't take no for an answer. They wouldn't wait for me to read the warrant like they're supposed to—and meanwhile, Mom was alone with more cops here in the city, at the apartment. I tried calling Dad but I couldn't reach him. As soon as the police were finished out at the house, I drove back in. And there's Mom with a big high-ball in her hand. Not really drunk, but acting disoriented . . . and looking the wrong way when I talked to her like she could hear me, but she didn't know where I was. I know diabetes puts her at risk for stroke. Maybe she *is* just drunk. But I didn't want to have to decide which myself. So I made her come in to the ER. I'm sorry to dump all this on you."

"Don't worry about it," I said.

"I thought about calling Vittorio and Alan," Geoff went on. "But you know Vic—he'd just start lecturing everyone in sight. What Dad needs now is a friend, someone sympathetic. Not Mayor Giuliani." He noticed my split lip, then my wrapped wrist. "What happened to you?" he asked, alarmed. "Did you get mugged?"

"I fell down the stairs," I said. "We'd better find your dad."

"Yeah," said Geoff. But as I moved off, he grabbed my arm. "Dad is the last person to admit he needs help. Could you help him anyway, even if he won't ask you to?"

"I'll do my best," I said. "But can I ask you something? That business about your grandmother's cook feeding her hallucinogenic mushrooms when he thought she needed a rest cure at the funny farm . . . ?" I trailed off, watching Geoff's face.

He looked away.

"It wasn't the cook, was it?"

Geoff shook his head. With some effort, he brought his eyes back to mine.

"Your father fed your grandmother those mushrooms himself, didn't he?" I asked softly.

"Yes."

"Because whenever she was on a drinking binge, he knew they would dry her out at this place they sent her to, this funny farm."

"Yes."

"Do the police know that?"

"I don't know," Geoff said.

thirty

"We ruled out stroke," I told Case and Geoff.

Case put his arm around his son's shoulder. "Thank God," he breathed.

"When you have a diabetic out of control like this, she can look like she's had a stroke," I explained. "The lethargy, confusion. But that's just the brain having trouble metabolizing glucose without enough insulin. We've given her a shot, and you can see her mentation is much better already. We'll run some tests."

"She's been under so much stress," Geoff murmured.

"Right. And the stress response triggers the release of large amounts of adrenaline, which in turn releases glucose into the bloodstream. But the body can't handle all that glucose without more insulin. So your mom's blood sugar was in the five hundreds. That was very alert of you to notice that her breath smelled fruity. You were right to bring her in."

Geoff looked considerably relieved to have his mother in good hands and his father nearby. "So what happens now?"

he asked. "Mom gets admitted and spends the night in the hospital?"

"Yes," I said. "She may have to stay a couple of days."

"I spoke with the endocrinologist," Case said. "She'll see her tomorrow, and we'll get her diabetes under control."

I had a couple of charts to do before they would be ready for Jackie upstairs, so I bowed out. Chip Nicholson came by at cruising speed and I shot out an arm and nailed him.

"Marie Powers, the possible hot appendix—the surgeon turfed her to GYN?"

"Right." He shifted an armful of sheets with a chart on top.

"What happened after the GYN saw her?"

"GYN did a full pelvic and signed off on her. She was released."

"Fine, but you need to document that. Look at what you've got in the chart. You saw the patient, GYN saw the patient, the patient went home. What are you going to do if that patient comes back at three A.M. with a ruptured appendix and Cabot says to you, 'Dr. Nicholson, why didn't you consult a surgeon?' "

"But I did consult a surgeon."

"You didn't get him to sign off on the chart. As far as I can tell, this woman was not seen by a surgeon. You also need to get Mark Ramsey to sign off on you. He's the intern, you're the med student. Twenty-dollar question—what's the most reliable way to rule out a hot appendix?"

"No rebound?"

I shook my head and smiled. "Ask the patient, 'If I could get you your favorite food, would you eat it?' If the patient says 'yes,' it's not appendicitis. If she says 'no,' get her ready for the OR. Any progress finding Seligman's chart?"

"ICU says it's gone to Admitting. Records Room didn't have it, so it must still be there. But Records did have the chart on Ramsey's sidewalk dump." He tipped his armload of sheets so the chart slid off.

I caught it. "Holy shit," I said, recognizing the surname of a famous wealthy American family. "No wonder she didn't want anyone to know she'd been dropped off with a heroin overdose. When she said she was worried about her boss, she must have meant Daddy." I took the chart and started flipping through it. There were Ramsey's notes from when the woman had broken her arm two years earlier: *Reverse Colles' fracture, radius displaced anteriorly.* Ramsey had been doing a summer clinical clerkship in University Hospital's ER, after his second year in medical school.

"Huh," I said. There was my own signature, under Ramsey's.

I started to laugh. "I gave Ramsey such a hard time for not remembering this patient—and here I don't remember her myself!" But now that I knew her name, of course it was jogging my memory. A vision of Ramsey pointing at the woman's X rays came flying straight out of my unconscious. *He's so shy with me,* I suddenly remembered having thought at the time, *but that patient draws him right out of himself. Because she's from his own milieu.*

Shy. That wasn't a word I would use to describe Ramsey today. Gregarious, outgoing, lots of nervous energy, eccentric maybe—but certainly not shy.

It was all coming back now: The three of us standing in front of the light box looking at the patient's X Rays—Ramsey, the patient, and me. I was asking Ramsey questions, he was answering them, and the patient was teasing us, asking questions of her own. Later I heard her and Ramsey discussing people they knew in common: guys who went to Ramsey's boarding school and pals from Yale, Harvard, Columbia, people who summered where Ramsey's family had summered when he was young and still had his parents living.

"Unfortunately, this woman left hours ago," Chip Nicholson was saying. "A guy in a spiffy Lincoln Town car came and bailed her out. He had a doctor with him who got the treatment plan from Ramsey, and off they went. Paid cash on their way out." He shrugged. "Records Room is a little behind." Charts often turned up hours after you requested them, often long after the patients were released. "I'll check Admitting for Seligman's chart."

I gave the chart back to Nicholson, shaking my head with a smile. Ramsey, *shy?* Not anymore. The accident had changed more than the way he looked.

I nipped in to see Jon Telsey, the bicyclist who'd hit his head and wasn't laying down new memory. "Mr. Telsey, you know where you are?"

"Um, University Hospital?" he asked.

"Very good. What happened to bring you here?"

He thought for a moment. "I fell off my bike?"

Telsey was much better than earlier. Although he didn't remember falling off his bike or whether he'd been wearing his helmet, he did remember what he'd been told the last time he asked.

"You know my name?" I asked.

"Uh . . . You helped me before?"

"I'm Dr. Sutcliffe. I helped you before." I smiled and patted his shoulder. "Anyone you'd like us to call?"

His sensorium seemed to clear right while I was standing there talking to him; suddenly he looked much more awake and alert. "Yeah, my hospital."

"Your hospital?"

"I'm a third-year resident in emergency medicine at Bellevue. You'd better call the ER down there and let them know where I am."

Jackie Hamilton was resting when I went in to tell her we were finally going upstairs. She opened her eyes and gave me a small smile. Fifty pounds overweight, pushing fifty, exhausted by her worries, depleted by her illness, not wearing any make-up—and she was still beautiful. The delicate crow's feet at the corners of her moss-green eyes seemed an adornment, the creases around her mouth a badge of good humor. She wore her honey-blond hair in an old-fashioned, shoulder-length pageboy, held back off her face by a black velvet headband. One could imagine her as anything: a member of a royal household, a *saloniste,* a university president, a model clamored for by Titian, Rubens, Rembrandt.

If Jackie drank enough to worry her son, I couldn't tell it by looking at her.

"Hell of a day," she sighed. She made it sound droll and amusing.

"Yes, it has been," I agreed. I checked her IV, and made sure her personal property bag was on the stretcher behind the headboard. "Your sugar was through the roof when you came in. How are you feeling now?"

"Like a damned fool. Case has so much on his mind. He doesn't need me to worry about. Where's my notebook?"

"It's in your property bag. I put it there myself."

"I'd like you to take the notebook and burn it," Jackie said. "If I'd had my wits about me when Geoff brought me in, I never would have let him bring that damn notebook. Yes, I keep my medical information in it—along with all kinds of personal information for my eyes only. I don't want it making the rounds of the hospital on the pretense that the medical staff needs to know my blood sugar levels. And I certainly don't want the cops getting their hands on it."

"I'll put it in my locker and return it to you when you're discharged," I promised.

I pushed Jackie's stretcher out of the emergency room, steered around a corner, and down a slight slope to the elevator banks.

"The walls have ears," Jackie said. "Stop this jalopy here for a moment. We might not get another chance to talk."

I stopped and went around to the side of the stretcher. Jackie took my hand. Speaking quietly but intensely, she said, "Someone's trying to frame my husband for Gary's death. You know it, and I know it. Whoever's behind this knows Case very, very well. All his soft spots and foibles, his disappointments in life, his failures. Case is a bitter and angry man who confides in no one. As a boy he was shamed by his father for expressing needs or asking for help or showing any kind of emotion. So, as a man, instead of asking for help, Case helps others. That's why he's here tonight, while the nurses are on strike. When Case is helping everyone else he can pretend that he himself needs no help whatsoever. Meanwhile, there were police searching our house. Where's my notebook?"

I rummaged in her bag and came up with the notebook, a plain spiral-bound type sold in the nearby University bookstore.

She went on: "He doesn't confide in me and hasn't for years. His great confidante in life was Pat von Laue. She was the only person he ever let help him. She's been dead for almost two years now, and without her Case is like a pressure cooker about to blow his lid. If he hasn't blown it already."

She lay back against the stretcher and closed her eyes.

I put the notebook in her lap. "What is it you want me to do exactly?" I asked.

"I'm going to be in the hospital for a few days," Jackie said without opening her eyes. Her voice was weary. "I'm not in any position to watch his back."

The elevator doors opened and we ascended. "Who do you think is trying to frame him?" I asked.

"I don't know. I was hoping you'd tell me."

"Jackie, don't drift off on me just yet. When was the last time you saw Gary?"

"Wednesday evening. Vittorio was in surgery. Alan called from the hospital looking for Case. But Case was off at an emergency meeting at the firm. Alan told me about Vic's accident, and I asked Alan if he needed me to bring anything to the hospital. Alan gave me a list—Vic's shaving kit, pajamas, that sort of thing—and I went downstairs and let myself into their apartment.

"I found Gary there in the study, sitting at Vittorio's desk. He had Vic's briefcase open, and he was reading through some files."

"Files? What kind of files?"

"Hospital files, it looked like. He hadn't heard me come in and he nearly jumped through the ceiling. I was just as surprised to see him. It gave me quite a fright. He immediately asked a lot of questions about Vittorio to distract me. Was the surgery over, what did the doctor say, how did Alan seem, that kind of thing. He said he was baking bread for Alan and Vic, then let it drop as casually as possible that he was going to call Alan's cellphone. So I would think that he was in the study to use the phone. There's a phone in the kitchen, but I wasn't about to challenge him—why should I? I've never understood Alan's continuing his relationship with Gary. If Vittorio wants to look the other way, it's not my place to say anything. Who knows what their arrangement is? Anyway, I smelled the bread baking. Gary called Alan and spoke to him. So I let it go. I packed Vic's things and left."

The elevator doors ground open and I pushed Jackie's stretcher out. We went down the hall, around a corner, and into the skywalk between buildings. Across the skywalk, through another set of doors. Around another corner, down another corridor. . . . Sometimes I felt as if I were pushing a patient clear across town when the distance was really only the equivalent of one city block. We stopped in front of yet another elevator bank, this time to go back down.

"Alan thinks Gary went to Case and Vittorio's reunion Friday night," I said.

"Really? Geoff mentioned that he saw someone there who looked like Gary. But why would Gary go?"

The elevator came. We got on. "When did Geoff think he saw him?"

"Friday, as you said. Some of the forms, including both Geoff's and Case's, were meeting in a bar in town. As Geoff came in, he said he saw a man who looked like Gary just going out the back. Geoff didn't see him, really, just a glimpse of him in profile. Then he was gone."

"Did Geoff see him again Saturday?"

"No. And Geoff looked for him. Because he couldn't think what Gary would be doing there."

I did a fast calculation. The school was in northwestern Connecticut, at least a four-hour drive from New York. Gary was in my apartment cooking by the time I came home for lunch on Saturday. If he'd left the school that morning, he could have made it easily.

The elevator doors cranked open; I pulled Jackie into the last corridor and around the last corner. We had reached our destination. But there was no one in the nurses' station to take my report. From down the hall came pitched voices:

"I don't care what the nursing home said, they always feed you some cock-and-bull—"

"Then *you* talk to the nursing home, Doctor!" A white-uniformed woman stormed out of a room. Rent-a-Nurse on a roll. She started toward us, then waved and called, "Just a minute, Doll!" and ducked into the ladies room.

There was the sound of a toilet flushing, then running water. The Rent-a-Nurse came out of the bathroom. A large woman with flaming orange hair and lipstick to match, she lumbered toward us with a warm, welcoming smile on her face. "Whatsa matter, Hon?" she said to Jackie in a backwoods Southern drawl, "You fixin' to check in?"

"I'm afraid my diabetes is a little out of control," Jackie said.

"Oh, I know what you mean—I'm diabetic myself. Don't you worry yourself, we'll get you all straightened out in no time." She narrowed her eyes at me. "I hope you're not going to give me any trouble."

"I wouldn't think of it," I said.

"You're one of the smart ones."

"Takes one to know one," I smiled. I gave her my report. She listened intently, glanced through the chart, and asked a couple of extremely astute questions. We wheeled Jackie into a private room and helped her climb into bed.

"How did you hear that Gary might have been poisoned?" I asked Jackie after the nurse left.

"Lauren called me at the apartment." She thought a moment. "I guess it was about seven Saturday evening. I told her that Case was still at the firm, and she reached him there. Case called me around eleven and told me that he'd been to the hospital, but was back at the law firm, and expected to stay at the firm until early morning. He said he had talked to Vic in the ICU waiting room, and had then visited briefly with Gary."

I felt my spine tingle.

"I'm surprised you didn't see him," Jackie said. "Weren't you and Phil keeping vigil in the ICU?"

"We were down the hall in the waiting room part of the time. Case must not have stayed very long."

"No, he wouldn't have. The crisis at the firm . . ." she trailed off.

I nodded and excused myself.

All the way back to the ER I thought, *Case visited Gary . . . and then Gary died. . . .*

Jackie took insulin, and Case had access to it.

I needed to get my hands on that chart.

thirty-one

"Help," Mark Ramsey pleaded as I came back into the ER.

"Sure. What kind?"

He walked over to the light box on the wall next to OR Three and slapped a couple of X Rays up.

"Mrs. Geller. Got up in the middle of the night to go to the bathroom, walked into her dresser, fell, and broke her wrist. Here's the fracture." He pointed. "Lower end of the radius, posterior displacement?"

"Right."

"What's that called again?"

"Colles' fracture. If the radius were displaced anteriorly, it would be a reverse Colles' fracture, or Smith's fracture—same thing." I shot a look sideways. Ramsey stared earnestly at the X Rays.

"Mark, your sidewalk dump patient—"

"Yeah," he said.

"She had a reverse Colles' fracture two years ago."

He lifted his hands helplessly. "I don't remember her at

all. Lost those brain cells when I drove the car into that ravine, 'We're going over!' " He punched his fist into his open palm. "Splat! What can I tell you."

It was hard to find fault with someone who humbly admitted that he didn't have a flying clue. Colles' fracture? What's that? I'd had incompetent interns under me a couple of times before, two of whom had in fact been dismissed from the emergency medicine residency program. The difference was, if they didn't know a Colles' fracture from a hole in the ground, they'd lie and bluff their way out of it. And that's what got them thrown out: the lying and bluffing to cover the incompetence.

"You feel competent casting this patient?" I asked.

"I think so," he said. "If I get into trouble, can I come get you?"

"Of course. But try to come get me before the plaster sets."

He laughed.

I looked at him a little more closely. "Ramsey, you have lipstick on your mouth."

"I do?" Blushing, he began to scrub at his mouth with the back of his hand.

The doors of the ambulance bay banged open and a gurney came through. Tsach and Oliveri again. A thin young woman lay curled in the fetal position, moaning very quietly.

"Boomerang," announced Oliveri. "You guys sent her home a couple of hours ago. Marie Powers, twenty-six-year-old black female, right lower quadrant pain, nausea, and vomiting, rebound tenderness, pain on cough. Can't get any more classic than that—my mother could tell you she's got a hot appendix. She says she saw a doc, a surgeon, and an OB-GYN. What happened to your face, Doc?"

"Fell down the stairs." I turned to the patient. "Ms. Powers, I'm really sorry. We'll get you admitted to the surgical service right away." I put my hand on her forehead. She was febrile. Damn.

Pulling the stretcher into Closet Two, one of the exam areas, I set to work quickly taking the patient's temperature, blood pressure, heart rate, and respiration rate. I drew bloods and sent them off to the lab. Meanwhile, I had the clerk chase down the patient's chart and page Nicholson.

"Who's the surgeon?" I demanded when Chip appeared, looking rumpled, his hair standing slightly on end. He'd obviously been napping. I glanced at my watch. Two A.M. It was going to be a long night.

"Oh, no," Nicholson moaned, seeing the patient. "I *told* Dr. Russell she had a hot appendix—he wouldn't listen to me."

"Get him on the phone. Tell him we're coming up."

Nicholson and I rushed Powers out of the ER and around the corner to the elevator. As we ascended, he paged frantically through the chart. "He never signed. Dr. Sutcliffe, I called him like you said and told him I needed him to sign off."

"Well, get him to do it before he scrubs in," I said. The elevator doors opened, we pulled the stretcher out, and raced down the hall.

Then, for us, the race was over. We handed the patient over to a Rent-a-Nurse and gave our report. Nicholson chased down Dr. Russell and demanded that he write a note. Russell wrote. Nicholson and I went back down to the ER.

As we walked down the exact same stairs I'd been thrown down earlier, I asked Chip if he'd had any luck finding Gary Seligman's chart.

"Yes," he said. A strange light flickered in his eyes, and his mouth set grimly. "Dr. Durbin has it."

Dr. Allison Durbin was the hospital's senior vice-president for medical affairs and associate dean of the University College of Physicians and Surgeons. In simpler terms, she was the chief of chiefs: the boss of all the directors of the various services, including Dr. Chris Cabot, my boss and the director of the emergency department.

"Really?"

"The clerk in Admitting says she came and took the chart personally. Durbin asked the clerk if he had billed anyone or entered anything in the computer or photocopied anything or filed it—and then she stood there while he went into the computer and made a note in the computer records that she had the chart. Gave the clerk a very stern lecture, he said, on how he was not to divulge any details about Gary Seligman to anyone including docs, or she'd have his job. Then off she went with the chart."

"Wow," I said.

"And there's a computer block on all his labs results. Can't get those either. However," he smiled, "it just so happened that Dr. Sachs had a copy of the chart on his desk. And I was able to copy that." He reached into his coat pocket and withdrew a sheaf of paper rolled up like a diploma.

"How did you get that?" I asked.

"Don't ask."

"Okay," I said after a moment, slipping the sheaf of papers into my own pocket. "You have any trouble with Russell, you let me know. I'll back you."

"Just what I had in mind," said Nicholson.

At 3:30 A.M. after seeing the last waiting patient, I told the clerks and chief Rent-a-Nurse that I was going to lie down for a little while in Holding. Julio, the ER ward clerk, made a note next to my name on the whiteboard in the nurses' station.

"Wake-up?" he asked.

I nodded. "Thanks, at six-thirty."

"Sleep tight, Doctor."

"Yeah," I said.

I went around the corner from the ambulance bay to Holding, where I found an unoccupied cubicle. Instead of lying down, however, I sat down at the small desk next to the stretcher. I pulled out the copy of Gary's chart that Nicholson had made for me, took a deep breath, and closed my eyes.

I wanted to clear my head. So I could look at the chart with new eyes, without a working diagnosis or foregone conclusions. Without anxiety, guilt, false sentiment or anger.

Yeah, good luck, I thought. *As if you could actually unpack all that.* But I made the effort.

When I had reached as zenlike a state as I was likely to achieve, I opened my eyes and set to work.

I personally had written all the ER section of the chart, except for the med student's notes, written by Nicholson, and a very brief nursing note, penned by Kathy Haughey. There were five signatures: mine, Ramsey's, Nicholson's, Haughey's, and that of the attending physician.

Nicholson had penned a rather long treatise summarizing his conversation with Poison Control, meticulously detailing the protocol for death caps, which we had followed. Med student diagnosis: "?ingestion psilocybin-containing mushrooms, ?ingestion cyclopeptide-containing mushrooms."

Professor Held believed that Gary had eaten muscarine-containing mushrooms, "the divine mushroom of immortality," *Amanita muscaria.* I scanned the routine labs. Nothing jumped out at me.

I made myself read my summary of the botched lavage and Gary's aspiration. Immediately my grief welled up, as if to punctuate the remote and unfeeling medicalese. Tears fell and pooled on the lenses of my glasses.

I fought for control and turned the page to the ICU notes.

An admission note scrawled by David Ulrich, the critical care fellow, co-signed by the attending. Nuncie Thomasson's precise, Catholic-school-girl hand recorded row after row of values in the nursing notes: blood pressure, heart rate, respiration rate, temperature, various readouts from the ventilator, cardiograph strips, etc. I scanned them all. All were values that could be expected in a sedated patient on a vent suffering from aspiration lung injury.

Pausing to blow my nose, I moved on to the code sheet. When a patient's heart stops and you call a code, a nurse sits down at a little table and begins a running log of the time and administration of all medications and what the docs say: the hospital version of the courtroom stenographer. The code sheet allows anyone doing chart review to reconstruct exactly what physical signs the patient showed during the code and what the docs did about it. Moreover, Admitting was going to bill someone for every single procedure performed, every single blood test sent, and every single drug administered.

Sunday night after Vittorio's dinner party, I'd sat up reading that pile of photocopies of articles on toxic and hallucinogenic mushrooms Nicholson had bird-dogged for me. Included in the pile were several case studies of patients who had presented to emergency rooms having eaten mushrooms later identified as *Amanita muscaria*.

But as I reviewed the chart, it became clear that nothing I'd read about *Amanita muscaria* answered the questions I still had about why Gary died. Any way I looked at it, muscarinic effects should not have been severe enough to cause Gary's death. One type of muscarine-containing mushroom mentioned in the articles had anti-cholinergic effects that might cause a rapid heartbeat, but not rapid enough for him to go into V-fib.

Face it, Sutcliffe, Gary died from the pulmonary complications of the botched lavage. The aspiration caused lung damage. Which resulted in a state of insufficient oxygenation. Which caused Gary's blood pressure to fall. He went into shock and died.

Unless.

I had made a big effort to hold one particular thought at bay while I read through the chart. It now leaped to the front of my mind like the proverbial cat leaped out of the bag:

Unless Case Hamilton gave Gary a whopping dose of insulin.

My heart beating, I started going through the computer printouts of lab results. I found the Chem 7 that was routinely ordered two hours before Gary coded. I compared it with the Chem 7 that was sent during the code.

The first Chem 7 showed that Gary's glucose was within normal limits. Two and a half hours later, according to the second Chem 7, Gary's glucose was 6.

The tears that fell now were tears of relief and anger: Mark Ramsey and I did not kill Gary Seligman. Someone who had looked in on the unconscious Gary did. That someone gave Gary a whopping dose of insulin. That's what caused his heart to stop. Not mushrooms and not the botched lavage.

But I found that I just couldn't make myself believe that that someone had been Case Hamilton.

I took my glasses off my face and wiped my eyes.

Normally when a patient develops heart dysrhythmias like Gary did, the docs check for metabolic derangement—low blood sugar—to see if the patient is diabetic. But we all knew Gary personally. We knew he wasn't diabetic. So we didn't check. And other physical signs that might have clued us in to the dangerously low glucose level were masked by the fact that Gary was sedated and on a ventilator.

We assumed that Gary's dysrhythmia was caused by insufficient oxygenation due to lung damage from the aspiration.

Whoever gave Gary the insulin knew there was a good chance that we would miss metabolic derangement as the cause of Gary's dysrhythmia.

And if that person was trying to frame Case Hamilton, he or she was doing a pretty damn good job.

*   *   *

"Ev."

I bolted upright. Somehow I'd made it from the desk chair to the stretcher and Never Never Land. I had no idea where I was, who I was, what day it was, or who the President was.

Case Hamilton was bending over me.

"Sorry to wake you. Wanted to make sure I spoke to you before, ah, ah—wanted to make sure you know how much I appreciate all you've done for me and my family." He swallowed.

I sat up and slid off the stretcher to my feet. "Is something happening? Is Jackie all right?"

But he gave up trying to talk and embraced me. I felt his nose and mouth against my neck.

Something jumped directly from his unconscious into my unconsciousness and sparked. "What are you talking about?" I asked sharply, coming fully awake. *Christ. He's going to kill himself.* "Why are you saying goodbye?"

And then Detective Ost and his partner, Detective Jude Rainey, pushed the curtain of the cubicle aside.

I'm dreaming, I thought. Behind Ost and Rainey I could see two uniformed police officers. With guns drawn. Pointing at the ceiling, just like on TV.

Case was still hugging me, unmoving and still. I pounded on his back. "Case!"

Unfortunately, this seemed to convince Detective Ost that I was being hugged against my will. Possibly even that Hamilton was assaulting or molesting me. Roughly, Ost grabbed Hamilton and yanked him away from me.

"Julian Case Hamilton," Ost barked. His eyes met mine without feeling. "You are under arrest for the murder of Gary Seligman."

There was the rasp of handcuffs.

"You have the right to remain silent. Anything you say

can and will be used against you in a court of law. Do you understand?"

"Yes, I'm an attorney," said Case. "I know my rights."

"You have the right to an attorney," Ost continued mechanically, fulfilling his legal obligation to read the suspect his rights whether or not the suspect knew them. "If you cannot afford an attorney, one will be—"

"Who should I call?" I asked.

"Vittorio."

"Anyone else?"

But the police were dragging him away. "Ev, I swear to you, I didn't send that basket!" Case called as they yanked him around the corner.

I ran after them. "You're making a mistake. Someone's trying to frame him," I cried. "Ozzie, please!"

"Not now, Doc."

"Elise Vanderlaende knows that story about the Hamilton family cook and the mushrooms on toast. She heard it at a Morningside Mycological Society meeting. She wanted to poison me so she could have Phil all to herself, and she needed someone to pin the poisoning on so she copycatted the cook's mushrooms on toast. Then she snuck into the ICU dressed as a doc and shot Gary full of insulin! Gary didn't die from the mushrooms or the aspiration injury—he died from an overdose of insulin!"

That got Ost's attention, but did not deter him from his mission. "Tell it to his lawyer."

They took Case out the ambulance bay entrance, sparing him the humiliation of being paraded in handcuffs past the nurses' station. Outside it was still dark. Except for a startled pair of paramedics staring from their rig, the street was deserted.

"Ozzie, wait," I said. "Please."

Ost handed Hamilton over to Jude Rainey, who put him

in the backseat of the police car, guiding his head with her hand so he wouldn't knock it as he got in.

Ost looked at me without expression. If he noticed my swollen mouth, he didn't comment.

"I'm afraid he'll harm himself," I said. "He has that look. Can you take his belt or whatever it is you do? Suicide watch?"

"Yeah," said Ost.

"Where are you going, the Two-Six?"

"Yeah."

Without another word he turned, opened the passenger side door of the police car, and got in.

thirty-two

At seven A.M. Tuesday morning the first University Hospital staff nurses returned to work. The twenty-four-hour nurses' strike was technically over.

The docs who supported the nurses lined up in the ambulance bay as the nurses came in, cheering and whistling and stomping their feet.

"California here I come," sang nurse Helen Yannis.

Not everyone could come back to work, however. In order to contract the Rent-a-Nurses, the hospital had agreed to hire them for a three-day minimum. That meant that the staff nurses they replaced could not come back until Thursday morning, which was about two-thirds of the normal staff.

"We are now officially off diversion for level-one trauma," Chris Cabot announced at five past seven. "The University Hospital emergency department is open for business. That could be good news, or bad news—you decide," he added with a crinkly smile.

Level-one trauma was blood squooshing in your shoes:

multiple-trauma motor-vehicle-accidents, gunshot wounds, stab wounds, jumpers from heights above the third floor.

"Bring on the blood and gore!" yelled someone from the trauma team. "I want veins in my teeth!"

"There's always someone who's sorry he wasn't at My Lai," Jazz Washington said as we broke ranks to await the first patients of the day.

"Dr. Sutcliffe, call for you." The ward clerk handed me the phone.

"How smart is this Elise Vanderlaende person?" the voice on the other end demanded without introduction. Vittorio, who else?

Since our first conversation at five-thirty when I'd called to inform him of Case Hamilton's arrest, Vic and I had achieved new heights of communication. Our first phone call had run thus:

"The cops just arrested Case and charged him with Gary's murder."

"When?"

"Just. Two minutes ago."

"You're sure he's been charged?"

"They read him his rights. 'You're under arrest.' "

"Where'd they take him?"

"The Twenty-sixth Precinct."

"He say who he wants for his lawyer?"

"No. He said to call you."

"Anything else I should know?"

"Yes, someone shot enough insulin into Gary while he was up in the ICU to stop his heart."

"Thank you, Evelyn." Click.

The second phone call was a two-liner:

"Where's Jackie?"

"Minuit, room two-oh-eight. Extension twenty-four thirty-nine."

"Thank you, Evelyn." Click.

To "How smart is this Elise Vanderlaende?" I said, "Very. Call Phil."

"Thank you, Evelyn." Click.

It was going to be a very long day. With only two hours of sleep under my belt, it was too long already. I decided to lose the plastic splint and Ace bandage. There was no way I could work with them.

"*Notificación.*" The clerk's voice rang out.

I could hear the sirens already, whoop-whoop-whooping down Amsterdam. The ambulance would be here before we finished talking to it.

"I'll take it," I said, limbering up my stiff wrist. It hurt, but not too badly.

The day was about to become even longer.

"Gunshot wound to the chest," the medic reported as he and his partner lifted the gurney down from the ambulance to the pavement. "Last BP eighty over forty, absent breath sounds on the left, IVs running wide and open!" Quickly they yanked the collapsible gurney up to waist height and we flew into the ER.

"OR One," I directed. "Julio! Get me Respiratory, page me Thoracic! Helen!"

The charge nurse appeared at my elbow, grabbed a Rent-a-Nurse, and ran ahead of us into the emergency room's OR One. Chip Nicholson materialized, still holding a cup of coffee. He hastily put it down on the counter at the nurses' station.

"Where's Ramsey?" I asked. There was no time to suit up; I grabbed a face shield and yanked on gloves. The medics had already intubated the patient; one medic pumped oxygen into his lungs with an ambubag. The patient stared up at me weakly. He looked to be in his mid-fifties, salt-and-pepper hair, well-groomed; a businessman maybe. "We know this guy's name?"

"David Al-Sharif."

"Mr. Al-Sharif, can you hear me?"

The patient nodded weakly.

"Okay, I'm Dr. Sutcliffe. We're going to take care of you."

The team worked in concert, quickly. While Helen revitaled the patient and called out the numbers, the Rent-a-Nurse cut off his suit pants, and Nicholson checked the patient's lines, I auscultated his chest. "We've got tachycardia and no breath sounds on the left," I said. "He's got a hemo-pneumo; let's throw in a left chest tube."

By now Respiratory was on the scene in the form of a young Latina who took over the bag from the medic. The medics bowed out and the cops came in; out of the corner of my eye I saw the uniforms. The room was filling up. "Julio!" I yelled. "Where the hell is Ramsey?"

"Sorry, sorry," said Ramsey, coming in at a run, knocking against a police officer. "I went upstairs to talk to Mr. Jhang."

"Put in this chest tube. I'll help you. Mr. Al-Sharif, I'm sorry, this is going to hurt. But you have blood in your lung and we have to let it out or you won't be able to breathe."

Grabbing a face shield and yanking on gloves, Ramsey reached into the chest tube tray as Nicholson and Helen braced the patient. Ramsey hesitated only a second before plunging the scalpel blade into the patient's chest and making the incision. The patient jumped from the pain and Ramsey apologized wildly. But seconds later, the tube was in and hooked up to the suction device. Blood bubbled noisily into the canister. The patient's lung reinflated.

"Ha!" cried Ramsey triumphantly. "*Ha!*"

I quickly briefed him on what he had missed. "What do you want to do?"

"Six units of O-neg, chest X ray, CBCs, type and cross-match!" Ramsey yelled happily.

"I concur," I said, smiling. I made a motion with my hands for him to quiet down. He took my point and started talking to the patient.

"Way to go, Ramsey," said Helen under her breath.

But a couple of minutes later the patient took a nosedive. "His pressure's down to sixty," Helen informed me. "Distended neck veins. Can't hear his heart sounds."

"Probably in tamponade," I said, glancing nervously toward the door. I could count on one hand the times I'd seen a chest cracked, and I had never done one unassisted. "Find Dr. Hollister for me, please," I told the premed. "Where the hell is Thoracic?" To Helen: "Set up a thoracotomy tray please."

Sixty seconds later neither the attending nor the thoracic surgeon had appeared but I couldn't wait any longer. Murmuring a prayer, I took the scalpel and cut horizontally and deeply through the muscles between the ribs, making a ten-inch incision from the breastbone on the left all the way around to the armpit. Helen handed me the large metal rib spreader, a ghastly device; if you didn't know what it was, you'd think it belonged on a car mechanic's bench. I inserted the device between two of the ribs and spread them wide enough to get both hands in. The cartilage popped noisily.

And there was the patient's heart, straining to beat. The sac around the heart, the pericardium, bulged from the blood that had seeped into it.

"You're doing fine, Ev," said a familiar voice behind me. Dr. Alex McCabe, chief resident on the Thoracic Surgery Service. I looked around and saw the attending, Dr. Jack Hollister, come into the room. The troops had arrived.

With surgical scissors, I made a tiny incision in the pericardium. Blood gushed out. The pressure relieved, the heart began to beat more forcefully. On the monitor, the blood pressure climbed to ninety.

"Very nice," said McCabe. "Let's take him up."

I was breathing like I had just run up six flights of stairs, my knees were shaking so bad I could feel the legs of my pants flapping in the wind, and my own heart was in my ears so loudly I could barely hear.

"Nice save, Sutcliffe!" The chief resident pounded me on the back. We were all standing around the nurses' station congratulating one another.

"Thanks. Ramsey here put in the chest tube." I wanted Ramsey to get his, too. I could see he was pleased as punch.

"Dr. Sutcliffe, phone for you."

"This is Dr. Sutcliffe," I said into the receiver.

It was Alan. "Vic asked me to call you and report that Case's attorney finally arrived at the precinct. But he still hasn't been charged. They're waiting for the D.A."

"Does Craig know anything?" I asked.

Next to me the conversation about our glorious save of Mr. Al-Sharif was still going on, and the detective in charge of the case was about to enlighten us with the circumstances of the shooting. Meanwhile, Nicholson had just asked Ramsey, "How's Mr. Jhang upstairs? Does he know his daughter?" I wanted to hear that, too. All the conversations mixed in my ears, while I tried to hear what Alan was saying.

"Craig got someone to tell him the police found Case's fingerprints on some of the mushrooms in the gift basket. That's all I know right now."

I stuck a finger in my ear so I could hear Alan. "What about Jackie?"

"Lauren and Geoff are with her. And the clan is gathering. All the other kids are driving down or flying up or whatever. I'll set up Camp Hamilton here and feed drop-ins. Berta and I are going over menus as we speak. Oh, one thing I wanted to ask you. Where's Gary's briefcase? Did you hide it somewhere?"

"What briefcase?"

"He had it with him when he came in Saturday, but Berta and I didn't find it while we were cleaning up yesterday."

I thought about that.

Across from me, the detective telling about Al-Sharif's shooting was making big swooping gestures with his arms.

"Maybe that's what the burglar wanted," I said finally. "Maybe he only took my computer and threw my stuff around to make it look like a burglary."

"Well, look for it when you get home, will you?" Alan said.

By the time I staggered out of the hospital late Tuesday evening my brains were fried. I walked straight out of the ambulance bay into a raging downpour and counted it as a shower. At the corner of Amsterdam, I stood dumbly waiting for the light to change without noticing that there was no traffic and I could cross unimpeded if I wanted. When the light changed I crossed.

Staggering dripping and wet into the doctors' residence, I stood in front of the elevator and waited like an automaton for the doors to open. On my floor I got out and lurched to my apartment. Once inside the door, I stepped out of my clothes and let them fall in a soggy heap on the floor.

Phil was already in bed asleep, sprawled on his back with his mouth open, snoring loudly. I took one second to appreciate how clean and neat the apartment was and two seconds to wrap a towel around my dripping hair before I fell into bed.

The briefcase, I thought.

Too late. By then I was sinking fast into oblivion.

The deeply resonant voice of National Public Radio's Bob Edwards penetrated my brain and coaxed me out of sleep. Sixten A.M. How did Edwards manage to sound so damned alert and awake at such an ungodly hour?

Next to me, Phil groaned. He thrust out an arm to see if I was there. "What time did you come in?" he yawned. "I must have been really out of it."

"You were. Me too."

"I'll say. Why do you have a towel wrapped around your head?"

"It was pouring. I was too tired to dry my hair." I rolled over, gave him a little kiss, then got up and staggered into the bathroom. The phone started ringing. "I can't get there before seven," I said over my shoulder as I closed the bathroom door. Jesus. Can't I even take a shower? What do they want, my blood?

I was sleeping standing up under the hot shower when Phil joined me and nudged me awake. "That was Vittorio. They arraigned Case finally at two A.M. and released him on five hundred thousand dollars bail."

"God—who posted that, Vittorio?"

"Apparently. Vic wants to know if Gary's briefcase is here."

The briefcase. "Oh, right—I was going to look for it." I quickly washed my hair, soaped and rinsed, and got out of the shower. Dashing around in my underwear, my blow dryer in one hand, I yanked open the closet and reached for a clean shirt and saw the dry cleaner bags Alan had brought home the day before. Through the plastic I could see the yellow silk dress he'd mentioned that I didn't own. As soon as the hospital returned to normal madness, I'd have to go to the cleaners and straighten out this business. Where were my clothes? Why did they keep giving me someone else's clothes?

But first: Gary's briefcase.

Phil and I searched the apartment, but no luck. Just as I was going out the door, however, on a whim I looked behind the living room couch. There, wedged between the couch and the wall, was Gary's maroon canvas briefcase.

Both Phil and I had to get to the hospital, so we could only quickly glance through the contents.

Two videotapes: *Trop Belle Pour Toi* and *La Retour de Martin Guerre*. Gary had loved French films. Although why he would be carrying videos around in his briefcase, I didn't know.

I took out two fat brown legal folders, the kind you can tie shut with strings. The first was marked "Union." Inside was Nurses' strike stuff, Xeroxes of newspaper articles about the strike, and papers relating to a case Gary was looking into of a nurse who claimed to have been unjustly fired from the ICU.

I opened the second file, which turned out to be stuffed full of Residency and Fellowship Committee matters, including memos addressed to Vittorio and copies of interns' and residents' blue-jacketed personnel files. I flipped through them, glancing at familiar names. Abigail Kubota, Keith Herrera, Jasmine Washington, Mark Ramsey, and my own, among others. I opened Mark's. Xeroxes of his original application to the residency program; correspondence asking to delay his entry into the program for a year, including three newspaper articles: ONE INJURED, ONE KILLED: BEST FRIENDS IN DRUNK DRIVING ACCIDENT; DRIVER ARRAIGNED IN DRUNK DRIVING ACCIDENT; and DR. MARK RAMSEY LEAVES HOSPITAL; the incident report I'd filed with Chris Cabot after Ramsey lost the guide wire trying to put in an arterial line; an article Mark had written for his boarding school alumni newsletter.

"What's Gary doing with those?" Phil asked, looking over my shoulder. "They're Vittorio's papers, aren't they?"

"Yes, you're right. Jackie Hamilton said she caught Gary going through Vic's papers the night Vic had surgery for his arm." I put Mark's file back and set the folder aside, reaching into the briefcase and pulling out a large intra-hospital envelope.

Inside were news clippings. "Look at this—here's all the dirt on Di Clausson's divorce." As one of the leading AIDS researchers in the city, her soon-to-be-ex, Dr. Hans-Albrecht Clausson, rated coverage in the gossip columns. But there was nothing new there; everyone in the hospital had read every scrap when the items first ran in August—including Phil and me.

I turned the briefcase upside down to see if anything else fell out. Nothing. I unzipped the inside pocket and found Gary's keys.

"Well, that was less than illuminating," Phil said.

"Wait." I was rummaging in the briefcase's outside pocket. I pulled out a glossy newsletter from Vittorio and Case's boarding school in Connecticut, along with a printed schedule of activities for "Old Home, October 11-12-13." On the back, the address label read "Julian Case Hamilton."

"Even less illuminating," said Phil.

I unfolded the newsletter. A blue correspondence card tumbled out.

" 'Gary,' " I read aloud, " 'I can't tell you how much I appreciate your meeting me for coffee to speak French! I really really need the practice, and your French is so fabulous!' "

"Give me that," Phil cried. He snatched the card. " '*Oh la la, quel boulot cette langue, avec mes sentiments chaleureux*, Elise Vanderlaende.' " He threw the card against the wall. "Jesus Mary and Joseph, is this woman going to worm her way into the bosom of every single goddamn person who knows me on earth?"

"I don't think that's the right question," I said. "I think the right question is, 'Who else is going to wind up dead?' "

We parked the briefcase next to the front door where Alan

could find it. As we left the apartment, Phil said, "Tomorrow I get a restraining order."

I locked the door.

"I hope that's soon enough," I said.

It might have been soon enough if we hadn't decided, completely on the spur of the moment, to spend Wednesday night at Phil's apartment.

Usually on Monday evenings Phil saw patients in groups. He got home late exhausted and liked to unwind by himself. So he stayed at his place and I stayed at mine.

Tuesday evenings I tried to go to yoga. Phil stayed late at the hospital to complete paperwork, then met with the shrink who supervised him. He got home late, exhausted and preoccupied, but stayed up another hour or two to go over in his mind what transpired at this session. So he stayed at his place and I stayed at mine.

Wednesdays after a full day at the hospital, we spent the evening together. I would cook a little something or we'd go down the street to the Greek restaurant, or over to Broadway to the Italian restaurant. Then he stayed over at my place.

Thursdays we stayed at Phil's, and he would cook a little something, or we'd order in from the Greeks, the Italians, the Indians, or the Chinese.

The weekend we stayed wherever, depending. Why we're so rigid Mondays through Thursdays and so flexible on the weekends I've never figured out, but there you have it.

And why we decided suddenly to go to Phil's on Wednesday night I haven't figured out either. Of course, Gary's death, the burglary, and the nurses' strike threw us both, to put it mildly. Phil had to cancel his usual sessions Tuesday evening, and we'd both been up most of the night Monday, so we decided to stay at my cleaned-up apartment Tuesday night, which I guess meant it was time to go to his on Wednesday. . . .

Which was how we happened to discover that Wednesday was the night Elise Vanderlaende liked to stay at Phil's.

Wearing my clothes.

Sleeping in his bed.

thirty-three

O f course, I'd have to walk in on Elise naked.

Not her. Me. Yet another reason not to sleep at Phil's that night: it was pouring again. We'd walked over from the hospital in the rain and come in soaked to the bone, and I'd shed my clothes in the foyer just as I had in my own apartment the night before, except that this night I hung them in the bathroom before proceeding to the bedroom—

I was so shocked to see her my feet actually left the floor in a bizarre airborne flinch. I came down full of adrenaline yet feeling at the same time that my heart had stopped. And there I was: stark naked.

While she sat calmly on the bed wearing my black silk chemise. With a bemused look on her face. She had a magazine in her lap and an apple in her hand, and as I executed my strange jeté she actually had the temerity *to turn the page and take a bite of apple and chew.*

I opened the closet, yanked out a robe, pulled it on, and tied the belt with a jerk. All kinds of things flashed through my head. *Don't turn your back on her. Does she have a weapon? Just because you don't see one doesn't mean she's not sitting on it.* And right on to: *Christ, it's all true. Phil's having an affair with this young, long-legged, long-necked, goddesslike girl-woman after all.*

"You're wearing my chemise," I said. Rage rattled my voice; in fact all of me rattled like a dilapidated shack in the wind. "How did you get in here?" Now I was barking and even angrier that she got to see me lose my cool. Vanderlaende one, Sutcliffe zero.

"I have keys," she said. She met my gaze and held it long enough to let me know she could look me in the eye. Then she glanced toward the bedroom door. In the kitchen, Phil had turned on the radio. I heard the mellifluous, intimate murmuring of WNYC's David Garland, then Chopin.

"How do you want to handle this?" Elise asked.

"Handle this?" I repeated. The force of her personality was flabbergasting. She was what—*twenty-one?* At twenty-one, I had been tentative and apologetic, testing the water with all ten toes, one toe at a time. In comparison Elise seemed capable of Olympic-level diving. I marveled that I had ever seen her scream. How could that young woman screaming in the ER be this young woman, cool and in command?

I found my own voice, the unrattled one. "Phil," I called. "Could you come in here, please?"

"How about a glass of wine?" he called back from the kitchen.

"Not right now. Come in here."

"You're sure you want to do this?" Elise asked. "It won't be pretty." When I didn't answer she shrugged, got up from the bed, reached for a pair of jeans neatly folded on the slipper chair, and pulled them on. "There's no reason to have a knockdown confrontation, you know." She tucked in the chemise— my chemise—and zipped up her jeans.

The she went back to eating her apple.

I moved to the threshold of the bedroom. "Phil," I called again. "Leave the wine for a minute and come in here—*now*."

The Chopin stopped in mid-phrase. I heard a door quietly open, then shut. Phil appeared at the end of the hall. He held his baseball bat with both hands, across his chest, like a police baton. "Is everything all right?" he asked conversationally. With raised eyebrows he lifted his chin toward the bedroom. I shook my head. He seemed to lower his gravity. Knees bent, long strides, he moved quickly toward me, then past, into the bedroom.

"Jesus Mary Mother of God!" he gasped.

"Hello, Phil," said Elise. She took another bite of apple.

For a long slow moment Phil looked in utter incomprehension from Elise to me and back to Elise. Then anger possessed him. Dropping his bat, in two strides he was upon her. "HOW DID YOU GET IN HERE?" he roared. He grabbed her by the shoulders and started shaking her. "You goddamned little bitch!"

"Phil!" I cried.

Elise brought her arms up and knocked Phil's hands away. "WITH THE KEYS YOU GAVE ME, HOW DO YOU THINK?" she roared back. Without looking she pitched her apple into the bathroom, ninety miles an hour and right over the plate; I heard it hit the wall and bounce into the sink. Hands on hips and feet wide, she faced Phil head on. Her anger was as formidable as his.

My breath caught. Phil sobered fast and backed away in a half-crouch. As he straightened up, I watched him morph into his shrink persona: Dr. Philip Carchiollo, attending physician and assistant clinical professor of psychiatry. "Ev, would you please call the police?" he asked quietly as if he were talking to Faith, the psych department secretary.

"And tell them what?" Elise snorted. "That you've got a

cat fight on your hands? That you forgot you had one girl-friend waiting for you, and you brought the other one home?"

"Don't listen to her, Ev," Phil said. "She's delusional. I did not give her keys to the apartment. I don't know how she got in here."

"Oh, please," said Elise. "If you buy that, Ev, you're a lot dumber than I would have thought."

I picked up the phone, dialed 911, and handed the receiver to Phil. When someone answered he gave his address, identi-fied himself, and explained that a deranged former patient had broken into his apartment.

"Oh, yeah, sure," Elise scoffed. "I'm so deranged."

"I don't think so," Phil said into the receiver, ignoring her. "But I'm not sure."

Elise rolled her eyes elaborately. "Now I'm supposed to be *armed?*"

"And she may be a suspect in an ongoing murder investi-gation," Phil went on. "Detective Ost of the Two-six Precinct has the case."

"You son of a bitch," said Elise.

"Thank you, I'd appreciate it," Phil told the 911 operator. He handed the receiver back to me and I hung up.

"Why are you doing this?" Elise asked.

"Why don't you tell me why you think I'm doing it?" Phil shot back.

"Why don't we go sit in the living room?" I suggested. I pointed at Elise. "You first."

She came around the bed like the young goddess she was, posture erect and head held high. As she passed Phil she gave him a sultry look. As she passed me she tossed her head triumphantly.

I followed Elise into the living room and Phil followed me. Elise sat on one futon sofa, I sat on the other. After detouring to the foyer to talk to the doorman on the house phone, Phil

came in and sat down next to me. Something flickered in Elise's eyes; I caught a glimpse of anger and surprise. Clearly
she'd expected Phil to sit next to her.

Feeling more and more as if I were wallowing in some
Kafkaesque quagmire, I decided to concentrate my attention
on not showing emotion to Elise. Phil was the shrink. Let him
handle her. Once the cops removed Elise, he and I could talk.

"You have some explaining to do," Elise said to Phil.
"You've been telling people I sent that basket of poisonous
mushrooms to Ev's apartment. You know I didn't."

Phil looked at Elise with interest. His *tell-me-more-about-that*,
interested-shrink look. "Can you prove you didn't?" he asked.
He managed to sound as if he believed her. The faithful and
concerned patient advocate, he was one-hundred-percent on
her side—and eager to help her bolster her story against her
detractors.

But it wasn't what Elise wanted to see or hear. "Can you
prove I did?" she shot back.

"It's not for me to prove or disprove," Phil said. "The matter is in the hands of the police."

Elise chewed this one over. I saw that her anger was
mounting. She didn't want Phil in his shrink mode. She
wanted him emotionally engaged, shouting at her and shaking
her as he had done in the bedroom. "You are so stupid," she
said. "You think I can't help you."

I remembered what Elise had said to Detective Ost: Why
don't you tell me, so I can help you?

"How can you help me?" Phil asked.

"First come over and sit next to me. Then find out."

"You know I'm not going to do that, Elise," Phil said patiently. "But I will listen to what you have to say."

"That's your problem, Phil," Elise countered. "You'll listen
but you won't *act*. Especially not when you have strong feelings involved."

Phil blinked. I probably did too—I don't know how many times I've said something similar to him. But before he could respond, I dove in. "I know you want to help, Elise. You *can* help. You can tell us what you saw."

I saw her almost take the bait.

If she had sent the basket, and if she had been clever enough to frame Case Hamilton, here was her chance to nail the lid on Hamilton's coffin. All she had to do was make up a story about what she "saw." And in her efforts to dazzle us with her ability to "help" us solve the murder, she might just slip and say something that would enable us to nail *her*.

She wanted to help. Offering help was the way she got power. If Phil accepted her help, he was weak, and she was strong. If he needed her help, he needed her. And if he needed her, that meant he must love her.

But right now she was savoring the power of knowing something Phil and I didn't. "You see how seriously the police take you," she taunted Phil. "Why aren't they here already?" She got up and went to the window, which overlooked Riverside Drive. "This is really such a nice view. The park, the river."

Her back was to us. *Tell her you need her help*, I mouthed to Phil. He shook his head questioningly; he didn't understand. "Elise, Phil needs your help," I said finally. "You were disguised in your kafiyeh, weren't you? Hanging around the doctors' residence, watching everyone who came and went. What did the man with the basket look like?"

Phil shook his head: *Don't play into her delusions.*

"Elise?" I called softly.

She posed a question instead of answering: "How did he get into your building?" Languidly, she stepped away from the window, stretched her arms out to the sides. Then she whipped her head to the side and lunged with one leg into a stance like the yoga asana called "archer." It was not a pose I

319

could have gotten into, let alone sustained—especially not while wearing tight jeans. But Elise's dancer's body held it easily.

In the distance, I heard a police siren.

"Here come your police," she said to Phil. "To help you choose between your women. Since you can't choose yourself. You're so weak." She lunged upright, stretched her arms to the ceiling, then bent again, straight-legged, until her head touched her knees and the palms of her hands rested flat on the floor. "Try this sometime," she said to me. "I bet you can't do it."

"You're right, I can't," I admitted. "Elise, I don't know how the person got into my building. You obviously do. Once the police get here, we're not going to have a chance to talk any more one-on-one. This is your chance to really dazzle me with what you know."

"The garage," she said. She reached from the floor to ceiling again and began the 12-pose sun-salutation sequence. Prayer pose. Arch back. Bend over. Leg back.

The sirens wailed closer. With a final blip, they stopped in front of the building. One car door slammed, then two. Then three and four.

"The Storrs Pavilion parking garage?" I asked.

"He had a key," Elise said from the push-up position. She lowered her chest to the floor and arched.

"A key to the door to the doctors' residence? The door in the garage?"

"Yes." She went into "down dog": Feet flat, legs straight, arms straight out in front of her, hands on the floor—and her firm, rounded ass pointed at the ceiling.

Behind me, I heard Phil get up and go into the foyer. He opened the front door of the apartment.

"What was he wearing?" I asked.

She lunged forward with one leg, then stood. She looked

around for Phil, didn't see him, and smiled to herself as she bent forehead to knees again. "A really, really bad wig," she told her knees. "Sunglasses. A white doctor's coat—long, like the attendings wear, midcalf."

"Did he come on foot or in a car?"

"A Volvo station wagon. Not a new one—maybe six or seven years old. Maroon, kind of beat-up. New York plates, K-P-R something. In the back there was a whatchacallit—you know, a cage-thing so the dogs don't jump from the cargo bay into the backseat."

Case and Jackie Hamilton's "country" car.

"Still think I can't help you?" she asked, straightening, then stretching into the arched-back asana.

"I never said you couldn't help us, Elise. Neither did Phil. You obviously can help us a lot. Did you push me down the stairs?"

She straightened up. The sun salutation was finished. Gazing at me limpidly—the exercise seemed to have aroused her, or sated her, or both—Elise said, "I have no reason to push you or poison you, Ev. I'm secure in Phil's love. He's the one with a problem—he can't make the final break with you because he's not willing to own up to his feelings for me."

I heard the elevator in the hall outside Phil's apartment open and close. Four members of New York's Finest came through the front door: two veteran uniformed officers; Detective Ost, and Ost's partner, Detective Jude Rainey.

They looked at us the way cops always do: showing interest. But showing force, too. One officer stood with his hand on his gun.

Phil stated the facts cleanly and professionally: he and I came home to find Elise here. She claims he gave her keys, but he didn't. She claims he's her lover, but he is not and never has been. He treated her once, in the emergency room, in July—the cops probably remember the shooting at the bank over on Broadway? Well, Elise was in the bank, in fact she was standing next to the guard when he was shot and got his blood and brains in her face and hair. Naturally, she suffered an acute stress reaction, and the cops code-P'd her and brought her into the ER. That was the only time Phil had ever seen her. She suffers from the erotomanic delusion that Phil loves her. She has stalked him, and there is even a good possibility that she's tried to poison him. "Which Detective Ost here can attest to," Phil concluded. "She's my own personal Mrs. David Letterman. We came home and found her in my bed."

All the time Phil spoke Elise stood, arms crossed over her chest, gazing at the floor. With a sardonic smile fixed on her face, she shook her head from time to time as if to say, Men will be men, and they can really be dopes sometimes.

"Phil knows perfectly well that I haven't tried to poison him or anyone else," Elise said mildly when Phil finished. "And I have keys because he gave them to me. The problem is not that he came home and I was here. The problem is, he has a scheduling conflict. He forgot I would be here tonight, and he brought Ev home by mistake, and now he's cooked up this cock and bull and called you to save face. So he doesn't have to admit to Ev that he's been seeing me."

"You see what I'm up against," Phil said. "She's very convincing. But I have paperwork at the hospital that documents the course of her illness."

"Yeah, he's been keeping that in case he ever had to deny our relationship," Elise said. "Covering his ass. You wuss. You have no backbone whatsoever, you know that?"

It was easy to see who was winning this argument. Not Phil. The two uniformed cops looked at him with a mixture of admiration, pity, sympathy, and envy. They looked at Elise with awe.

They didn't look at me. I was the wronged woman, and out of respect and embarrassment, the uniforms averted their eyes. Jude Rainey glanced at me from time to time with her characteristic impassivity; I suspected she'd noticed my split lip.

"You got anything to say, Doc?" Ost asked me.

"She's a serial stalker. She used to stalk Professor Robert Held at the University. He'll talk to you. He says she's a mushroom expert. She probably got keys to this apartment by taking Phil's keys from his desk at the hospital, duplicating them, then returning the key ring. In the late summer Phil 'misplaced' his keys one time, then 'found' them again about six hours later. She gets into the hospital wearing scrubs and a white clinical coat. She also apparently has been going in and out of my apartment—my keys are on Phil's key ring—and stealing my dry cleaner's tickets off my fridge and replacing them with her own. That way, when I go to the dry cleaners, I get her clothes, and when she goes to the dry cleaners, she gets mine. That's my chemise she's wearing now."

"You flatter yourself, Ev," Elise snorted. "Why would I do that? You think I actually want to wear your clothes? As if. No, Phil gave me this chemise. If I'd known it was yours, I'd never have touched it. I assure you." She shot Phil a scalding look and moved to leave the room, but Jude Rainey took her arm. "Can I just go to the *bathroom?*" Elise demanded theatrically.

"I'll escort you," Rainey said.

When they had left, I said, "*And* I still think she killed Gary Seligman." Although by now, I wasn't so sure.

"We're looking into it," Ost said. "But I can't discuss it. Who hit you?"

"Someone pushed me down the stairs at the hospital. I didn't see who. Right before it happened, I did see Elise dressed for surgery, near the stairwell where I was pushed."

"I want to bring charges of battery against Elise for pushing Ev down the stairs," Phil said. "And breaking and entering."

Ost shook his head. "Difficult to prove, Doc. Dr. Sutcliffe here just said she didn't see who pushed her. And if she has keys . . ."

"I don't care," snapped Phil. "I didn't give her keys, and I want justice. If the judge doesn't believe me, he can throw it out."

Ost was still shaking his head. "Gotta get past the D.A. before you even get near a judge, and I'm not sure any D.A.'s going to buy this. Like it or not, Vanderlaende sounds just as convincing as you. My advice? We remove her from the premises and you call a locksmith. Then you get a restraining order, and *next* time we charge her with aggravated harrassment." He added under his breath, "If we don't arrest her first for a related matter."

"Thank you, Ozzie," I said. To Phil I whispered, "Don't let Elise upset you. That's what she wants."

"You're right." He put his arm around me and kissed the side of my head, just in time to have Elise see him do it as she returned from the bathroom. Her jaw dropped. "You are so two-faced I don't believe you!" she cried. "Just when are you going to tell her?"

She had changed into her own clothes, and now wore a white cotton tee-shirt and beige cashmere cardigan with her jeans. And boating shoes. The kind I wore in the ER.

"Empty her bag," Ost told Rainey.

"Hey!" Elise protested. "You can't do that. You need a warrant."

"Wrong," said Rainey. She took Elise's black oversized shoulderbag and carefully upended it over Phil's coffee table.

All kinds of stuff tumbled out. Notebooks, books, pens, checkbook, cosmetics case, and a huge ring of keys, like the super of a building might have, or the hospital's night watchman. Rainey tossed the keys to Ost, who handed them to Phil. "Any of these yours?"

Phil and I picked over the keys. On a braided leather keychain, Elise had keys to Phil's apartment, to his mailbox, and to his office at the hospital. She had a key to his brother Sal's car and a key to Phil's father's house in Hicksville, out on Long Island.

And, as I had realized earlier, she had keys to my apartment.

Including the key that opened the door leading from the Storrs Pavilion parking garage into the basement of the doctors' residence.

"She either saw who delivered the basket with the vegetables, or she delivered the basket herself. She just told me she saw a man with the basket enter the doctors' residence through the parking garage using a key—"

"You bitch," said Elise.

"—wearing a really, really bad wig, sunglasses, and white clinical coat—long, like the attendings wear."

"That so?" said Ost.

"Yeah, except she's leaving out the important part, the Volvo station wagon," Elise sneered. "Maroon with K-P-R something plates."

She turned to me. "Because you know whose car that is. You think you're so smart! You think the cops won't notice how you're protecting Case Hamilton!"

thirty-four

P hil poured me a large Jack Daniel's on the rocks. He poured himself a neat two fingers of Glen Morangie single malt.

The cops were gone. Elise was gone, for the moment, too. Although they wouldn't promise anything, Ost and Rainey had taken her in for questioning. Phil and I were in Phil's nice, eat-in kitchen with the French bicentennial wallpaper, recently remodeled by his brothers in the construction business.

We sat down at the table.

"*Ein Prosit,*" I said. We clinked glasses.

"So what were you trying to do in there?" Phil asked. "Trip her up with her own delusions?"

"I was trying to find out what she knew. I was hoping to be able to tell whether she delivered the basket herself and she's framing Hamilton, or she saw who did deliver the basket."

"I couldn't tell, could you?"

"No."

Phil sipped a little Glen Morangie, rolled it across his palate, and swallowed. "Damn that's fine stuff."

"Did you ever talk to Held?" I asked.

"Yeah. He wasn't much help. He said he realized in the thick of it, when she was writing him all these strange notes and telling other people he was her boyfriend, that the only way he was going to keep his sanity was by accepting the fact that she was part of his life. He couldn't do anything about her. But he could do something about how he responded to her."

"Very twelve-step," I said. "Don't try to fix the other person, fix yourself."

"Anyway, Held said nothing new," Phil said. He took my hand. "Thanks for standing by me and not letting Elise gaslight you."

"You're welcome." I leaned across the table and kissed him.

When the phone started ringing, we almost didn't answer it.

"Oh, thank God," Alan breathed when I picked up. "You're there. I think Vic's having a stroke."

"Tell me exactly what the problem is," I said. Putting my hand over the receiver, "It's Alan. He thinks Vittorio's having a stroke."

"Oh no." Phil ran into the other room to get on the extension.

"Or maybe it was the mussels," Alan went on in a rush. "You can get paralyzed, can't you? You don't think he's having a stroke, do you? Remember Bubbeh Hazel staggering around, and her eyelid drooped?"

"Never mind Bubbeh Hazel. Tell me what's going on with Vittorio."

"He's having trouble seeing and his speech is slurred!" Alan yelled.

"Is his mental status clear?"

"Um, yeah."

"The trouble seeing and speech slurred—how long has this been going on?"

"He seemed okay this afternoon. I went out to Zabar's and Citarella's. Then I came back and cooked him dinner, *moules marinières*, his favorite. He ate that okay, and had only one glass of wine. So I didn't notice at first that anything was wrong, but then he started crashing into stuff, and I said, 'What's going on?' "

"And he said what?"

" 'Leave me alone, I'm getting smashed.' Then he wants to read some papers, and I notice he's squinting like he can't see straight. He's already having trouble talking clearly, but I thought that was just the wine. Then he gets up and sort of falls over the hassock. So now I'm thinking, Wait a minute— I've seen him drink two liters of wine before. He's big, over two hundred, he can handle his liquor. Then I notice his left eyelid is drooping, like Bubbeh Hazel—"

Alan's fear pulsed into my arteries. "Does he have any history of migraine?"

"No."

"Does he have a headache now?"

"He says he doesn't. I asked."

"Vomiting?"

"No."

"Nausea?"

"I don't think so."

"Diarrhea?"

Alan considered this. "No."

"What about a fever?"

While I talked, Phil came back with the living-room phone, reeling out the cord behind him, so we could sit at the kitchen table and listen to Alan together.

"I felt his forehead," Alan said. "He's not hot. Ev, could

you just come over here? He's got drooping eyelid! And he's crashing into stuff!"

As if on cue, there was a crash in the background. "Fuck," I heard Vittorio curse loudly in the background.

"I'll meet you in the emergency room in ten minutes," I said. "Don't bother with an ambulance—come in a cab."

"He won't *go*, Ev!" Alan was beside himself now. "He says someone will kill him just like they killed Gary! Why do you think I'm calling you? I need you to come over here and make him go!"

Vittorio took the phone from Alan. "Nothing 'a matter," he insisted. "Drunk."

"Listen to me," I said in my best I'm-the-doctor-here voice. "I know you hate having to get medical attention, but this is no time to be macho. *You must go to the emergency room!* You have cranial-nerve symptoms. I am concerned that an air embolus from your fractured arm has gone to your brain. Or you could be having a stroke; you're of an age. Please meet me in the emergency room in ten minutes."

"Not going inna hospital. Had enougha hospitals."

"Did you hear what I said to you? *Life-threatening!*"

"No," said Vic. "Just drunk."

"*Vic*," I said sharply, "it could be serious!"

He hung up without answering.

I replaced the receiver in its cradle.

"Well, he's drunk," said Phil, as we waited for Alan to call back. "What do you think?"

"In terms of most life-threatening, I'm worried about an air embolus. Second, some other kind of cerebral event. Or maybe ciguatera poisoning from the shellfish—"

"Alan could be right," said Phil. "He has excellent intuition."

"Or he could be poisoned. With God only knows what." The phone rang under my hand. I picked up.

"We'll come there," I told Alan.

329

                    *   *   *

Phil and I arrived twelve minutes later, having shanghaied a police cruiser outside the hospital when we couldn't get a cab. A lucky thing, too—the officer driving, a Vietnam vet, was probably one of the few people in New York capable of piloting a vehicle through the monsoonlike downpour without having an accident. I was sure if we'd gotten into a cab we would be dead by now, drowning in the gutter after a five-car pile-up.

I dashed from the patrol car to Vittorio's handsome, pre–World War II building, Phil hot on my heels. We ducked under the awning over the front door. Rain pounded on the canvas like gunfire and bounced knee-high off the pavement. The uniformed doorman, expecting us, let us in, looking worried. We dashed into the elevator. Ascended to the ninth floor. Dashed out again.

Alan stood in the open doorway to the apartment at the end of the hall. We dashed into the apartment.

"Where is he?"

"Living room. Give me your coats, I'll hang them in the bathroom." He took our dripping slickers.

"Lotta nonsense," called Vittorio from the living room. "Can't a man enjoy a glass of wine?"

I went through the French doors with their antique astragal hardware into the living room, for once oblivious to the trappings. My eyes went directly to Vittorio.

He sat half-reclining in one of the chintz chairs, sunk low in the down-filled cushions, his chin on his chest as if napping. He straightened up as we came in.

He didn't look like he had a thing wrong with him. He was impeccably dressed, as always. Gray flannel trousers. Blue cotton business shirt, open at the neck. Red cashmere socks. Tassel loafers. He glared at us imperiously, his chin tilted back now to regard us out from under his drooping left eyelid as if he had been born with that defect and had compensated for it all his life. He held his fractured arm in its ex-fix across his belly as Napoleon might, or Lenin. He *was* noticeably short of breath. Had I been coming into the room unenlightened by Alan's phone call, I would have laid his rapid breathing down to passion, or political ideology. The King rouses himself. The lion roars.

"Hey, Vic," said Phil, sitting down in front of him on the large chintz hassock. "Alan called us. He's concerned you might need medical attention."

"Just drunk," said Vittorio.

"Well, you know, you could be drunk *and* have something else going on," Phil went on, in his reasonable, nonthreatening shrink voice. "Maybe something very serious, a stroke, or an air embolus to the brain, or some other kind of cerebral event. Or maybe ciguatera poisoning from the mussels you ate for dinner. Why not let Ev have a look at you? As long as we're here."

"You could be poisoned, Vic," I said. "I'd like to take your blood pressure. May I?"

"Suppose no choice," Vic said. He spoke slowly and deliberately. "Okay. Do your worst."

"Your speech is slurred," I told him. "You've noticed that?"

" 'Wine is a mocker.' "

"And what's that quote from, Vic?" I opened my "black bag," in reality a canvas boat tote from L.L. Bean, with a zipper top—why advertise to the criminal crowd that I might be carrying drugs?—and took out my blood pressure cuff and stethoscope.

"Bible. Proverbs."

"Uh-hum. Can you lie down on the couch for me, please?"

I watched him as he got up and moved to the couch. Definitely some kind of difficulty with coordination, which he tried to conceal from me. He sat down carefully on the couch, kicked his shoes off carefully and slowly, one at a time, and lay back, flopping down. "What's this difficulty with coordination you're having?" I asked.

"Be all right tomorrow," he insisted.

"I hope so. Have you been taking your IV antibiotics?"

"Took them morning."

"You taking any other medications?"

"No."

"No blood pressure pills, aspirin, allergy medications?"

"No."

Looking around, I saw Phil and Alan disappearing into the dining room. Probably going to sneak a look in Vittorio's medicine cabinet.

"You have to tell me exactly what you've eaten in the last twenty-four hours." I pumped up the BP cuff.

I wrote down his blood pressure (140 over 80, normal for Vic), popped a thermometer into his mouth, took his pulse (78, high for an athlete) and counted his respirations (22, a cause for mild concern). His temperature was 98.8°. I asked him to stand, and took his blood pressure again, to see if it changed from lying down. It didn't.

Vittorio sat back down on the couch and I sat next to him. His face was strangely impassive, without expression. "Dinner, mussels," he said slowly. "Lunch, cheese, carrot, apple, cookie Alan made. Breakfast, egg, toast. Coffee Starbucks."

"What about dinner last night?"

"Ask Alan. Forget." He was having a great deal of trouble getting his mouth around the words. I couldn't tell if this was drunkenness or cranial nerve symptomology or both.

I held up two fingers in front of his face. "How many fingers am I holding up?"

"Two."

"Follow my finger with your eyes without moving your

head." I sketched an H in the air. He followed, albeit slowly and deliberately.

I looked in his mouth. Tongue and mucous membranes were dry. "While you were crashing around and falling over the furniture, you didn't hit your head, did you?" I palpated his head, checking for lumps and bumps. There were none.

"No," said Vittorio.

I checked his pupils with my penlight, looked in his eyes with my ophthalmoscope, examined his neck, and listened to his heart and lungs. "You're short of breath, and you're wheezing," I told him.

"Allergic," he said.

"Allergic to what?"

"Cat."

"You have a cat? Since when?"

"Okay, dog."

"Jesus," I muttered under my breath. "Close your eyes and tell me where I'm touching you." I trailed a finger across the left side of his face.

"Cheek."

"Good. Now where?"

"Right arm."

I had him wrinkle his forehead, close his eyes tightly, and smile. I stuck a tongue depressor in his mouth and he said "ah." When I asked him to stick his tongue out and move it rapidly from side to side, however, he had trouble. And there was the worrisome drooping eyelid. "Decreased tongue motion and ptosis," I said. "These are neurological signs that something is going on with your cranial nerves. Now I have to ask you something. When was your last test for HIV?"

"September." He seemed to be having even more trouble getting his tongue around the words. "Negative."

I sat with him for a moment.

He had the same symptoms as Thomas Kennaugh, the yuppie heroin abuser.

Kennaugh was now lying in the ICU on a ventilator, his respiratory muscles temporarily paralyzed by the botulinum toxin.

Could Vittorio have wound botulism from the dirt-contaminated wound in his arm, at this late date?

If so, all the antibiotics in the world were not going to help him. Any minute now, the creeping paralysis of the botulism poisoning would reach his diaphragm. It had already affected his cranial nerves.

"Vic, you have to go to the hospital. You may have wound botulism from your broken arm. Very shortly now, you're not going to be able to breathe. But we can get antitoxin at the hospital for you."

"No hospital."

"Then I'll take you against your will. You're not competent to make medical decisions on your own behalf."

An expression of surprise spread across Vittorio's face. He looked at me helplessly and staggered to his feet, groping for his throat with his good hand. The surprise turned to fear as he fell to his knees.

I bellowed for Phil and Alan.

"Vic!" Alan shrieked, running in. He flung himself to his own knees, next to Vittorio.

"Can't breathe," Vittorio gasped.

He toppled over.

thirty-five

I called Hatzolah because they had a better response time than EMS. When someone isn't breathing the difference between three minutes and nine minutes is a lot.

"This is Dr. Evelyn Sutcliffe," I barked into the receiver as I checked my watch and wrote down the time in a small spiral notebook. "I'm a medical doctor. I have a patient who has stopped breathing and I need a bus right away at—"

Behind me there was controlled chaos as Phil and Alan stretched Vittorio out on the floor and began rescue breathing. Alan kept his CPR certification current, and knew what to do. Kneeling next to Vittorio's head, he tilted Vic's chin back, pinched his nose, and blew into his mouth. Phil began to count out loud for him: "One-one-thousand, two-one-thousand, three-one-thousand . . ."

I called the doorman on the house phone to alert him that an ambulance was coming. "Hold an elevator for them," I commanded.

I called the ER to alert them we were coming in. "The

patient is Vittorio von Laue and I want B-O-T"—Board of Trustees—"in large letters across the top of the blue slip. Have a pulmonary fellow waiting on arrival."

By the time I got off the phone the ambulance crew was coming through the door to the apartment, wheeling a collapsible gurney complete with oxygen tank, jump kit, tube kit, Lifepac, and an orange plastic trunk with white lid—the ambulance drug box, which I had forgotten to request and they had thankfully brought up on their own.

I quickly glanced at their shoulder patches to see their ratings. Only then did I think to look at their faces. The EMT was a swaggering young Israeli god. I'd worked with him a few times and didn't like him—but I had to admit he seemed good. The paramedic I knew well; he was a very old hand, seasoned without being jaded, and utterly unfazable. I almost wept with relief: *Thank you, thank you, for people who know what they're doing.*

"Hey, Doc," said Frank Kuperstein quietly. A balding guy with a long face, he was a calm sort who had the ability to work very, very fast yet still look plodding. "What's up?"

He moved into the living room and greeted Vittorio with calm concern—"Hey, Mr. von Laue, let's see if we can help you get some air"—as if Vic were sitting on the sofa reading a newspaper instead of sprawled on the floor with Alan giving rescue breathing. To Alan, Kuperstein said, "Keep going for a minute." As he spoke, he hooked up the oxygen apparatus and the bag-valve mask, which is attached to a balloon that looks like an inflatable football. You squeeze and unsqueeze the football and this inflates and deflates the patient's lungs.

Kneeling, Kuperstein said "May I?" to Alan, brought the mask down on Vic's face, and squeezed the bag. And all this before I had finished saying, "Vittorio von Laue, forty-eight years old, no history of cardiac or respiratory problems, went into respiratory arrest three minutes ago, rescue breathing since then. He may have botulism poisoning."

Poor Vittorio followed us with his eyes. Although unable to breathe, he was not unconscious. Nor mentally incapacitated in any way, although he was clearly still having vision problems. I saw him struggle to focus on Kuperstein's name tag and that of the EMT, Ari Ben-Dov, then turn his gaze on their shoulder patches just as I had done when they'd come in the door. Amazing. He can't breathe, but he still wants to know who these guys are and what their training is.

"You feel any easier with the oxygen on you, Mr. von Laue?" Kuperstein asked.

Vittorio looked at him and gave him a weak thumbs-up.

Alan was as white as a sheet. Now that Kuperstein had taken over, he had nothing to do. Nor could he hold Vittorio's hand because we were all crowding around with gear.

Ben-Dov had charge of the pulse oximeter, a little clamp that goes on the finger, shines an infrared light through the nailbed, and gives you a computer readout on a little screen of how much oxygen is in the blood. "Pulse ox ninety," he said.

"Vic, we're going to have to intubate you, okay?" I said. Even as I spoke, Ben-Dov was snapping open the buckles on the orange intubation kit. He offered me the open kit with its "grab-and-use" arrangement of laryngoscope handles and blades, oral airways, and endotracheal tubes in different sizes. Using the thumb and pinky of my right hand like a tape measure, I measured Vittorio mouth-to-ear for the right size airway, and selected what I needed. "Ready when you are," I said.

Frank gave Vic several deep breaths in quick succession, then took away the bag-valve mask. Taking my own deep breath and holding it, I swiftly lifted Vittorio's jaw and slid the blade of the laryngoscope between his teeth, advancing until I could see into the larynx. Ben-Dov slapped the endotrach tube into my hand and I snaked it down Vittorio's throat. His absent gag reflex helped. But by now Vic was waving his hand frantically for me to hurry. I nodded, still holding my own breath. Ben-Dov slapped the airway into my hand. I snapped it onto the endotrach tube. Held out my hand for the tape. Taped the airway to Vic's cheeks. Kuperstein was ready with the bag-valve mask, and I exhaled explosively as he squeezed the bag. Watching to see Vittorio's chest rise and fall, I then auscultated both lungs with my stethoscope. Although I could have relied on Vittorio to tell me that the endotrach tube was in place. Putting his hand on my arm to get me to look, he gave me the thumbs-up sign.

The tenor in the room changed as we all relaxed slightly. But it was only the eye of the storm; there was still urgent work to be done. Ben-Dov took Vittorio's vital signs and called them out; I got an IV going in Vic's left arm in case we needed to give meds.

"What happened to his arm?" Kuperstein asked as he pumped the bag.

I explained the ex-fix.

He nodded, and for the first time since he came through the door, glanced around appreciatively at his surroundings. But his attention wandered only for a moment. "We're going to move you to the stretcher now, Mr. von Laue," he said. "We'll make you comfortable and strap you in, and then we'll get going."

Phil handed me my slicker. I asked Alan to take Vic's wallet and jewelry.

Alan had born up well until now, but as he removed Vic's Swiss Army watch and slipped his gold-and-onyx signet ring from his finger, his face crumpled. "I'm sorry," he apologized, chagrined that he would embarrass himself this way while Vittorio was being so brave.

Vittorio raised his hand, perhaps to touch Alan's cheek.

But we were already going out the door. The touch turned into a wave. Kuperstein, Ben-Dov, and I rolled the gurney into the elevator and got in.

The doors closed. We descended.

Outside the wind hit us like a sideswipe as we ran out under the awning of the building, and the rain came horizontally, as if the world had been knocked over by Mother Nature. Half-crouched, we sped the gurney to the ambulance. I was Vic's lifeline now, his breath between my hands as I pumped the ambubag, squeeze-unsqueeze, inhale-exhale. I had his IV bag clipped with a hemostat to the collar of my slicker and it slapped on my chest as I ran all-out for the goalposts. The back doors of the ambulance swung open. We heaved. The wheels of the gurney landed and rolled forward.

We were in. I moved swiftly around the gurney, which was low to the floor, and threw myself into the captain's seat, holding my breath again to remind me that Vittorio was without air until I settled and resumed the bag. I reset the mask and squeezed and we both breathed. Rainwater dripped from my face to his as I sat over him, my elbows on my knees, one hand on the mask and the other working the bag. Our eyes locked. I saw fear in his. I hoped he didn't see fear in mine.

The siren wailed and we hurtled into the monsoon. In my peripheral vision Kuperstein moved around, one hand on the overhead grab rail. As the siren oscillated I could hear water under the wheels and the thwap-thwap of the windshield wipers. Rain pelted the roof and sides and windows. We were in another world, a flying-forward womb in which Vittorio floated and we with him. Kuperstein locked the gurney to the floor. Unclipping the IV bag from my collar, he hung it on a hook set into the ceiling. Swept away the tarp that we had covered Vic with.

"Just a few minutes now," I said to Vic. Were his eyes going out of focus?

"Oh-two ninety-six percent, heart rate one hundred," said Kuperstein.

He had just sat down on the crew bench and was leaning forward to check the oxygen tank between Vic's knees when the ambulance swerved first to the left, then to the right. My shoulder slammed into the wall, and Kuperstein was thrown across Vittorio's lap. There was the frightening sensation of hydroplaning before the wheels grabbed the pavement again.

"*Yoter l'at!*" Kuperstein yelled at Ben-Dov in Hebrew. Righting himself, he said to Vittorio, "I'm sorry, Mr. von Laue," and went about his business, muttering under his breath, "I should have driven, I was in 'Nam. Ari here learned to drive zooming tanks around the Sinai—a lot of good on a night like this."

Looking back, I can't say that I had a sense of foreboding. But my heart was pounding and I suddenly found my breath coming faster than I was pumping the bag—did Vittorio need more air or did I? There seemed to be two of me, one working the ambubag while the other let go of the mask for the briefest of moments to reach into my inside pocket and get out my spiral notebook, and shake it open to a blank page—and toss it onto Vittorio's chest. I pressed a pen into his hand.

I was horrified to hear myself say, "I need you to tell me now in case there's not another chance. Who do you think poisoned Gary?"

I could see Kuperstein looking at me with a puzzled expression as if I had a second set of eyes to turn on him while the first set remained locked to Vittorio's. I was in a dream. It was unfolding very slowly. Vittorio fumbled for the notebook. Kuperstein leaned over to hold it for him.

I remember the horrible grinding of metal.

I don't remember the ambulance going over on its side.

*   *   *

Voices.

"Oh Jesus—somebody call the cops?"

"Is he dead?"

"Don't touch him. There's blood everywhere."

Wind-driven rain. The siren that had wailed as close as my own heartbeat now wailed away, somewhere else.

No, coming closer. Coming this way.

Where?

Pain stabbed my back and shoulders and I opened my eyes—what was that smell?

Gasoline.

Wet pavement.

Amazingly, my glasses were still on my nose. I was all crunched up on my shoulders and back with my legs somewhere higher. When I looked I saw far above me the captain's chair where I'd been sitting, and the radio behind it. There'd been an accident. We went over on our side. I was in the passenger-side door well.

I started yelling. "Vittorio! Frank! *Frank!*" I tried wriggling out from under myself.

And then I was groaning from the pain. I got an arm under myself and tried to sit up but I was blacking out again. I couldn't see, dizzy . . . I moved a jump kit off my chest and the ambubag fell with it. *Oh God no—who was bagging Vittorio?* I called for Vittorio and for Frank and Somebody we need help in here! Then finally the top part of me was upright but my feet were still above my head. Somehow, I got my feet down and under me and very slowly stood.

Vittorio was still strapped in his gurney. The gurney, locked into the floor, hung in midair. He lay in his straps as if in a hammock, his arms and head dangling lifelessly.

"There are people in the back! Can we get this back door open?"

"Oh God, Vic," I breathed.

Wheels in water and sirens, close nearby, whooped then stopped. Doors opening and closing. All the while the rain pounding in sheets. Frank Kuperstein was lying against the cabinets that should have been above the crew bench but were now below it. He groaned and stirred. Now on my knees, I reached up to probe my fingers into Vittorio's neck, searching for a pulse, willing a pulse, *demanding* a pulse. There. I felt it. His eyes fluttered open.

Holding my breath again I searched for the ambubag, found it, reconnected the oxygen, hooked up the bag to Vic's endotrach. I let my breath out explosively as I started pumping air into Vittorio's lungs. He looked at me weakly, then closed his eyes.

The doors of the ambulance yawned open. Cops and medics took Vittorio out into the rain and onto another gurney and into the back of another ambulance, while I yelled after them, "Have them test for botulism! Get Dr. Clausson; she knows about it!"

They took Kuperstein out into the rain and onto another gurney and into the back of another ambulance, too. He was semi-conscious, moaning in response to pinching and verbal commands, so he got to lie down while they "collared and boarded" him—strapped him head to foot to a long wooden board to immobilize him in case he had spinal injuries. Since I was walking and talking, they collared and boarded me standing up soaking in the downpour, because the act of lying down could paralyze me for life if I had spinal injuries. Then they took me down onto a gurney and loaded me into the back of yet another ambulance.

I kept telling them someone was going to try to poison Vittorio in the hospital.

But I couldn't get anyone to listen.

thirty-six

The lights in the emergency room seemed very, very bright. Abby Kubota was on duty, a welcome sight. She peered down at me with concern, spoke quietly, and worked efficiently. The attending, a retired military man who reminded everyone of Colin Powell, circulated from room to room, directing and supervising care. Frank Kuperstein was still unconscious; they were rushing him to CT scan.

Phil came in finally.

"Where's Vittorio?" I asked.

"CT scan. He's on a ventilator. He's conscious. Di Clausson is coming in to evaluate him, as you asked. Since she's the on-site botulism expert."

"Alan?"

"Upstairs with Vittorio."

"Tell Alan not to take his eyes off him. Vic's afraid someone's going to shoot something into his IV like they did with Gary."

Kubota looked up, startled, as Phil ran out.

"Come right back!" I yelled.

I was afraid now that someone was going to shoot something into my IV, too.

I had to stay collared and boarded until I was X-rayed to rule out spinal injury.

By now I'd been totally immobilized for at least forty-five minutes.

I'd had time to think.

And realize what we'd all missed.

The ceiling went by as Abby Kubota rolled me personally to X Ray. "You can't leave me alone collared and boarded like this, Abby," I was saying for at least the fourth or fifth time.

Kubota was beginning to look worried. She clearly thought I'd suffered some type of head injury to make me paranoid. "I could give you a little Valium, if you like," she offered.

"I don't want any Valium. I want you to not leave me alone. With anybody. Look. Why don't you just untie me? I'll lie perfectly still, I promise."

"The X Rays won't take long," she said. She parked my stretcher outside the X Ray suite and went in to find the technician.

I lay on my stretcher thinking about the IV in my left arm, and how vulnerable I was. My neck was in a C-collar, a stiff plastic job that kept my neck still. My head was packed with big orange foam blocks strapped down with adhesive tape. My vision was severely limited—since I couldn't turn my head, all I could see was the ceiling. If someone wanted to talk to me, I couldn't see that person unless he or she leaned right over my stretcher. My arms were restrained, as were my legs.

I felt like one of those damsels in distress in the old silent movies, tied to the railroad tracks by the villain with the big black mustache going heh-heh-heh.

344

I wondered how long it would take the poisoner to hear where I was and what had happened and show up at bedside.

I wondered whom he considered more dangerous: me or Vittorio?

And whom he'd try to kill first.

Damn it. I had to get Kubota to untie me.

A shoe creaked.

"Who's there?" I cried.

"How you doing, Ev?" someone said softly. "I came as soon as I heard."

"GET AWAY FROM ME!" I shrieked, straining against the adhesive tape and orange foam to look around. "GET AWAY FROM ME NOW!"

There was a tug on my IV.

"KUBOTA! HELP!"

Running footsteps. Kubota's face came into view, angled over mine. Her forehead creased with concern over her black, almond-shaped eyes.

"Who was that just now?" I demanded. "Who was that here?"

"Nobody's here, Ev. Just me. Try to calm yourself."

"Look. Someone's trying to kill me. Promise me if I become unconscious, you'll treat for insulin shock."

"Ev, why don't you let me give you something?"' she responded, ignoring me. "Really. A little Valium—"

"Do not give me anything, Abby. I DO NOT want any Valium. Nothing, do you understand?"

"Then you have to calm down," she said. "Right now."

"Fine. I'm calm."

Her face disappeared from my range of vision. I heard her kick the brake off my stretcher.

I watched the ceiling go by as she wheeled me into X Ray.

The chief resident on the radiology service, summoned by the BOT alarm I'd set off when I'd called in Vittorio's impending arrival to the hospital, scrutinized my X Rays and humm-hummed quietly under his breath.

Finally he pronounced me fit and sound.

The radiologist and Kubota began to untie me. They started with my head: off came the tape, the big Styrofoam blocks, the C-collar. I could turn my head again. Next they untied my hands, then my feet.

Kubota handed me a cotton ball and took the IV needle out of my arm.

"Thanks guys," I said. "You probably won't appreciate this, but you just saved my life."

"I never would have known you to be so melodramatic, Ev," Kubota said with a smile.

I headed directly to the phone on the doctors' desks in the nurses' station. The call was answered on the first ring.

"Where are you?" he demanded. "What's going on? Vittorio has food poisoning? A stroke? What?"

"I think somebody shot something into his IV," I said. "But we got him to the ER on time. Now we have to make sure no one shoots anything else into his IV. He's going to be up in the ICU for weeks. How soon can you be here?"

"I'll come as fast as I can."

"Wait. I need a favor before you come." I described what I wanted.

There was a long pause on the other end of the phone. Footsteps went away and came back. "My God, you're right," the voice finally said. "How could we all have been so blind? Plain as day, right in front of our faces all this time—*but only Gary noticed?*"

"Only Gary noticed." I hung up the phone and dialed again.

"Hello?"

"It's Ev Sutcliffe. We need to talk."

"Now?"

"Yes."

"What time is it?"

I looked at my watch. "Two A.M."

"Where?" he asked.

"Meet me at Sami's."

Stopping in the emergency room, I armed a scalpel holder with a blade and slipped it into my pocket. Just in case. *Although*, I thought, *what's he going to do?* He's a coward at heart. I'll tell him what I know, we'll argue, he'll back down. We'll be in a public place, a restaurant.

I actually talked myself into thinking that.

Bad move.

It was still raining, although not as hard as earlier. I wrapped my silk scarf around my neck and pulled up the hood of my slicker. Standing a moment under the overhang of the ambulance bay, I looked out at Amsterdam Avenue.

Then I stepped out into the cold wet autumn night thinking, *Be scared—be very scared.*

thirty-seven

Morningside Heights that night was like a movie set. One with a rain machine gone berserk. The rain was gentle for a little while. Then it sluiced down in sheets. Then it tapered off again.

I stood under the awning at Sami's Café across the street and a little down Amsterdam from the hospital. It was dark and shuttered. I read the note that Sami, the proprietor, had taped to the inside of the glass door:

SORRY VERY MUCH
ON FURTHER NOTICE CLOSED 2–5 A.M.
BECAUSE ILLNESS OF SAMI'S BROTHER

My heart in my throat, I wondered how I was going to handle this now. I closed my hand around the scalpel handle in my pocket.

I looked across the street at the strange statue on the Cathedral grounds. It was a playful statue, designed for children, with animals and figures from fairy tales. The only problem was, it looked like the unicorn was mounting the animal in front of it. Or maybe it was an antelope. I squinted through the rain.

I was full of adrenaline. My mind was running on idle.

A cab pulled up. He got out, wearing a trenchcoat with its collar up, a nineteen-forties-style hat like Bogart's at a jaunty angle. He saw me standing in front of the café and ran across the street, his shoulders hunched under the rain like you hunker down under helicopter blades.

I watched the cab drive off. Its red rear lights refracted off the raindrops and the wet tarmac. Damn.

The rain pounded on the awning as Mark Ramsey ducked under.

"Hell of a night," he said. He put his arms around me. I let him hug me, even raised my own hand to his wet back.

He read the notice Sami had posted.

Trying to decide what to do, I told Mark about Vittorio's collapse. I rambled on about wound botulism, the kind you get from World War I trenches and dirt in your wounds and contaminated heroin. Mark attributed the botulism to Vittorio's broken arm. I didn't contradict him. Not yet.

Mark and I might have had a conversation about botulism poisoning earlier, regarding Thomas Kennaugh, our yuppie heroin abuser. If I had remembered to have it with him.

Although it didn't matter now that I'd forgotten.

What mattered was the train of thought that unfolded when I'd started thinking about it.

Diana Clausson used an injectable form of purified botulinum A toxin in her Ear, Nose and Throat Clinic, to treat people like her patient the Rev. Dr. David Keller. Nicholson's voice rang in my ears: *Treatment of choice local injection of purified botulinum A toxin, which is well-suited for many of the dystonias, including blepharospasm, spasmodic dysphonia, and swallowing dis-*

orders. The toxin acts by weakening the strength of the involuntary contractions, without interfering with fundamental neural mechanisms.

Vittorio had symptoms of botulism poisoning. He could have wound botulism from dirt trapped in his arm after the surgery, but I didn't think so. And Vittorio was afraid someone would shoot something into his IV if he went into the hospital.

Suppose someone had *already* shot something into his IV?

Who had access to injectable botulinum A toxin?

Diana Clausson.

Who had access to Vittorio's IV?

After Vittorio's dinner party Sunday night, I'd shown Case Hamilton how to hook up Vittorio's IV, flush it with saline, flush with heparin, then administer the antibiotics he needed. But the plan was for Vittorio to ask Mark for help, since he lived in the building, too—and he was a doc.

So either Mark or Case could have shot Vittorio full of botulinum A toxin while he was about it, and knowing Vittorio, I'd bet he hadn't even been watching very closely.

And Case *could* have procured botulinum A toxin from Diana Clausson, I supposed. But I didn't think so. Ramsey was the one who was having on-again-off-again sex with her.

Just two days ago, he'd had lipstick on his mouth.

Lauren Sabot had said that she'd stumbled on Ramsey listening to his phone messages Friday night. After which, he'd been upset.

That was the night that Gary had gone to Chase and Vittorio's boarding school reunion. The night Geoff Hamilton had gone to his own class reunion. At the same school.

The same school that Mark Ramsey had attended with his friend Scott, whose last name I had forgotten, if I'd ever known it to begin with. Scott, who had later been killed. As Ramsey and he were driving home from the graduation parties to Ramsey's house in Greenwich, Connecticut.

Graduation parties. People drink a lot at those parties.

Which might explain why one of the two men might have been driving the other's car. Because he was the designated driver.

"You never go to your class reunions at boarding school, do you?" I asked Mark as we stood under the awning in front of Sami's Café, watching the rain come down.

"I can't bear to go," Mark said. "I haven't been since Scott died. Usually, some of my form mates call me to see how I'm doing, though. They know it's difficult for me."

"Did one of your form mates call you Friday night?"

"What do you mean?"

"Your phone messages. When Lauren Sabot let herself into Case and Jackie's house—*her* house, actually—to raid the liquor cabinet. You let Lauren believe that you'd had a steamy message from Di Clausson."

Ramsey furrowed his brow. "I don't know what you're talking about, Ev."

"I think you do, Mark. I think one of your form mates called and left a message for you, to let you know that a guy named Gary Seligman was at the reunion, pretending to be an alum. And that he was asking difficult questions about you. And about your friend Scott," I added softly.

Ramsey gazed across the street at the statue of the possibly fornicating nursery-rhyme animals.

"You're really Scott, aren't you?" I said.

He shook his head. "People mixed us up all the time. I'm not surprised you've made that mistake. When Scott was alive—" choking up, he broke off.

"You're so good at medications," I said. "We just couldn't figure it out. How could someone be so bad at reading X Rays, so bad at suturing, but so good at drugs?"

He was crying openly now. Tears ran down his cheeks.

"I've had a couple of interns under me," I went on, "who've had a rough start. It took them a while to get a grip. Some we've had to put on probation or threaten them with probation. Two or three we had to wash out of the program entirely, for fucking up and lying about it.

"Everyone kept saying that you might not know what you were doing, but you never lied to cover your mistakes. That time you lost the lead wire in the patient's chest when you screwed up putting in his central line, you came and got me immediately. The patient had to go to surgery to have the wire removed, but no worse harm was done because you confessed, right up front. If you had lied to cover, the patient would have died. So when you screwed up, we all kept saying, 'but he's honest.' "

He got out his handkerchief and wiped his face and blew his nose.

"But of course you wouldn't know how to suture or read X rays. You never went to medical school. That was the *real* Mark Ramsey. You're good with drugs because you went to pharm school."

"Scott Renfrew is dead," Mark said. "He died in the accident. I'm Mark Ramsey. You know that."

"I had Case Hamilton look up your pictures in his son Geoff's yearbooks from boarding school."

"The school mixed up the pictures. They were always mixing us up. We were best friends, we had similar coloring, similar builds. And we had similar backgrounds. No families. Orphans. Alone in the world. But we had each other. We went everywhere together."

"You didn't go to Yale together," I said. "Mark Ramsey went to Yale. You went to Saint John's University. Case Hamilton gets the Yale yearbook every year—he's got a whole set in his library. That was not your picture in the Yale yearbook."

"You knew me when I was a med student. You know I'm Mark Ramsey."

"You know how many med students and interns I supervise in a year? Yes, I remember Mark Ramsey when he was here as a med student—vaguely! And you look just enough like him that when you came up to me your first day and introduced yourself as Mark Ramsey, I was snookered. Besides, you'd already had several of the plastic surgeries meant to make you look even more like Mark Ramsey than you already did! So yes I thought you were Mark Ramsey. But now I know you're not. Gary must have had his suspicions from the beginning. And when he acted on them—when he went to your boarding school reunion and started asking difficult questions—and when your form mate called you and left you a message that Gary was there wanting to know peculiar things—you had to act. *Immediately.* You acted even before you could come up with a coherent plan. So you grabbed a few mushrooms from Case Hamilton's potting room, you drove his car into the city Saturday morning, put on that ridiculous disguise, and delivered the basket."

"No, Ev, please. The basket was for your new healthy eating plan. I got you a basket of nice vegetables because you said you'd made a resolution to eat healthier foods. I don't know how those mushrooms—" he stopped. "They had Case Hamilton's fingerprints on them," he said firmly.

"Might as well poison all of us," I said. "We were the people Gary would be most likely to confide in if he decided to share his suspicions with anyone. What happened—they misidentified you at the hospital after the accident, and you just let them go on thinking you were Ramsey? Or you switched wallets with Ramsey before rescue workers came on the scene, once you saw he was dead?"

"I don't remember the accident!" he said sharply. "I don't know what happened! I'm Mark Ramsey! It was my car! I was driving!"

And then I got the blank stare.

Which was when I realized that Scott Renfrew really, really needed to believe that he was Mark Ramsey.

353

Because Scott Renfrew had been driving. He couldn't live with the guilt of having been responsible for Mark Ramsey's death. So he became Mark Ramsey.

That way Scott Renfrew "died" for the sin of killing Mark Ramsey, and Mark Ramsey, innocent, "lived."

I felt a stab of fear.

The man who stood in front of me was just as deluded as Elise Vanderlaende.

The difference being, Elise had not shown herself willing to kill for her delusions.

While he had.

"Tell me you know I'm Mark Ramsey," he said. "Tell me now."

He moved his arm slightly and I heard a click. I knew what that click was.

But before I could react, he had my arm in a viselike grip.

And the point of a switchblade knife in the soft hollow of my throat.

He marched me across the street to the Cathedral gardens. We passed under the three-story-high animal sculpture. Then we were out of the light and into the shadows.

It was still raining steadily. I couldn't tell if the wetness on my neck was blood or rain. He held the blade pressed firmly against my skin, and as we jostled each other walking he pricked me several times. My hand in my pocket gripped my scalpel, but I was afraid to use it. I prayed to God that neither of us stumbled.

There had been several rape-murders in the area, with the bodies found in Morningside Park, half a block away. If they found my body in the Cathedral gardens—

"Listen," I said.

"I'm not going to listen to you anymore."

"Why did you shoot botulinum toxin into Vittorio's IV?"

"Tell me when you think I did that," he said. "I was with you all day at the hospital. Or didn't you notice?"

"You weren't with me all day. You were scheduled for night float this evening. You went home to sleep." I couldn't believe we were having this conversation. He was holding a knife to my throat! *Think*, Sutcliffe! *How are you going to get away from him?*

I couldn't trip him. He'd bring me down with him and I'd fall right on the knife.

What, then?

I said, "I'm sorry I said everything I did. You're obviously Mark Ramsey or you wouldn't be behaving this way. You feel so bad that Scott died while you were driving, you can't bear to listen to these accusations I'm making against him. I'm sorry if I've said anything to call his honor into question. I know how much he meant to you."

He faltered slightly. For a split second I felt the blade of the knife leave my throat. But then it was back again. "He was my best friend," he said grimly.

"I know he was," I said. "I know how much you miss him."

There was movement in the bushes. "Baksheesh!" A man wearing a soaked, dirty blanket over his shoulders jumped out at us. "Give me money! It's a mitzvah!"

The diversion was enough. I knocked away the knife. Then, I swung with all my force and thumb-punched Mark-Scott in the throat. My thumb connected with the delicate cartilage of the trachea and the trachea collapsed.

I heard a high-pitched whistle as he gasped to breathe. The knife clattered to the ground. Both of his hands went reflexively to his throat. But there was nothing he could do. He knew as well as I that within three minutes, he would lose consciousness from lack of oxygen. The collapsed trachea had the same affect as if he'd just got a large piece of steak stuck in his throat: he was choking to death.

But this choking couldn't be fixed with the Heimlich maneuver. The only thing that would help him now would be for someone to make an incision in his trachea to insert a breathing tube.

We were less than two blocks from the emergency room and life.

He had sunk to his knees, his hands still at his throat.

Taking a big breath and holding it, I yanked him to his feet and pulled him along. In a panic, he came along for a few strides without protest. We passed under the animals who might be fucking. We reached the sidewalk. We turned north.

Then he dug in his heels, stopping short.

"You've got to come with me Mark," I cried, pulling him along. "I'll crich you. You'll be all right."

He shook his head vehemently.

"Too bad. I won't let you commit suicide." I kept pulling.

With his last ounce of strength, he rushed me in a flying tackle. He got his arms around me and we fell heavily to the ground, me under him, his weight crushing me. He probably weighed no more than Phil—maybe 180—but as dead weight that was enough to knock the wind out of me.

And with his last conscious thought, he locked his arms under me in a death grip and inched his weight up over my chest and fainted dead away.

I struggled to get out from under him. Rain fell on my face.

By the time I dragged him to within screaming distance of the ER and people ran out to help us, his heart had stopped.

thirty-eight

Driving to the cemetery, we kept passing houses with ghosts hanging in the trees.

"Did you hang ghosts in the trees like that when you were a kid?" Phil asked as he slowed for a stop sign.

"Some kids dressed up as ghosts," I said. "I don't remember hanging any in the trees."

"Me neither. What I remember is carving the pumpkin, and my mother would roast the seeds in the oven while we were out trick-or-treating. So we'd come home to that wonderful smell."

It was the Sunday before Halloween. More than a week had passed since the harrowing night Vittorio's ambulance crashed, and Mark Ramsey aka Scott Renfrew held a knife to my throat. A full two weeks had passed since Gary's death.

I was a ghost hanging in a tree myself.

I didn't seem to be the same person I had been before Gary died. I had hoped by now to meet the new me—the me I would be now that Gary was gone—at his funeral. But the service was so hastily thrown together, and Gary's poor mother and sister so deranged by grief and jet lag (having just arrived home from China), and the rabbi who presided so flat and rote, and the funeral home so impersonal, that I couldn't find Gary there to say goodbye to, and the new me never put in an appearance. The memorial service at the hospital was better. But I still felt disconnected, disassociated, not home, not me, and deeply depressed.

"Here's the Post Road," Phil said. "Left or right?"

I consulted the directions I had scrawled on a yellow legal pad. "Left."

"Greenwich, Connecticut," he sighed. "Home of the American dream. Old money, new money, the pot of gold at the end of the rainbow."

I looked out the window. More ghosts.

Everything seemed up in the air, twisting in the wind.

We did have one thing to be thankful for: Vittorio was on the road to recovery. Although it would be a long road. While no longer intubated—the docs had done a tracheostomy—he was still ventilator dependent because his chest muscles and diaphragm remained paralyzed. Which meant that he couldn't speak.

With the aid of anti-toxin administered by Clausson shortly after his admission, Vic was slowly regaining muscle control. He was now at the point where he was able to write a few words at a time on a small whiteboard with a magic marker. But he was not much help in reconstructing events. The brief oxygen deprivation he had suffered during the accident with the ambulance wiped out whatever short-term memory he'd laid down about that day. He remembered breakfast. That was about it.

It would be three to four months, Clausson said, before he'd be able to breathe on his own again. But she expected him to recover fully. No permanent damage.

Scott Renfrew—who still claimed to be Mark Ramsey—had lain for a few days in the next bay of the ICU from Vittorio. He did suffer permanent damage from his oxygen deprivation. He woke from his brief coma unable to read. When he was encouraged to walk the halls of the hospital with assistance, it was discovered that he could not orient himself in space—if he walked so much as twenty-five yards down the corridor, he couldn't find his way back to his room. His speech was unimpaired, and his sensorium seemed clear. But he insisted he did not remember anything that had happened since his motor vehicle accident a year and a half earlier. He was determined to leave the hospital immediately, to attend to Scott Renfrew's funeral.

Nine days after I punched Ramsey-Renfrew in the throat, he was remanded to the Kirby Forensic Center on Ward's Island in the East River. Kirby was a maximum security hospital for the criminally insane. There Mark-Scott would stay until a judge decided whether he was fit to stand trial.

"Do you think the judge will find him fit to stand trial?" I asked Phil now.

"Who, Mark?"

Phil flipped on the blinker and slowed. "He'll probably have to stand trial. Technically, whether or not you remember what occurred, if you're now able to say, 'I understand that I'm being charged with murder, and I understand that you're my attorney, and this is the judge, and we're in America,' you're fit to proceed. Your lawyers can then put forward an insanity defense in front of the jury to try to get you off."

We turned into the church parking lot, parked and got out. After the dramatic turns of weather the previous week— unseasonably mild one minute, and a ferocious northeaster the next—today seemed more October-ish: partly sunny, breezy, and cool. Most, if not all, of the trees had changed color. The ground was covered in fallen leaves.

"But how can he get a fair trial?" I asked. "He can't assist his attorneys by providing any details, or any exonerating evidence on his own behalf—he doesn't even know what happened. Or so he says." I touched the spot on my neck where Ramsey-Renfrew had pressed the knife into my flesh. The small cut he had made was nearly healed.

"It doesn't matter," Phil said. "There's a case, what's it called . . . This guy shot at a bunch of people, and then fired on the police when they showed up. The police shot him in the head. When he woke up, he couldn't remember anything about the shooting. The court ruled that he was not an incapacitated person just because of this retrograde amnesia, and that he was fit to stand trial. People versus Francabandera."

We went around to the front of the church, as Batty Coleman had directed. A gaggle of small children dressed for a Halloween party clattered by, herded by a coven of soccer moms. Passing under an arch in the cloister, we continued down a driveway to the cemetery behind the church. The late afternoon sun broke through the clouds and slanted through the trees.

"I can't get used to the time," Phil said. We'd changed the clocks the night before. "Look, the sun's about to go down already."

But I had other things on my mind. "I can't believe they're really going to dig up Mark Ramsey's and Scott Renfrew's parents to test the DNA."

"Why not? It will prove once and for all whether Mark's who he says he is—or isn't. Neither Mark nor Scott have any living relatives, or they'd test them."

"Still," I said. "Batty says it doesn't matter whether he's Mark or Scott. Scott was the sole beneficiary of Mark's will. He would have gotten the money anyway."

Phil shook his head. "He wouldn't have gotten the Yale

M.D. Batty's got a very narrow focus. He's in complete denial about the crimes committed."

Walking now into the cemetery, I was beginning to think that I was in complete denial about the crimes committed. The loss of Gary was a resonant, constant throb under my breast bone. I worried about Vic's medical condition, and the psychological toll it would take on him—and on Alan, who hovered bravely at bedside. Yet at the same time, I fretted obsessively over the details of Mark-Scott's legal problems. I even found that I missed the Mark Ramsey I used to know, touchy-feely, nervous Mark, the honest intern who never bluffed. *But he killed Gary!* I reminded myself from time to time. *He tried to kill Vic!*

And I tried to kill Mark-Scott. I thumb-punched him in the throat, knowing full well that that might kill him. Of course, it was self-defense. But I went around and around with it, chewing over that line from *Romeo and Juliet,* after Romeo killed Tybalt: "Romeo slew him; he slew Mercutio. Who now the price of his dear blood doth owe?"

It got me nowhere, except back to the beginning. As we had at the dinner party at Vittorio's and Alan's, I seemed to be winding along the detour via Mark Ramsey Road. I couldn't bear to talk about Gary any more, so I kept talking about Mark instead.

Maybe that's why I was here today. To talk about Mark instead of Gary.

"Now which way?" Phil asked.

"We follow the slate path to the right. Batty says there's an obelisk, and we'll see it from the path. You know, one thing I can't figure out . . . when Scott was in the intensive care unit after the accident, after Mark died . . . Why didn't he say, 'I'm not Mark?' He wasn't fully conscious, so he couldn't possibly have had his wits about him enough to *impersonate* Mark. Did he actually think he was Mark?"

361

"Yeah, I've been wondering about that, too," Phil said. "What we're talking about here basically is the full range of motivation for any behavior—what's going on at the conscious level, what's going on at a less-than-conscious level . . . Was Scott just being opportunistic? Mark had more money, he went to Yale, he got that M.D. degree. Maybe Scott always wanted to be more like Mark. Then, suddenly, there's the opportunity to have everything Mark has, to *become* Mark. Scott just grabbed it.

"On a less-than-conscious level, Mark's and Scott's lives had become so intertwined that, in a sense, they'd become almost interchangeable. Batty says that Mark and Scott wore each other's clothes, and had keys to each other's cars and apartments. There must have been some fusion of identity fostered by the repeated losses and abandonment of the parents' dying—Scott and Mark only had each other. And since they were so similar, they became like one person."

"So if one dies, it might be unclear to the other which one is really dead? I dunno, Phil, that seems a little far-fetched."

"Not really. But let's factor in Scott's head injuries from the accident. A blow to the head can put someone into an incredible fugue state. I've had patients go for years assuming a different identity. Because of head trauma, or some odd type of seizure activity, suddenly they don't know who they are. But you can't go through life like that. When someone asks you, 'Where are you from?' you can't answer, 'I don't know.' You need to fill in the blank, so you confabulate a lie. Demented people do this all the time. They start inventing answers, then they come to believe them."

Like we're doing now, I thought but didn't say.

"Maybe none of the above," I speculated. "Maybe Scott's lying there in a semi-conscious state, and all he has on his mind is, he was driving that car, he killed Mark. So he's moaning, 'Mark, Mark!' And he happens to be moaning that when the doc comes in and says, 'Squeeze my hand. What's your name?' 'Mark! Mark!' He's not answering questions, he's just completely obsessed with Mark."

Phil shot me a look, then laughed. "Common-sense ER doc trumps shrink, offers better explanation," he said as if reading a newspaper headline. "Say more."

I spied the obelisk and pointed. Phil and I left the slate path and set out across the grass. Leaves rustled and crunched underfoot. The sun sank behind its clouds, and the orange and yellow warmth of the late afternoon chilled into the blue of dusk.

"O.K., let's say Scott is coming out of his haze," I went on, handing Phil the flowers while I paused to take my sweater from my shoulders and pull it on, "and as he gets clearer, this knowledge that Mark is dead really starts to sink in. Scott realizes that he can't cope. But there's a way for him to avoid having to cope. They all think he's Mark by now anyway, why not just buy into it?"

"So it's an impetuous decision, but once he's made it, there's no turning back," Phil said, nodding. "Makes sense. He can become this friend who in his mind had everything, or perhaps was everything Scott ever wanted to be . . . There's only one problem. The real Mark Ramsey did a clerkship at University Hospital. Someone was bound to suspect that Scott wasn't Mark. And someone did. Gary."

We knew by now that Gary had confided his suspicions to Vittorio the week before he set out for Vic's and Case's—and Geoff's and Mark's and Scott's—boarding school reunion. Vittorio had said exactly what anyone would have expected him to say: By all means, find out as much as you can before you make any accusations. With any luck, you'll find you're wrong.

Ask about other matters as well, Vittorio had advised Gary. Be discreet. That way if you *are* wrong, you'll avoid embarrassing Ramsey. You don't want it getting back to him that you were up there asking questions about his accident.

Good advice, which Gary unfortunately didn't—or wasn't skilled enough—to heed. It had gotten back to Ramsey-Renfrew that he was up there asking questions. And Mark-Scott panicked. He grabbed a handful of mushrooms (probably confusing the *Amanita phalloides* death caps with the *Amanita muscaria* fly agarics), drove into the city early the next morning in the Hamiltons' station wagon, stopped at his West End Avenue apartment building, dashed in to collect the basket of vegetables he had specially ordered for me the day before—as he had said, because of my Rosh HaShanah resolution to eat more healthful meals—got back into the car, drove to the hospital and down into the Storrs Pavilion parking garage, got out of the car, ran down through the tunnel over to the hospital proper, where he grabbed the first clinical coat he could lay hands on—Ilan Moskowicz's—ran back again to the car, put on the sunglasses and wig (part of a costume, it had turned out, from a Wiffenpoof event at Yale that Geoff Hamilton had sung in), grabbed the basket (now with its lethal addition of the poisonous and hallucinogenic mushrooms), and went off to find Sava Hadzic. Whom he bribed with fifty dollars to put the basket in my fridge.

We came to the Ramsey family plot, marked off by rusting iron railings. In the center of a dozen or so gravestones, the obelisk rose at least fifteen feet into the gloaming, crowned with a stone urn and wreathed in stone garlands.

" 'William Talbot Ramsey,' " I read off one side of the obelisk, " 'died April twenty-six, eighteen-hundred and seventy-five, aged seventy-one years, eight months, and six days.' "

Phil looked around and whistled. "There are six or seven generations of Ramseys here." All four of Phil's grandparents had come from the old country. As had three of mine.

In one corner of the plot stood a white marble bench inscribed "Rest and Remember" on the seat, and "RENFREW" on the side. A few feet away, we found the gravestone, set flat into the ground: Scott Jason Renfrew, Beloved Friend.

I began to feel chilled. The breeze, light and cool when we had first arrived, had strengthened to a cold wind. The far reaches of the cemetery dissolved into shadow. I set the bouquet of flowers down on the bench and pulled my cardigan more tightly around me.

"So many children died in the old days," Phil murmured, bending to examine a row of small stones whose names and dates had worn away over time.

What am I doing here? I wondered.

"The impetuosity might explain why Ramsey sent that basket with poisonous as well as edible mushrooms," Phil picked up the conversation where we had left off. "The whole thing seems so ill-thought out. Or maybe it was, as Rob Held thinks, ambivalent."

I shook my head and sat down on the bench. "No, I think Scott just couldn't bear the responsibility. He took Mark's identity because he couldn't bear the thought that he'd 'killed' him in that accident. So when he decides to go after Gary, he leaves it somewhat up to chance. He can then stand back and say, 'I didn't kill Gary. He can tell the difference between an *Amanita* death cap and a Portobello. If he chooses to eat a toxic or hallucinogenic mushroom, it's his own damn fault!'"

"Nice," said Phil. He sat down next to me. "That's the argument that guns don't kill people, people do. But what about the insulin? Scott didn't leave that up to chance. And he had to steal the botulinum toxin from Di Clausson before he could inject Vittorio. That's pre-meditated."

"By then the resolution had sunk in, I guess," I conceded. "And once he resolved to kill Gary, it was easier to resolve to kill Vic. But there are still missing pieces of the puzzle."

"Yeah, like how Scott knew that Gary had shared his suspicions with Vittorio."

The gloom deepened.

And then I saw him.

About fifty yards away, walking slowly—perhaps a better word was *gliding*—along the far reaches of the cemetery. Wearing a black monk's robe with the peaked hood drawn up over his head. Grasping a long-poled scythe in his left hand.

I dug my nails into Phil's thigh. "Do you see *that?*" I gasped.

He jumped. "What? See what?"

"Over there. In the shadows."

The figure, perhaps hearing us, turned and paused. His robe billowed in the wind. It was too dark to see his face.

If he had one.

"Where?" Phil asked.

"There." On my feet now, I pointed.

For a long moment, the figure seemed to gaze back. Then he turned and disappeared into the nightfall.

"What? Ev, Honey, you're shaking."

Immediately, I doubted my own eyes. "You didn't see him?"

"See who?" Phil looked where I was looking. "There's nobody there," he said.

Almost as soon as the hospital board of trustees voted to pursue negotiations toward a merger with St. Eustace Hospital, rumors flew that Eustace planned to close University Hospital and turn it into an outpatient unit. Hospital management, galvanized by Dr. Diana Clausson, staged a successful coup against those trustees who still declared for Eustace. Before you could say "Talks broke down," University left Eustace standing at the altar and eloped with Mt. Scopus. Together they announced in the *New York Times* plans to form a single-parent corporation to oversee both hospitals.

The new corporation would not be a merger per se. Each hospital would maintain its own board of trustees, manage its own assets, and be responsible for its own debts. "How supposed to work?" Vittorio scrawled on his whiteboard when Case Hamilton broke the news. "Mt. S $25 mil surplus last year, Univ $6 mil in red. Mt. S pumps money into Univ—for what?"

"We need to fill beds," Case explained. "They need the space."

Without pressure from Eustace to dramatically reduce the nursing staff, University Hospital was able to negotiate a deal with the nurses that even Gary would have accepted. The number of nursing positions to be eliminated was halved. The hospital agreed to a "no bump" clause, giving up its right to move nurses without their consent from one department to another. In return, the nurses agreed that unlicensed aides would take over some nursing duties. "I guess we have to get with the program," Kathy Haughey sighed. "Medicine is changing."

Because the new corporation would not be a merger per se, the residents and interns would not have to reaffiliate with the Albert Schweitzer School of Medicine, and our residency programs would not be disrupted.

"That's a big relief," I told Gary in my head early in November. I had taken to slipping into the hospital chapel to whisper Kaddish for him, and while I was there I would tell him the news. The chapel was Christian, with stained-glass windows depicting Jesus, and technically I wasn't supposed to be reciting Kaddish without a minyan—actually, I wasn't sure whether you said Kaddish for someone not your relative to begin with—but I didn't think Gary—or God—would mind.

Since I had seen Death in the cemetery, I had become both more defiant and more philosophical.

Di Clausson, adjusting her sails to the winds of change, set out to woo the powers that be at Mt. Scopus. The last I heard, she had completely charmed Dr. Luke Christmas, the Director of Medicine there. There was a very good chance she would be appointed the director of the new Mt. Scopus-University Hospital Center for Cranial Base Surgery when it opened the following year.

"What was that fight you had with Gary Seligman a couple of days before he died?" I asked her out of the clear blue sky one day.

"My affair with Mark," she said easily, surprising me. "Dr. Christmas is born-again. Before he got Jesus, his name was Nathan Goldblatt. Apparently he's rabid on the topic of adultery. Gary threatened to mail all the *Post* clippings about my divorce to Christmas unless I took the pressure off Keith Herrera. As if anyone could pressure Herrera. Or Christmas for that matter."

Scott Renfrew had been found fit to stand trial, I told Gary one morning in chapel. His attorneys gave notice that they planned to pursue the insanity defense. I took the day off to go to court to watch the proceedings. Oh, and speaking of court, guess what! I completely forgot to tell you about Elise Vanderlaende!

Amazingly, she slapped Phil with a medical malpractice suit at the end of October, alleging that he had seduced her over the course of several months of psychotherapy. Phil was able to convince the judge that he had never treated her, except for that one time in the emergency room, and that there was never any psychotherapy or therapeutic alliance. Professor Robert Held gave a deposition to the effect that Elise had also stalked him. He handed over this big stack of letters she had written him, and Phil handed over his big stack, and these were all entered into evidence, as was the Latin note— from which the police were able to lift one good fingerprint, it turned out—hers. Apparently, Di Clausson's translation, "One woman's meat is another woman's poison" was right on the money. The judge dismissed the charges.

But I'm leaving the best part to the end.

Over the course of several weeks, Elise spent enough time with her new attorney to decide that he was in love with her.

So she's no longer our problem.

Phil seems more himself since Elise has left him alone, and switched her attentions. The Prozac seems to have helped, although Phil's thinking of stopping that now, and trying St. John's wort instead. Since he's less depressed, he's less insistent that we marry. And since he's less insistent, I'm less anxious. I might almost be ready to talk about it.

I sat quietly in the chapel, imagining Gary's response. He'd probably hug me and say something encouraging about Phil. Or maybe he'd make a joke about Elise and laugh.

Let's see, what else? Alan has decided to stop apologizing for liking his life. He says he's been going around with this big chip on his shoulder, imagining that people look down on him because they think he's a housewife, and he's just not going to do that anymore. His new attitude is, Who cares what they think?

He misses you. A lot.

So do I.

Vittorio's still vent-dependent, but it really hasn't slowed him down much. He spends his time writing notes to people. Anything important, Alan types up for him.

So Case comes in to visit Vic one morning and Vic hands him a list, typed up and printed out ahead of time by Alan:

You & Jackie go for credit counseling
You get a budget and cut up all your credit cards
You appoint me your financial advisor
I manage all your affairs
I give you an allowance
You apply to medical school, I pay

Case was insulted, but Jackie and Lauren are working on him. I can't decide whether Vic's offer is Solomonic, or just pours salt in Case's wounds. Probably both.

I miss your laugh . . .

I sat especially quietly for a few minutes to see if I might hear Gary's laugh one last time. After a few minutes when there was no laugh, I got up and left the chapel.

That's O.K., Gary, I thought as I walked back to the emergency room.

I have your laugh in my heart.